"TASHA, PLEASE STAY— AND MARRY ME AGAIN."

She glanced up, her eyes expressionless. "Does this mean you're in love with me?" she asked.

A slow flush rose over Ben's face, and he answered reluctantly, "I'm sorry you asked, Tasha, for I'm trying to have done with lies. I think love would come."

"Then you don't love me," Tasha concluded unemotionally.

"I didn't say that, either. Dammit, I just don't know!" he protested. "Perhaps I've spent too many years hating you, hating the kind of woman you are. From hate to love is too much of a jump. I can't change overnight."

"Then it seems that your low opinion of me hasn't changed, either," she remarked dispassionately. "No, thank you, Ben," she added with immense civility. "I'd rather be married to Max."

AND NOW...

SUPERROMANCES

Worldwide Library is proud to present a
sensational new series of modern love stories —
SUPERROMANCES

Written by masters of the genre, these longer,
sensuous and dramatic novels are truly in keeping
with today's changing life-styles. Full of intriguing
conflicts, the heartaches and delights of true love,
SUPERROMANCES are absorbing stories —
satisfying and sophisticated reading that lovers
of romance fiction have long been waiting for.

SUPERROMANCES
Contemporary love stories for the woman of today!

ABRA TAYLOR

A TASTE OF EDEN

A SUPERROMANCE FROM

WORLDWIDE
TORONTO · LONDON · NEW YORK · SYDNEY

Published February 1982

First printing August 1981
Second printing December 1981

ISBN 0-373-70012-1

CHAPTER ONE

"FOR GOD'S SAKE, Tasha, grow up!"

The photographer, Jon Lassiter by name, glared with exasperation at the tall slender model who was posing, along with several others, for the day's shoot. Against the background of Stonehenge, with huge white clouds building like aerial monoliths in the blue sky beyond, everything was perfect—except for Tasha Craig. She looked stunning enough; Tasha always did. Like most good high-fashion models, she was beautiful in a totally individual way. Not one of Tasha's features was perfect, but put together they were marvelous—brown almond eyes with that overlarge look often a sign of defective vision; long straight black-silk hair; elegant hollows beneath wonderful cheekbones; a certain unfulfilled promise about the mouth.

Yes, Lassiter thought to himself, Tasha had what it took to turn this into a great picture if only she'd shed that touch-me-not air. Sexy sophistication, that was the feeling he wanted today—a city-slicker look to contrast with the primitive background of stone and sky. And Tasha Craig had just finished refusing to lower the zip on the front of her outfit by even one more inch.

For God's sake, Tasha, grow up. The words stung Tasha now as they had stung so many years ago, when Ben had said them. *Ben, don't think of Ben,* Tasha told herself, *not now, not in public*. Even across the years and the miles, the excruciating memory of Ben Craig, her husband and yet not her husband, still had the power to wound. The old hurts had been put away in the secret hiding places of her heart; it was only in the loneliness of the night that she thought of him now. Why did Jon have to use those particular words, bringing a host of old aches flooding back?

Perhaps, if those words had not been spoken at this precise moment, in that precise way—explosively, although with less bitterness than had been in Ben's tone—perhaps, if the photographer had used some other method of urging Tasha to do as he wished, none of what followed might have happened at all.

But he did say them; and perhaps after that there was an inevitability to everything that took place. Tasha's immediate response was a higher tilt of her head, a somewhat stubborn look about her full lower lip, a certain hardness of eye that effectively concealed the surge of feeling inside. Unconsciously, she fell into a slightly more defiant pose.

"Let me try it once more, Jon. I'm sure I can get the look you want without showing more skin."

"For a high-fashion model, you're a bloody

prude," Lassiter told her grumpily. But after directing several more poses, he said more kindly, "Now you're beginning to get it. But I still want more! Sexy satin against Stonehenge—sophistication in a primitive setting! The contrast, Tasha, the contrast. Can't you see what I'm getting at? Look at Lisette. That's what I want—that air of a girl who's just been made love to."

"You should know, Jon," came a wicked little comment from one of the other models. It was a well-known fact that Lisette lived with Jon Lassiter in a thoroughly modern arrangement. Several titters followed.

Lisette, very much a Brigitte Bardot type, stuck out her tongue at the girl who had spoken, then directed her words to her apartment mate: "Don't tell Tasha to imitate me, Jon darling. She wouldn't know how. We all know how active *her* sex life is."

Normally, Tasha was quite capable of defending herself with her tongue. But today, with memories of Ben chasing through her mind, she found herself unable to leap into the verbal fray. Lisette's catty comment was only too true.

"Sheath your claws, Lisette love," Jon Lassiter said in a placatory tone. "How about it, Tasha, can you do it or not? If you can't I'll have to take you out of this shot. Oh, God, I *can't*—the editor will kill me if I don't show that particular outfit. So let's try it once again. That touch of defiance is good, Tasha, but I want *sex*. Maybe a few more clothespins will help."

He motioned to his female assistant, who moved behind the models and added a few more plastic clothespins to those already clamped down Tasha's spine, giving her from the rear the uncomfortable look of a porcupine and causing the fabric to strain revealingly against the front. The outfit was seal-brown satin, a match for Tasha's eyes, and consisted of slinky pants and a top fashioned like a zipped windbreaker. At the moment the zipper clasp was poised just below center of her breasts, revealing little more than a bathing suit would have done.

"Now pull the collar aside a bit," Lassiter. instructed, and the assistant moved around to Tasha's front. "Muss the hair, let that wind catch it . . . dammit, it's still not quite right. The zipper has got to go."

Tasha opened her mouth to protest, and her hand moved into a defensive position. High fashion dictated that there be no brassiere beneath; there was none.

"Don't worry. I'm not about to show a damn thing," Lassiter told her irritably. "A little titillation for the readers, that's all. Nudity may be into the high-fashion mags, but not for this particular shot! If anything shows that shouldn't, I'll personally burn the negatives."

"Can't show something that's just not there," came Lisette's voice a trifle too sweetly, taking advantage of Tasha's unaccustomed silence, and perhaps also taking some revenge. It was well known that Lisette liked to be the center of attention, and today she had not succeeded. "You were quite right, Jon darling. In some ways Tasha isn't grown up, and that's one of them! If I were built like Tasha, I'd be modest too!"

"About time," Tasha said spiritedly, at last recovering enough to give as good as she took.

But seconds later, when the assistant's hand again reached for the slide fastener, Tasha allowed it to do its assigned task. The zip went down and Tasha's chin went up—eyes stubbornly avoiding the deep V of skin now bared to her navel.

"That's it—now you've got it! Hold it, everyone...good. Now another. Lean forward, Lisette, cleavage is in this year! Again...again...shift a little, girls! Try another pose. Wet your mouth, Tasha! No, don't push that hair out of the way—just let it blow across your eyes...it looks terrific!"

SIX MONTHS LATER, when the photograph hit the front cover of the fashion magazine, it had been cropped to include only Tasha's top half. All the other models had succumbed to the scissors. As Jon had predicted, the shot looked marvelous. A few strands of silky black hair winnowing across a pale gold complexion; huge brown eyes defying the camera; chin in an aggressive tilt and mouth parted in a moist promise. The breasts were revealed to the limits of decency, but as Jon had promised, no more. All the same, there was a considerable expanse of flesh. Certainly enough showed to give the lie to Lisette's last catty comment.

The effects of the photograph were far reaching, even more far reaching than Tasha would ever have guessed on that windy day on Salisbury Plain, as she'd stood in the shadow of the megaliths of other centuries.

Nor could she have any premonition of its consequences when she first saw the picture. Her initial sensation was relief: the shot was not totally indecent after all. Second came elation. The cover of a magazine! Now the model agency would have more calls for her; it all helped toward paying the enormous debts left by her father's death some years before. The third and strongest sensation was something else that came flooding back to her unbidden—the memory of the exact words that had sent that zip down to a level somewhere in the vicinity of her navel.

For God's sake, Tasha, grow up. It was ironic that when Ben had said those words, nearly seven years ago, he had not known how young she was. He had had no idea of her real age when he married her, although he had learned that night: their wedding night. What should have been their wedding night. Why had Ben made no effort all these years to put an official end to the marriage? Or had he done so, with some seedy divorce in some far-off corner of the globe? Perhaps not. It was possible that Ben found the marriage useful, as she did herself, in preventing entanglements. Ben had never wanted to marry; he had made that clear the first time they met. And certainly, as long as he was legally bound by some piece of paper, he could never be trapped again, as he had been trapped by Tasha. . . .

She had just turned seventeen the year she met Ben Craig. Seventeen. She was still Tasha Montgomery then, shortsighted Tasha Montgomery with horn-rimmed glasses not contact lenses, five-foot-nine-and-a-bit in her stocking feet, only two weeks out of the French *lycée* she had attended since her mother's death. Her father was English; but her mother had been French, as tall as Tasha herself, with an inherited family height that was rumored on no good authority to be the result of a certain visit to Paris of a certain Romanov duke more than a century before. The French school had been a necessity, so that Tasha could live with her grandparents during the school term.

Seventeen. . . . Memories seeped through Tasha's defenses like water through a flawed dam. Tall, gangly, bespectacled, she had developed her height early and her shape late. Sensitive in the extreme, she had soon learned to hide her adolescent miseries behind a prickly defensive tongue that—had she only realized it—kept swains at bay far more effectively than the height or the horn-rims. There had been no mother to ease her through a painful puberty, and while her grandparents had been warm and loving, they had not understood all her needs. Nor had her father. Good-natured but absentminded, Charles Montgomery was little aware of the vulnerable young person who took refuge behind a bright laugh and a layer of seeming insouciance.

As a teenager Tasha had accepted, unwillingly, the fact that she could not live with her father. Before his death, Charles Montgomery, a zoologist, was forever off on some expedition or other, to places like the Galapagos or Hawaii's Leeward Islands or some other wildlife preserve. But he kept his comfortable home in London and always made a point of returning to England every year for the summer months to visit Tasha and prepare his latest book or paper for publication. That, he often told her, was the important thing for a scientist: to publish. His books were noncommercial, strictly for the scientific community, but he had made some good friends in the publishing business, and it was from one of them that the invitation came.

When her father had informed her that he wanted her to attend the cocktail party with him, Tasha had barely managed to conceal her dismay. "Oh, papa, I can't go," she had said.

"Of course you'll go! There'll be lots of young folks there, and it's time you met some of them. You've been out of this country too long, Tasha. It's time you made some friends here."

Tasha had demurred, but Charles Montgomery had insisted. "I want a companion for the evening, Tasha, and I'd just as soon it's you. If I take some other lady I'll have to dance attendance on her. And there's going to be a fellow there I want to have a good talk with, an American who's spent a lot of years knocking about the globe in some of my favorite places. Why, he knows the Indian Ocean like the back of his hand. I've never met him, but I've read some of his articles, and they're good."

"A fellow zoologist?" asked Tasha, with a show of interest that concealed her consternation. If her father was going to abandon her at the party, she certainly didn't want to go.

"No, just travel pieces. Jim Arthur is toying with the idea of putting out a collection of some of this man's work, on my suggestion, I might add. So you see why it's important for me to go to this affair. I can't understand why you don't want to attend. Surely you're not afraid to go out in public?"

"Of course not," Tasha said brightly.

"Then I have to assume it's because you don't want to be seen on the arm of a dry old stick like me."

"Oh, papa...." Cringing inside, Tasha said the only thing that would make her father happy. "Of course I want to be seen with you! It's just that I have absolutely nothing to wear. I've put on six pounds this year, and nothing fits except my jeans—and a few skirts and sweaters."

"Then go shopping," her father replied logically enough, sensing none of the real reason for her reluctance. Already his attention was turning back to a book on species of iguanas. With his usual lack of prudence for all things financial, he added, "Charge anything you want, Tasha. Or go up and raid your mother's clothes closet. I think you've grown tall enough to wear her gowns."

In the end, that was exactly what Tasha had done.

It was not the first time she had tried on clothes from the marvelous treasure trove of expensive designer dresses that had once belonged to her tall elegant mother; but it was the first time she had filled out the seams. Now, years later, Tasha realized that the wardrobe had been far too sophisticated for a seventeen-year-old, but at the time, she had been aware only of a transformation she could hardly believe. Well, except for the glasses—and as she could not see herself at all clearly in the mirror once she had removed them, she could only guess as to what the effect might be without.

She had settled, after much indecision, on a clinging apricot-colored silk jersey. Superbly cut, it had a high choke neck in front, but the back was totally bare, from shoulder to shoulder and from neck to waist. Charles Montgomery, his mind still several thousand miles away in some tropical paradise, had not noticed its unsuitability—and who else was there to say her nay? As Tasha's father had pointed out, her acquaintances in England were by this time few and far between, and most of them were her father's fellow scholars. She wore the dress.

And the dress did things for her: gave her a veneer of sophistication; turned her from all angles to all curves; accentuated the good bones and graceful carriage that would later lead her into modeling; emphasized the golden tint of her skin and the dark gloss of her hair. It made her look years older, especially with makeup applied more lavishly than was suitable for her age, with her hair pulled back in a smooth French knot, with her mother's antique gold pendant nestling between the newly burgeoned breasts. And without the glasses. On a last impulse, she tucked those firmly into a dresser drawer before finding her half-blind way down the stairs to the living room, where her father waited for her, inspecting a display case filled with some rare and beautiful moths.

Charles Montgomery noticed the dress not at all, but he did comment on the lack of glasses. "Mmm. You look very decent without those things on your nose."

Tasha squinted at him, delighted by the compliment. "Do you think so? Once I've taken them off I can't tell! My face is just a blur in the mirror. Do I really look all right?"

"Not bad at all," her father told her. "We'll have to get you a pair of contact lenses, Tasha. Why don't you go for a fitting on Monday? You may turn out to be quite as beautiful as your mother." And he led her off proudly to the reception.

There had been perhaps two hundred people there. With her imperfect eyesight, Tasha was aware only of a sea of milling humanity, which was confusing at first. Her father had been pulled away almost at once for an introduction to the man he wanted to meet. Tasha saw him join a circle of people, mostly women, clustered around some person she could not see.

She turned away, quite prepared to find a quiet corner from which she could observe the dancing that was part of the night's entertainment. But it was not to be.

"Clever of me to get rid of him so neatly, wasn't it?" came a voice from over her shoulder, and she turned to see the same man who had dragged her father away, only moments before. "In payment I expect the first dance—and maybe the second, too. Now don't pay any attention to those other men trying to catch your eye; I have first claim. . . ."

And so began the whirl. Partner followed partner at a dizzying pace; Tasha could hardly believe what was happening. The quick tongue she had developed to shield her through her awkward adolescence stood her in good stead, allowing her to keep up a pretense of self-possession and fend off the amorous advances with some semblance of sophistication. She was at first astonished, then delighted, then secretly thrilled at the attention. Her self-confidence blossomed as the night wore on.

Halfway through the evening, wanting to escape a dance partner who had whispered a lewd suggestion in her ear, she had made some forcedly bright excuse and found her roundabout way to a flagstoned terrace that looked out over formal gardens. It was a starry June night; the perfumed air issued invitations to the senses. But it was a little cool for her backless dress, after the hot dance floor. Leaning over a stone balustrade to peer unseeingly into the shadowed garden, she huddled her bare arms together and shivered, half in consternation over the alarming directness of her last dance partner, and half in a haze of wonderment that so many men were paying attention to her.

"Oh!" She gasped as something soft and warm landed over her shoulders. It was a summer-weight dinner jacket, still holding the heat of a man's body. Startled, she turned to the donor of this gift and had to look upward by quite a number of inches to see his face. At five-foot-nine plus high heels, she was not used to men several inches taller than she was; certainly none of her dance partners had had such height. In this dim light and with her eyesight, she could discern no more than a blur of craggy features. She swayed a little closer to the man—a movement dictated by the shortness of her vision, but one that was unknowingly provocative.

"Who are you? I don't believe I know you," she said in a voice more husky than usual, with a little catch to it. There was something about the man's physical presence that took her breath away—a sort of overpowering virility and vitality that exuded a primitive magnetism. He had the solid, well-knit build of an athlete; one sensed there was not an untoned muscle in his body. In this light his hair appeared to be dark brown. Later, she was to discover that it had a bronze cast where it had been streaked by sun, and that his eyes, too, seemed bronze in certain lights—although they were really a tawny tortoiseshell brown, several shades paler than her own.

But for the moment she did not know that. His eyes were only pools of shadow in the deeply tanned face; but she could feel them sweeping her in a manner she had not yet learned to take for granted.

"I don't know you," she repeated.

"That makes us even." His strong mouth quirked into a smile that revealed white even teeth. "I don't know you, either. But I plan to know you—very well, by the time the evening's through. I've been watching you for some time, but nobody could tell me who you are. I may as well declare right now that my intentions are serious—and totally dishonorable."

The moment filled Tasha with awkwardness. She hid her nervousness, as she often did, with a bright little laugh. "That's an odd way to ask someone to dance," she said.

"I'm not asking you to dance. I'd much rather talk." There was a vibrant intimate quality to his voice that thrilled Tasha to the core. "You can start by telling me your name—unless you insist that I find someone to introduce us properly, in which case I'll go looking again. Somebody here must know you."

It seemed terribly important to Tasha to impress this man. In her seventeen-year-old inexperience, he seemed enormously self-assured and old—at least thirty-five, she was sure. Later she found out that she had put her guess several years too high; at the time Ben had been less than thirty. How old would he be now? Thirty-five, thirty-six? Reliving the past, Tasha realized that she had not known Ben long enough to find out his birthday. Only long enough to marry him. . . .

"I'm Natasha Montgomery. Tasha, if you prefer," she had said at once, afraid that if he walked away now he would not return. She tried to sound blasé, as an older woman might. "I don't particularly like dancing, either. It's so boring, isn't it?"

Ben had sounded amused at her bored air, and true to character, he had immediately set about trying to explode her small pretense. "Only the very young get bored that easily. Just exactly how old are you?"

Tasha was stung that he had seen through her, but the habits of some years came to her rescue. "Fifteen," she said promptly, with a cool smile.

"Now that," he said, "is an outright lie."

"Don't you know that a woman always lies about her age? Besides, you haven't answered my first question. Who are you?"

"Ben Craig."

"Do you make a habit of pickups, Mr. Craig?" Tasha tilted her chin in the slightly defiant attitude she always adopted when situations unnerved her. "You might start with this." And, pushing the jacket from her shoulders, she dropped it over the balustrade into the garden ten feet below. Then, forcing indifference into a small serene smile, she brushed past the tall male frame and walked her unseeing way toward the dance floor, thoroughly conscious of her naked back gleaming beneath the soft yellow pools of outdoor lighting.

He caught up with her before she left the terrace, and an arm like iron barred her way. Beneath the silky fabric of his white dinner shirt, she could feel the press of muscles, the warmth of firm flesh. His fingers curled around her slender wrist, making it captive, sending shivering sensations to untried regions of her body.

"Sorry for asking your age. Just double-checking, that's all. I don't go in for cradle-robbing; beginners aren't my style. But dammit, you did seem to enjoy the dancing earlier, and your remark seemed to be quite—"

"Juvenile?" She broke in, still fighting him with her overlarge dim-sighted velvet eyes. Then, forgiving him suddenly as something melted inside, she smiled more endearingly than before. "You're quite right, I was lying about the dancing. I love it."

"In that case I'll relent, too. We'll dance—even though I hate it. Come while I get my jacket."

"I'll wait here for you."

"I don't trust you out of my sight," he said, and without asking for permission he drew her down into the dark shadows of the garden while he retrieved his jacket. Something about the way he touched her arm had warned Tasha that he wanted to kiss her. Half in fright, half in anticipation, she had moistened her lips. The kiss had not come. Instead he had laid a hard warm hand on the cool bare skin below one shoulder. It was a gesture more intimate than a kiss, and one that reaffirmed his intentions with no word said. She had not moved away from his hand.

After that, they had danced exclusively with each other. And because he had not tried to hold her too close, as her other partners had, they had managed to fit in a lot of talking, too, and laughing. Ben had a dry sense of humor that found a foil in Tasha's ready tongue. For once she found herself using it not for defense, but because she enjoyed hearing that husky vibrant laugh that was as masculine and compelling as everything else about him.

She soon found out that he was the man her father had wanted to meet, something she had not suspected at once because his accent was not typically American—the result, he told her, of leaving the States at a very early age. Bennett Craig was his full name. Ben suited him better—it was a plain name, powerful like the man. She discovered that he had been sailing single-handedly around the Indian Ocean for the past few years, exploring, observing, learning, writing articles for travel magazines to pay his way. He had flown to London to discuss the possibility of rewriting some of his pieces so that they could fit together coherently, into a book. He had arrived only this morning; soon he would be leaving again.

"To an existence as nomadic as before?" Tasha asked.

"I haven't decided. There are times when I think about putting down roots...but don't get ideas, brown eyes. Marriage is very definitely not in my plans. So don't tell me later you weren't warned."

Somehow Tasha managed to keep up the pretense of being older than she was. She tried to avoid direct lies by the use of verbal fencing wherever possible, but there were some outright lies, too, for she knew that to tell certain truths would be to lose him—that he would walk out of her life, perhaps forever. Hadn't he said he wasn't interested in beginners?

"What have you been doing for the past few years?" he asked her after the first hour had sped by. They were still on the dance floor, his hand intimately lodged against her naked spine.

"Going to school," she answered without thinking, soft brown eyes shining up at him, basking in the glow of his attention, for by now it was clear to her that more than one woman in the room envied her.

He pulled away from her a fraction. "You never did tell me your age. Are you sure you're old enough for me?"

"Can't you guess by looking at me?" she stalled, heart hammering wildly lest he should, indeed, guess.

"Twenty-something? You've got one of those eternal faces, Tasha—wonderful bone structure and skin like a baby's. I suspect you'll look exactly the same ten or fifteen years from now. I wouldn't dare guess in case you cut me down to size, as you did out on the terrace."

How old was old enough? Tasha took a wild stab. "I'm twenty-four," she lied with a smile. "But of course, I'm lying again. A woman always does."

"Which university?"

It was not as easy to equivocate to that question. Tasha told him the name of a famous one in France; and also her reasons for attending school out of England. The reasons were true enough; only the school was false. "I just graduated," she said. Well, that much was true.

"What course?"

"Zoology," she said with no hesitation at all. It

was a lie; she had not yet decided what course to take. But she had considered entering her father's field. With that curious need to explain oneself that often comes with a lie, she babbled brightly on, using knowledge picked up from her father. Ben appeared interested, filling Tasha with feelings of dismay lest she should have to answer too many questions. "I've been specializing in ornithology," she finished on a sudden inspiration, sure that would put an end to the conversation. What man wanted to talk about birds?

"You, a bird-watcher? Somehow I can't picture you—"

"Well, it just goes to show how wrong you can be," she countered lightly. In truth, she felt wretched because one lie seemed to be leading to another; she was fast becoming caught in a tissue of fabrication.

To her relief, Ben left the subject then, and the dance floor. Scooping her into an arm, he told her, "I'm taking you home. Tell your father we're leaving."

"But—"

"Tell him, Tasha," he commanded quietly, and she did not need good vision to sense the message in that unsmiling mouth. The air between them crackled with electricity, as though there were no others in the room.

"I'll tell him," she agreed, her heart palpitating with the knowledge of Ben's stated intentions: *dishonorable*.

Fortunately—or perhaps unfortunately—Tasha's father was deep in discussion with a fellow scientist, and he waved her good-night abstractedly, without inquiring as to her escort.

Ben drove her home without talking. Squinting now that her face could not be seen, she watched his large capable hands mastering the steering wheel and wondered what it was going to be like. Her imagination didn't go beyond a kiss, and perhaps a caress of the breast. At the *lycée*, her best friends had been two petite and popular French girls, who had described such things to her in intimate detail. On several occasions, they had fixed Tasha up with blind dates who had been far too overawed by the height and the horn-rimmed glasses to attempt any similar feats. Ben, she knew, would have no such reservations; and that knowledge set her flesh to quivering with anticipation.

But inside the front door, the kiss she expected didn't come. She was sick with hurt and clammy with relief. Ben looked around, taking in the quiet furnishings and Charles Montgomery's various collections from around the world. Tasha watched the tall hazy outline of him prowling the room, every movement a study in unconscious virile grace. He was so big, so powerful, so vital. Inexpressible yearnings filled her heart to bursting.

"I'd like a drink," he said finally. "Do you mind? I'll get it if you like."

"No, I will." She moved to the liquor cabinet, glad of the fact that she was sometimes asked to do this for her father. She knew exactly where everything was kept, without having to peer closely at labels. "What would you like?"

"Scotch on the rocks," he replied, lowering himself into a chair—an unpretentious one, but it seemed now to dominate the room. Tasha prepared the drinks, including a plain ginger ale for herself, and for a time things became more comfortable as they began to talk again, lightly, about this and that, with Tasha quite skillfully evading all personal topics lest they lead to more lies. Her lingering sensitivity about not being kissed lent an extra superficiality to her chatter. At first, when Ben inserted the casual question into the conversation, Tasha could hardly believe her ears.

"I beg your pardon?" she said with widening eyes.

"I asked if you would like to go to bed," he repeated calmly.

Her heart tripped over itself. Ben Craig, inviting her to go to bed. A full-grown, forceful man she had met only two hours before and was already desperately infatuated with, with every fiber of her adolescent being. She closed her eyes and forced a small bright laugh. "You ask me just like that? You haven't even kissed me."

"I don't need to kiss you to know it's going to be one hell of an experience. Sorry to be so blunt, but surely you understand that there are times when a man gets into a state of considerable frustration. I don't think I can cope with the preliminaries, Tasha—I've been at sea too long! I have no intention of letting myself get aroused by a woman who intends to say no ten minutes later. Surely you must have guessed why I didn't want to get too close on the dance floor; you're not that naive. Believe me, in normal circumstances I wouldn't be so circumspect."

But she was that naive. Such a possibility had never occurred to her, and now she was faced by the sure knowledge that Ben needed a woman; and if he could not have her he would soon find another one. Tasha's head spun sickly with the dilemma. It was as well her feelings were still shuttered behind closed lids.

"I thought I made my intentions perfectly clear when I introduced myself," he said gravely. "I'm sure you understood. If you've been playing me along with thoughts of something other than a brief encounter, Tasha, then you've wasted your time and mine. If you find my suggestion offensive, please ask me to leave."

So it had not been some magical magnetism, after all. He had concentrated his efforts on her tonight only because he thought the rewards had been implicitly promised. It was true enough that Ben had warned her time and again; the first fine flush of romance had blinded her to the full and frightening implications of what he wanted. Despite her infatuation, Tasha was not prepared to make a commitment like that—and yet, she felt she could not bear it if Ben Craig walked out of her life.

Her eyes came open to the blur of his well-knit frame halfway across the room. "I'd rather you stayed. But I don't fall into bed with any man on a first date." She tried very hard to make her voice flippant. "It takes a little longer than that."

"Ah." He was silent for a time. "I'll only be in town for six days, Tasha. Will I be wasting my time if I see you every one of them? How long do I have to keep up the courtship ritual?"

"Oh, I never relent before the seventh day," she returned as lightly as possible, trying to make a joke of it without discouraging him altogether.

"I'll take my chances, then," decided Ben abruptly. "But be warned. I'm not a moonstruck teenager and matrimony is nowhere in my mind. If you allow me to kiss you, I'll want—more."

He saw her every day for the next six. Terrified that the truth about her age and inexperience would come out, Tasha kept all conversations on a light superficial level, parrying Ben's attempts to learn more about the person beneath the surface. She also went to some lengths to prevent a meeting between Ben and her father, maneuvering that was made easy because Charles Montgomery spent most days at the library. Tasha kept raiding her mother's closet; the horn-rimmed glasses spent most of their time in the dresser drawer. She became practiced at not squinting. She and Ben walked; they talked; they dined out; they went to movies, which Tasha pretended to see; they laughed a great deal. Tasha fended off Ben's occasional laconic suggestion that it was time for the relationship to progress further. He touched her very little—a brushing of shoulders, a hand resting lightly on her hip, fingers running once through her loosely flowing hair. Little touches; electric touches. And no preliminaries.

On the sixth day, leaving her at the front door, Ben kissed her lightly on the forehead. Tasha said good-bye with a brave bright face, refusing to weep until he had walked down the front steps and out of her life, a life that seemed to crumble overnight.

But the next day, just after her father had left for the library, the doorbell rang. Tasha, clad in jeans and wearing her glasses, answered it with a heavy heart, expecting no miracles.

It was Ben.

"It's the seventh day, Tasha," he said easily, and stepped inside. "You know, that's the first time I've seen you with those glasses and without makeup? You look about sixteen."

"Ben!" She snatched the glasses from her nose, and thrust them into a hip pocket. She had laughed and she had cried, and she had hung herself like a necklace around his shoulders. Ben, Ben, Ben. Every secret of her adolescent worship must have been revealed in that moment.

"Are you alone?" he murmured into her ear.

"Yes—for the afternoon," she told him, and at the time she believed it to be true.

He had kissed her then, and she had kissed him, allowing her body to instruct her in the knowledge she lacked. Even now Tasha could not permit herself to think of the deep expert kisses that had aroused her so; of the skilled hands that had rioted over her awakening body with a fervor all the more intense for being too long denied. Those were memories best left alone; forcibly she blanked them from her mind.

Force it all away, everything, everything...until that moment when her father arrived unheard, not more than ten minutes later, at her bedroom door. She had been naked, already in bed; Ben, shirtless and removing the belt from the trousers that hugged his powerful thighs, had been standing tall beside the bed.

"What's going on here?" Charles Montgomery had demanded in disbelief and outrage. Tasha snatched a sheet up to her chin, and sat stunned and shivering.

"Surely it's obvious," Ben replied levelly. Tasha couldn't see his expression, but she could hear the self-assurance in his voice. He had not sounded ashamed.

There had been more protestations, more recriminations from her father, half directed at her, half at Ben. At first Tasha had been too shocked to say anything in her own defense or Ben's.

"A man of the world like you, taking advantage of.... Why, you should be ashamed of yourself! Get out of this house and never let me see you again! Moreover I intend to speak to Jim Arthur about—"

"Papa!" She heard her voice intruding into her father's tirade. The words simply spilled out of their own accord, with no forethought for consequences. "Ben's done nothing wrong! He's asked me to marry him."

Her father, faltering in his indictments, turned toward Ben. "Is this true?"

Tasha could feel Ben's eyes turn in her direction.

The heat rose to her cheeks and her lashes fell, shielding her from the accusation she knew must be there.

"She hasn't given me her answer yet," Ben said slowly, with a touch of scorn in his voice.

The tensions in the air were broken by her father. "You might have waited until she gave it," he said angrily. "Well, Tasha, what *is* your answer?"

Even to protect herself or Ben, Tasha knew she should not trap him by saying yes now. He had never even told her he loved her, and he had certainly made his views on marriage clear. But there were too many pressures to contend with, not least of them her own heartsick adolescent adoration of the tall, forceful, virile man who had stormed into her life only a week before.

"Yes," she said, head in a sick whirl.

"When you're decent come downstairs and we'll talk about it," Charles Montgomery had said stiffly and vanished. Ben followed more slowly to the door, pulling his shirt over broad tanned shoulders as he went.

"I'm sorry I did that, Ben," whispered Tasha in agony, knowing her father would be waiting just beyond earshot, in the hall. "Oh, Ben. . . you didn't actually have to propose."

"It seems to me," Ben said dryly, "that I didn't. For once, the answer came before the question."

"You don't have to go through with it," Tasha started to protest, but already Ben was gone. By the time she reached the living room, hurrying in order that Ben and her father would not be alone together for too long, it seemed her life had already been arranged for her. Charles Montgomery had said nothing to betray Tasha's age, possibly because he assumed that Ben already knew it; but he had made it clear that his views on marriage were old-fashioned and that he had no intention of allowing Tasha further opportunities to compromise her virtue. There was to be a quiet ceremony in the Montgomery home in six weeks' time. Tasha and her father would have to make all the arrangements; Ben had matters to attend to elsewhere. Already he had delayed his flight to be there that day.

"I'll return two days before the wedding," he told them, his voice now crisp and businesslike. "I've promised Mr. Arthur I'll be back in London about that time. He's drawing up a contract, now that we've come to an agreement on how the book should be handled."

"Oh?" said Charles Montgomery without further comment. But for once, he did not sound vague.

Ben had no close family to invite. His parents were long since dead, and the man who had been his guardian during most of his youth was now a semi-invalid, unable to travel—although it was he, Tasha now discovered, who had taken Ben abroad at an early age. It gave her a curious knotted feeling to realize that her relationship with Ben had been so superficial that she had not even learned those things. Moreover, the superficiality had been her own fault—the result of too much verbal fencing during the past week. Ben had tried often enough to get through the barriers, and Tasha, caught in her web of lies, had not allowed it.

During the weeks that followed Tasha alternated between deep misery and a bittersweet haze of anticipation, as she considered the prospect of her adolescent dreams of romance coming true. She consoled herself in optimistic moments by thinking that if Ben were truly unwilling, there was nothing to make him turn up for the wedding. And then, at the very prospect of his not turning up, she would be once more plunged into deep despair.

For the first time in his life Charles Montgomery seemed aware of her innermost sensitivities. "What's troubling you, Tasha?" he asked somberly about three weeks before the wedding, when she laughed too brightly over nothing, her eyes too shiny beneath their new contact lenses.

"Oh, papa. . . ." All at once she was in tears, and she sobbed out her doubt and her heartbreak and her certainty that Ben would not turn up as promised.

"Don't worry," Charles Montgomery said with a grimness and determination Tasha had never heard before, "he'll be here."

It was not until later that it occurred to Tasha that her father might have brought pressure to bear on Ben through his friend Jim Arthur. That thought offered no consolation; it left her wretched beyond belief. Though totally miserable, she was almost relieved when Ben did not turn up two days before the wedding as promised.

But he had turned up for the ceremony itself, half an hour late. His tardy appearance gave Tasha no comfort, for it was clear that he was in a volcanic frame of mind. His mouth was drawn, his eyes black-rimmed; and when Charles Montgomery asked him stiffly where he had been, Ben did not even answer. And what had followed that night was still, in Tasha's mind, too hurtful to contemplate; but the worst of it all had started with those words:

"For God's sake, Tasha, grow up!"

Picking up the fresh new copy of the fashion magazine, she ripped the front cover off and shredded it savagely into pieces.

CHAPTER TWO

THE RESULTS OF THE PHOTOGRAPH were not long in making themselves felt. A call came from the agency a week later. Tasha was to present herself at the House of Fabienne, most fabulous of all cosmetic companies, headquartered in London, despite the French sound of the name.

"I think they must be looking for a new Fabienne woman," the manager from the agency told her on the telephone. "So look your most beautiful, Tasha! This could be very lucrative for all of us if Max Fabienne likes you. I hear that each year he personally picks the model he wants to use."

"And dates her, too," returned Tasha dryly. "I don't really want to be the latest filly in Maximilien Fabienne's stable."

"You can handle him," came the cheerful answer, showing more confidence than Tasha herself felt. "And some girls don't think Max Fabienne is a fate worse than death, you know. He's very distinguished looking. Generous, too—and quite a charmer, I hear."

"I'm sure. He's had plenty of opportunities to practice his charms. A new one every year."

"Oh, Tasha, he's not like that. Word is that he doesn't actually *do* anything with his models—just likes to be seen with a pretty girl on his arm. It's all part of the public image! Well, can I confirm this for Thursday?"

"I'll go, but I won't promise to do it."

"I won't promise you'll be offered it," returned the woman. "But try, will you?"

The House of Fabienne was all chrome and glass and space, and decorated with the most stunning receptionists Tasha had ever seen. Only one female, a crisp homely woman of about sixty, was less than gorgeous. She inhabited an office next to Max Fabienne's and clearly vetted anyone who was to pass through to the inner sanctum. She introduced herself merely as Morley; Tasha was unsure whether it was first name or last.

"Just Morley," smiled the woman in a way that did nice things for her plain face. She spent a few minutes chatting with Tasha before leading her in to meet Max Fabienne.

He greeted her in an office the size of Tasha's whole apartment, furnished with a lavish use of glass and pearl-gray suede, even to pearl-gray suede on the walls. Max Fabienne was a remarkably well-preserved man, fit and tanned, with distinguished graying temples and the manner of an old-world gentleman. He was, Tasha guessed, in his middle years, probably near fifty.

The object of the interview, it seemed, was not to discuss a contract, but to discuss Tasha. Max Fabienne had a way of remaining polite and detached without being aloof—a subtly reassuring manner that was almost that of the professional listener, doctor or counselor. His impersonal interest allowed Tasha to answer his questions without becoming uncomfortable. His voice was soft and soothing, rather like the pale pearl suede on which Tasha sat, herself a complement to the muted decor in an understated couturier suit of nubbly white wool.

"I'm happy to see you're so prompt, Miss Craig," Max Fabienne observed as soon as Morley had left them alone together.

"Thank you, but it's Mrs. Craig," she corrected him, deciding it was best to set that matter straight immediately.

"You're married?"

Tasha reflected that if she was indeed offered this assignment, it would be impossible to conceal the truth, as she often did from temporary clients. "I've been separated for nearly seven years," she admitted.

His brows lifted at her answer. "You don't appear to be of an age for that," he murmured.

"I recently turned twenty-four."

"Married so young?"

"Yes. It didn't last long."

"A long time to go without a divorce," he observed.

Tasha looked him straight in the eye. "I've always found the marriage useful," she said coolly. "It prevents entanglements. I'm not interested in entanglements—of any kind."

Max Fabienne left that matter for the moment and turned to various questions about her schooling. The answers seemed to meet with his favor. "How long have you been modeling?"

"Six years, but only one as a photographers' model. Before that, I was doing showings in small Paris salons."

"Not too much magazine exposure then; that's an advantage. What made you decide on the career?"

Tasha hesitated and then, because Max Fabienne had turned out to be a surprisingly comfortable sort of person, she told the truth. "I was desperate to earn money, quite a lot of money, and as fast as possible. My father was a zoologist and he died leaving enormous debts. He'd been helping to finance one of his own expeditions, and he seldom troubled himself about things like money, except to borrow it. One of my school friends had started modeling in Paris about that time, and she eased me into it. Being tall helped, too."

"And these, ah, crushing debts?"

"I've just finished paying them off." Suddenly, Tasha found herself wanting this job very badly: there had been too many lean years.

"I take it your husband has never supported you." It was a statement, not a question.

"That's right." For an instant Tasha glanced down at her slender tapered fingers with their polished pearl-pink nails, but other than that, her expression remained totally serene. When she looked up again she smiled composedly. "I've never asked him to," she said.

"If I decide to use you it might be better if you divorced him. Or would he be difficult about it?"

Tasha weighed her answer for a moment. So far, she had been impressed by Max Fabienne; he certainly did not seem the type to have ulterior motives. "No, he wouldn't be difficult. Ben was never the marrying type, and if he hasn't sought a divorce himself there's only one reason." At the polite question mark in Max Fabienne's face, she added dryly: "He can hardly get caught in a marital trap if he's already in one."

"Then you could secure a divorce."

"If I wished." Or an annulment, she added in her head, without saying it out loud. "It would be no trouble."

"Mmm." Max Fabienne paused as if in thought, and for a few minutes contemplated Tasha through half-closed gray slate eyes. A square buffed fingernail tapped against a plate glass tabletop next to the chair he occupied. "Do you have any objection to traveling? Most of our shots are done on location."

To Tasha's relief, the questions now became less personal. At the end of the interview, she had no idea whether she had been hired or not. But that evening, a florist's box arrived at her apartment. It contained two dozen long-stemmed roses, accompanied by a small card with instructions to return to Max Fabienne's office on the morrow. Nestling amidst the flowers was an exquisite pearl necklace with a dia-

mond clasp. Cynically certain that she now understood Max Fabienne's intentions, she returned the
necklace by messenger the following morning without explanation and failed to appear for the second
interview. To her surprise, the phone in her small
apartment rang an hour later.

"Max Fabienne here," said that soft well-
modulated voice. "Did you misunderstand me,
Natasha? I may call you Natasha, may I not? I'm offering you the opportunity to be the Fabienne woman
for this next year. You must know what that means—
fame and fortune. My models are only the best. They
do rather well for themselves after leaving my
employ."

"I understand perfectly well, Mr. Fabienne,"
Tasha replied coolly. "The job sounds fine. It's the
fringe benefits I don't like."

"Ah, but I think you do misunderstand me. The
pearls represent our newest cosmetic line, Essence of
Pearl. They have no—how shall I say it—no strings
attached. To be the Fabienne woman calls for public
performances, not private ones."

"I wish I could believe that."

"Perhaps you will after lunch. I've made reservations for one o'clock. My chauffeur will pick you up.
He will have the pearls with him. Wear them," he
told her, and with a few more instructions, he rang
off.

Curious now rather than hopeful, Tasha attended
the lunch, in a restaurant famed for its astronomical
prices as much as for its exquisite cuisine. Max Fa-

bienne was suave and attentive and a perfect gentleman, and it was hard to disbelieve him when he told
her of the reasons behind his actions.

"The pearls were my way of finding out about
you, Natasha. After more than a quarter century of
dealing with the modeling profession I have found
there are too many women willing to thrust something my way that I haven't asked for. Had you accepted the pearls and appeared for the interview, I
would have thanked you politely for your time—and
wished you goodbye. In sending them back you
assured yourself of the job, especially as Morley ap-
proves of you, too. I'm hiring a model, my dear
child, not a mistress. By the way, I highly recommend the *salade niçoise*—the chef here has a way
with greens, and they're marvelous for the complexion. Shall I order for you? One can't be too careful
about such things as diet. Well, Natasha...yes or
no?"

"To which question?"

"Will you be the new Fabienne woman?"

"Yes—I will," agreed Tasha, "as long as we
understand each other."

"Good. Then that answers my other question. I
will order for you." After doing so, he went on, "I
must warn you that I'll take an intimate interest in
every detail of your life—except the one aspect you
seemed to be worried about. What you eat, what you
wear, where you go—all these things are a part of the
public image you must project, a public image I intend to orchestrate. Even such small things as the

necklace you must accept, and other trifles as well. There's nothing personal in these gifts. You see, Natasha, my own public image is also involved. People expect me to shower you with gifts and attentions, and it makes good press. I want every woman in the world to know that Max Fabienne can make a woman feel like a woman—protected, pampered, cosseted, loved, whirled into a world of excitement and romance beyond her wildest dreams. What the public sees in the man they see in the product, and what they see in the product they buy. By the way, I've arranged for a box at the theater tonight. An opening benefit performance. It will be a rather formal affair with a reception afterward.''

Tasha, dismayed by the speed with which her life was being rearranged, demurred. "I'm not sure I have suitable clothes, Mr. Fabienne. I live a very simple life.''

"Max, from now on," he corrected her. "And you will have suitable clothes. By the time I deliver you back to your apartment—Morley will find you a better one, by the way; your address is not very fashionable—there should be quite a choice. Several couturiers are delivering selections I chose personally this morning. I recommend the white crepe, if it fits. It has a certain elegant simplicity of line. Naturally, from now on, your clothes will be especially designed for you on my personal instructions. Several fittings are scheduled for tomorrow, starting at noon. A little late, it is true, but after the theater tonight, you will need your beauty sleep, hmm?''

And so it all began—the whirl of existence punctuated with long and exhausting photography sessions. Max Fabienne, Tasha had to admit, had reached the top of his profession for good reason. He took advice from no one but Morley, who had been his woman Friday since day one. He was tireless in his pursuit of perfection; no detail was too small for his attention. He passed judgment on everything: Tasha's gowns, Tasha's shoes, Tasha's jewels and furs, Tasha's new apartment, the color of her lipstick and the shade of her eyeshadow. Only her hair he left alone, other than to decree the exact shampoo she must use every morning. "Perfect," he told her. "Black, silky, sensuous—a siren's hair. But the length and the straightness give a touch of innocence, hmm? Like Aphrodite emerging from the sea, still untouched but with all the knowledge of the ages in her bones...ah, that is the image I want for my new line, the Drenched Look. We must photograph it by the sea."

Tasha had learned by now that Max's thought patterns revolved incessantly around the cosmetics industry. That was his first love, his life, his obsession. No wonder there was no room for any woman in his existence, beyond the current Fabienne woman!

Therefore, when he proposed three months after taking over her life, she listened with a surprise bordering on shock. He had come into her apartment for a nightcap; they were seated in sumptuous surroundings, on a velvet-covered couch of pale gray— Max's favorite color for Tasha's apartment, as well as for his own office.

"Purely a business arrangement, my dear Natasha," he told her in an emotionless velvet voice. "I've been intending to marry for several years now, and only circumstances have prevented me from doing so. And I feel I must marry a Fabienne woman—the image, you know. Frankly, I would have asked the last one but for the fact that she made the mistake of advertising herself as too available to other comers. I couldn't afford infidelity in a wife! And the one before that became engaged to some previous boyfriend. In any case, I decided after meeting you that a divorced woman might suit my purposes best; then, there will be less talk of a winter-spring affair. I've been watching you closely. You have a certain fastidiousness that appeals to me. Perhaps I should state that more plainly?"

"Please do," Tasha requested, playing for time. Her mind spun crazily; Max Fabienne had become almost a father figure to her, and she could still not conceive of the idea of becoming his wife.

"It's difficult to put it delicately. Shall I say you seem to have no particular interest in the opposite sex? Well. . .have I observed correctly?"

Tasha decided that honesty was the best approach; by now, she knew Max Fabienne well enough that she could be quite outspoken. She answered him quietly, "I suppose you're right. My small experience of marriage put me off men. I used to date on occasion, but I soon found that the men involved expected more than I was prepared to give. After a time I decided it was easier not to date at all. It's true, I don't have much interest in men.''

"Ah." Max regarded her through narrowed contemplative eyes. "For myself, I have a fierce interest in women—but for all women, and in the purest aesthetic sense. Women as objects of beauty, not as subjects of some rather distasteful athletic enterprise. And yet a wife would be very useful to me. I'm a realist, my dear. I'm quite aware that my years of appearing to be a dashing Lothario are nearing an end. My time is running out, Natasha. Facelifts can do only so much!'' Max Fabienne appeared, or pretended, not to notice the curious glance Tasha cast him at this revelation. He went on, "An elderly man escorting a stunning young model around town becomes an object of pity—not envy. I'm sixty now; did you know that?''

Tasha was startled; he seemed no more than fifty. "No, Max, I didn't realize.''

"I thought it best to be honest if we are to enter into a new kind of contract. Does it frighten you? Ten, perhaps fifteen years of serving as companion to a man in his declining years.... Someday you would be a very wealthy woman, Natasha. Well, have I your answer? It should not take more than a few months to put an end to your charade of a marriage.''

Tasha licked her lips. "I doubt it would take that long, Max. To tell the truth, I could have ended it years ago, if I had cared to.''

Max raised a quizzical eyebrow.

"An annulment," Tasha explained. "It was never consummated. I was only with him one night and nothing... happened." Remembering now how painful that "nothing" had been, Tasha hid the memory behind a light defensive laugh. "I suppose I could use the evidence now," she said.

Max seemed alarmed. "I'd prefer you didn't do that, Natasha. People are bound to be curious as to why the marriage was never consummated. It would do my image no good if people thought I was marrying a woman who was, er, incapable of satisfying a man."

"But that's exactly what you are doing," Tasha pointed out with a mirthless smile.

"Ah, but that's a secret between you and me, my dear. No, this must be done by divorce. In fact, after some thought on the matter I've decided it's best if your husband divorces *you*—naming me as corespondent. We could provide him with evidence of infidelity, hmm?"

Tasha stared at Max with deep surprise, and only the fact that she did not wish to offend him prevented her from giving voice to a laugh that would have been quite genuine this time.

"Manufactured out of whole cloth, of course," Max elaborated silkily to Tasha's relief. "Surely your husband would be amenable."

"I don't know," Tasha said slowly. Ben would have no compunction about shedding her, she knew; but in his own time and in his own way. It was entirely possible that, if asked for his cooperation, he would not give it. "He might take a notion to refuse. Ben can be very...stubborn."

"Money might be an inducement," Max suggested.

"With some people, yes. Somehow I don't think it would in this case."

"Yet I imagined he was not a wealthy man. Didn't you say he had never supported you? I had visions of a rather feckless fellow—a rolling stone, as it were."

Tasha became uncomfortably conscious of her heartbeat. Why did even the thought of Ben make her hurt somewhere in the region of her ribs? "A rolling stone...yes, I suppose he is that. But I imagine he's not badly off by now. His latest book did quite well—an account of how he sailed single-handedly around the world. He's not the first to do it, but there's always an audience for that sort of thing."

Max's fine eyebrows raised a fraction at that piece of news. "Craig, Craig...not Bennett Craig, by chance? Yes, I've read some of his articles. His ketch is called *Adam's Folly*, I believe? An adventurer, then, of sorts."

"That's right. Ben's the independent type. He can also be very blunt when he chooses. If you offered him money he might tell you to...to...."

"Go to hell? Or will his language be even cruder than that?" Max gave a short, soft cynical laugh. "My lawyers can be very persuasive, Natasha. If you give me some idea of where your husband can be reached...."

"I have no idea where he is," Tasha said, suddenly feeling exhausted. "In any case, Max, I think Ben would be more cooperative if I contacted him myself. I could probably manage to do that through his publisher."

"Excellent, excellent. Then, if he seems uncooperative, you can divorce *him*. Infidelity, I think, would make better press than desertion. . . . Ah, yes, a little publicity suggesting that your former husband is a womanizer would do my image no harm, no harm at all! We'll marry as soon as—"

"Max," interrupted Tasha, "you haven't actually heard my answer."

"But, my dear, I have." Max picked up her unresisting hand from the edge of the velvet-covered couch and deposited a discreet kiss on her fingertips. "You gave me your answer when you offered to get in touch with your husband. Do you know, I believe fire opals would suit you very well. Or perhaps black pearls. . . ."

And so, because by then she was indeed quite fond of Max—and perhaps also because she was to some extent beginning to enjoy a life that was organized for her into reassuringly luxurious compartments— Tasha accepted, two days later, an engagement ring that was an enormous black pearl encircled with diamonds of no mean size. She also made the phone call to Ben's publisher—not Jim Arthur; Ben had given him his walking papers years before—and left a message implying some urgency.

Certain that Ben was in some remote corner of the

globe, she expected to hear nothing for several weeks. Surprisingly, the call came late that same night—or perhaps, to be more exact, at two o'clock the following morning, moments after Tasha had returned from a very dull and long-drawn-out embassy reception. She answered the ringing phone with no particular expectations, wondering if someone had dialed the wrong number.

"I thought you were in a hurry," came Ben's cool voice, exactly as if it had been only yesterday that she had spoken to him last. Tasha's stomach knotted as though in the grip of a giant fist. His tone was so casual that he might have been phoning from somewhere in London, and only the static of poor long-distance communication told her it was not so. "I've been trying to get you for four hours. Where have you been?"

Tasha tried to still the thudding of her heart; she was sure it could be heard across the wires. Was it possible that the mere sound of his voice could bring back all the uncertainties of her aching adolescence? Her voice, when she managed to find it, came out as a parody of itself, brittle and artificial, all natural huskiness lost in the shock of the moment. "I might ask the same of you, Ben. Only I've been wondering where you are for a lot longer. Seven years, in fact! You took off in a terrible hurry after our wedding, didn't you?"

"Not fast enough," he said, his voice measured but coolly insulting. "What's the big urgency to talk to me after all these years?"

"I want a divorce," she said.

"Done," came the prompt and mocking answer. "And now that you have it, I'll say goodbye. Don't call me, I'll—"

"Wait! Don't hang up. I'm not joking, Ben, I really do want a divorce, and I need your help."

"Ah." There was a short heavy silence. "Why don't you just get an annulment, as you should have done years ago? Don't bother answering that; I imagine it's because the proof has long since been tampered with."

Tasha felt her insides curdling and took a tighter grip on the telephone wire to steady herself. "I'm going to be married, Ben. I'd like that divorce as soon as possible."

"Go right ahead," he said coolly. "I'm not stopping you. Who's the unlucky man? Don't bother answering that, either; I really don't care."

Tasha stiffened. "The man is Max Fabienne," she said.

"That excuse for a human being who's been squiring you around for the past couple of months?" Ben chuckled, not too pleasantly. "The two of you deserve each other. Now, if you'll excuse me, there's someone waiting for—"

"Ben!" Tasha spoke swiftly, communicating her urgency. "This is important. I want you to divorce *me*. Max and I will provide you with evidence."

Her words stopped Ben in the act of hanging up. Tasha heard him laugh again, this time quite nastily. "Well, well. I can only think of one reason for going about things in such a backhanded way. I always thought there was less to Max Fabienne than met the eye. As I said, brown eyes, a very good match for you.''

"Will you do it or not?"

"Do what?"

"Divorce me."

"I told you, Tasha," came the derisive answer, "I already did. I divorced you years ago."

"You...what?" The words were faint, quite unlike Tasha's usual self-possessed tones. She had always known this was a possibility; there were places in the world that catered to short-order divorces. All the same, it took her by surprise.

"Oh, didn't you get the papers? Must have been an oversight."

To help her through the awkward moment, Tasha laughed—a trilling little laugh that was nerves, pure nerves. "Some oversight! Really, Ben, I do think you might have let me know!"

This time the silence on the other end of the phone was so long, so laden, that Tasha finally said, with another bright manufactured laugh, "Ben? Did you drop dead? Or is that just wishful thinking?"

"I'm still here," he said at last, his voice now no longer mocking but cold and controlled.

"Do you have proof of this divorce? Some papers?"

"Yes," he said in a flat tone, "I have proof."

"Can you send me something? A notarized copy, perhaps?"

Tasha could hear Ben's breathing in the phone. "If you want the proof," he said slowly, "you'll have to come to where I am and get it."

Tasha took a deep swallow. "And just exactly where are you?" she asked with a lightness she did not feel.

"I'll tell you in a minute." His tones were low, unemphatic, and yet in the very stillness of his voice there was an implicit warning that told Tasha he meant every word he said. "But first let me tell you this. If you don't come where I want, when I want, I'll fight you every inch of the way. You'll never find out where I got the divorce, for one thing. And if you set about trying to get another one...why, I'll just have to make it as difficult as possible for you. You did say you were in a hurry, didn't you?"

Tasha controlled her temper. "I'm sure I can get a divorce without your cooperation, if I must."

"On the other hand," Ben went on with a mock geniality that fooled Tasha not at all, "do as I say, and I'll cooperate in any way you want. Why, I won't even spread nasty rumors about you and your popinjay friend Max—not that I would anyway, but—"

"That's enough, Ben," she said coldly. "Just give me a small hint about your motives. After seven years of not giving a damn about my whereabouts, it's hard to believe you're suddenly anxious to see me. Why do you want me to come to...wherever it is?"

Ben hesitated. "Let's just say," he suggested softly, "that I have a sudden irresistible urge to see you."

Tasha's heart did a quick flop, then righted itself at once when she heard a muffled wheedling on the other end of the line. "Ben, you said...." The rest of the sentence was cut off. Tasha guessed that Ben had covered the telephone with his hand, but not before she had recognized the interruption as coming from a woman.

"Exactly where are you?" she asked lightly, when he had come back on the line. "I assume it's some-place civilized, for a change. If you were at the ends of the earth, you wouldn't be running across gossip columns about me and Max."

"I saw those a couple of months ago, when I happened to be in London," he came back imperturbably.

"Then you can't be so very anxious to see me after all."

Ben laughed derisively. "Very perceptive of you. So I'll just have to leave my motives to your imagination. If you want my cooperation, I'll expect you here...let's see, as it's an overnight flight, I don't think you can make it before the day after tomorrow."

Tasha gasped. "I certainly can't do that! I have fittings for the next two days and then I leave for Greece."

"Then change your plans," he warned softly.

"I can't! There's a whole planeload of people involved, and deadlines to meet. I can't reorganize my whole life just for you!"

"You're asking me to reorganize my life for you,"

Ben pointed out tauntingly. "Now I could hang up and get back to the very pressing business that's waiting here at hand...."

Tasha heard a muffled throaty gurgle in the background at his end and compressed her lips. Well, at least she suspected that Ben's motives, murky though they might be, included no designs on her own person. "I'll have to ask Max if the shoot can be postponed," she conceded in a brittle voice. "Exactly where is it you expect me to be?"

"The Seychelles," he said.

"Is that a place—or part of a tongue twister?"

"They're the islands I call home—or as much of a home as I have." Ben's level tone made Tasha feel a fleeting sense of shame for her waspish sarcasm, especially as she had indeed heard of the Seychelles, although she had only the vaguest notion of their whereabouts.

"They're off the east coast of Africa," Ben told her now. "Plan to stay for a week. I'm in Victoria right now, the capital. I'll meet you at the airport, the day after tomorrow. If I happen to miss you there, I'll contact you at your hotel. I'll make a reservation for you at...let me see, The Boulders should be civilized enough for you.... And to answer your question, no, I'm not."

"Not what?"

"Bedding down at the same hotel," came the deeply mocking reply. "I have other sleeping arrangements."

Tasha managed to maintain her breezy manner.

"Do you mind giving me her number? I'll have to contact Max and call you back in a few minutes with my answer. Or would you prefer I didn't call for an hour or two?" She forced a light lilting laugh. "I wouldn't want to interru—"

And then she halted and started shaking uncontrollably, because Ben had hung up and she was talking to the burr of an empty line.

CHAPTER THREE

TASHA'S NERVES were still jangling thirty minutes later, when despite the hour she put a call through to Max. After she had given him a quick summary of the conversation with Ben, she added, "I wouldn't have listened to him at all, Max, except for those veiled threats he made. The whole thing is preposterous, of course, but I thought it was best to check with you."

"Your husband—or should I say your ex-husband—sounds like an altogether preposterous man," Max noted smoothly. He sounded totally alert and calm, although Tasha's call had wakened him from a deep sleep. "Perhaps, Natasha, it is best to take the man at face value and consider doing as he asks."

"Max! You don't mean that, do you? Why, I can't possibly be there the day after tomorrow. . . and after the way he hung up on me, I really don't want to go."

"An understandable reaction," Max assured her. "Nevertheless, I believe we should give some thought to his bizarre request. Why do you think he has made it?"

"I have absolutely no idea," Tasha replied truthfully. "The last time I spoke to Ben was by telephone shortly after our wedding night. He told me he never wanted to see me again in his life."

Max's small silence ended in a silky and mildly reproving directive. "Perhaps it's time for you to tell me more of what happened that night, Natasha. If this outlandish man has some knowledge that could be hurtful in some way. . . ."

"There's very little to tell, Max. Ben was in a very black frame of mind that night. I'm sure it was because he felt pressured; he didn't want to marry me in the first place."

"Why did he marry you, then?"

"I don't know," Tasha returned with the small feeling of helplessness that always came to her when she contemplated that very question. "At the time I thought it was because my father had some influence with a publisher—James Arthur—who was considering taking Ben on. Oh, it was true enough that my father had been trying to exert pressure. But I found out later that Ben had told Mr. Arthur where to get off in no uncertain terms. He ended up with a different publisher altogether. So I have to assume he married me for some other reason—a sense of honor, perhaps."

"Hmm," said Max. "'And what went wrong on the wedding night?"

"He got very angry. I don't know exactly why, but I think it was because he was feeling trapped—for whatever reason." Why had Ben been in such an explosive mood that night? Tasha's head began to throb, as it always did when she considered the happenings of that night. But she could not tell Max everything, and so she said simply, "He walked out on me. It wasn't until a couple of days later that I found out Ben had married me for some reason of his own, nothing to do with my father's pressures at all. Not that it would have made any difference, Max. By then Ben had vanished into nowhere. He simply . . . didn't want to be married to me."

"Then there's no possibility he's thinking in terms of a reunion of some kind?"

"None at all." Tasha was emphatic about that. "He doesn't even like me very much, Max. I can't imagine why he wants to see me."

"Hmm," said Max thoughtfully. Then, coming to a decision, he launched into a smooth flow of instructions. Max was less ignorant than Tasha on the subject of the Seychelles; it seemed he had once considered filming a television commercial there.

"Prepare to leave tomorrow evening, my dear. It will indeed be an overnight flight, as you were told. I'll phone Morley at once and have her make arrangements. With the amount of traveling we do, I imagine we have all the proper immunizations, hmm?"

"We?"

"I intend to come with you, of course. I have to protect my investment! Do you think I would risk the Fabienne woman in the hands of such an outrageous man as your husband? If he has some kind of revenge in mind—"

"My ex-husband, Max," Tasha corrected with a lightness that denied the dull ache in her heart. "And somehow, I don't think Ben's intentions involve bodily harm."

"Max Fabienne takes no chances," came the velvety reply. "Your face, Natasha, is my fortune."

"But Max, the fittings for the Drenched Look...."

"The clothes," he proclaimed with absolute certainty, "will fit. You'll understand, Natasha, when you see them. Morley will phone you tomorrow to confirm flight arrangements. Pack the wardrobe that was intended for the trip to Greece; it will do very well for an interlude by the sea. For the flight tomorrow, wear the new Halston—the moss-green silk. I believe it will resist creasing very well...."

Tasha absorbed Max's instructions automatically, with the professional part of her mind. Gradually, as Max injected a note of ordered sanity into the venture, Tasha began to accustom herself to the idea that she must screw up her courage to face Ben again. Perhaps it would not be so hard with Max along— and doubtless Morley would be there, too; she always traveled with Max.

"Are you sure you can get airline tickets for us, Max?" she inserted suddenly into the one-sided conversation.

"As we shall travel by the House of Fabienne jet," Max said, "I foresee no need for tickets at all."

"The jet! That's a lot of airplane for two or three people."

Max's small chuckle was typically silky. "But, Natasha, there will be many more than two or three people involved. Do you think I will waste a week of your time—or mine? This will be a working trip, my dear. Those photographs for the Drenched Look—I can do them in the Seychelles. The locale should be just as suitable as Greece, hmm? Now go back to bed and rest; I must phone Morley at once. And take heart, Natasha. What can possibly go wrong?"

With Ben, everything, a little warning voice told Tasha; and although she followed Max's advice and tried to rest, she spent the rest of the night tossing fitfully, reliving the aches of that awkward adolescence she had long since put behind her.

Somehow, Max had everything arranged before the deadline. His whole week had been rescheduled, and so had everyone else's. The power of the House of Fabienne breaking all barriers, including that of time, Tasha reflected wryly. When Max talked in that gentle silken voice of his, everyone listened—and jumped. By the time Tasha arrived at the airport the following evening, squired by Max in his limousine, everyone and everything was waiting: luggage, equipment, cameras, photographer and photographer's assistant, art director, wardrobe assistant, cosmetician, seamstress, prop girl, the invaluable and ever-cheerful Morley, a secretary, Max's personal masseuse, and four men who looked more like bodyguards than anything else. They had a vaguely familiar air; had she seen them before?

Tasha was unsurprised to see that the photographer on this trip was Jon Lassiter. She was not the only person to benefit from the cover photograph; Max had been impressed enough that he had taken to awarding a good number of assignments to the young photographer. Tasha was surprised, however, to see that Jon, whom she quite liked, had Lisette, whom she didn't, in tow. Max, too, seemed taken aback by this and somewhat annoyed. Tasha heard him exchange a few quiet words with Morley on the subject and gathered that Jon had succumbed to his paramour's pressure to bring her along, and had in fact refused to come without her.

"Well, well," Lisette purred *sotto voce* to Tasha, as the whole assemblage began to file onto the plane. "Haven't you been the busy little girl since last we met."

"Very," Tasha said discouragingly.

"And I hear it's all because of our last assignment together—the day you came unzipped. I take it you've stayed that way? I can't think of another reason Max Fabienne would be using you."

"Keep thinking," Tasha said coldly. "It's a good exercise for an idle mind."

"My interest is not exactly idle, darling. I've been dying to meet Max Fabienne for a very long time. If someone's scissors hadn't slipped on that cover photograph, I'm sure I'd have succeeded instead of someone else. How does it feel to be the Fabienne woman? Or rather, how does Max Fabienne feel? As smooth as he looks?"

"Ask his masseuse," Tasha came back promptly.

Lisette arched her eyebrows and smiled. "The Swedish girl? Really, darling, I wouldn't dare, in case she took offense. She looks as though she could level me with her little finger."

Tasha opened her mouth to voice the retort for which Lisette had left herself open, but suddenly she found herself sick and tired of the meaningless exchange. So instead, she merely trailed a cool look from Lisette's artfully untidy hairdo to Lisette's immaculately shod toe. In between, there was a good deal of décolletage—all of it, Tasha decided, on display for Max Fabienne's benefit. "I'm very tired, Lisette. Do you mind if we have this conversation some other time?"

"My, my, we are below scratch, aren't we. And big black circles, too. Was Max frisky last night?"

Lisette's innuendos came to a halt as Max arrived at Tasha's elbow to escort her onto the plane. He chose to sit next to her, a gesture of reassurance for which she was grateful, even though he spent the first part of the trip dictating into a small tape recorder. It didn't occur to Tasha to question the fact that Max should continue to attend to business. To Max, the cosmetics industry was everything; he had never pretended anything else. Tasha sensed that he had developed a certain detached fondness for her; but she also knew that her main function in his life was that of an investment. A troublesome one at the moment, to be sure; but an investment all the same, and one not easily replaced.

Max put the tape recorder aside when a meal arrived after they had been aloft for about an hour. "I believe I'll allow you a little champagne this evening, Natasha. It may help settle you for the night. One glass only, though; a hundred extra calories is concession enough."

Tasha sipped at the unaccustomed champagne, which was if nothing else a welcome change from Perrier, and picked at an exquisitely prepared but lonely-looking lamb chop flanked by perfectly cooked asparagus tips. Usually her tastes ran to more than Max allowed her, but tonight it was not so. "I know so little about the Seychelles, Max. Exactly where are they?"

"In the Indian Ocean," Max told her. Tasha's brow knotted briefly as an elusive memory tantalized her brain. *He knows the Indian Ocean like the back of his hand....*

"North of Madagascar," Max went on. "Don't do those things to your forehead, Natasha. It injures the skin. The islands used to be French long ago, British more recently—but no longer. They're independent now. A little more remote than Greece, but I believe they'll be quite satisfactory from our point of view. And with their new international airport, not so very remote after all. We'll charter a boat and scout for locations. Morley has brought extensive travel literature with her. During this flight she'll read up on the pertinent facts and give us a report tomorrow when we arrive. You're not nervous, are you, Natasha?"

"Not at all," Tasha lied; for in truth the recollection that the Indian Ocean was Ben's territory had left her mouth dry and her palms damp. She put her fork down, giving up all pretense of eating food she did not want.

"The bodyguards are for you, my dear," Max told her, confirming her suspicions about the four burly men who sat silently in the banks of seats behind them. "They have orders to watch you night and day, in shifts. Two men to guard over your every move, at all times. Each of them is handpicked, Natasha, and skilled in the martial arts. How can you come to any harm?"

"I'm sure they won't be necessary, Max. I don't really think Ben plans anything physical."

"And yet," Max murmured, surprising Tasha with his perception, "you are more upset than you admit."

For once, Tasha did not try to hide behind a smile. She sighed, "Ben left a lot of emotional scars, Max."

"They show only in the interesting hollows of your face, Natasha my darling. So even emotional scars have a use, hmm? By the way, you haven't asked me yet about the outfit for the photographs."

"What is it?" Tasha asked automatically, trying to feign an interest she did not feel.

"Blue jeans," said Max triumphantly.

"Blue jeans?" Even Tasha's other worries could not totally eclipse her sense of surprise. The Fabienne woman in blue jeans?

"Blue jeans wet from the sea," Max told her. "Not really from the sea of course—the salt would be much too hard on your skin and hair, especially as

you may have to remain wet for several hours each
day. We'll douse you as needed with fresh water, and
perhaps some special emollient to protect your skin.
Wet blue jeans and a simple white T-shirt, clinging
and provocative. Perhaps lying on a rock, or leaning
against a large boulder, spray about your feet. . . ah,
I can see it already. I've brought dozens of T-shirts
and jeans to choose from; all custom-made, of
course, from special fabrics I've chosen. A master-
stroke! The Fabienne woman as everywoman—and
every young woman will be able to see herself as you!
I'm quite excited by the whole prospect. So much
more creative than a bathing suit or even a wet evening dress, don't you think?''

"Yes," murmured Tasha, feeling for once quite
overcome by Max's obsessive dedication to his life's
work. She sensed he had been trying to distract her;
nevertheless she was quite relieved when he returned
to his dictating machine shortly thereafter, leaving
her to her own thoughts. It was not long before exhaustion from the previous night drove her into a
deep and dreamless sleep.

They crossed several time zones and stopped twice
for refueling. Although Tasha's unadjusted watch
showed an early hour, it was midmorning when the
order came to fasten seat belts for the last time.
Beyond the plane window a cluster of dark, mountainous mist-shrouded islands loomed out of a jewel-
like sea as the plane began its descent.

"Mahé," Max told her, consulting a map, "is the
name of the main island, the one where we will be

landing. The other islands seem to have a strange mix of French and English names. La Digue, Bird Island, Curieuse. . . ."

They cushioned down onto the runway, and moments later Max and Tasha and their oddly assorted entourage spilled out of the plane. It had rained recently; the breathtaking forested slopes of the island's upward-jutting interior were steaming beneath the equatorial sun. It was hot and humid but, with sea breezes to cool the air, not impossible to bear. Nevertheless, Tasha was glad of the printed silk decreed by Max for the trip; it was suitably light and fresh in appearance, despite its sophistication.

In the terminal, there was no sign of Ben. Not so surprising, thought Tasha wryly; he would be watching for the regular flights. All the same she felt a curious frisson of something—doubt, disappointment, premonition of disaster?—across her skin, despite the heat of the tropic air.

Morley had managed to arrange accommodation for the entire party in the hotel mentioned by Ben. After a short delay at the airport while visitor passes were secured, most of the party piled into a coach that would transfer them to the hotel. Tasha was too distracted to note Lisette's envious glance at the large, sleek black limousine that had been laid on especially for more favored members of the party.

Morley joined Tasha and Max in the limousine, as did one of the bodyguards, who took his place beside the driver. Morley, who had a photographic memory, was by now thoroughly conversant with the facts in her guidebooks.

"First," Max instructed as the vehicle set off, "tell me about this hotel we're being taken to."

"The best on the island," the invaluable Morley assured him, without having to refer to any of the literature she had read. "On the sea, of course; nearly all hotels here are. The Boulders is owned by an elderly retired American who lives on the island of Praslin. I should tell you about that island, Max. There's a very curious valley there, and the story is that—"

"Stick to the point, Morley," Max reminded her softly.

"I believe The Boulders would have been your own choice, Max. It's about ten miles from here on the other side of the capital—a tidy tropical town called Victoria, by the way; we'll pass through it soon. The hotel has air conditioning, telephones, television, swimming pool, separate cottages luxuriously appointed...."

Tasha hardly heard Morley's description of the hotel, because at mention of the town of Victoria she had gone on instant alert. Her heart palpitated more quickly as it became clear they had entered the approach to the town.

"This is Mont Fleuri Road," Morley said, without reference to a map. "The hospital's over there, then the botanical gardens. There's an aviary there and giant land tortoises. There are also some very interesting palm trees, if you—"

"The vegetation," Max interrupted, "is of no particular interest at the moment. Nor is the wildlife. If I wish to know such things I will ask. What else have you learned?"

"The Seychelles were first sighted by Vasco da Gama but weren't colonized until about two hundred years ago—by the French, and by freed slaves from Africa. There's a very strong streak of mysticism and superstition in the islands. The African heritage, no doubt."

"Interesting," murmured Max.

"The population is mostly Creole, because intermarriage has always been common. The Seychellois pride themselves on having no color barriers. Only the shopkeepers—East Indians, most of them—tend to keep to themselves. Other than that you'll find English, Europeans, Chinese, a very heterogeneous mix. Both English and French are spoken here on Mahé, but for everyday use the Seychellois speak a Creole patois—archaic French heavily larded with English, Hindustani and Bantu words. Guttural and virtually incomprehensible to the untrained ear, I understand."

As the car nosed its way along sleepy streets, Tasha saw a mixed population much as Morley was describing. Nowhere was there a tall lithe man with bronze lights in his hair. Most of the islanders were considerably shorter than Ben, with complexions ranging from pale café-au-lait to nut brown.

The town of Victoria seemed to grow out of the very hillside, its corrugated roofs nestling amidst exuberant vegetation and lush-leaved trees. To the east, morning sun sparkled on the water of the harbor. Morley pointed out various landmarks—the yacht club, the Stade Populaire, the docks where ferryboats departed for other islands.

As the limousine rounded a corner and aimed away from the waterfront into the heart of the town, Morley noted, "Oh, he's going to show us Gordon Square. It's named after one of the more famous visitors to the Seychelles—General Charles "Chinese" Gordon. He came here several years before he died in Khartoum; and later, Max, you must let me tell you that story. But right now, have a look at the clock tower. Odd, isn't it, to see it in miniature in the middle of a tropical town? Why, you'd think you were right back at the Houses of Parliament if you half closed your eyes."

In the center of the square was a fenced-in cast-iron replica of London's most famous clock, perfect in every proportion although it was only three or four times as tall as a man. Tasha gave it no more than a glance; her eyes were too busy screening sidewalks and store entrances, hoping to catch a glimpse of Ben among those unhurried figures that ambled along the streets, straw-hatted against the heat of the equatorial sun.

It was not until the limousine had worked its way through the town and joined a road leading through the island's lush interior, that Tasha subsided into her seat and began to pay attention to Morley's words again.

"You know, Max, one of the writers said these islands were the perfect setting for a comic opera, and I think he might be right. There are such lovely local customs. For one thing, they say the town ends just at that point where the Seychelles women take off their shoes—or put them on, depending on which way they're heading. And do you know, I saw someone doing that a minute ago?" Morley laughed in a warm cheerful way that seemed to light up her unbeautiful face. "Another custom is that the clock—a different clock, the one in the cathedral—always chimes each hour twice. It chimes on the hour, and then again a couple of minutes later—a second chance, I suppose, for those who missed it the first time. That's the kind of country it is."

"Whimsical," murmured Max, "but hardly essential to our purpose here. Now tell me about the food."

"Creole cuisine based largely on seafood, and quite spicy."

"No spicy foods for Natasha; they interfere with the digestion. See if the hotel will agree to take on a French chef while we are here. Fly one in if necessary. If the hotel is uncooperative, try to contact the owner; I may consider buying the establishment. I'll want to charter a boat, Morley; undoubtedly the hotel can arrange it. A craft suitable for scouting purposes. Make sure there is also a competent guide familiar with the shorelines. Have him present himself at ten o'clock tomorrow morning."

"Yes, Max," Morley answered promptly, and Tasha knew Max's orders were as good as done.

"I'll meet the man to explain the kind of location we're looking for. Our art director and photographer can do some preliminary scouting tomorrow morning; I'll pass judgment on their choice in the afternoon. We start shooting the day after tomorrow."

"But Max," started Tasha, "what if Ben—"

"Relax, my dear." Max laid a cool reassuring hand over hers. How did he manage to have cool hands, Tasha wondered, when the surrounding air was so warm? "Tomorrow you will be at the hotel all day, trying on blue jeans for the shoot. Although they were all made to your specifications, there are minor variations of detailing that I wish to pass judgment on. Your ex-husband will have plenty of opportunity to contact you. No doubt he will do so this afternoon, hmm?"

For the few remaining minutes of the trip, Tasha slipped back into her own thoughts, no longer listening to Morley's recital of facts. Curiously, despite her reluctance to see Ben, there was an ache of disappointment deep inside that he had not been on hand at the airport. It brought back all too clearly the agonizing feelings of her youth, when Ben had not shown up by the hour of the wedding: the awful gnawing sense of hurt and despair she had tried to hide behind the frozen mask of her face. And then, when Ben had arrived, he had been like a stranger. . . .

The hotel was opulent, as Morley had promised. The main building was low, modern, architect designed, and constructed of local granite with a lavish use of glass, which afforded splendid views of the sea and ubiquitous palms. The gleaming scalloped shoreline of white sand was strewn with enormous primeval boulders, a feature, Morley had told them, of Mahé. Closer to the hotel, flowering vines climbed many of the tree trunks, lending splashes of color and spilling heavy blossom scents into the humid air.

The lobby was cool, but even here faint floral fragrances seemed to invade the air-conditioned space. Rough stone textures, smooth mirrored surfaces and potted plants gave the hotel a contemporary ambience that had not been present in the somnolent tropical town of Victoria, with its old-fashioned frame structures and its relics of colonial years.

The motor coach had arrived some minutes earlier, and most members of the entourage had already vanished to inspect their cottages. Max, Tasha, Morley and two of the bodyguards remained in the lobby; the other two, Max explained, had gone to inspect the accommodation to be used by himself and Tasha. Within seconds the smile-wreathed hotel manager appeared.

"Ah, Mr. Fabienne." He spoke in English. His features and skin betrayed his Creole ancestry, and his voice bore strong traces of French. "This is indeed an honor! As manager of this hotel, may I say I am delighted you have chosen to stay in our establishment. I confess there was some trouble to find enough space for your party, but. . . ."

Tasha listened with no particular interest while the hotel manager went through his paces. During the exchange, she stood several steps behind Max, furtively looking over the people in the lobby and those coming and going at the entrance of what appeared to be a dining room. No one was tall and broad-shouldered with vital bronze-streaked hair and tawny tortoiseshell eyes. The only tall broad-shouldered men in the lobby were the two bodyguards, of whom she remained uncomfortably conscious as they moved unobtrusively around in the background, inspecting potted palms as though they expected them to conceal Ben.

"Oh, by the way, Mr. Fabienne, a message came a few moments ago for some member of your party. Is there a Miss Montgomery with you?"

It took Tasha a moment to realize that the manager was talking about her. Max, too, seemed momentarily nonplussed, until Tasha signified that the message was directed to herself. The little lurch of feeling occasioned by Ben's use of her maiden name was well concealed as she listened to the manager's words.

"It was a man who left the message. He said only that he would not be able to see you today. He left no name."

"Was he. . . here in person?" asked Tasha.

"No, the message came by telephone."

"Did he say when he would call again?"

"I am afraid not," the manager said pleasantly and turned his attention back to Max.

"There are some special things we shall need," Max said serenely. "Expense is no object. My assistant has a list. . . ."

Tasha sighed and forced herself to think of something other than Ben. Her spike-heeled custom-made sandals, mere slivers of creamy leather that made her two inches taller than Max, were beginning to hurt. She longed to slip them off. She flexed a foot and rubbed its toes surreptitiously against the ankle of the other.

"Tsk, Natasha," said Max mildly, at last turning away from the desk and leaving the rest of the arrangements to Morley, "that ruffles the ankles of your nylons. And it's very inelegant; only certain strange birds stand on one foot. If your feet are troubling you I'll send my masseuse in to you."

Tasha felt a sudden and unaccustomed surge of annoyance. Why did Max have to notice every little lapse? "My feet would prefer a barefoot walk on the beach, Max. Or am I permitted to do that?"

If Max noticed the trace of sarcasm in her voice, he politely refrained from commenting on it. "Certainly, Natasha," he said patiently, "if the sand is free of sharp objects such as shells. I'll have it inspected this afternoon."

"I'm not made of glass, Max."

"Nevertheless, one of my men will check the beach," Max said smoothly as a hotel employee led them through the lobby and out onto a shade-dappled path. Ahead lay a curving row of sizable palm-thatched cottages set back from the shoreline under the fringing fronds. Tasha became conscious of the two bodyguards following not far behind.

"Do they have to follow us everywhere?" she asked with a stab of irritation.

Max angled her a mildly surprised glance. "They have a way of fading into the background, Natasha my dear. Perhaps your senses are overly acute today."

"I realize you've arranged this because of Ben, Max. But doesn't it occur to you that he mightn't want to see me with all these people around? Besides, I don't particularly like the thought of being shadowed all the time."

Max's smile was gentle and indulgent. "Don't think about it, then. You never have before."

Tasha stared at him with widening eyes and a deep sense of shock. "Do you mean...?"

Max patted her hand. "Now, Natasha, what did you expect? Every Fabienne woman for the past thirty years has been protected. Do you know how many millions of dollars are invested in that beautiful face of yours this year? And you, of course, are even more important to me than those who have gone before, for your role is not to end when the year is over. Put it out of your mind. Once we settle into our accommodation, the men will become invisible."

The private cottage she was to share with Max—he in one bedroom, she in another, with a connecting living room between—was discreetly luxurious in every detail. At Max's behest, Tasha spent most of the day trying to rest, but in reality wrestling with her very mixed emotions about Ben—and about Max. The discovery that she could anticipate a life of being shadowed at all times unsettled her not a little. Could she bear to live with the power of the House of Fabienne, even to protect herself from the kind of heartaches given by men like Ben? The opulent existence of the past three months had been an adventure and one she did not regret, she reflected to herself with a certain rueful self-honesty. It had been the kind of whirl every woman might dream of, for at least once in her lifetime. But it had nothing to do with reality. It didn't touch the core of life and it didn't touch the emotions.

Oh, God, she thought to herself, why would she want her emotions touched? Although she had learned not to show it, she had always been far too sensitive inside. At least the House of Fabienne was a wall against the world—a giant shatterproof glass wall that Ben and his hurtfulness could never penetrate.

Lunch, a light salad, was served in the privacy of the cottage, and it was not until the dinner hour that Tasha emerged on Max's arm. It was dark and balmy, with stars spangling a palm-crossed sky.

"I think, Natasha, I'll allow you an alcoholic beverage again tonight. Nothing sweet, of course. Would you fancy a small Campari and soda?" Max asked the question as soon as they were seated in the hotel's dining room, an attentive Seychellois waiter hovering in the background. At tables less fortunately placed, other members of the entourage were already enjoying the Creole cookery for which the establishment was justly famous.

Tasha accepted the drink but only toyed with it. Max's private detectives were well out of sight tonight, but the knowledge of them left a taste as bitter as that of the Campari, a drink she had always hated.

Morley soon joined Max and herself at table, and her presence allowed Tasha's mind to drift. She paid enough attention to learn that virtually all of Max's requests had been attended to during the course of the afternoon. The French chef had been installed, by special concession, in the kitchen. The hotel had arranged for a suitable boat. A detailed chart of the island of Mahé had been provided. A guide had been arranged, a Creole by the name of Le Rouge who was familiar with these waters. No, there was nobody by the name of Bennett Craig in the Seychelles telephone directory. Discreet inquiries by the hotel manager had produced the information that he did not have an unlisted number, either.

Tasha had come alert at the mention of Ben's name, and so she listened with more care to the next part of the conversation.

"One becomes suspicious," Max noted thoughtfully as he toyed with a wine goblet, "when the man fails to show up after bringing Natasha so many thousands of miles. I think it best, Morley, to take some precautions. Something he said to Natasha suggested that he considered these islands his home. See if you can procure a list of property owners in the Seychelles."

"For all islands?" asked Morley. "There are nearly a hundred in the whole group—many of them no more than flat coral flyspecks with no population at all.''

''Need you ask, Morley? You are usually more acute.''

The silky disapproval in Max's voice would have shriveled many a person, but Morley only laughed. ''And so are you, Max. I've already requested all that information, for it occurred to me that Mr. Craig was being a little too elusive, and certainly his motives are obscure. But it also occurs to me that he must be on an island with a telephone system—at least, he was today.''

''Ah, Morley. What would I do without you?'' Max turned to Tasha and murmured, ''Once we determine the man's whereabouts, I intend to assign special investigators to look into his romantic life over these past years. It's best to think of everything. I'm sure we'll discover that your ex-husband has some attractive skeletons in his closet, hmm, Natasha?''

''I suppose,'' replied Tasha in an unusually dispirited tone. What she had overheard two nights ago had not sounded like the voice of a skeleton. It was the one part of the call she had not divulged, nor did she intend to divulge it now. To Max's mild surprise, she declined the grilled grapefruit he had ordered for her dessert.

''By the way,'' Max added as an afterthought as they stood up to leave the table, ''have you a photograph of your ex-husband, Natasha?''

''I didn't know him long enough to get a photograph," she admitted, and in her state of deep depression did not bother to add a physical description.

"Well, I suppose we may be able to find one on a book jacket. See to it, will you, Morley?"

The sour taste of the evening lingered long after Tasha had retired with some sleeping powders especially provided by Max. "Morley procured them before we left London," he told her, "from my own Harley Street specialist. I thought the need might arise. And as you failed to drink your Campari, I think you should take them, hmm?"

It was not much past dawn when a jangling phone awoke her. Aching in every bone and still groggy from her sleeping draft, Tasha stumbled blindly to the telephone, pulling a silk wrapper over her nightgown as she went.

"Tasha?" said the voice that had such power to make her defenses crumble.

"Ben, oh Ben...." For a moment she could say no more. Although she had expected to hear from Ben today, she had not expected this. As yet there were no defenses to crumble: the day's armor had not yet been donned.

"Welcome to my lair," came a lazy voice into the void on the telephone. Tasha's hands shook. Then, somewhere in the back of her consciousness, she noted a tiny sound—could it be Max, picking up the extension in his own bedroom? The possibility gave her the strength to continue in a forcedly controlled tone.

"How like you to phone at such an ungodly hour, Ben! It's hard enough to digest you at the best of times, but on an empty stomach you're impossible."

"Do I give you morning sickness, Tasha?" came his mocking reply. "Once I wanted to. How little I knew you then."

"How little you know me now." Tasha tried to will wakefulness into her bones. Or was this sensation of numbness and faintness entirely due to the sleeping draft? "Get to the point, Ben. Where shall I meet you and when? I'd like to get our little confrontation out of the way, so I can get back to the business of living."

"Ah, such touching eagerness for a reunion. Sorry, Tasha, you'll have to contain yourself. I'll be too busy to see you today."

"Ben...." Anger built inside her, bringing total wakefulness at last. "After bringing me all these thousands of miles? You can't be serious!"

"I'm deadly serious, Tasha my love. Something important has come up. My life doesn't quite revolve around you, you know! I'll be tied up all day today. Perhaps I can see you tomorrow. I'll let you know."

"And yet *I* had to drop everything and come here on a moment's notice. Do you know how many people you've inconvenienced?"

"As a matter of fact, I do," he said coolly. "I saw you all piling off the airplane. Yes, brown eyes, I was at the airport—watching from a respectful distance."

Her heart missed a beat. Had Ben been that close yesterday? Surely she would have sensed it. And then she remembered the shiver of premonition that had traveled over her skin, like fingers on flesh....

"We could have done all our business from an even more respectful distance," she reminded him tautly in a voice that revealed none of the fire-and-ice tremblings inside. "Frankly, Ben, I don't trust you."

"Is that why you've brought that human barricade along?" There was something deeply sardonic in his tone, and for a moment Tasha had visions of contemptuous eyes and a dangerously hard line of jaw. "Surely you don't need quite so much protection, brown eyes! There must have been twenty people pouring off that plane. Several of them looked like strong-arm men."

Tasha's knuckles turned white over the telephone cord as she tried to control her wayward emotions. "Of course I didn't bring them all to protect me," she told him in a frosty half lie. "This is a working trip, Ben. They're here to do photographs."

An ironic "Oh?" was Ben's only response.

"We'll be starting to shoot tomorrow," Tasha went on, "and if you don't make it today, you'll have to see me at my convenience."

"Well, I can't make it today. So I'll have to see you tomorrow."

"I told you, Ben, I'll be on a shoot tomorrow!"

"Then I'll see you after the shoot," he said laconically, "...maybe."

Frustration and other emotions tore at Tasha's lungs, but she was determined not to give Ben the satisfaction of sensing that he upset her. She reminded herself, too, that Max was undoubtedly listening in on the other line and would not be impressed if she lost her temper. "Perhaps we could meet for dinner then," she suggested icily.

"Perhaps," came the uninformative response.

"Why did you insist that I come all this way, Ben? Now that I'm here you don't seem in any hurry to see me."

There was a small pause on the line. "I'm not in a hurry as long as you have those heavy shadows in the background," Ben conceded. "I prefer to see you on my terms, which include privacy. And as it seems we're not going to get it any other way, I've made up my mind to do something about the situation. I always prefer to warn people of my intentions. Is your boyfriend's ear still glued to the telephone?"

"Ben, how can you suggest that Max—"

"Yes, Mr. Craig, I'm listening," came Max's instant admission. "So please, no threats to my fiancée."

"Threats?" Ben feigned innocence, fooling no one. "Have I been making threats?"

"I sense you are about to," Max returned in a soft implacable voice that was equally as dangerous as Ben's deep mockery. "What is this. . . thing you have decided to do, pray tell?"

"Kidnap her," Ben said, and to the sound of his contemptuous laughter, the line went dead.

CHAPTER FOUR

"CONTROL YOURSELF, Natasha, my dear. Can you imagine a Fabienne woman with puffy eyes? Tears today will only show in photographs tomorrow! The arrogant fellow is only trying to upset you, and I can't allow that. His threats are idle. How can he possibly come within a hundred yards of you without my knowledge? Now get dressed at once; we have a full morning of fittings. Ah, good, I knew you would control yourself."

"Oh, Max. I don't cry that easily...and...and even when I do, I never get puffy eyes." Tasha even managed a small smile at Max, who had appeared in the doorway of her bedroom immediately after Ben's parting rejoinder. "I'll be all right, Max, really I will. Now do you mind leaving while I get ready?"

In the afternoon, after the fittings, Max had gone off to pass judgment on the locations selected by the art director with the help of the Seychellois guide.

"A scruffy uncouth Creole, this fellow Le Rouge," Max told Tasha at dinner, with a small shudder. "But I must admit he's come up with an excellent spot. White sand and great granite boulders along the shore. Spray dashing in and purple mountains in the background. Altogether spectacular! And there's even a road that leads fairly close to the scene. The last short distance to the beach is a little rough, but it can be done by four-wheel drive. The hotel has arranged for a suitable van, very well fitted, so it will serve as a dressing room, as well as transport for the last half mile or so. The crew will start setting up at dawn; I want morning light for this shot. That means an early call so Pierre can work his magic on your face, my dear. Five A.M.—no, four-thirty, for there's your shampoo to think of too. I do believe," he added, eyeing her critically, "that you neglected to attend to that this morning."

Tasha felt some concealed inward mirth, which she hid behind a polite smile. What a single-track mind Max had! What was the use of reminding him that her hair was to be soaking wet for the shot, as if she had emerged from the sea? And could he not appreciate that a shampoo had been the last thing on her mind this morning, after Ben's unsettling phone call?

But it was easy enough the following morning to put Ben from her mind. Photography sessions were hard exhausting work, despite the fact that they were usually nine parts standing around waiting while people fussed with light meters and reflectors and lenses and props. Moreover, Max had posted one of the bodyguards along the road where the limousine had to be left. The man had a walkie-talkie and would warn of anyone's approach—whether Ben, or just a curious sightseer who wanted to gape at the odd assemblage on the beach.

"No, don't douse her with water yet! Pierre, move in and do something to salvage that lip gloss. And Natasha, do not nibble at your lip again. It's not like you to be so unprofessional. Have you no appreciation of the fact that it took Pierre fully two hours to achieve that natural look? And Jon, I fail to see why you cannot understand my instructions about the camera angle. Palm trees are all very well, but I want mountains out of focus. I see this as a symphony of rock and sky and sea...."

Tasha sighed inwardly and resigned herself to the fact that the day's session would not be a swift one. Not that sessions ever were, when Max Fabienne's perfectionist instincts took over. A score of people were present, and for three hours Max had plied them all with a steady stream of instructions, paying attention to every tiny detail. Max had not once raised his voice, but Tasha knew there were many present who were stinging under the velvet lash of his disapproval.

"An ordinary star filter?" Max was saying to Jon Lassiter, his voice silky with displeasure. "Yes, I want a star effect where the sun glints on water—but softer, Jon, softer."

"I haven't got a human-hair filter with me," Jon said, sounding disconsolate. Poor Jon: he had suffered the brunt of Max's displeasure.

"Yet I notice you did not come unprepared in other respects," Max chastised softly with a nod along the beach. "Perhaps if you had left your lady friend, Lisette, in London you would have paid more attention to packing up your camera equipment."

"I'll start making a hair filter tonight," Jon promised unhappily, "if I can get Lisette to donate the wherewithal."

"In that case perhaps your girl friend will come in useful after all," Max noted coldly.

What an extraordinary, surrealistic business modeling was! The art director carefully combing the sand beach and redistributing cowrie shells to make it look more "natural." The photographer's assistant busy setting up huge reflectors because some of the shadows looked *too* natural. The prop girl off trying to find a bird's nest, with Morley's help, because Max had decreed one would look *very* natural in a niche of the spectacularly huge boulder against which Tasha was to lean, sea swirling about her feet, for the photographs. Tasha had half expected to hear him ask for a live bird, if one happened to be within salting distance; that was the kind of day it was.

And yet, reflected Tasha, with a twist of wry humor, that was only one-half of the insane scene! Pierre, the cosmetician, was clucking around Tasha like a mother hen, while she sat beneath an awning that had been raised to protect her skin from the sun's rays, another natural effect that would have drawn some deep displeasure. Lisette was sunbathing a short distance away and looking sulky because she had not managed to attract Max Fabienne's attention, even by dint of removing her bikini top half an hour ago. And Jon Lassiter was looking sulky because Lisette had attracted some other attention; several employees of the hotel, there to cater and carry, were ogling her openly.

And now, after Max's last critical words, Jon looked more put out than ever. Poor Jon!

At last the refreshed lipstick passed muster, and so did the sand beach, and the cowrie shells, and a bird's nest Morley had found, and numerous other details, as well. Pierre did a last-minute check of Tasha's false eyelashes, and finally everything was ready.

"There! Move into place, Natasha, and Jon will take over. Don't worry about the sea spray; they're going to douse you now. No, wait a moment—did someone remember to put the emollients in the water? Ah, good...yes, now...."

Submitting to the tepid dousing was no shock to her system. That didn't come until Tasha had eased herself against the huge boulder. She glanced downward to adjust her feet to a slightly different angle, as instructed. Suddenly she was all elbows and knees, gangly and awkward as a teenager again. Coltishly, she hugged her arms around her breasts and looked around wildly.

"Natasha, what *is* the matter?" called Max.

"M-Max, I can't wear this T-shirt!" she cried in dismay, cradling her dripping breasts to hide them from view, a move that succeeded only in riveting the attention of the normally blasé onlookers. "Look what the water does to the fabric! It's totally transparent!"

"Well, of course." Max's voice didn't rise a notch, but it held a note of reproof all the same. "I selected it very carefully for that exact purpose. Don't be childish, Natasha. You can't expect...."

But Tasha did not stay to hear the rest of Max's admonishment. To the startled stares of the many assistants scattered around the scene, she bolted. Feet flying, wet hair flying too, she raced for the only private enclosure within easy reach—the van that was to serve as a dressing room, should fresh T-shirts or blue jeans be needed. It was parked in a reasonably level grassy place, backed up to the beach for easy accessibility; Tasha reached it in seconds.

Max, who could move with astonishing alacrity when he chose, arrived at the van just as Tasha yanked the rear doors open and climbed in.

"Natasha! You cannot behave in this irrational fashion. I absolutely forbid it."

From the relative safety of the van interior, Tasha turned to face him, reaching for the van doors with the intention of closing them in Max's face. "I'm not something you can put on display like a *Playboy* centerfold," she said in a low fierce voice. "I'm your fiancée, Max! How can you think of allowing my picture to be taken as if, as if...."

"This false modesty is unbecoming," Max said in a decidedly chilly tone. "Do you really wish to create a public scene?"

"Better that than a public spectacle!" flashed Tasha, and then, because Jon Lassiter was hurrying to the scene, camera and light meter still dangling about his neck, she slammed the van doors. Through the double windows in the doors she could see Max's expression growing unnaturally apoplectic; he was not used to such treatment.

It was at that moment that the engine of the van leaped into life with a noisy twist of the ignition. In the frozen second before it accelerated, Tasha gathered her wits enough to rattle at the inside handles of the doors she had just slammed; they were locked and would not open. And then, in a screech of tires and a cloud of dust, the van took off.

Through the rear windows in the van doors she could see Max, momentarily paralyzed and dumb-founded by this untoward turn of events.

"Natasha!" he screamed as the van took off. "Jump! Run!"

But it was clear she could not; and so it was Max who ran—immaculate Max, in his knife-creased gray flannel trousers and Italian sports shirt. It all happened so swiftly, and the distance between the van and those behind was growing so fast, that Tasha received only fleeting impressions—figures converging at a run from all sides, shouting voices, waving arms, Jon Lassiter for some reason snapping pictures as rapidly as he was able, Max in frantic chase after his fast-vanishing investment....

Max? That bone-bald man running in a cloud of dust, with a handsome gray-tinged toupee flying in the air behind him? It was a Max who looked utterly foolish and years older, and Tasha no longer needed to wonder why Jon Lassiter was so busy with his camera. Not that she cared; she was far too alarmed by her own predicament.

Of course she knew it was Ben's doing; it could be nothing else. How had he managed to get through Max's early-warning system? Or had he bribed the driver of the hired van to do this? Or. . . .

As she realized the devastatingly simple truth, rage ripped through her system, replacing alarm. She wrenched her gaze away from the confused collection of wildly gesticulating people quickly receding into the distance and directed an angry glare toward the front of the van. A sturdy partition separated the rear from the driver's seat, but there was a small window to allow communication. A blind had been lowered for privacy. With some difficulty, for the van was now bumping along at a fair clip, she made her way forward.

She had caught a glimpse of the driver early this morning, but had paid him little attention in the confusion of last-minute arrangements. Max had nodded to the man curtly and with faint distaste, drawing Tasha's eye briefly to the heavy-shouldered Creole in baggy shirt and trousers, slouched over the wheel of the van. She had seen enough to note a dark brown beard and a shapeless straw hat flopping low over his face. She had even heard him address a few remarks, in the guttural island patois, to one of the hotel employees. And then, Max had whisked her into the limousine that was to transport them for the first part of the trip; and she had not given the man another thought—until now.

She raised the blind only to find that there was glass behind it. Just as if he had eyes in the back of his head, the driver chose this exact moment to reach a teak-tanned hand to a button on a control panel and lower the tiny window automatically. He did not glance backward, nor was there a rearview mirror in which she could see his face. But he had cast aside his floppy straw hat, revealing that the hair beneath was shades lighter where the sun had bronzed it than the scraggly brown beard that had caught her attention earlier.

"Welcome to Mahé," said a mocking voice, just as the van negotiated the last bumpy stretch and ricocheted onto the road, passing Max's parked limousine. Tasha hardly noted the casual greeting salute of the bodyguard Max had posted there; evidently no one had yet gathered wits enough to contact him by walkie-talkie.

"You...!" Her eyes shot poison darts at the back of Ben's head. There was no need to see the face now; she knew who it was.

"Thanks for making it so easy for me," Ben said with enraging coolness, not turning to look at her. The van was whipping along smoothly now that it was on the road. Ben was driving at breakneck speed, evidently wishing to give Max and his cohorts no chance to catch up. Through her tiny window, Tasha could see little of the passing scene, beyond the winding road directly ahead.

"At a loss for words, my darling?" he taunted. "I can suggest a few choice ones for you—in the Sey-

chelles patois, if you prefer." He added a few evidently earthy phrases, and although Tasha spoke
French as fluently as if it had been her first language,
she understood no more than a word or two. "All of
which was my opinion," Ben added, "of that im-
probable scene back there. Frankly, I almost missed
noting your arrival at the van; my eyes were too busy
elsewhere. Do all your smart-set friends sunbathe in
the demi-nude?"

Tasha clenched her teeth inelegantly just as Ben
glanced fleetingly over his shoulder, giving her a brief
view of his darkly tanned and bearded face.

"Don't do that with your teeth, Natasha," Ben
mimicked in a cruel and creditable parody of Max's
velvet tones. "You'll grind them into nothing and
how will that look? Oh, yes, my love, I did pay a little
attention to your part of the scene earlier—until your
friend distracted me with her considerable charms."

"You, you. . . ."

"Surely I can be forgiven for watching. It was
clear she wanted an audience, and besides, I was
beginning to despair of your ever turning up for a
change of clothes. Frankly, I thought it was unlikely
once I had investigated the wardrobe in the back of
the van—boxes of jeans and T-shirts, just more of
what you're wearing. Why did you come to change?"

The worst of Tasha's shock was over now. Her
pulse had slowed somewhat, and self-control was
beginning to reassert itself. Ben's words made it clear
that he had witnessed very little of what had trans-
pired back at the beach, or if he had witnessed it he

had not understood what he had seen. And she certainly had no intention of enlightening him!

"I saw you running and Max chasing you to the van. What happened?"

"I stubbed my toe," she declared tightly. "How do you think you're going to get away with this, Ben? Kidnapping is a very serious offense. Within fifteen minutes every policeman on Mahé will be out looking for you."

"Within fifteen minutes we won't be on Mahé," he informed her coolly, as the van veered off the road again and Ben shifted the gear that engaged the four-wheel drive. Directly ahead lay a stand of trees and bushes, and beyond that water. With bone-jolting speed, Ben aimed for it, and within seconds the van was parked behind some thick shrubbery, invisible from the road. He jerked on the hand brake and turned his full attention to Tasha, twisting in the seat until he had the small window and her soaked head in full view.

He studied her in mocking silence for a moment, his lids drooping over eyes more derisive than Tasha remembered. Had they always glinted like that—as if there were little gold flecks buried deep in the tortoiseshell irises? Nor could she recall those tiny crinkles at the corners, pale against the deeply sunned skin of his face. But then, the only time she had ever seen Ben with benefit of contact lenses had been on her wedding day, and he had not been smiling then. . . .

"Surprised, brown eyes?" he murmured. "I didn't

expect you to recognize me this morning. Amazing what clothes will do for a man. A dirty shirt, a pair of trousers tied up with an old rope, a month's foliage on my chin. . . why, I didn't even have to hide behind the hat, except when you were around. Your fancy friends shuddered with disgust and kept their distance. Today has been a very amusing day all in all.''

"For you!" Tasha snapped. For some reason she felt no fear at all—only a great wash of anger at Ben's highwayman tactics. "Max will have your neck for this!"

"He'll have to find it first," Ben said equably. "Now come along, brown eyes, we have no time to waste. We're switching to the sea."

From her limited vantage point, Tasha could not see the water now, but she could remember an indistinct glimpse of a sizable two-masted sailboat that had been anchored a small distance from the shore. "You had this planned to the last detail, didn't you!" she accused.

"Barring the unforeseen," Ben agreed imperturbably. His strong bronzed fingers hovered over a control panel. "Now don't bother running when I unlock that rear door from up here; I can beat you in a sprint any day."

Tasha glared at him balefully, long enough to see the brief white grin that broke through his ruffianlike beard. Then, gathering her wits, she flashed a glance over her shoulder to look at the rear doors. Ben might have locked them automatically from up front, but evidently he had forgotten that there was a strong bolting arrangement on the inside, too. Even as she heard the click of the releasing lock she made a dash for it; and by the time he rattled at the rear door the heavy bar had been lowered into place. Let him try to kidnap her now! Within minutes searchers would be combing the island, and Ben could hardly transport a whole van on that ketch of his!

She could hear a deep annoyed sigh and then silence. She backed away from the doors, negotiating her way through boxes of clothing, and sat down on one of the benches that ran along the sides of the van, eyes still fastened on the rear windows where Ben's big body could still be seen, head for the moment just out of frame. He was strong, but surely he wasn't strong enough to break through that barricade!

A head appeared in the window. In order to look into the van, Ben had to bend slightly; his well-knit body was propped almost casually against one hand as he peered through the glass. Some unruly part of Tasha's mind thought, *How tall he is, I really had forgotten....*

"That's a very fetching T-shirt," he said, his deep voice only slightly muffled by the barrier that stood between them. Tasha's arms flew back into defensive position over the clinging garment that had been the least of her worries for the past few minutes.

"And don't bother covering up, brown eyes. If you were willing to show that much in a photograph, there's no point being a prude for me. If I'd known you were on display, too, I mightn't have paid so much attention to your topless friend back at the beach. Very enticing altogether and much more erotic than bare flesh.... Now open the bolt. I'm not a patient man.''

The back windows had small blinds, too, installed on Max's express instructions, so the van could be used as a change room. Tasha reached them in several steps and yanked them down, closing out Ben's leer altogether. She could hear his earthy chuckle and made a face that expressed about one-tenth of the outrage she felt.

''I could try to force this door right away,'' she heard him say mockingly, ''but I'm of a mind to be generous. I'll give you five minutes, brown eyes, to change into some of the dry clothes in those boxes. We've a long trip ahead of us and I don't want you catching pneumonia.''

''I'm not going anywhere,'' Tasha retorted angrily. Mulishly, she settled herself back on the seat, arms still wrapped about her transparent T-shirt. Let Ben do his worst!

''Five minutes' truce, Tasha,'' he said softly, ''that's all. After that you're coming out, ready or not. Now start changing; I'm counting.''

She maintained a stubborn silence, unwilling to give him the satisfaction of sustaining the dialogue. What could he do, anyway? Two minutes passed, then three. As the silence stretched she became more aware of the inadequacy of her wet garments. What if rescuers did arrive? She had no desire to be found in these clinging clothes. And it seemed that Ben intended to honor his word;

there had been not a single rattle of the door handles.

With a sudden spurt of activity to make up for time lost, she snatched a towel, one of a pile left in the van that morning along with other accoutrements of the shoot. She doffed the heavy dripping blue jeans first, starting with her lower half because it seemed by far the most vulnerable part, should she happen to be caught naked. More haste, less speed. She could find no fresh underwear to replace the soaking bikini briefs she had just discarded, and so she pulled a pair of dry blue jeans directly over her bare skin. Her fingers fumbled for precious seconds with the clasp of the zip, and then she dived for the box of T-shirts. At least there had been no warning signs as yet; surely she still had time!

"Coming, brown eyes? Your five minutes are up."

"I certainly am not!" she cried to the face she could not see. "And I suggest that you take off on that silly boat without me, Ben Craig, if you value your own skin!"

"Ah, Tasha," he taunted. "Do you really think I've gone to all this trouble only to take off without you? I have no intention of leaving you behind."

And with that there was a mighty splintering crash. Tasha froze in the very act of peeling off her clinging see-through shirt. On the door of the van, a great gap had appeared near the handle, where a glint of lethal-looking metal showed through. Before it was withdrawn, she recognized it as an ax blade. Another crash...and then Ben's large long-fingered hand reached through the widened aperture and knocked the heavy bolt out of place as if it had weighed no more than a feather. The doors of the van were wrenched open and Ben stood there, looking incongruously calm as if the act he had just perpetrated had not been violent at all.

"A very useful five minutes," he drawled. "You didn't really think I allowed it only in order to let you change, did you? I needed time to fetch an ax from my boat. Thanks for not running."

"You despicable bastard," she gasped, eyes flashing fire. She tried to shield herself with a hand while she pushed the tangle of the wet T-shirt back below her midriff.

"Coming? Or would you prefer to be carried?"

When his mocking words met with no instant response, Ben ducked his head and levered himself into the van interior. In the next instant a steely grip fastened over her wrist, and she found herself slung, fireman fashion, over a broad shoulder, her head and arms dangling down his back and her legs inelegantly clamped at his front in the circle of one powerful arm. She flailed at his back with her free hands with no effect whatsoever, except to hurt herself.

"Damn you, Ben Craig...d-damn you! At least let me get dressed!"

He ignored her struggles and her howl of outrage. "That yours?" he asked, aiming a small kick at a leather case that rested on the floor amid the boxes of spare T-shirts and jeans.

It was Tasha's model case, an ample and well-fitted suitcase of hatbox size, such as all models carry. Although she had not expected to need it that day with Pierre along to attend to every tiny detail of her makeup, she had brought it along as a matter of course; the habit of carrying it on all assignments was by now thoroughly ingrained.

"Yes," she choked out, still struggling ineffectively.

Ben half kneeled and snapped the case open with his free hand. It was already partly filled with the various paraphernalia of Tasha's profession—sprays, lipsticks, lotions, powders, all neatly nested inside. "Sorry I don't have time to repack," he said grimly, thrusting a large handful of fresh T-shirts into such free space as remained in the case. He clicked it closed.

"Shoes?" he asked. "You'll need shoes."

"Let me go, you, you. . . ."

Ben spotted the Italian thongs Tasha had worn earlier that morning when leaving the hotel. Despite their low heels they were thoroughly impractical, little more than a criss-cross of leather attached to a flimsy sole. "You didn't come too well prepared, did you?" he noted disapprovingly as he hooked the sandal straps over a finger and hoisted the model case in the same hand.

Tasha gave vent to every ounce of her considerable lung power as Ben manhandled her out of the van.

"Forget it, brown eyes," he said with some amusement in one interval when she paused to catch her breath. "That limousine parked back at the scene of the crime isn't going anywhere in a hurry. I managed to filch the keys this morning, after it delivered you and your fancy boyfriend. Why, I doubt the police even know about your predicament yet.''

She sputtered into indignant silence as Ben aimed across the beach toward an inflatable dinghy that waited at the water's edge. He seemed in no particular hurry now. His stride was wide but measured, his lack of haste infuriatingly self-confident. The sheer size and animal strength of him served to make her alarmingly aware of her own vulnerability. The rough texture of his shirt scratched through her wet one, and his powerful arm held her legs as easily as if she had been a small child instead of a full-grown and very tall woman.

He placed the model case carefully aft, and then with far less ceremony dumped Tasha into the dinghy. Despite the air-cushioned softness, the impact knocked the remaining breath from her lungs, stunning her momentarily. Ankle deep in water, Ben stood beside the dinghy for a moment, openly and wickedly assessing Tasha's very scantily concealed breasts.

"Very nice," he judged, with the eye of a connoisseur. "You win over your well-endowed friend, hands down. Not in quantity but in quality."

Tasha recovered enough to struggle to a sitting position and conceal herself with her hands. Not that it mattered by then; Ben's eyes were directed elsewhere. With the litheness of a born athlete and a competence earned by many years at sea, he pushed the dinghy from the shore and leaped in lightly as it came free of the sand and glided toward deeper water.

He turned his attention to the oars. As he started to insert them into the oarlocks his back was half-turned to Tasha. Wits by now fully regained, she came to a crouching position preparatory to leaping off the boat. She certainly had no intention of making this easy for Ben! In the next instant she found herself flung bodily backward, pinned into place by a long, large and very virile body.

"Didn't you know I'm a mind reader?" he taunted. His face was so close she could see the texture of his skin and feel the prickle of his beard against her chin. The full weight of him was on her, crushing her body against the pillowed place where she lay. She could feel the beat of his heart, the cadence slower than hers; and the warmth of his breath stirred against the moisture of her parted panting lips.

"What are you...going to do...with me?" Her breathing was ragged, her eyes huge. "What do you...want of me?"

"I leave you to guess," he murmured, the smile in his eyes fading. Something hostile gleamed in those eyes—contempt, perhaps? Tasha was conscious of every inch of him, lying warm and heavy over her body. He had no need to use force to pinion her into place; the superior size of his well-muscled limbs dominated her easily. "You're a big girl, Tasha, and a very clever one, too. Surely you can figure out why I've done this if you set your mind to it."

"You didn't. . . want me. . . for a wife."

"Only too true," Ben agreed.

"Then why have you. . . done this?" It seemed the air would explode in her lungs, and yet somehow she managed to voice the breathless words. "You. . . divorced me. Or were you lying about that?"

"No."

"Then what is it. . . you want?"

Ben's eyes glittered briefly with some emotion she could not quite define. "Unfinished business," he said, "from our wedding night."

Tasha's heart seemed to stop for one topsy-turvy moment; there was only one thing Ben could mean. "Why. . . now," she whispered, when she found her voice again, "after all these. . . years? Does it mean you want me. . . for your wife. . . after all? Oh, Ben. . . ."

The tawny tortoiseshell eyes were watching her narrowly as if assessing her reactions. "Of course I don't," he said, his mouth twisting in a hard unfriendly line. "My small experience with you cured me of any desire for marriage—to any woman. Surely you don't think I snatched you out from under your fiancé's nose for the cause of true love? A very romantic notion. . . but I'm not a romantic man. No, brown eyes, my intention is much simpler than that, and perhaps if you use your imagination. . . ."

Tasha could and did. As Ben's voice trailed off meaningfully, she flared, "Is that what you always do with women? See what you want. . . and take it? Whether they're willing or not?"

Ben's eyes turned mocking and darkly slumberous, as they fastened themselves on her carefully painted lips. "Does the thought perturb you?" he murmured, clearly enjoying her moment of unconcealed consternation. "Good. That will give you something to look forward to. Think about it, Tasha, one stolen week...."

"One...week?"

"That's when I'll return you to your charming fiancé—if I'm through with you by then." His face moved closer, so that no more than a single inch separated their mouths. His voice became low, husky, intimate, almost like a caress. "I'm not sure I will be...."

Tasha told herself that the little tremor of excitement in her lower limbs could not possibly be desire; that was a feeling she had not experienced for many years. It must be fear that clogged her throat and turned her hands clammy and made her so overwhelmingly conscious of the fact that Ben's virile body was beginning to react to her proximity, proving quite palpably that he was very well equipped to carry out his threats.

Ben's heartbeat had quickened, too; and now his hands slid into her damp tangled hair, one at each ear, holding her face in place. "God knows why a man in his right mind would want you," he muttered thickly as he lowered his mouth to hers.

He had no need to tease her lips apart. Some terrible weakness seemed to prevent Tasha from closing her mouth against his kiss. The roughness of his beard against her face, the deep probing explorations of his tongue, the erotic movements of his powerful and knowing fingers at her ears, the heavy textured weight of his chest against her damp breasts—all combined to rob her of defenses. For one moment of madness she almost found her traitorous hands stealing around his shoulders, and then, recovering some degree of sense, she used them instead to scratch.

Ben's head jerked away, but he did nothing to prevent the raking of her fingernails. "You silly bitch," he said scornfully. "Keep that up and I'll personally take a pair of manicure scissors to your nails. I'm sure I saw some in that ridiculous case of yours. And what will Max say about that—when he sees those pretty painted claws cut to the very quick?"

But she did accomplish part of her purpose. Without haste, Ben freed her body and turned his attention back to the oars. This time he was careful not to turn his back—not that it mattered. In the few minutes since the dinghy had been freed from the beach, it had drifted farther from the shore. The waters of the lagoon were perfectly clear, and it was possible to see the sand bottom dotted with the beautiful shapes of shells. With a well-hidden wince Tasha realized the inflatable dinghy had drifted beyond her depth. Swimming was one art she had never acquired; there would be no more attempts at escape for the time being.

With her arms huddled protectively around her semi-exposed breasts, Tasha watched Ben's long arms bending to the oars, their movements firm and

economical. She did not need to see beneath the loose
ragged shirt he still wore to know the strength of
those sinews, those muscles, those well-formed
biceps. She shivered, despite the tropic heat and the
sun that poured like golden syrup out of a blue
equatorial sky. Had she really nearly reacted with
passionate abandon in the arms of a man who made
no pretense of even liking her? A man who had virtually admitted he intended to take her by force? No,
she thought, revising that slightly: Ben would not
take her by force. He was too sure of his potent
physical attractions to do that. Damn him anyway!

"Stop looking so offended," Ben mocked as he
stroked toward the larger boat. "You enjoyed every
minute of that kiss—despite the last-moment resistance."

Some innate strength came to Tasha's rescue now;
she was damned if she wanted to admit any weakness
to Ben. The hard learned arts of modeling helped as
she strove to regain her aplomb. Despite the humiliating semi-nakedness that still caused inward writh-
ings, she managed to don a haughty sophisticated
expression.

"You haven't changed at all," she said coldly.
"Arrogant and impossible and so damn sure of yourself. I allowed you to kiss me only because I was
afraid you might bite my lip if I didn't. In my work I
can't afford a wounded lip. That was submission,
not response. You didn't touch my feelings at all."

For some reason that observation wiped the cruel
mockery from Ben's mouth; his eyes clouded and his

face closed over. "Did I ever?" he muttered as he
turned his attention back to the sea. Seconds later
they had pulled alongside the ketch. In a swooping
movement that rocked the smaller boat alarmingly,
Ben picked Tasha up and deposited her over the side.
She gasped but did nothing to resist; how could she,
short of risking a tumble in the water?

As Ben himself boarded he kept Tasha's model
case well out of her reach—a deliberate and infuriating gesture that Tasha knew was intended to
upset her. Unwilling to let Ben see her reaction, she
put on a bored expression and settled herself by a pile
of spare sails in the fore of the large cockpit. Unhurriedly she reached for an edge of sail canvas and
draped it over her breasts, at last able to abandon the
undignified huddling of arms.

After Ben had stowed the inflatable dinghy, he
yanked a rope to start a small auxiliary engine.
Clearly he wished to take no risks by remaining any
longer in this danger zone; he made no attempt as yet
to set the furled sails. Within seconds he was
squatting by the tiller, one watchful eye on Tasha
as he steered toward a channel through the reef. His
big frame looked deceptively relaxed—for it was
ready, she knew, to uncoil like a spring should she
show a single sign of diving off. Would to heaven she
could!

Tasha sat in baleful silence for a few minutes,
pondering her predicament. It seemed she could expect no reprieves for the time being. The shoreline of
Mahé was fast being put behind, and there was no

sign of rescue on the horizon. "Where are you taking me?" she asked tightly at last.

"Away from it all," Ben said unrevealingly, his voice dry with mockery.

"Surely you're not planning to keep me at sea for a whole week," she said, looking askance at Ben's boat. It was large, unluxurious and thoroughly seaworthy with its neatly coiled lines and unpretentious practical fittings—not an easy boat to handle, she guessed, with the amount of sail it carried. Spitefully, because she sensed Ben was probably proud of his boat, she added, "This little dinghy doesn't look too comfortable."

"It's not a dinghy, it's a ketch," he corrected. If he had taken offense at her deliberate insult, it didn't show in the derisive glint of his eye. "And your comfort is the least of my concerns for this next week. However, as you have so little love for the sea, you'll be glad to know I'm taking you to another island."

Tasha's small shaky laugh was purely a nervous reflex, dredged up to conceal the jangle of her nerves. "Am I supposed to be grateful?" she asked.

The laugh seemed to set Ben's teeth on edge: it was as if she had twanged a raw nerve. For the first time he seemed momentarily off balance. A dull red color rose in his face, and he jerked his eyes away from her altogether. Somewhere in her brain, Tasha stored away that useful piece of knowledge. All very well for him to laugh, she reflected poisonously: he didn't seem to like it very well when she managed to do so.

"Someplace civilized, I hope," she added malevolently.

"On the contrary, it's very remote," he snapped. His averted face was hard and set, his lips drawn back in a manner that indicated utter exasperation. "The whole idea is to get you alone—and away from civilization."

At this reminder of her vulnerability, Tasha's fingers tightened over her skimpy canvas protection, part of a spare sail she could not disentangle enough to allow herself freedom of movement in the boat. "May I please have my makeup case?" she requested with an idleness she did not feel.

Clearly her moment of advantage had passed; Ben was once more in firm control. His gaze trickled over her lips with devastating thoroughness. "What for? Where you're going, you won't need that kind of fakery."

"I'd like a change of clothes. My T-shirt is still wet and uncomfortable."

"Then take it off," he said. "I'm not stopping you."

Tasha simmered, but could not risk arguing too much until she had secured a fresh shirt. "I don't want to go pink in the wrong places," she said lightly, gesturing gracefully at her draped chest.

Ben's eyes traveled in the opposite direction: upward to her nose. "Good thinking," he said insultingly. And with that, the nondescript hat he had worn earlier landed smartly in her lap.

Tasha shrugged the hat aside and hid her resentment behind a glacial expression. "I'm talking about my bikini line," she said, pointedly.

"What bikini line? My guess, brown eyes, is that like your fellow fashionplate you're quite used to sunbathing in the buff. I'm willing to bet you're a healthy all-over gold."

It was true; but the effect was the result of secluded and carefully timed sunlamp sessions, fifteen minutes a day, as prescribed by Max. But she had no intention of telling that to Ben—or, if she had her way, of letting him see the result. "Nevertheless, I have sensitive skin," she said angrily.

Ben's dark brows quirked upward contemptuously. "Really? I hadn't noticed. If you want your case, come and get it."

He spent the next thirty seconds enjoying the spectacle as Tasha tried to hook the leather handle of her case with one naked toe. At length she gave up the awkward attempt and abandoned modesty in favor of dignity. Sail edge dropped, she made her way to the case and retreated with as much hauteur and speed as crawling on all fours would allow. Within moments, turning her back, she had restored decency and also donned her sandals.

The boat had now left the calm lagoon and entered open, lightly ruffled waters. Ben spent a brief moment squinting at the seas and the skies, making Tasha wonder irrelevantly whether that was how he had acquired those little indentations that fanned out from the corners of his eyes. "Be thankful you're *not* in a dinghy," he said dryly. "We've a fair way to go and the wind's too light today to take us there in a hurry. We'll be lucky to reach the island before dark, even in this ketch. Its name, by the way, is Mystique.''

"I thought it was called *Adam's Folly*," Tasha said—and then could have bitten her tongue off for betraying that she had read Ben's book.

Ben's eyes glittered with open amusement at this indisputable evidence that he had the upper hand. "I was talking about the name of the island," he corrected softly as he moved forward to attend to the sails.

Bested for the moment, Tasha curbed her tongue. Not wanting to watch Ben's long loose-limbed body or his easy competence with the sails, she turned her mind to speculation about the island he had named. It was not one she had heard of or noted on any of the maps Morley had shown, but with nearly a hundred islands in the Seychelles group, that was not so extraordinary.

Mystique. It was an intriguing name, she had to admit. It conjured up visions of a tiny enchanted island lost in a lonely mist-shrouded sea, a place as beautiful as it was mysterious. It was as if the name itself exerted some strange spiritual force, as of a place half-remembered or half-imaginary. For one moment Tasha found herself thinking, *I've been there before, in another existence*...and then, she pushed such fleeting and foolish thoughts from her mind and returned to contemplation of her present and very real predicament.

Sails secured on a port tack, Ben settled back at the helm. He draped his muscular body against a small pile of life preservers, folded his arms behind his head and took to studying Tasha openly. His silence and the small enigmatic smile that played over his lips unnerved her; they told only too well that he was enjoying himself in some twisted way.

"I'll try to answer your many questions about the island," he said at last with deep irony. He paused long enough to verify that there were no questions forthcoming and then proceeded, "It's a granitic island, small but mountainous, and heavily forested. No more than a couple of hundred inhabitants. A patois is spoken. French is understood; English isn't. No radios or any other manner of communication with the outside world, beyond a copra trader that calls every couple of months. No police force—law enforcement nonexistent. Electricity nonexistent. Entertainment nonexistent, except of one's own making." He hesitated reflectively. "By the way, how's your swimming?"

"Nonexistent," Tasha replied acidly. "I can't swim a stroke, and I don't intend to learn in the next week—especially from you."

His derisive grin broadened. "Glad to hear it," he said. "I was afraid you might have unsuspected Olympic talents. The closest island is a good six miles away, but I was afraid you might just take a notion to strike out on your own one day." He added as an afterthought, as if he had read Tasha's mind, "And don't think about stealing this rig for any spectacular escapes, brown eyes. It takes some knowledge to handle a ketch this size; and just to make certain you don't attempt it, I plan to dismantle the odd part beyond your capabilities to reassemble. By the way...."

Coming to an upright position, he seized one of the life preservers and chucked it in Tasha's direction. "Nonswimmers wear lifejackets in this boat," he ordered brusquely. "Put it on."

Tasha was nervous enough of the water that under normal circumstances she would have obeyed; but Ben's tone of command raised her hackles. She smiled distantly, reached instead for her makeup case and pulled out a mirror.

"Gracious, my lips are quite denuded," she said coolly. She extracted a lipstick tube and started to redefine the outline of her mouth with infinite care, noting well that Ben's irritation was building. Another thing that annoyed him. Good!

"Put it on!" he warned with more steel in his voice. "Now!"

Tasha pretended she had not heard. She flattened her lips to paint a more pronounced line on the upper, applying lipstick with a more generous hand than usual. It was a small gesture of defiance, not too effective, she knew, but the only one available to her for now. With studied artfulness, she flicked away an imaginary grain of sand and patted some compressed powder onto her nose. Out of the corner of her eye she could see Ben's fingers flexing as if he wanted to do nothing more at this moment than spank her; she expected him to force the issue momentarily. Some part of her quivered with a little trill of fearful anticipation, and another part wanted very badly to win this battle. She added to his irritation by pulling out her hairbrush and starting a languorous stroking of her long tresses, now very nearly dried.

Ben's glowering silence continued for several minutes, but he made no move to employ force, as she had expected. At last Tasha finished her leisurely and intentionally irritating preoccupation with face and hair and tucked the brush back in her case.

That done, she lifted her lashes—or rather, the long lashes Pierre had so carefully glued into place early that morning. She looked at Ben with a small triumphant smile that told him she thought she had won this round.

Too late she realized he had been waiting for this exact moment when her gaze was locked with his. Ostentatiously, he began to unbutton his shirt, revealing the deeply tanned and muscular flesh beneath. Tasha at once knew his intention; but to look away now was to acknowledge defeat, and so she forced her eyes to remain steady. The little smile on her face was now purely pasted on and indicative of none of the panic that rose to fever pitch as his hand traveled to the rope that tied his trousers in place.

His eyes still held hers in a mute challenge when he stood up and stepped out of the baggy pants he had worn as part of the day's disguise. She had thought he would stop short of that; and despite every intention of behaving in a blasé manner, her eyes skidded for safety. The wordless battle lost, she now wrenched around until she was facing the mast, her back turned to Ben and her heart beating triple time at that too intimate glimpse of his overwhelming masculinity.

Seconds later a very large, very well-knit and uncompromisingly nude body strolled into the new line of Tasha's vision. As he reached the mast Ben grinned wickedly and turfed the clothes overboard. The beard roughening his chin seemed to accentuate his roguishness. He looked vital, virile and totally piratical—and every wildly misbehaving nerve ending in Tasha's body jangled at the message in those sun-bronzed biceps, that iron-hard stomach, those whip-cord thighs.

As though he had all the time in the world, Ben propped one hand against the mast and studied her expression with cool amusement. Pride would not allow Tasha to turn her back a second time. She pretended an intense interest in an imaginary fleck of foam visible somewhere in the ocean, beyond the line of Ben's knee.

After five or six painful minutes, he said casually, "I have a duffel bag of clean clothes below decks, along with other stores. Would you prefer I put something on?"

"That's entirely up to you," Tasha said with glacial lack of concern. It was a creditable acting job; in truth she was on the brink of hysteria.

"On the contrary," came the sarcastic rejoinder. "It's entirely up to *you*. When you put something on, so do I. You know what I mean."

Her capitulation came about one minute later, when she could bear the status quo no longer. Only when he had seen that she was well and truly buckled into the ungainly orange jacket did Ben finally duck his way into the compact storage cabin below decks. Within two minutes he was back, now decently clad in close-fitting mud-colored Levi's and a checked shirt that remained unbuttoned over that tanned, textured disturbing chest.

"Next time," he threatened softly as he settled back at rest, "remember I like to have my orders obeyed. All my orders. Forget that, and I'll make your life a misery for this next week. Now put on the hat before you get sunstroke."

As if assuming she had no other choice, he turned his attention to the sea. This time Tasha obeyed with what grace she could muster. It was growing close to noon, and although the sails had afforded some protection earlier, now the hot tropic sun was relentless in the way it beat down on her head. Nonetheless she cursed Ben inwardly as she punched the hat into shape and arranged it over her head at a jaunty and not unflattering angle. Like any high-fashion model, Tasha had a way of making the shabby and the ordinary look soigné; on her, the hat—like the jeans and the T-shirt—took on a whole new elegance.

Damn Ben anyway. Did he really think he could dominate her so easily? Well, despite his ultimatum she intended to fight him at every turn; he'd regret his actions before the week was through!

Was it to be like this for the next seven days—a

seesaw of wits and wills, with Ben always gaining the upper hand? How easily he seemed to be able to cut her down to size—whether with his superior physical force or with his potent sexual attraction or with his taunting words. And the worst thing was that some part of Tasha, spirited though she was, wanted to be mastered.

What purpose did Ben really have in going to such lengths as to kidnap her? Surely not just the satisfaction of some sexual fantasy. For men like Ben, women were never a problem. Moreover, he was the type for sexual realities, not fantasies. Tasha was too much of a pragmatist to think that her own attractions were greater than those of dozens of women he must have encountered in the intervening years. Reading between the lines in his latest book, one knew there had been casual encounters...short idylls in Valparaiso and Manila and Sydney and a dozen other ports he had touched during his round-the-world trip. He had not needed to spell out his prowess with the softer sex in so many words; Tasha knew perfectly well that women would fall like ninepins for a man so devastatingly masculine, especially one with the air of a rugged and rakehell adventurer. In Ben's life, casual encounters would be the norm, and in these days of sexual liberation no doubt he could pick and choose almost any woman he wanted.

So why would he risk possible incarceration just to sample one week of forbidden delights with a woman he had forsworn years ago? His every word made it clear he despised her; and certainly he had discarded her seven years ago without a backward glance.

Could it be possible that his motives were not sexual at all? If seduction was the only thing on his mind, it would have been easy enough for Ben to approach her in some other way. With some soft words to ease old aches, she would not have been immune to his virility and sex appeal—she recognized that now. But he had made no attempt; in seven years he had given no hint that he was even aware of her existence.

And yet, ever since the day she had spoken to him by long-distance telephone, he had been like a hungry lion sniffing the air and circling for the kill, his attention directed to one thing only: her, his prey.

No, she decided, Ben had not revealed the full truth about his motives.

The possibility presented a tiny ray of hope, especially as she was relatively certain from personal experience that Ben would not take her by force. He could be volcanic in his emotions, yes; violent in his passions, yes; but he was no rapist. Their wedding night had proved that much, for if he had ever wanted to take her by force, he could easily have done so then.

As this most recent thought presented itself to her, she felt a need to look at Ben, to study his face for clues. During her reflections she had been watching, without seeing it, the light wake created by the ketch on its present tack. Without advance warning, her eyes shifted direction—and for a frozen second the entire world seemed to stand still.

Ben was looking at her, his guard for the moment down. In the instant that their eyes connected, his glazed into a total enigma—cool, mocking, challenging—but not before Tasha felt a little shock of recognition at the hostile emotion she had surprised in those tawny depths.

Hatred. Could it be anything else? It had certainly not been desire. And if he hated her, why? According to her memories of their short and ill-fated marriage, she had done nothing to earn that kind of detestation. Had it been only in her imagination? Oh God, it must have been. . . .

The moment shook her in a way that nothing else had so far. Feeling totally alone and chilled to the core despite the heat, she closed her eyes and tried to make her expression a total blank.

"I've some ham-and-cheese sandwiches back here," Ben informed her in a tone so matter-of-fact it seemed almost surrealistic after that smoking intensity of a moment ago. "A case of beer, too, if you want one. Or is beer too plebeian for your champagne tastes?"

When she did not answer, he repeated with exaggerated patience, "Do you want to eat or not?"

"No," she said, her lips barely moving to voice the only word of which she felt capable at that moment. Her eyes remained closed.

"Suit yourself." He sounded cynical. "This time I'm issuing no orders. Frankly, I don't give a damn if you happen to dehydrate yourself. I'm not offering again; so if you want anything you'll have to beg me prettily."

Which was enough to keep Tasha's lips sealed all afternoon—long after hunger and thirst had become a crying need that replaced all her agitation over the brief but burning hostility she had glimpsed in Ben's unguarded eyes.

Nightfall came swiftly in this clime, not many degrees distant from the equator. With eyes determinedly closed, Tasha was not aware that the sun had lowered to within a half hour of its western bed when Ben spoke again, his voice vibrant with mockery.

"Open your eyes, Tasha, and have a look at the island of Mystique—the romantic little retreat where you'll spend the next week or so. Nature in the raw. A return to...." Ben hesitated perceptibly, then chose his words carefully as if changing direction. "A return to the origins of man," he finished.

Her false eyelashes felt starched into place along with the expression on her face, but somehow she managed to open them. They were in a lagoon, and directly ahead a pattern of dark green peaks and valleys loomed. The island had a strong and savage beauty about it. It was primal, misty, mysterious, not so different from the way she had visualized it, except that a number of scattered thatched dwellings were visible here and there on the steep and densely forested slopes of the island; all of them were farther to the south, at some distance from the small cove the ketch was now entering. On the white rim of sand, monumental boulders studded the shoreline, as they had on Mahé.

"Well, what do you think of the place?" Ben asked dryly.

Tasha cast him a spiteful glance. "I don't think I can tell you," she said. "It wouldn't be polite."

Only the barest flicker of a muscle in Ben's temple betrayed any annoyance at all. "I couldn't agree with you more," he said levelly. "Fact is, I've avoided Mystique like the plague since I bought a small place here seven years ago. Honeymoon hideaways have a way of palling when the honeymoon turns sour."

"You intended to bring me here for our honeymoon? How quaint."

If Tasha hoped that her caustic tone would wound, she could take little satisfaction in Ben's reaction. "I used to think I could find the real you in this place," he said without inflection. "I don't mind admitting I've made a few bad mistakes in my life. Buying a place on this island was the second worst of them."

Something in the very flatness of his tone was far more hurtful than scorn would have been, for it seemed to reveal Tasha's flippant efforts for the petty jibes they were. Stung into silence, she attended to doffing the hat and lifejacket while Ben anchored some distance from the shore. He had lowered the sails earlier during the approach to the island, and entered the lagoon on auxiliary power only. Leaving the stowing of the sails for now, he eased the rubber dinghy over the side for the last short leg of the trip.

"I'll take you ashore in the inflatable, and you can wait in the shade while I do the rest," he suggested. Although the sun had already dropped behind the serrated peaks of Mystique, it still beat down with some intensity on the ketch. Ben eyed Tasha critically. "You've had more than enough sun for today, despite your coverings. Now come along."

With that, he swooped down and scooped her into his arms before she could protest. In the embrace one large hand closed over a breast, cupping it; he deliberately looked her in the eye to see her response. Tasha turned giddy and hid behind the long veil of Pierre's lashes. For an instant, banked there against the hard wall of Ben's chest in the swaying boat, she fought the irrational sensation that she had come home at last; that this was all happening as it had always been meant to happen.

"What an obliging female you are," murmured Ben. "I expected a little more fight."

His mocking tone restored her reason and her spirit. "I bruise easily," she said sharply, "and I can't afford that. If you want a sparring partner find some other woman! Surely you didn't bring me here just to see who could last ten rounds in the ring? I don't care for fisticuffs."

"Except verbal ones," he taunted. His eyes glinted down at her derisively.

"Can you bring my model case, please?" she asked tautly, hoping the extra burden would force Ben to release her breast. A helpless little quivering had started in the extremities of her body, and she was afraid that all too soon he would sense the springing response of her flesh.

"I'll bring it next trip."

Tasha gave a tiny laugh faked to order, with the full intention of unsettling him as much as he unsettled her. "I never take a single step without it," she improvised.

Ben tensed; that little laugh had clearly bothered him once again. His jaw worked for a moment and he growled with rough impatience, "If you want it, you can damn well pick it up yourself." Without releasing her breast, he leaned over so she could retrieve the case with one outstretched arm. Moments later he had deposited her in the inflatable dinghy and was stroking toward shore with strong measured sweeps of his muscular arms.

"You mentioned another island. Where is it?" Tasha asked, her curiosity not entirely idle. She was aware that she would never be able to cope with the intricacies of a two-masted sailboat like Ben's ketch; but it had also occurred to her that there must be other boats on Mystique. Perhaps some local fisherman might aid in an escape?

"Off to the northwest," Ben informed her. "You can't see it from here." Reaching shallow water, he shipped the oars and rolled his denims to his knees, uncovering the corded calves with their light dusting of body hair. He splashed off the side and pulled the inflatable into inches of water. "Out you get," he ordered.

Tasha started to unbuckle her sandals for the short wade to dry beach.

"Oh, for God's sake," Ben said impatiently, "a little water won't hurt. I'm in a hurry, Tasha. I have a lot to do before the sun goes down."

"Oh?" She slowed herself deliberately, and in the next moment found herself seized bodily and with no particular gentleness. This time, out of pure reflex, she started to struggle as Ben stalked angrily a short distance onto the beach. Perhaps in payment for that, he dumped her on the sand with no ado—stooping to within six inches of the ground and then simply letting her go.

Tasha gasped but recovered quickly, nothing hurt as much as dignity. Standing, she brushed the sand from her offended bottom, while Ben fetched her case from the boat. She retrieved it and walked toward the trees without comment, but with murder on her mind.

She inspected the island as she went. No dwellings were visible from here, but thick tropical vegetation lay directly ahead behind a fringing of palms. Surely there was someplace on this island she could hide from Ben—someone who would help her and shelter her if she told her story! Had Ben forgotten that she spoke French as fluently as she spoke English?

She could feel him watching her as she reached the trees. Knowing he would not set to work until she was settled, she chose a boulder of about the right height and made a show of dusting it off fastidiously with a large leaf. That done, she lowered her jean-clad legs daintily onto the rock and draped her hands over her knees. With the elegant tilt of her head, she might have been modeling a Dior. The dying-swan look, she thought to herself humorously—one of those model poses that were part of her stock-in-trade. She trained a vague Vogue look in the direction of the blue horizon. Let Ben do a little tooth-grinding about that!

Her actions had a stronger effect than she had dared to hope for. After Ben rowed back to the ketch, he turned his back to the shoreline and ignored her altogether as he began furling the sails, snapping them into place around the boom with a vigor that could have been efficiency, but might very well have been plain anger.

It was ten minutes before Ben turned his attention back to the trees, and by then, Tasha had vanished.

CHAPTER FIVE

SHE STUMBLED HER WAY upward through a tangle of undergrowth, catching at roots and branches to aid her progress up the difficult slope. Adrenaline coursed through her system, giving her a strength and speed she could not normally have achieved. She scrambled over stark slabs of granite that tore at her fingernails and scraped the knees of her jeans. Forked branches caught at her shirt, causing a few small rips that Tasha did not even notice in her desperate bid to reach help, any kind of help, before Ben took up the chase. Thank goodness for the thick curtain of greenery that would conceal her progress from his view!

She came to a panting halt after about ten minutes when her advance was temporarily impeded by a dense growth of bushes directly in her path. Through a heavy screen of vegetation she glanced back and down toward the angle of the shoreline, and was surprised to find that she had covered no more than a hundred yards. From her concealed vantage point in a thicket of greenery, she could see the ketch clearly.

The ketch. . . and Ben.

During the past few minutes Tasha's heart had

been in her throat, but now it relocated itself in the region of her ribs as she realized that Ben was not in hot pursuit. He was standing on the ketch, arms akimbo in an attitude of exasperation, staring at the very spot where Tasha had been so elegantly posed a short time ago, and where she had abandoned her model case. He stood stock-still and so did she— hardly daring to breathe, because even at this distance it seemed to her that Ben would be able to hear everything, including the wild ticking of her pulse.

And then, with a surprise bordering on disbelief, she saw him shrug. Ben had shrugged! Didn't he even care that she had vanished? He turned his attention back to the ketch as if, indeed, he did not. Unconcernedly he began to load boxes of supplies onto the inflatable, illustrating clearly that her presence or absence was a matter of supreme indifference to him. Tasha expelled her held breath with a vehemence akin to anger. How dare he bring her into the land of nowhere, and then be so cavalier as to not even give a damn what happened to her! Why, in this thick vegetation she might encounter heaven-knows-what hidden dangers. . . .

For the first time a chill of apprehension for her predicament shivered down her spine, a sensation that now had nothing to do with the age-old chase of the hunter and the hunted.

She dragged her eyes from Ben and the ketch and looked at her immediate surroundings with new eyes. Away from the cooling breezes afforded on the beach, there was a steamy rain-forest quality to the very air. The vegetation seemed to press in upon her from all sides, contributing to a sense of unreality. Her pulse rate increased in direct ratio to her imagination. What dangerous creatures lurked among those twisted roots. . . behind those gnarled trunks. . . beyond those jagged rocks. . . even in those tall trees? Were there snakes? Tarantulas? Poisonous lizards? A line of tiny ants was working its way toward her unsuitably sandaled toe; she jerked her foot away quickly. She had seen enough specimens collected on her father's various expeditions to know that appearances often lied; the most innocuous-looking could be the deadliest of all.

Gritting her teeth, she forced herself to take stock of the situation more rationally. Oh, if only Max had allowed Morley to proceed with her information on creatures indigenous to these islands. The thought reinjected some sanity; surely, if poisonous creatures abounded on these islands, Morley would have informed Max of this? Now, although Tasha still looked askance at the ants and spiders around her, she did so with a less unreasoning eye.

But soon other doubts intruded on her mind. She thought she was aiming in the direction of the thatched huts she had seen from the shore; but was she? From here the huts were not visible, as they had been from the lagoon. No sounds of human habitation reached her in this spot, except for the cheerfully tuneless whistling Ben had taken up seconds ago.

Her eyes turned in that direction again, and she

saw that he was still within view. He had brought the inflatable to shore once more and was midway through unloading boxes of supplies onto the beach. As if that mattered more than finding her! As Ben deposited the last of the boxes on the sand and straightened to his full six-foot-four height again, she noticed some small things in his hands. Could they be the remnants of the beer and sandwiches she had been too proud to ask for earlier? The thought of them served to remind her that she had had nothing to eat or drink since breakfast—and a very spare Max-type breakfast at that: one soft-boiled egg without salt, one sugarless grapefruit, one butterless piece of toast. A hunger pang, surprising her with its intensity, invaded the hollow of her elegantly slender stomach.

Her surmise had been correct: Ben was in possession of her uneaten lunch. Standing arrogantly with one hand on his hip, he threw back his bearded head and raised the beer can to his lips. He did not lower the can until it was, she was sure, empty. As he wiped his mouth with the back of his hand, an earthy enjoyment was written in every muscle of his long easy body—almost as if he knew she was watching! Her fingers tightened involuntarily over a twig. Even as she watched, he raised the sandwich to his lips and took an enthusiastic bite.

"I despise you, Ben Craig," she muttered maliciously beneath her breath. She snapped the twig in two and angled it crossly into a nearby clump of bushes, then jumped in dismay as something large and dun-colored flapped out of the bushes and screeched past her face in a rush of wings and a blur of feathers.

"Oh...!" It was the softest of exclamations; she had managed to swallow her scream. A quick alarmed glance in Ben's direction assured her that he had not even cocked his head at the bird's sudden and noisy takeoff. His attention, in fact, had been diverted by another occurrence altogether. Down on the beach, there had been a score of new arrivals. Many of the Seychellois who lived on the island—men, women and children—were straggling across the beach toward the ketch. Well, at least the welcome party would keep his attention from her!

But the moment of panic at the bird's appearance had served to remind her that she must move on. Darkness was not very far away, and she must try to reach help before it fell. A rational appraisal had allayed most of her initial apprehensions about the nature of wildlife on this island, but she had no desire to spend the night curled up on a bed of anthills.

But perhaps, she reflected murderously, that was exactly the fate Ben had in mind for her!

Donning a look of grim determination, she pushed aside the bushes that had brought her flight to a halt and pressed on as quickly as she was able.

Darkness advanced more swiftly than she. It took time to work her way through the tangle of bushes, and within minutes the encroaching gloom threatened an obstacle of a new kind. It was with relief that she stumbled through a screen of trees and emerged at what appeared to be a path. It was not much of a path, but it was very definitely there. Trees pressed close on each side, and the arch of branches almost closed out the sky, which had turned a gloomy twilight purple.

Which way to go: up or down? She made an instant decision and turned her hurried footsteps to the rise. At as much of a run as her impractical footwear would allow, she raced upward on the winding path until—at an eyeblink—the light of day was extinguished.

She stood, panting, trying to get her bearings. She investigated the black void with her hands and found nothing that told her which direction the meandering trail now followed. Only a few stars winked through the canopy of trees. She waited, but night vision restored no visibility. A twig crackled. A cricket chirped. A low cooing sounded, seemingly at her ear. Something soft and moth-winged brushed her face. But these things told her nothing, except that she had stumbled into a sightless alien world she did not comprehend in any way.

Suddenly a match flared, almost under her very nose. Tasha jumped back, and this time, to stifle a scream, she had to place her hand over her mouth.

The apparition directly ahead of her did little to settle Tasha's by now severely shaken nerves. By the light of the match, the almost totally toothless smile that confronted her appeared otherworldly. But it was a smile; very definitely a smile, and after the initial shock had finished reverberating through her system, Tasha tried to smile back.

A wizened hunched little woman, a wrinkled brown raisin of a face, a halo of wispy white flyaway hair, a thin gold wire twisted into one ancient ear, a dress like a sugarsack patched until the original fabric had all but disappeared—all these things Tasha saw in the moment before the match burned out.

"Venez avec moi," quavered the voice of a very old woman. Tasha's heart pounded as a thin bony hand came to rest on her wrist. But the woman's touch was as light as a dried leaf, reminding Tasha of parchment and rose petals, and when the gnarled fingers slipped into hers, all apprehension vanished as if it had never been.

"Venez avec moi," repeated the very old voice, as if the woman had been expecting Tasha all along. There was a lullaby quality to that wavering voice that seemed to rob the dark of danger; and enfolded by it, Tasha started to follow the urging fingers as if in a dream. As the old woman shuffled along, holding Tasha's hand ever so lightly, she mumbled to herself in a patois of which Tasha could understand only a few phrases. Occasionally she slipped into traditional French, although she seemed to be talking not to Tasha but to herself, commenting on things they passed. How those ancient eyes could see anything in this dark night was beyond Tasha's ken, but it seemed that indeed they could.

"Oh, oh, oh, I do not like that *bois tangue* over there, it might strike me dumb...but then, perhaps I can remember not to chew it.... Is this a *fruit de*

cythère? Yes, yes, it must be. . . see the little apples
that have fallen on the ground. . . and here, oh, oh,
oh, I must not touch the *herbe poison*, its juice is
very bad for the eyes. . . . That big *cèdre* I see, it
is nearly a century old. . . . Oh, yes, I can remember
when it was a little seed. . . I think. . . . Oh, it is nice to
walk where the lemon grass grows, I like the smell of
the oil that lives inside. . . ."

Soft fragrances wafted through the night as they
brushed past the branches of strange plants and
tropical trees, and trod on the ferns and grasses that
grew along the narrow path. The old woman's mumbled monologue told of exotic names—*modestie* and
sangdragon, *bois de natte* and *langue de boeuf*,
ouatier and *vieille fille*, *monstera* and *vetivert*. At
times she seemed to be reminding herself, with some
confusion, about the properties of each growing
thing, whether fern, fruit, tree or flower.

"Is that an Indian licorice tree? Oh, oh, the
réglisse has such pretty seeds to bear such evil. . . and
no, tonight the tree is not asleep, so there will be no
storm. . . I think. . . . Or is it the bad seeds of the
tanguin that sleep? I forget. . . but tomorrow I will
remember. . . . At least I see no strychnine tree, such
poisons I do not like, I will not have them in my
hut. . . . Oh, yes, the *patchouli*, that is a good
plant. . . . Its oil is good against the moths. . . or is it
mosquitoes? Moths, I think. . . . I must gather some
tomorrow. Yes, tomorrow; my memory will not
desert me tomorrow. . . maybe. . . ."

At last the woman came to a halt, and the dessicated hand squeezed a soft command to Tasha's fingers. "Wait," she said. Then the ancient fingers released their grip, and Tasha stood alone waiting in a black void, listening to shuffling sounds in the dark. For some reason, she felt no apprehension whatsoever; the old woman's crooning voice and dried-leaf of a hand had vanquished all fear.

A moment later another match flared, and this time it was used to ignite a badly bent kerosene lantern of very primitive design, evidently fetched by the old woman during her short absence from Tasha's side.

Directly ahead, in Tasha's path, stood a tiny grass hut in the middle of a small clearing. A couple of crude plank steps led up into the abode, which was raised a foot or so above the ground.

"Come," beckoned the old woman from the doorway. Tasha could see her more clearly now than during the one brief glimpse by matchlight. She was extremely old—so old and so frail that it seemed a puff of air might blow her away. Her brown face was mapped with a network of wrinkles, her white hair sparse; her shapeless ankle-length dress was covered all over with variegated patches, like a Jacob's coat of many colors. That seamed sunken smile appeared warm and friendly now, no longer weird and alarming as it had been on the path.

"Come," repeated the tremulous voice, and Tasha mounted the unsafe-looking steps.

The hut was a single room, and its appearance was odd indeed. Bunches of drying herbs and roots hung from the supports of the low palm-thatched ceiling so that few steps could be taken without ducking one's head. At the far end of the room, on roughly constructed shelves, were dozens and dozens of ill-assorted glass jars, many of them chipped and all containing dried leaves, pieces of bark and more roots. There were also a number of dented tin cans, labels carefully peeled away, and Tasha surmised that these contained more of the same, or perhaps cooking supplies. A nearly empty sack of rice, two coconuts and a large bruised breadfruit occupied some shelf space, too.

The room smelled of wild vanilla and dried flowers and a potpourri of other pleasant scents Tasha could not identify. It was clear the old woman was some kind of herbalist; but it was not only the oddity of this profession that gave the hut its strange appearance.

It was the chairs.

Nearly every inch of floor space in the tiny hut was occupied by chairs. They were all wooden chairs of indifferent design, and every one of them seemed to be in a sad state of repair—some missing rungs, some missing legs, some with broken seats. There were at least a dozen of these tatterdemalion chairs in the tiny hut, leaving enough floor space for only one small and lumpy-looking wooden framed cot and a few narrow passages to different parts of the room.

"Come," the old woman said for the third time, and patted the seat of what was evidently the most serviceable of her possessions, a stiff wooden chair of which one arm had been broken and mended with some kind of homemade twine. Tasha ducked her way to the chair, by now so bemused by the unreality of the scene that she had almost forgotten how she'd come to be there. It seemed right to do as the old woman asked, whether the chair looked unsafe or not.

Lantern in hand, the old woman peered at Tasha closely. Despite the great age that had long since robbed the ancient eyes of lashes, the eyes themselves were like brown beads, warm and curious behind the crow's feet of wrinkles. They blinked at Tasha several times.

"I have forgotten why you came to see me," the old woman quavered at last. "But do not tell me, I will remember.... Is it *catépen* that you want? But I can see you have no ringworm...oh, oh, oh...why did you ask for *catépen*? You are trying to confuse me...*catépen* is not for bruises. Or is the *catépen* for someone else?"

Tasha gaped a little and blinked once or twice. "I didn't ask for anything," she said, "at least, not yet."

"Oh, oh, oh," said the old woman, "it is a long time since anyone has come to me with a bruise. I will have to think what to use...if I can remember...."

Tasha skimmed a puzzled look at her arms, the only part of her anatomy that was bared to the view. A cursory inspection revealed not a single bruise.

"No, no," trembled the aged voice. "You are trying to pretend to an old woman. Oh, oh, I have good eyes, do you think I cannot see?"

And with that, she bent down and lifted one cuff of Tasha's blue jeans. At calf level a dark mark was already beginning to appear. Tasha blinked again in surprise. The damage must have occurred during her precipitate flight from Ben—but how had the old woman known? Some telltale abrasion of the denim, perhaps, that was hardly visible to Tasha's eyes?

"Oh, oh, oh," clucked the old woman. Leaving Tasha's side, she squeezed a passage between chairs to the shelf that held her herbal remedies. The gnarled fingers reached up and secured a jar. Muttering to herself in her creole patois, she removed several pinches of its contents and set to work with a crude mortar and pestle. Tasha watched, too fascinated to remember the urgency of her need for help, while the old woman added sprinklings of dried leaves from other jars and clear liquid from yet another container. The resulting thick paste was then spread on a large fresh leaf of some kind, and the old woman shambled her way back across the room, apparently well pleased with her concoction.

"Oh, oh, oh," she muttered as she stooped to Tasha's leg, "why did you think I had forgotten what to do for a bruise? It is good you came to me while the bruise is still fresh. By tomorrow, there will be not a single mark."

Tasha submitted to the poultice without complaint. It smelled of cloves and was agreeably cool and soothing to the area of the bruise, which had begun to hurt during the wait. The old woman's eyes darted blinkingly around the hut as she looked for some method to tie the dressing into place; and at last, with a rueful sigh, she unfastened the rough twine that had been securing the arm of Tasha's chair.

"O-o-oh," she mourned sadly as the arm of the chair came away in her hand.

"It doesn't matter," Tasha said quickly, "I can hold the leaf in place."

"No, no, no, it must be done in the proper way." With a loving pat and a wistful sigh, the old woman put the chair arm in a safe spot; and then set to work with trembling fingers to tie the poultice into place on Tasha's leg. "And tomorrow I will make a new rope of coconut fiber... I think I know how...."

At last she stood back and nodded, satisfied. Tasha decided it was time she gave some account of herself.

"My name is Natasha Craig," she said, and then— belatedly remembering the divorce—amended, "I mean, Montgomery."

"You are trying to confuse me again," the old woman accused in a quaking sorrowful voice. "Why do you tell me a name that is not yours?"

"I'm sorry, it's because...." Tasha bit her lip, wondered how to explain, and then decided against explaining at all. "Natasha Montgomery is the correct name," she said.

"Oh, oh, oh. Why do you lie to an old woman?" She leaned down and studied Tasha's face intently. "But... you are not laughing at me, so perhaps... you are just confused yourself...."

There was no point in pursuing the matter, Tasha decided; let this old woman believe what she wished. She might be muddled in her thinking, but she had been kind, and Tasha had no desire to say anything that might be mistaken for mockery.

"Thank you very much for treating my bruise," she said politely, "and for finding me in the dark. You've been very good to me, considering I'm a perfect stranger."

"Stranger? Oh...." The ancient hand picked up the kerosene lantern again and held it close to Tasha's face. Something the woman saw there caused her to moan softly, a sound as soft as the shush of autumn leaves scattering underfoot. "Surely you know old Eulalie," she trembled. "And I, I have seen your eyes before...no, no, it is only that you remind me of someone. Oh, oh, oh...you do need Eulalie's help. Why did you tell me you were troubled by a bruise? A bruise is a very little thing compared to what I see in your eyes. Oh, I will give you something to help. But first, I will soothe you a little."

"Really, I don't need anything," Tasha denied as Eulalie once more breached the obstacle course of chairs. But already the old woman was reaching for a dark glass bottle, one of two that stood side-by-side on a shelf.

"Are you afraid to drink what an old woman offers? But it is only *calou*...oh, very weak, it was only tapped from the palm yesterday...or was it last month? No matter, that will make it even less strong.

Even a child could drink it. And you so thirsty, so hungry. . . ."

Moments later she was back at Tasha's side with the bottle, as well as a bowl containing a few scraps of vegetables and a little cooked rice. "First the *calou*," she suggested, pressing the bottle into Tasha's hands. "It will loosen your tongue to tell me of your troubles. Oh, oh. If you do not drink, I will think you only pretend to want my help. . .and why did you come here, if you do not want my help? Oh, yes. Such a long way you have come, and just to find Eulalie. . .yes, take the whole bottle. . .oh, oh, oh. How did you find my hut in the dark?"

Fortunately, the old woman Eulalie did not seem to expect an answer to this last question; she rambled on about other things as she watched Tasha down the bottle of the liquid known as *calou*. Its taste was reminiscent of turpentine and altogether unpleasant. Only an extremity of thirst, along with a strong desire not to offend Eulalie, overcame Tasha's initial revulsion. Once she grew used to the taste, the effect was quite pleasant, rather like a mild beer. When she finished, Eulalie's withered face broke into a smile.

"Now the food," she said.

"I'm really not hungry," Tasha demurred after one look at the unappetizing dish. Fortunately Eulalie did not insist; in fact she looked somewhat relieved.

"If I had remembered you were coming tonight," she said tremulously, "I would have baked my bread-fruit. Oh, oh, oh. To think I have expected you for so long and not to be ready when you come. You must forgive me, at times I grow confused.... Now tell me. Why are you running from the man who is tall like a tower?''

Tasha stared, momentarily dumbfounded. Then reason took over, and she realized that Eulalie, like herself, must have been able to see Ben through the screen of trees high on the hill—that she had probably, in fact, witnessed their landing. All the same, after Eulalie's other confusions, it seemed to be an extraordinary piece of insight.

"Tell me," urged Eulalie sympathetically, "unless you already did. For it seems to me I know, and yet...oh, oh, oh. Perhaps you should tell me again. I think I must have forgotten.''

Tasha's explanation started simply enough, but soon became less so. Perhaps it was the oddness of the surroundings, perhaps the lamplight, or the keen interest in Eulalie's wizened brown face; perhaps it was the aftermath of the day's events, or the after-effects of the mild *calou* on an empty stomach. But for whatever reason, she found herself recounting things she would normally not have told to a stranger.

When the recitation was over, Eulalie began to croon softly and shake her white-crowned head in a woeful rocking motion, as if in lament for all the sorrows of mankind. And there was no mistaking the compassion in those bird-bright eyes.

"Will you help me then?" pleaded Tasha. Her eyes traveled briefly to the bed. "I realize I can't ask to stay here. But perhaps there is someplace you could take me? If there's someone of authority. . . ."

"There is one man on this island who can help," trembled Eulalie, "if I can remember who he is. . . ."

"Please try," Tasha said with some urgency.

"Oh, oh, oh." Eulalie screwed her eyes tightly closed. "Let me see what I can see with the eyes in my mind."

Her lips moved in little muttering motions, but no sounds came out. All of a sudden her eyes sprang open and she leaned forward, enormously pleased with herself.

"The clock," she said. "I saw the clock."

Tasha was speechless. Had Eulalie understood nothing of what she said? And yet, it seemed rude to point out the total lack of logic in Eulalie's train of thought.

"I don't think that's what I need," Tasha said carefully, once she had recovered her wits.

"No? Well, then. . . ." Eulalie's briefly disappointed expression changed to one of reflection. She began to rock slowly back and forth, and her voice took on a singsong quality, as if she was repeating to herself something learned long ago. "*La coquette* for the pimples," she crooned, "*rose amère* for the worms. *Morongue* to draw the blood and *citronelle* to dull the fever. . . oh, oh. How about. . . but no, she has no warts, so why would she want that? *Pignon d'Inde*? No. *Monte au ciel*? No. Oh, oh, it is hard to think when you are old. *Bois malgache*, perhaps? But no, he would never try to poison her. . . . Then there's root of the paw-paw, but what is it for? If I could only think properly...."

"I don't need any medicines," Tasha said, despairing.

Suddenly Eulalie sprang to her feet, her face wreathed in satisfaction. "Oh, oh, why did I not think of it sooner? No medicines. Of course. Now I know what she needs."

Tasha watched, round-eyed and with a growing sense of helplessness, while Eulalie sidled over to her crowded shelves once more. One bony hand rooted around in a tin container and emerged triumphantly with a needle. It was becoming apparent, Tasha reflected, that Eulalie in no way understood the nature of the problem. And yet, with someone so very, very old, what could one expect?

And why was Eulalie removing that thin gold wire from her own desiccated earlobe?

Tasha remained quiescent as Eulalie advanced toward her once again. It was not until she saw the direction of the pointing needle that she leaped to her feet.

"Oh, no!" she gasped, trying without success to retreat into the sea of chairs. "You're not going to stick that in my ear!"

"No?" Eulalie halted at once and her bright old eyes turned troubled. "It is good for the thing that ails you."

"I...I...thank you very much, but no thank you. I don't want my ear pierced. That's not the kind of help I need."

Eulalie looked at her piece of gold wire forlornly, then shrugged and twisted it back into her own ear. Her disappointment was evident, and she spent the next minute blinking at Tasha and sighing. "Well, then, I will see what else I can do.... Do you have a pinch of sand from his footprint?"

Tasha felt bubbles of hysteria rising in her throat. "No," she said.

"Oh, oh, oh, this will be very hard," Eulalie quaked. "Why did you ask me to help? You take none of my advice...oh, oh, oh...and you did not even bring the pinch of sand...or is it a piece of his fingernail I asked you for? I forget...."

As Eulalie advanced once more to her shelves, the ludicrousness of the whole scene overcame Tasha, and she sat down again heavily, close to tears of frustration. How on earth could she explain? She watched Eulalie rummaging around, gathering pinches of this and that with her gnarled fingers and placing them all on a piece of scrap brown paper that appeared to have been saved for many years.

"There is one thing missing, but what is it?" muttered Eulalie to herself. "Oh, oh, oh, it is so long since anyone has asked me for one of these. Yet I knew that she was coming and I knew that she would ask. And all these years I have tried to remember, so that when she asked, I could help.... Oh, oh, what have I forgotten? Let me think...."

After a few moments of reflection, she plucked a hair from her own head and added it to the tiny pile. At last, satisfied, she folded the paper very carefully and sealed it with several licks of her dry old tongue.

"I appreciate what you're trying to do," Tasha begged, attempting to keep the despair from her voice. "But really, what I need is a bed for the night. I don't think that little packet will help."

"No?" Eulalie paused, looking thoroughly downcast and somewhat puzzled. She blinked uncertainly at the brown paper packet in her hand.

"I'm running away from someone," Tasha explained earnestly, and with an anxiety she could not completely conceal.

"Oh, oh, oh. Why did I not think? I have not soothed her enough." Eulalie tucked the little packet into a pocket of her patched dress. Before coming back across the room, she picked up what appeared to be the second bottle of *calou*, not without a wistful glance and a deep sigh at the empty space this left on the shelf. She dusted a thick gathering of cobwebs from the neck of the bottle and padded back to Tasha's side, negotiating her way through the chairs.

"Oh, Eulalie. . .don't you understand? All I want is a place to stay for the night. I'm having trouble with my husband, my ex-husband I mean. Is there no person on the island who can help?"

The words seemed to be deeply distressing to Eulalie. Her lips started to tremble as though she wanted to cry, and her eyes took on a decidedly watery look. "I am helping," she wavered accusingly, "and I am on this island. . .I think. . . ."

"Oh, Eulalie," said Tasha helplessly, "you've been wonderful. But I'm looking for someone in charge, a priest or a chief man. Is there anyone like that?''

Eulalie shook her head as if to straighten what was inside. "Oh, yes, I said there was a man. I told you there was a man. And oh, oh, oh, you did not laugh, but you wanted to.''

Suddenly it occurred to Tasha that perhaps it was she, not Eulalie, who had been lacking in perception. The word for clock, in French, was *horloge*; and that was the word Eulalie had used earlier. Could it be the name of a man—just as Le Rouge had been the name of another man on Mahé? Yes, it was possible. It was a curious name, but on this strange island, the curious seemed commonplace.

"Is there a Monsieur L'Horloge?" Tasha puzzled out loud.

Eulalie looked vague and confused as if she was sure Tasha was trying to make fun of her. "Oh, oh, oh," she mourned. "I am old, only old, I am not mad at all. Why do you think me mad? I told you there was a man and you would not listen.''

Tasha struggled to maintain calmness. "Please, Eulalie, I don't think you mad at all. This man who can help, is it a Monsieur L'Horloge?''

Eulalie's eyes meandered for a moment or two, but she appeared somewhat mollified. "Oh, **y**es, he can help...I think.... Oh, yes, I am sure. He is **the** man you need to see.''

Tasha breathed a sigh of relief; at last it seemed they were getting somewhere. "Can you take me to him?''

"Yes, I will take you to him...if I can remember the way...but first you drink this." She pushed the dusty bottle into Tasha's hands. "Oh, yes, very soothing."

"Really, Eulalie, I don't need any more soothing."

Once more Eulalie's wrinkled lips began to quiver pathetically. "Why did you ask me for it then? Oh, oh, oh. You should not ask an old woman for favors if you only intend to refuse them. And I would have given you anything, even my chairs, because of the sorrows I saw in your eyes! You are trying to confuse me...you want me to forget my own name...I do that sometimes, too...."

"I'm sorry, Eulalie," Tasha said quickly, if with a well-hidden inward grimace at the bottle in her hands. The first bottle of *calou* had been very mild in its effects after all; surely she could manage to down another bottle? "It's me that's forgetful. I did ask for this. And I appreciate everything you've done."

Fortunately, the second bottle was not as atrocious as the first. It had a sweeter woodsier flavor; apparently the longer shelf life altered the taste for the better. All the same Tasha, who was quite unused to alcoholic beverages, had considerable trouble downing the contents; she choked several times. But Eulalie now looked so pleased, blinking with intent and watchful interest as the level of the liquid dropped, that Tasha felt she had no recourse but to finish it to the last drop.

"What was it you asked me to do?" blinked Eulalie, while Tasha was still trying to regain her breath after the last difficult swallow. "Oh, yes...I will take you to his hut. We will need...what? A lantern? Oh, oh, oh...if you had good eyes like mine, we would not have to waste the light. Oh yes, with my old eyes I can see what other eyes cannot...I think...."

Tasha followed the beckoning finger into the night, and soon they were on the narrow path once more. This time, with the lantern in Eulalie's hand lighting the way, Tasha had the odd impression that she was traveling down through a winding tunnel of greenery. The sensation was dizzying, as if she was moving through time as well as space. Her head grew lighter and her feet heavier, and Eulalie's mutterings, once more resumed, only added to the feeling of otherworldliness.

"Oh, yes, the *bilimbi*, that will take the stains from my clothes...but if I pick the fruit, what will the black parrot eat? Oh, better a stain than a hungry bird.... See, the pitcher plant has been eating tonight...and so will Eulalie, soon.... Oh, why did she take so long? I am so old, so tired of waiting. Oh, oh, oh, is that where the *brède martin* hides? I had forgotten, I must make a soup of the shoots...."

At last Eulalie halted just where the embracing trees came to an end. Directly ahead lay a large moonlit clearing, and beyond that a majestic grove of palm trees. They were enormously tall, easily twice the height of any palms Tasha had ever seen. There was a hushed cathedral beauty to the grove. The moon, visible here where it had not been before, silvered the fronds of the giant palms beyond the clearing and filtered down to cast luminescent patterns on the lacy ferns and vegetation that lay beneath.

Tasha caught her breath at the unearthly loveliness, and a strong sense of déjà-vu came over her, perhaps accounting for the reeling of her brain.

Eulalie waved her lantern in a slightly different direction, toward one side of the sizable clearing. Tasha's gaze followed and found a palm-thatched hut. It was bigger and considerably less decrepit than Eulalie's; it had a large veranda for one thing. A bright light burned inside, visible through the shuttered windows.

Tasha turned to Eulalie, trying to steady her senses. "Is that where Monsieur L'Horloge lives?" she asked.

The alert brown eyes blinked at her once from their bed of wrinkled skin; and then, without answering, Eulalie lifted the primitive lantern and blew.

Startled, Tasha reached out to touch her. Where Eulalie had been standing only seconds before, her fingers encountered empty air. "Eulalie?"

There was no answer. She listened and heard no footsteps retreating on the dark narrow path where no moon reached. Perhaps Eulalie preferred not to hear protestations of thanks? Perhaps she did not wish to visit this neighbor of hers with the odd name? Perhaps she had extinguished the light only to conserve kerosene and was standing no more than a few feet away? There was no way of telling, and as Tasha received no response to her soft callings, she finally turned toward the only oasis of sanity in this surrealistic night: the patches of light shining through the windows of the hut.

The ground of the clearing, though overgrown with grasses, was easily negotiable. Nevertheless Tasha found it unaccountably difficult to walk the distance to the hut. Her feet flagged as she mounted the double step. The door onto the veranda was open. She walked through to the second door and rapped, supporting herself on the doorjamb because she felt so dizzy.

"Come in!" called a voice, and she turned the knob.

A man was sitting at a table, shaving. He was powerfully muscled and naked to the waist. His back was turned to the door, but his clean-shaven face was reflected in the mirror propped in front of him. His razor did not miss a stroke.

"Hello, Tasha," Ben said coolly. "Won't you come into my parlor?"

CHAPTER SIX

"SAID THE SPIDER to the fly," she felt impelled to whisper, through lips that were curiously stiff.

Perhaps there had been too many shocks that day; this latest one produced nothing but paralysis. A giddiness assailed her and her feet felt leaden, rooted to the wooden floor. There seemed to be a Greek-tragedy inevitability to it all, a sense of the fates taking over—as if she had been meant to come here all along.

"Exactly," said Ben with total calmness, half-turning as he wiped the last traces of lather from his jaw. The skin beneath the beard-line was scarcely paler than elsewhere; it showed very tanned against the white towel he was using.

Tasha swayed in the doorway, trying to pull together the jigsaw pieces of the room that seemed to swirl before her eyes—a crude table, four chairs, closely shuttered windows, two unpretentious metal-framed beds along one wall. And Ben. Surely the gods were making mock of her futile efforts to escape; she had been delivered well and truly into his hands.

"Ah, that feels good after a spell at sea," Ben

noted conversationally, just as if her reappearance had been totally predictable. He paused and tested his jaw with lean long fingers, then put the towel down and turned his full attention to the door.

"I was hoping you wouldn't put your nose in until I finished. Getting rid of a month's growth is no fun, and I confess it produces more than a fair share of cuss words." He busied himself with pulling the checked shirt over his rippling shoulders and buttoning it. "Normally I shave almost as soon as I put to shore, but this time I had other things on my mind. That message from you arrived just as I landed at Mahé. Good timing, Tasha; you must have extrasensory perception. I'd been at sea for a full month, and I hadn't been in touch with my publisher for some time. Now come on in, your supper's all ready and.... Good God, why are you looking at me like that? I assure you I'm not a ghost. This is me, very much in the flesh."

Tasha tried without success to battle the unreal sensations that were turning her stomach to butterflies and her brain to butter. A sense of fatality and futility gripped her, along with a thickness of tongue she could not control. "How did you know I'd come?" she asked unsteadily. "It's as if you...expected me to walk in just now."

Ben looked mildly surprised. "Of course I expected you," he said somewhat sardonically. He stood up and began to tuck his shirttails into the mud-colored Levi's that molded his powerful thighs in ways that were not conducive to Tasha's peace of mind. She tried to refocus her eyes elsewhere—an exercise that seemed unaccountably difficult.

"That bird you disturbed gave me a very good idea of where you were and exactly where you were heading. I knew you'd stumble on this little valley within a minute or two. It was directly in your path, and you couldn't possibly reach the other huts on the island without passing by mine."

Tasha blinked slowly and tried to concentrate. Had she really been so close to this place earlier? And where had she been a short time ago, if not at one of the other huts? Had she imagined everything? Was she imagining this now? Certainly something very strange was happening to her senses, which seemed to be gradually deserting her.

Ben went on, not remarking on her silence. "I counted on your love of civilization, brown eyes. As most of the islanders were down at the beach, I knew you wouldn't be able to tell whose hut was whose. With nightfall only minutes away, I didn't think you'd go stumbling any farther—unless you spotted me coming after you. So I simply stayed away from here until dark, when it was too late for you to do any more running. Were you watching from the coco-de-mer grove?"

A great heaviness in her limbs contributed to the sense of time out of joint. Her powers of reasoning appeared to have gone askew. Nothing Ben said seemed to make much sense, and yet in an odd way she knew that it did.

"Once night fell, I hardly thought a city-bred girl

like you would run away from the only light in sight." For once, Ben's unflattering sarcasm was wasted on Tasha; she was too busy clutching the door frame for support. "I also knew," he said, "that before the night was through, something was sure to drive you inside. I doubt even the Garden of Eden could turn you back into the original Eve, Tasha; it's too late for that. What was it—falling coconuts?"

Tasha's head swirled with the effort of following Ben's logic. Garden of Eden? Eve? Coconuts? He was making no sense at all.

"Falling coconuts?" she repeated dazedly, with a cotton-wool tongue.

"They fall more frequently at night," Ben informed her in a dry tone, eyeing her narrowly. "Well, if it wasn't coconuts, I suppose it was a scare of some kind. You look quite distraught. You can start pulling yourself together, brown eyes; likely, it was only some small nocturnal creature like a bat. Now come on in and eat. Nothing fancy; just a job fish I pulled in on a handline this afternoon. I cooked it Creole style, with coconut oil and onion and garlic, and—"

"There was an old woman," Tasha blurted, interrupting Ben midsentence. "I've been at her hut...or perhaps I just imagined her...."

It was Ben's turn to stare in disbelief. Something in Tasha's face, an unusual wildness of eye perhaps, at last communicated itself. He came quickly across the plank floor, in three long easy strides.

"What are you talking about?" he asked, frowning down into Tasha's ashen face. In the earlier chase through the undergrowth, her hair had become tangled, and a day of chewing lips had quite demolished the careful paint job she had applied on the ketch. But the eye makeup remained intact and contributed to her expression of staring bewilderment.

"Tell me," Ben commanded, his eyes narrowing.

"An old woman.... Oh, Ben...." She swayed forward, forgetting that not so very long ago she had tried to escape those strong arms; and realized only when her head was muffled against the reassuring bulk of Ben's chest that she was shaking all over and was very dizzy, too.

"I've been so...." Scared was the word she had intended to use, but something stopped her from saying it. And it was not strictly true in any case. She had not been scared of Eulalie at the time—only during these past few minutes since Eulalie had abandoned her on the path.

"I've been so confused," she whispered, wondering how she could convey the aura of the supernatural that had enveloped her since the moment she had sighted the grove of tall palms. Needing something real and human to reassure her, she rubbed her face against the little crispness that prickled through the light cotton of Ben's shirt. Her ears were ringing. She felt close to tears, and yet at the same time the giddiness that tingled through her head was not entirely unpleasant. "Oh, Ben...."

He led her across the room, one strong arm about her shoulder to guide her wavering footsteps. Not relinquishing his hold, he lowered both their bodies to a sitting position on the edge of one of the beds. With one hand he directed her face so that he could watch her expression; his own head bent close to hers. "Tell me about it," he said gravely.

And so she did, little by little. She found the telling difficult, for her wits were becoming more fogged by the minute. Some cautionary instinct prevented her from mentioning fears of the supernatural; she did not wish Ben to laugh at her. Gradually, as he listened without scoffing, the shaking ceased. Now only the dizziness remained and a slurring of voice that seemed to grow worse as she talked.

"Eulalie," said Ben thoughtfully when she had told almost everything. He rolled the name on his tongue again. "Eulalie—why, she must be the island's *bonne femme di bois*. I did hear there was one, but remember I haven't set foot on this property since I bought it. The *bonne femme di bois* generally lives in solitude, well back in the woods. Sort of a local witchwoman."

"Witchwoman?" came Tasha's faint rejoinder.

Ben laughed lightly, restoring some aura of reality. "Well, that's putting it a little strongly. The Seychelles government frowns on that kind of mumbo-jumbo, and if Eulalie were really practicing it, she'd be in deep trouble. She's probably more of a herbalist as you suggested. I imagine her infusions don't do any harm, and they may even do a mild amount of good. Those old herbal remedies often do."

"All the same, it was so odd...." The room

reeled, seemingly revolving around the little golden lights in Ben's eyes that were too dangerously close to her own. "She came to...to meet me on the path...."

"Heading down to see the action at the shore," Ben said, injecting a note of sanity. "Like everyone else on the island."

"And all those chairs...."

"That's easily explained, too."

Tasha formed an "Oh?" with her mouth, but the sound never emerged. Ben's face seemed to loom close to her lips for one moment of madness and then recede again. Or was that imagination, too?

It must have been, because Ben now frowned—as if he did not like being close to her at all. Still steadying Tasha's shoulders, he moved a little away and explained Eulalie's peculiar penchant in a brusque tone of voice.

"On these islands chairs are a symbol of prestige. Often they're a woman's proudest possessions, her mark of standing in the community. Who knows, perhaps Eulalie grew up in a family where there was dismal poverty and no chairs at all. Undoubtedly that would give her a yen to own as many as possible. Perhaps she persuaded some of her customers to pay her in that way, in exchange for dispensing *gris-gris*."

"*Gris-gris?*" Tasha asked thickly, swaying toward her vanishing support.

"Charms, I think, would be an appropriate translation. Or amulets. They're usually little packets containing bits of this and that. You can guess the kind of thing—cloth, hair, bits of rusty iron, sand from the footprints of an enemy...."

At the brief startled look in Tasha's eyes, Ben smiled grimly and remarked, "Don't let that alarm you. I suspect Eulalie's *gris-gris* don't work very well."

Tasha blinked in slow motion and licked her lips, an exercise that took a painfully long time. "Why?" she managed to say, at last.

"Because the chairs sound like the worst kind of castoffs, from your description," Ben replied with a dry logic that Tasha, in her muddled state of mind, could not possibly dispute. "If Eulalie's customers were satisfied, don't you think they'd have done a little better for her?"

"But why...." Tasha halted and tried to gather her thoughts. What had she been going to ask Ben? With effort she remembered. "Why...bring me... here? She...was taking me...to a man...a man called...oh...."

"Perhaps she was confused," Ben suggested with a watchful smile. "It seems to be catching."

"She...wasn't bringing me...to you?"

"Never met the woman in my life," Ben said flatly. "Perhaps she meant to take you to some other hut and lost her way in the dark. Now don't give the woman another thought. She sounds like an addled old soul with a good heart; that meal she offered you was undoubtedly her own. I warrant you she wouldn't harm a fly."

Unaccountably Tasha giggled, something she had never done before in her life. "Said the...spider," she said.

Ben scowled and made no effort to join in Tasha's moment of mirth. "Although I do wish she hadn't given you so much *bacca* to drink," he said disapprovingly.

"*Bacca*? Not *bacca*...." She tried to remember what it was that Eulalie had urged upon her, but without success.

"The first bottle was undoubtedly *calou*—palm toddy, a fermented sap taken from the tip of a growing cocopalm. But the second...well, didn't you say the bottle was very dusty? Palm toddy starts to deteriorate about four days after it's tapped, and the taste doesn't improve with age. The second bottle must have been something else, and *bacca* seems likely. It's made from sugarcane juice, and it can be like a time bomb. In fact it's forbidden to sell *bacca* more than three days old, because it gets so potent. Not eating all day wouldn't help, either. You, my love, are more than a little drunk."

Tasha almost sobbed with relief, and in trying to stifle it hiccuped instead. So that was the explanation! No wonder so many odd sensations had been assailing her. No wonder she had felt unable to run from Ben a second time. No wonder she could not resist him now, as his powerful arms came around her again, offering support. And now that she knew the trouble, she could give in and stop trying to fight it.

She wrinkled her nose, blew away a strand of hair that had fallen over her face, and sneezed.

"Moreover, I think you're having a delayed reaction," Ben said, looking at her oddly. "An explosive one, too."

Tasha giggled again and nose-dived toward Ben's collar opening, where the column of his throat was revealed. "It's about time," she murmured, snuggling in. And then, for the life of her, could not think what reaction he was talking about.

With a firm grip on her upper arms, Ben eased her away from his body. His lips were compressed in a line of sufferance. Steadying her, he puffed a pillow, then laid her down on the bed.

"I think you can forgo the meal tonight," he muttered, leaning over her, his face marked with lines of concern. "I don't think you're in shape for anything but bed."

"Thanks," she giggled, reaching up to wind her fingers around his neck. A warm lassitude crept through her limbs.

Ben groaned again and unlaced her fingers. "I'm not taking advantage of a woman in your condition," he said, sounding angry.

Offended, Tasha sprang to a sitting position and put on an air of injured dignity. "I'm not in...that condition," she said haughtily. "Babies and bikinis...don't mix. Besides," she hiccuped, "Max doesn't...do that...kind of thing."

"Lie down, Tasha," Ben said firmly, easing her back into a reclining position on the bed. "Right now

I'm not tempted to do a damn thing except give you a good paddling. For the love of heaven, don't wriggle that way for the next few minutes. All I want to do is get you ready for bed.''

She sighed with acquiescence and a great happiness washed through her. She closed her eyes. When she opened them again some seconds later she could not think why Ben's head was bent in evident concentration at her midriff. He seemed to be moving at half speed, flexing his fingers as if he did not want to undress her after all. Lamplight bronzed his hair, which looked rumpled, as though he had been raking it. His brow was knotted, his mouth compressed in a murderous line. A muscle worked in his jaw. And all that just because his hands were poised at her waistband. She giggled.

She heard a muffled curse and something snapped open. Then a brief tugging at her waist and another curse.

"Damn zip," muttered Ben. He seemed to be attacking it very viciously; why was he doing that? Then Tasha remembered that she had no undergarment on and giggled again. No brassiere, either. Max's doing.

"Max says...no," she said seriously, waggling a finger at Ben. "No...underwear."

"Damn Max all to hell," Ben muttered furiously, just as the zip came free and he discovered this for himself. Gritting his teeth, he left the bed and rummaged through a duffel bag until he found a pair of silky white cotton pajamas. His brow had turned to thunder, his mouth to a slash of lightning.

Tasha sobbed and hiccuped as he returned to her side. "Not...fair," she moaned in desperation. "You...have...pajamas...I don't."

Ben slanted a glowering and unamused look in her direction. With no particular gentleness he lifted her hips and began to wrench off the skin-tight jeans, keeping his eyes determinedly averted from the flesh thus revealed. Deep tinglings started in every inch of skin that came into inadvertent contact with his bronzed fingers. Tasha moaned and writhed and wished that Ben would not keep snatching his fingers away as if the very touch of her burned him... wished he would undress her slowly, lovingly, branding her with kisses, as he had done once so many years ago....

His moment of fury subsided when the jeans reached calf-level, revealing the leaf that Eulalie had tied into place.

"What's this?" he frowned, holding her knee still with one hand, while the fingers of his other hand probed lightly at the edges of the primitive poultice. "A bruise? Well, I'll leave the dressing for now. Who knows, it may even be all right by morning."

"Mmm," sighed Tasha in dizzy agreement. Ben's warm hand felt wonderful on her knee. Her eyes flagged closed, and a faint happy smile touched her lips. A great warmth radiated upward from the very spot on which Ben's hand rested. But why was he removing his hand now? And what was that slide of silk coming up over her legs? And why was he tying something around her waist, too tightly? Tasha's eyes came open again, focusing on the vicious clench of Ben's teeth. Her fingers groped for the offending pajama tie, found it, and pulled.

"Oh, God!" Ben exploded, and with a look of grim determination he set about securing the tie once more. This time, before she could rectify the situation, he wrenched the covers over her, and tucked them into place in a series of rough spastic movements very different from the controlled grace with which he usually moved. He leaned across her to straighten the pillow beneath her head, bringing the open collar of his shirt into her line of vision. The hard line of his newly shaven jaw, the strong throat, the taut set of his powerful shoulders—all contributed to the whirling of her senses. Dizzied by his closeness, she extricated one hand from beneath the covers, reached upward and nipped a tiny curl of chest hair between two lacquered fingernails.

She heard a deep groan and released the hair at once. "I...hurt...you," she sobbed, repentant on the instant and totally desolate, too. She squeezed her eyes closed because she wanted to cry so much. "Oh...oh...oh."

"Pull yourself together, Tasha," said a disgusted voice. "I don't get hurt that easily."

She opened her eyes wide and Ben swam into focus again. "You...don't?" she said in a daze of happy wonderment. She licked her lips, because Ben was swaying closer now, as if he very much wanted to kiss her, despite the enraged expression on his face. His eyes were burning with banked fires that she recognized, hazily and happily, as desire. One of his hands hovered near her head, as if it ached to smooth the long silky tangle of her black hair against the pillow. A deep bliss welled up inside her because she knew he wanted her badly now. She could see it in the way his gaze was riveted on her lips; she could feel it in the tensions that seemed to hold him there, like invisible chains binding them together. She sighed in deep contentment, closed her eyes again, and parted her lips for the kiss that must surely come.

"Oh, for God's sake," Ben muttered furiously, and left the bed altogether. An overwhelming sense of self-pity struck Tasha, and she sobbed and sniffled intermittently as she watched him move around the room, doing things she did not understand. Why did he look so angry? It seemed cruel that he should sit down and eat a meal, frowning through it all as though he did not like the taste of the food. It seemed cruel that he should go and stand at the door, looking out onto the dark veranda and rubbing his hand wearily around the back of his neck, as if he could find nothing better for his hand to do. It seemed cruel, but at length she dozed. . . .

Her eyes clicked open at the very moment he extinguished the light. She could hear sounds of him undressing in the dark—the soft thud of a shoe, the rustling of a shirt, the descending of a zip. Surely she would not be lonely much longer; Ben had given in to his needs at last.

But seconds later, she heard the creak of bedsprings elsewhere in the room and, dizzy with disappointment, realized that he had no intention of coming to lie beside her in the night. Perhaps he did not want her after all? A sense of deep hurt turned her lips to trembling, but she lay in silence until she heard the regular breathing that told her Ben was now asleep. She began to drift again. . . .

She awoke to the sound of a low moan from the other bed. It was a moment or two before she conquered her giddiness enough to realize that Ben was groaning in his sleep and tossing restlessly. So he wanted her after all! With a warm ecstasy flooding her heart and a lack of propriety she would never have displayed if she had had all her wits about her, she sidled out of bed. Half-tripping on the pajama legs, she tiptoed to where he lay. She fumbled for the sheet, and seconds later she was slipping in beside the long warm male body.

She rolled close to him at once and touched his face with tentative fingers. It was drenched in cold sweat—more evidence that set her heart to singing, for it seemed to denote to her muddled mind that he must want her very badly. "Ben," she whispered.

He awoke at once, tensing, as Tasha wrapped her arms around his neck and began to stroke the crisp vital ends of hair at his nape. "Don't. . . worry," she slurred, "I'm. . . here now."

"Oh, hell," muttered Ben. He jerked his head upward from the pillow. His face hovered over Tasha's so that she could feel the warm come-and-go of his breath fanning her face. "You'll have to go back to your own bed," he said, his voice sounding nearly as unsteady as her own.

"I don't want to...sleep...alone...anymore," she whimpered, sniffling unhappily. "I'm...dizzy. So dizzy."

Ben uttered another muffled curse. But he pulled her fiercely closer into the spoon of his near-naked body. A hand started to stroke her hair, easing the long strands away from her face and lodging them gently behind her ear. Her ear? One last thought penetrated the hazy pleasant fog of anticipation in her mind.

"My ear," she mumbled, thinking of one of Eulalie's actions that Ben had not explained, although she had described it to him. "Why...my...ear?"

In the darkness, she felt lips moving at her temples, and the slow slide of a hand at the small of her back. "Because of your eyesight," Ben murmured, the timbre of his voice unusually thick. "She only wanted to improve your eyesight."

Tasha's eyes blinked open as she remembered dizzily that she had not removed her contact lenses. "But...how...."

"I'll explain tomorrow," said Ben huskily, sealing her lids with his lips. "Now for God's sake, go to sleep."

"How...did she...know...."

"Hush," Ben muttered, pulling her head close against his chest, until the animal heat of him enveloped her. Tasha sighed contentedly, secure in the knowledge that everything would indeed be all right by morning. Of course Eulalie knew. Eulalie knew everything, except where to find Monsieur L'Horloge.

And then she forgot Eulalie altogether because Ben's mouth was fierce in her hair, and because she felt the wanting in his hard body, and because she heard the thud of his heart like loud thunder in her ear.

Tick tock, Mr. Clock.

"Big...Ben," she slurred, reaching down to release the pajama tie once more. "Big...bad... Ben...."

CHAPTER SEVEN

THE FIRST THING that impinged on her consciousness was her eyes. The insides of the lids felt like glue. Her lashes felt stuck together, too. She opened them very carefully and encountered dim light. Nothing looked familiar. Without turning her head, she directed her eyes toward the source of light. The door onto the veranda was open, and a tall tense figure stood there in silhouette, brooding out at the morning. She realized she was indeed wearing her contact lenses as she recognized the broad shoulders and the long powerful limbs and even the mud-colored Levi's....

Remembrance flooded back. She closed her eyes quickly so that if he turned around, he would not see she was awake. What had happened last night? She could recall nothing beyond the moment she had slipped into Ben's bed. And after that...? The speculation gave rise to a peculiar tingling that started somewhere in the deep regions of her body and traveled slowly upward to her face, warming her cheeks.

Moving very gingerly so that Ben would not hear, she shifted her fingers beneath the covers and felt the warmth and slight depression left by another body. It seemed to confirm the worst of her fears. The palm of her hand moved again and encountered naked hip. So she had slept with no clothing whatsoever on her lower half—or was that a pair of pajama bottoms tangled around her thighs? The T-shirt was still in place, twisted uncomfortably around her waist; but that was woefully inadequate to protect her from the kind of embrace Ben had no doubt subjected her to in the night. She started to straighten the pajama bottoms surreptitiously, but stilled the movement at once when she heard sounds of footsteps coming back into the room.

Oh, Lord. What had happened last night? Or rather, had last night really happened? The strangeness of it all swarmed back in full force. That odd hut in the hills. That mystical sense of inevitability. That old woman who seemed to understand nothing and everything. That dizzying journey through a tunnel of trees, to find Monsieur L'Horloge. And instead finding Ben. . . .

Ben. A hot shame coursed to Tasha's cheeks as she remembered various details of her behavior the previous evening. All the same, it was Ben's fault entirely; if he hadn't brought her to this island, nothing would have happened at all. Oh God, what was she going to do?

After a slight pause the footsteps continued into the main room of the hut, coming in her direction. There followed another sound as of a shutter being opened; this conjecture was confirmed by the sudden increase of light penetrating her closed eyelids. She kept them determinedly closed.

"You're awake," Ben stated flatly. "Don't bother pretending, brown eyes. I saw your hand moving around under the cover a minute ago. Besides, your color's giving you away. I'm glad to see that shame is one emotion you haven't forgotten."

At Ben's taunt Tasha at once opened her eyes and put on a haughty expression. She was damned if she'd let Ben lord it over her because of anything that happened the night before! "It seems to me," she flashed back at him, "that the person who should be ashamed is you."

Ben compressed his lips and eyed her with a distinctly sour look. "Oh, really? Don't try me, Tasha. I had a very hard night last night."

"So did I," she returned coldly, "considering the way you took advantage of the situation."

His eyes swept her with something very like disdain. "Unless you know something I don't," he said acidly, "the only thing you lost last night was one of your eyelashes."

Tasha stiffened imperceptibly. So nothing had happened, after all! The knowledge gave her a fluttery feeling and no particular comfort, for it only meant that the worst was still to come. To hide her momentary lack of composure, she tucked the sheet carefully around her middle and began to investigate her eyelids with her fingertips.

Ben pulled up a wooden chair, straddled it backward and sat there scowling at her. "You'd better take off the other one, too. You look lopsided."

The words sounded too much like a command, and

although Tasha had been about to yank off the one remaining eyelash, she abstained.

"Do you always wear those wretched things? You never used to."

"I feel altogether undressed without them," she lied airily, and out of sheer perversity began searching the rumpled sheets for the missing lash. At least it kept her from being mesmerized by the way the taut fabric of Ben's lean-hipped denims molded his muscular thighs, tightening to an alarming extent because of the way he sat astride the chair.

"Don't bother looking," Ben growled. "I threw it into the bushes first thing this morning."

"You didn't!" Her eyes snapped back into dangerous territory.

"Damn right I did. I'd have dispensed with the second one too, but I didn't want to wake you up. So you'll just have to feel naked, won't you?"

Tasha glared at him as imperiously as possible, considering the state of her eyelashes. What an arrogant impossible man! Why had she ever thought otherwise long enough to marry him? "Speaking of naked," she said tartly, "may I please have my jeans? I'd like to get up now."

"No."

Tasha opened her mouth to utter an angry objection and then thought better of it. She forced herself to slow down and take stock of the situation. It was clear that frustration had put Ben into a very bad mood this morning, and considering her own present state of undress, it was probably best not to antagonize him too much.

She raised her eyebrows and put on her very best you-can't-be-serious smile. "You can hardly expect me to go naked for a whole week," she said with an attempt at reasonableness.

Ben's scowl hardly flickered. "I've considered it," he said unsmilingly.

"You're joking! Eyelashes is one thing, but—"

"This valley is enormously private, Tasha; that's one of the reasons I bought it. And yesterday, when the islanders came to greet me at the beach, I made a point of asking them to stay away. You'd never be seen by anyone but me."

Tasha quelled a brief impulse to hysteria, but it was impossible to pretend that Ben's words did not unsettle her. Her fingers tightened protectively over the sheet that was draped around her middle.

"It occurs to me," Ben went on dourly, "that you can hardly go running for help without decent clothes. So I'll make you a deal. You get your jeans back if you promise not to take any of your silly stories to the people on this island. I don't want you upsetting them."

"Silly stories! Oh...!" If looks could have killed, hers would have done so at that moment. Once again, she fought for poise and found it. "No deal," she managed at last in a frigid voice. "Now will you please tell me where to get washed up? I feel quite filthy this morning—as though I'd slept in close contact with a snake."

Ben's jaw tightened. Abruptly, he stood up and turned his back. "There's a stream across the clearing," he informed her in a curt voice, "and primitive facilities, too. Don't bother running, for I'll be outside, and I can see if you head for the trees. Not that you will. You'd never let yourself be seen in public looking the way you do."

All the glaring in the world succeeded in making no dint in those uncompromising shoulders. And so at last Tasha made a nasty face in Ben's direction and set to work gathering herself into some kind of decency. She pulled the pajama bottoms into place, secured the tie at the waist and sidled out of bed. Even though her legs were long, the pajama bottoms were at least five inches longer. When she tried to roll the silky fabric to her ankles, it did not hold. Well, she was damned if she would do a Charlie Chaplin walk across the clearing under Ben's hostile eyes!

"Did you bring my makeup case to the hut?" she asked with an immense dignity she did not feel.

"What do you want it for?"

"A fresh T-shirt," she lied, "and some soap."

"Good," Ben said rudely, "it's about time you scrubbed the rest of that junk off your face." Complying with her request, he came close to the bed, lowered himself to his haunches and slid the case out into view right at Tasha's feet. Unwillingly, she noted the virile aroma of him, a compound of clean smells that reminded her of newly turned earth and unscented soap. Straightening, he deposited the case on the bed beside her and studied the ravages that

sleep had worked on Pierre's careful eye makeup. If
the lopsided look amused him, it did not show in the
insolence of his expression.

"A vast improvement already," he said insultingly. "Good God, yesterday you had so much makeup
on you looked like an armadillo."

She opened the case, determined not to rise to his
baiting. "You do have a way with words. Need I remind you that I was out on a shoot when you so rudely interrupted? I don't wear that much every day."

"While you're around here you don't need to wear
any at all. There's nobody to see but me, and I prefer
the natu— What the deuce are you doing with those
scissors?"

"An amputation, what else?" Tasha said sweetly,
dropping part of a pajama leg on the bed. The nail
scissors advanced toward the other calf.

Ben glowered, but he did nothing to stop her. The
second pajama leg succumbed to the scissors, revealing the leaf that Eulalie had tied in place the previous
night. And because that did not look very dignified,
either, Tasha removed it. Beneath the makeshift
dressing, the bruise was considerably worse than
before; now it was a dark blue purple, turning brown
around the edges. So much for magical mystery
cures!

"Well, did your lily skin survive?" asked Ben, who
could not see from his vantage point. Scorn was in
his every syllable.

Tasha concealed her slow burn by standing up and
taking some seconds to arrange Ben's guillotined pa-

jama bottoms over her calves, as carefully as if she had been wearing a Paris original. The two legs were different lengths and looked ludicrous. On a last thought, she picked up the scraps of fabric she had scissored off and threw them into her model case, snapping the lid closed as if in answer to Ben's question.

"I asked," Ben reminded her tightly, "whether Eulalie's potion had worked."

Tasha tucked her toes into her expensive Italian sandals, picked up her case and stalked across the room. "Thanks for your concern," she flung over her shoulder airily, "but I think she gave me the cure for warts."

"It's not nice to make fun of an old woman!" Ben shouted after her, evidently unamused.

It gave Tasha no comfort to hear a burst of mocking laughter just as she reached the stream across the clearing; she knew it was directed at her appearance. How Ben must enjoy seeing her in such a disreputable state!

"It's not nice to make fun of a young one, either," she muttered furiously to herself. "I'll teach you, Ben Craig."

And she set about the business of getting ready to face the day.

The stream was set in a grassy depression of land shaded by a brilliant parasol of a tree covered with dazzling red flowers. About thirty yards to one side lay the thick woods from which she had emerged the night before; at an equal distance to the other side loomed the grove of enormous cocopalms that had seemed so awe-inspiring by moonlight. But this colorful tree by the stream—a flame tree or flamboyant, Tasha later learned—was the only large tree in the clearing, and a quick appraisal of the situation convinced her she could not make a dash for better cover without being intercepted by Ben.

"If you think a lack of clothes will keep me here, you're mightily mistaken," she whispered determinedly to no one in particular as she set about the morning's preparation.

She counted on Ben's stubbornness, and it worked. It was a full hour and a half before he came to find her, and that had allowed her time to do everything. Well, nearly everything. She was still working on her eyelashes.

Ben came to a halt on a grassy knoll a dozen feet away and surveyed Tasha's makeshift dressing room with a jaundiced eye. She was seated Indian-fashion near the stream, with a mirror propped in front of her and jars of paste and pomade spread everywhere.

"I might have known you'd carry spares," Ben noted contemptuously, watching the second eyelash go into place.

Tasha leaned forward and examined the final results minutely in the mirror. For Ben's benefit, she craned her neck elegantly, licked a finger and smoothed one immaculate eyebrow. "I knew you'd be pleased," she said. She gathered up the various tools of her trade and tucked them back into the case. Along with everything else went a small emergency sewing kit she had used to turn Ben's pajama bottoms into a hastily-stitched dirndl skirt. With time and fabric at a premium, she had not taken time to sew a proper hemline; instead she had ragged the bottom edge into artistic and not unflattering tatters. *That* would stifle Ben's cruel laughter!

She snapped the case closed, then rose to her feet and posed elegantly with one hand on her hip. "No comment? Or do words fail you for once?"

Ben's expressionless gaze trickled down slowly over the finished effect. With legs planted apart and thumbs hooked into his hip pockets, he might have been appraising a racehorse. "You do have a way with pajama bottoms," he observed at last, sardonically. "I had no idea you were so talented with a needle and thread."

"Once upon a time I did make some of my own clothes, Mr. Craig. It's amazing what you can accomplish on a shoestring." She took a few deliberately mincing steps and preened like a peacock. "I did consider doing something with fig leaves, but—"

"Knock it off, Tasha," Ben grated. "You're not on a runway now."

"Oh, you like it? I'm so glad. It's the scarf." She flipped one end of the floaty silk fabric she had tied around her waist, a Hermès scarf that was kept in her model case to protect her hair on windy days. "Makes the whole costume come together, don't you think? And would you believe matching bikini briefs, underneath? It's my back-to-nature look. Very crude, but then so are the surroundings. I chose the makeup to go with it. Rage Sauvage, this lipstick is called—Wild Rage, to you. And the eye makeup is Oeil Mauvais. That's Evil Eye, in case you didn't—''

"Stop it!" snapped Ben. "I know damn well you're trying to irritate me. Don't you ever think of anything but your wardrobe and your face?"

She smiled sweetly, taking a vindictive delight in the knowledge that her barbs were finding their mark. "Sometimes I think of my stomach, too. I haven't eaten in more than twenty-four hours and I'm starved. I thought I smelled coffee.... Is breakfast ready?"

"Anytime you want to cook it," said Ben curtly, and turned on his heel to stride away.

Tasha's moment of spiteful satisfaction evaporated. "If you think I'm going to cook breakfast for you, you're very much mistaken!" she cried after him angrily.

Ben halted midstride and turned slowly to face her again. Contempt curled his mouth, and his large powerful body looked faintly menacing. "Did I ask you to cook for me? I've already eaten. I did consider cooking for you, but you took too long putting on your face. Now come along and I'll show you the larder."

Something, either hatred or hunger, seemed to be burning holes in Tasha's stomach. But she was not about to let Ben see that he distressed her in any way!

"I'm perfectly capable of looking after myself. I do know a little bit about cooking, too." With immense hauteur, she picked up the model case and headed toward Ben's hut, deliberately dawdling along the way.

Ben had transferred the supplies from the boat into tin boxes, which were kept in a low cupboard on the veranda. He opened it and peered in. "Rice," he pointed out. "Flour. Sugar. Coffee beans. Cocoa. Lentils. Peppercorns. Salt. Tea. A few vanilla beans in that tin, I think. Sorry, there's no fish left from last night; in this climate it simply won't keep. Eat it when you catch it, that's the rule."

No prepared foods then. No doubt Ben found this very amusing! "Is there any fresh fruit around?" she asked with a pleasantness she did not feel.

Ben waved at the great outdoors, in a sweeping gesture. "Whatever you can find in this valley," he told her, amiability evidently fully restored. "In the Seychelles you mustn't filch things off anybody else's property; nothing's lying around for the taking—except perhaps breadfruit. The people are very poor, and every fruit or nut might be a part of someone's livelihood. So if you find a banana just leave it hanging, unless it's on my property."

Bananas! Tasha resisted asking the obvious question for fully five seconds, at which time hunger overcame hatred.

"Where are your banana trees?" she asked in a cool voice.

A lazy golden gleam grew in Ben's eyes, and with a wave of intense hatred Tasha realized that he was beginning to enjoy himself immensely, that he was playing her along much as he might have played a game fish. "I don't have any," he said.

With strained patience, Tasha forced a civilized smile. "What is on this property, then?"

"Breadfruit, but that takes a little time to bake. Some edible greens very like spinach. Wild mustard. A herb resembling thyme.... I'll point them all out to you. Not very filling, but they do add flavor. Lots of coconuts, of course." His eyelids drooped reflectively as if he were trying to reach some decision. "As part of a short course in survival, I'll even introduce you to the *panga*," he offered magnanimously at last.

Panga? Could that be some fruit akin to the mango? Tasha's mouth watered. She pasted a small distant smile on her lips and pretended idle curiosity. "Is that a tree? Or a vine?"

"More like a machete," Ben pronounced firmly. "Once you learn to handle the thing, it's not so very hard to open a coconut. Different strokes for different kinds of coconuts, though. A good ripe one can usually be split in two with a single stroke. To open a drinking coconut you approach it as though you were sharpening a big pencil.... Oh, it's not too hard once you get the knack. Then a dozen swift chopping strokes and—"

"Never mind," Tasha said, with a growing tightness to her voice. "I'll stick to coffee and tea. That stream water is drinkable, I hope?"

Ben nodded; his eyes gleamed. Indolently, he scratched his chest where a dusting of hair roughened his skin at the opening of his partly buttoned sports shirt. "Wise decision, brown eyes," he congratulated her. "The green drinking coconuts don't fall anyway, and I hardly think you're dressed for climbing trees. I'd boil the water, though; you never know when somebody's been washing upstream."

"Am I supposed to catch my own fish, too?" she asked tartly. "It's evident that your short course in survival includes a healthy dose of starvation."

Ben's sliding gaze measured Tasha from top to toe and apparently found her wanting. "No, actually, I'd like to fatten you up a bit. So I'll make you a deal. You gather the shellfish, and I'll bring in the finny kind."

"Very funny! I wouldn't know an edible shellfish if I saw one."

"This afternoon I'll show you where to find tec-tec," he offered, mocking her with a cruel lift of one dark eyebrow. "They make a wonderful soup, quite a specialty on these islands—if you can manage to get the sand out of them. And if my memory serves me rightly after seven years, there are some oysters, too, if you're willing to go wading in the lagoon."

Oysters! Tasha's taste buds tingled in anticipation. Oysters were not your ordinary everyday breakfast, but at least they could be eaten raw. Visions of wolfing down a dozen nonstop danced in her head. "Will you direct me to the lagoon then?" she requested with feigned pleasantness.

"Just follow the stream through the coco-de-mer

grove,'' Ben directed. His eyes traveled down to Tasha's unsuitable footwear and he put on a frown. "Those aren't exactly the kind of thing I'd choose to use in the lagoon, though. However, better a wrecked shoe than rip your feet to shreds on the coral. Tell you what; I'll make you a deal. I'll lend you an old pair of army boots if—"

"Never mind," she interrupted tautly. "I'll stay on sandy bottom. I'm sure that's where the oysters are found, anyway."

"True," Ben nodded sagely. "How are you going to open them? With your manicure scissors? They don't come on the half shell."

Tasha paused midway through the door; that had not occurred to her. She turned back to where she had placed her ubiquitous case and began to rummage through it without deigning to comment on Ben's words.

"Oh, by the way," he said offhandedly, "there are some other things you should watch for, even if you stay on sandy bottom. Turkey fish, rabbit fish, barbel eels, some kinds of jellyfish." He looked at the open-toed sandals critically. "Perhaps you'd better wear those anyway. They won't do much good against sea-urchin spines, but they might help if you step directly on top of a stonefish. You do know about stonefish, don't you? Absolutely fatal! Very well camouflaged devils, too; they can hardly be seen on the sandy bottom. Unfortunately I have no antivenin—not that you'd have time to reach it. Excruciating, but at least the agony lasts only a few minutes. And oh, by the way, if you cut your foot, get out of the water as fast as you can. The sharks have a nose for things like that, and I've seen them attack in six inches of water. They'll practically throw themselves on the beach just to.... Why, Tasha, whatever is the matter?''

He paused and smiled genially at Tasha's rapidly paling face. ''Well, is it a deal? Fish in exchange for shellfish? If so, gather enough oysters for me.''

Tasha deposited her manicure scissors back in her case and made a silent wish that had to do with Ben and an entire bed of stonefish in intimate embrace. Well, rice wasn't the best breakfast in the world, but it was palatable. Considering her state of semi-starvation, even old shoe leather would have been palatable. ''Just show me where to find the cooking utensils,'' she said through tight lips. ''I need a pot to fetch the cooking water.''

Ben waved in the general direction of the closed door that led into the hut's main room. But when Tasha reached for the knob he said, ''No, not in there. Out back, behind the house. And here....'' He tossed her a small tin. ''Matches. You might as well get your fire going first. It's been a while since I ate, and I imagine my coals are getting cold.''

Tasha opened her mouth, snapped it shut again and headed out into the open. Damn Ben all to bits! How like him to find such cruel amusement in her predicament! Well, if he thought she couldn't light a fire, he was in for a nasty surprise!

Discouragement set in at the actual sight of the dying fire Ben had laid earlier. An iron pot hung on a blackened stick that was propped on two forked branches. It still steamed and was demonstrably too hot to handle.

But if the pot looked hot, the fire did not. A few smoking gray ashes were all that remained, and a preliminary inspection revealed that although there was a neatly stacked pile of casuarina logs nearby, there was absolutely no kindling within sight. Perhaps the embers would be enough to start a fire? But first, she must remove the pot.

Valiantly, she grabbed a stout green stick that lay nearby and attempted to snag the iron pot off its perch. She succeeded, but not without collapsing the entire structure that had held it over the fire. In the process, the pot dropped, too, spilling its contents. The last of the embers hissed into sodden death.

Vexed and frustrated almost to tears, Tasha threw the green stick onto the doused fire and added a mental curse. But she would not give in to Ben! Involuntarily, her eyes flickered toward the woods, trying to find the path from where she had emerged the previous night with Eulalie.

"Make you a deal," said a cool voice from behind, and she spun around to discover Ben leaning indolently against the corner of the hut, a dozen feet away. With one strong hand stroking his newly shaven jaw, he looked infuriatingly smug. And also, Tasha fumed silently, enragingly well fed. Her toes curled with the effort of maintaining self-control, and she forced her facial muscles into a tight excuse for a smile.

"I don't like your deals," she proclaimed with a coolness that verged on acidity. "Now if you don't mind, I'll take that lesson in machete handling right away."

"Just to get kindling? I'll give you a little household hint, brown eyes. Old dried palm fronds work perfectly well, and you'll find lots over there in the coco-de-mer grove." He tilted his head toward the oversize palms that lay behind him. "Unfortunately they're heavy, but I think you can manage to drag one or two this far. Or you might look for spent coconut shells. They make a very smoky fire, but you don't mind getting your face dirty, do you? It's easier than cutting kindling. And green wood won't do, in any case."

"Cutting kindling wasn't exactly what I had in mind," she said, with a spiteful and pointed glance at his throat. She tilted her nose in the air and started a determined march toward the grove of palms.

"Wait," Ben commanded, intercepting her. His fingers closed authoritatively over her arm as she swept past him. "Aren't you going to listen to my deal?"

There was no easy way to get away from him; his grip was far too strong. Overpowered by it, she gave in with grace and even made a pretense at having stopped of her own volition.

"If you insist," she said aloofly, trying to look bored, a performance she found exceedingly difficult, with her skin tingling where Ben's insistent fingers dug into the flesh.

"It's clear to me that you're not cut out for the Robinson Crusoe life," he drawled. His eyes, glinting with mockery, directed their attention toward Tasha's immaculate lipstick. "So I'll make you an offer. I did intend to feed you, brown eyes, until you performed your little miracles over by the stream. I had thought the state of your wardrobe would keep you from running. Now I could take away the clothes you've managed to fix up, but...well, I'm inclined to be generous...."

"I haven't heard your offer," she reminded him tautly.

"You'll never manage to light that fire, let alone cook anything on it. So I'm prepared to do the providing, if you promise not to run—" he paused significantly to lend emphasis to his next words "—and not to fight off my advances."

She tried to shrivel him with a glance—unsuccessfully. "Can you please show me where to find the spinach?" she asked in a saccharine voice. "I'll eat it raw, if necessary."

"In other words you still plan to run for help at the first possible opportunity?" Ben smiled broadly, drawing her unwilling attention to those strong even teeth. The smile did not touch his eyes, which had now turned hard and assessing. "Let me tell you a little more about this island, brown eyes. There's nothing much any of the inhabitants can do for you, even if they wanted to. Are you going to walk up to some perfect stranger and ask him to house you and feed you, just like that? Most of the people around here have enough trouble putting food on the table for their own families, and the huts are very small— often several people sharing a single room. Chances are they'll pay no attention to you anyway. Yesterday, when you so ill-advisedly ran away, I told them you were a little...." Ben made a corkscrew motion in the air, with one finger directed toward his own head. "Well, frankly, *amarrée* was the word I used."

"Tied up? A very good description!"

"In creole parlance, it means fixed up by a sorcerer. The islanders are good Catholics, but they're superstitious, too; deep down they believe that kind of nonsense. They think you're temporarily mad. Under a spell, so to speak."

As if to demonstrate that she indeed was, Ben now released her wrist, slowly. His hand traveled upward and for one wild moment she thought he intended to trace the curve of her lips that seemed to hold so much of his attention. Suddenly her legs felt very wobbly and her feet incapable of movement.

But Ben's goal lay elsewhere. He reached into the breast pocket of his shirt, pulled out a chocolate bar, folded back the paper wrappings and nibbled thoughtfully at its edge. "Whatever wild story you tell now," he said with unconcealed satisfaction, "they're likely to dismiss it. Most of them would do exactly as Eulalie did—bring you directly back to me. Well, brown eyes, which is it? Give in to me gracefully—or starve?"

Despite her best intentions, Tasha could not wrest her eyes from the chocolate. Involuntarily, she swayed toward it—and Ben. "Where did you get that?" she asked faintly.

"Oh, I have a few ready-to-eats tucked away here and there," Ben informed her derisively. "Your breakfast, for one. Yes, I did cook it for you. But as you see I'm still a trifle hungry; I'm thinking of eating it myself, unless...."

"You're a monster," she moaned weakly.

Ben's strong mouth curled into a sardonic twist. The smile was not a friendly one, despite the crinkles it described at the corners of his eyes. "A monster of the first water," he agreed. The chocolate bar vanished back into his pocket, followed by Tasha's longing gaze. He closed his eyes and sighed. "Paw-paw," he murmured reflectively. "Some little brown eggs I found this morning. Coconut milk. And yes, there is some coffee left, too...." The eyes feathered open again and he added, "Last offer, Tasha. Is it a deal or not? And, oh yes, I nearly forgot. I made some wheatcakes, big golden ones. They're keeping warm over a spirit lamp, and—"

"You win," Tasha choked out.

Gradually Ben's mocking smile faded and something sensuous took its place. There were hungers of a different kind in that last lingering gaze. But he thrust them aside abruptly and turned on his heel.

"Good," he said. "Come on, then. The food's all laid out inside on the table."

How horrified Max would be, Tasha reflected fifteen minutes later, if he had seen what quantities of food she had managed to tuck away! Not even Ben's watchful mockery or the knowledge of what she had agreed to had interfered with her very hearty appetite.

"I don't know how you stay so thin," Ben observed dryly when she had tucked away the last of a stack of wheatcakes that would have given pause to a stevedore. He gathered up the dishes and placed them all in a pail. "These can wait," he said crisply. "You can wash them at the stream when I go to the lagoon later on to see to our supper."

"But the lagoon sounds so dangerous," Tasha said without thinking. "Surely with sharks about, you can't—" She bit back the words, chastising herself mentally for taking any interest whatsoever in Ben's safety.

His eyes derided her again. "Mostly little sand sharks," he said, "and not dangerous at all. The big tiger sharks and hammerheads tend to stay out farther in the daytime; they don't like to feel the reef behind them. Concerned, brown eyes?"

"I don't like to be lied to," she said coldly. "If the lagoon's not dangerous you could have spared me the descriptions."

His expression became serious once more. "Ah, but it is dangerous for novices. I wasn't lying about that. But you'd be safe if you were to go swimming with me and wear a pair of flippers or canvas shoes on your feet."

"I think I'll pass on that offer. Need I remind you I don't swim?"

Ben sighed, apparently annoyed by her tartness.

"It wasn't exactly an offer; I didn't plan to take you with me. Now come along and I'll give you a tour of the property. All on dry land, I assure you."

"I'm not sure I want that, either," she retorted airily. Nourishment had fully restored her self-possession, and with it her spirit. "I agreed not to run away. I didn't agree to follow you around like a puppy dog!"

"I insist," came the dangerously quiet command. Ben's eyes glittered as he reached for her arm and pulled her to her feet. The height of him and the animal heat of him seemed overpowering in this small room, and Tasha's heart thudded alarmingly— bringing back for one brief moment the dizzying sensations she had experienced the previous night. Only this time, they could not be put down to Eulalie's potent *bacca*.

"I...I'll come," she said in a voice too unsteady to sound like her own. "You don't need to use force."

"I should hope not," Ben remarked acridly as he freed her arm and waited for her to precede him across the room.

He led her toward the cathedral-like palms that dominated the valley, walking a little ahead and not turning to see if she followed. Soon they were moving beneath the arch of trees, past tall straight trunks like graceful pillars stretching to the very sky. High above, there was a soft incessant rattling sound that had a curiously restful effect; Tasha realized that it was caused by the gentle clash of huge, rigid fanlike

fronds stirred by a light breeze that did not penetrate
to this dank moss-laden place far below. Sweet heavy
scents hung in the humid air. Here and there were
palms that Tasha took to be seedlings—a startling
sight, for although they had not developed the immensely tall straight trunks of their parents, the stiff
shiny fronds appeared fully grown, like treetops
spanning many feet and springing from the very
earth itself. An enormous peace pervaded the grove
despite the swoop and chatter of birds disturbed by
the slow progress of human intruders.

In a quiet voice as they walked, Ben pointed out
different species. "The Seychelles sunbird," he said,
indicating a somberly clad small bird of very dark
gray, probing a flower with its needlelike bill. "The
toc-toc. The Seychelles fody. The colibri.... I used
to think you'd be fascinated by these birds, until I
found you weren't studying ornithology at all. They
look very ordinary to the eye, but most of them are
found nowhere else in the world. The Seychelles are
something of a paradise for bird-watchers. I even saw
a *cateau noir*—a black parrot—in this valley seven
years ago. And they're supposed to exist in only one
place in the world—the Vallée de Mai on the island of
Praslin." Ben pronounced the name "prahlin," as
Morley had not done. "It was when I spotted that
black parrot that I decided to buy this valley for
you—for us."

"Oh," said Tasha, feeling humbled in a way she
could not express. Had Ben really done that for her,
so many years ago? She felt the fight and the

antagonism ebbing away from her, like water seeping through sand after a high tide. And when the next wave of feeling washed through her, it was very like regret. . . .

"As looks go, the black parrot is nothing to rave about. With your love of fine feathers, I doubt you'd even turn an eye." The scornfulness in Ben's voice forestalled Tasha, just as she had been about to place a hand on his arm. "Its song is the prettiest thing about it. Altogether, it's not a very exotic bird to live in the Garden of Eden."

"The Garden of Eden?" Tasha repeated in a numb voice, to hide the sudden and inexplicable cold that clutched her. What was it Ben had said last night about the Garden of Eden?

He squinted high into the trees and thrust his hands deeply into his pockets. Beneath the fabric, she could see his fingers tensing and untensing. With a peculiar tightness in her throat, she looked upward at his face and listened.

"This valley is very like the Vallée de Mai on Praslin," he told her in an expressionless monotone, as if he had rehearsed this speech a thousand times. "And that's been likened to the Garden of Eden. General Gordon came to the Seychelles some years before he died in Khartoum, did you know that? Well, he was the first to get excited about the possibility that he had found the original Eden. Others have toyed with the idea since, possibly because it's believed that the Seychelles were at one time attached to the mainland of Africa, and East

Africa is known to be the cradle of all mankind, the place where early man first appeared. General Gordon's belief that he had found the Garden of Eden stemmed from his excitement over seeing the coco-de-mer palms. If you look closely, you'll see they're very unusual, and not just because of the height.''

Tasha's eyes traveled upward to where sunlight filtered through huge graceful fronds nearly a hundred feet above their heads. She felt unable to ask questions, but Ben needed no prompting.

''The male tree and the female,'' he said evenly. ''General Gordon thought he had found the Tree of Life and the Tree of Knowledge. You can distinguish the male because it's about twenty feet taller, and it bears those drooping yellow catkins instead of coconuts. Even to the untrained eye it looks like a male; there's an anatomical similarity you can hardly miss. And the female is very unusual, too; the nuts it bears are like no other coconuts you'll ever see. Each nut takes seven years to mature, for one thing. Look, I'll show you at closer range.''

He turned his attention to the ground, sweeping it with a practiced eye until he saw what he was looking for—a mature fallen nut in good condition. The nut was huge, and it was indeed like no coconut Tasha had ever seen. It was more like a double nut really: two nuts indissolubly joined.

Ben dropped his long limbs to the moss-soft earth beside the nut, hefted it into one hand and used the other hand to brush the exterior free of insects. Obedient to some inner command she could not understand, Tasha lowered herself slowly to a crouching position not two feet away. As if hypnotized, she watched him smooth the nut with fingers gentler than they had been on her own flesh fifteen minutes before.

"The coco-de-mer palm grows naturally nowhere else in the world," he went on in his low level voice, "although a few examples have been grown elsewhere as showpieces. Even in the Seychelles it's found on only a few islands. Originally it grew only on the islands of Praslin and Curieuse, with the stand in the Vallée de Mai being the largest—there are four thousand trees there, some of them eight hundred years old, it's believed. Sometimes you'll hear that valley referred to as the Valley of the Giants. The trees you see here are much younger. Early settlers transported specimens to a few other islands in the Seychelles, including this one. Perhaps they thought they were going to make a fortune. These nuts, you see, were once worth a great deal of money."

Tasha watched Ben's bent head, the forelock falling over his mahogany-tanned face, the strong hands spanning the nut as he turned it contemplatively. In her heart there was a heavy dull ache. Ben had said it took the coco-de-mer nut seven years to mature; that period of time had a significance to Tasha that hardly bore thinking about, especially in light of Ben's clear and oft-stated dislike of her. What was it Ben had said last night? *I doubt even the Garden of Eden could turn you back into the original Eve... it's too late for that....*

Fiery Passion. Forbidden Love. Free.

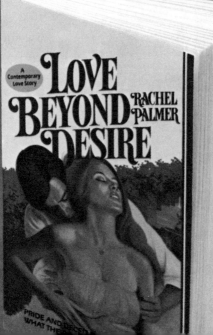

...At his touch, her body felt a familiar wild stirring, but she struggled to resist it. This is not love, she thought bitterly.

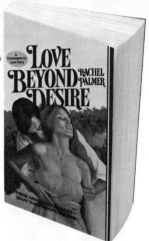

Bring twice as much romance into your life, beginning today. And receive *Love beyond Desire*, **free.** It's yours to keep even if you don't buy any additional books. Mail the postage-paid card below.

SUPERROMANCE
1440 South Priest Drive, Tempe, AZ 85281.

↙Mail this card today for your FREE book.

A compelling love story of mystery and intrigue... conflicts and jealousies... and a forbidden love that threatens to shatter the lives of all involved with the aristocratic Lopez family.

← Mail this card today for your FREE book.

"Years ago," Ben went on, "centuries before the Seychelles had even been sighted by early mariners, the occasional coco-de-mer nut used to wash up on the shores of the Maldives or Ceylon or India. Men believed that they were the fruit of a strange tree that grew beneath the sea; that's why the name. Princes and potentates paid exorbitant prices to obtain the coco-de-mer—often, the nut's weight in gold and precious jewels. Perhaps that will impress you even more when I tell you this is a smallish example; the coco-de-mer nut can reach forty or fifty pounds. In the Middle Ages, men would almost kill to obtain one."

After a time Tasha interjected a small "Why?" into the silence.

Ben frowned at the nut in his hands. "It wasn't just the rarity; it was partly because of the way the nut is formed. If you look closely you can see it resembles nothing so much as the lower half of a woman. The resemblance grows when the nut is shucked and polished. Because of that, men came to believe that the fruit was possessed of great powers. They considered it the most potent aphrodisiac known; oh, sometimes they used it as a specific against poison or paralysis, too, but it was as a love potion that the coco-de-mer nut was really prized. Some Seychellois still believe it's an aphrodisiac. General Gordon wasn't interested in the love potion of Indian rajahs, but he did believe he had found the forbidden fruit of the Garden of Eden."

For a time Tasha turned her eyes up to the trees

and studied the patterns of light and shade that strained through the softly clashing fronds. For some reason she wanted to cry but knew she wouldn't—not in front of Ben. "And do you think that, Ben?" she whispered at last. "That this is the Garden of Eden?"

Suddenly Ben heaved the weighty nut to one shoulder and hurled it angrily at the bole of a tree. A score of small birds scattered into the air, shrieking indignantly. Tasha tensed; the mood of a moment ago had been irrevocably broken.

"No," scowled Ben, "why would I think a ridiculous thing like that? I'm not superstitious, and I'm not a Bible fundamentalist like General Gordon. I don't believe in Adam and Eve, and if there's an original sin it's man's inhumanity to man, nothing more. There is no Garden of Eden! Good God, I'd as soon believe in Eulalie's *gris-gris*!"

A second coconut went hurtling through the air and crashed into a feathery stand of fern. Tasha remained very still, glad of the long curtain of dark hair that swung forward to hide her expression. Sensing that Ben's sudden vehemence could just as easily be turned on her, she virtually held her breath until the brief fury passed.

"There is no Garden of Eden," he repeated, subsiding but now sounding cynical. Out of the corners of her vision, Tasha could see the way his fingers tightened, forming fists against his knees. "And even if there were, it's a paradise long lost to man. But this place does have a certain primitive charm, and once upon a time, I had some crazy notion that by bringing you here I could save you from yourself."

"Save me," repeated Tasha, momentarily stunned. She pushed back the long swing of hair and looked at Ben more closely. His attention was directed not at her but at an insignificant-looking bird of drab brownish gray, perched some distance away on a laurel bush. Idly and with none of his earlier rage, he threw a small stick at the base of the laurels. The bird winged upward in alarm, vanishing at once from view. Tasha's throat tightened as the impulse to tears became overwhelmingly strong.

"From the kind of person you were becoming even then," Ben went on, his voice once more flat and unemotional. "Shall I go through the list? Superficial, shallow, selfish...."

He did not stop there. As she listened to Ben's recitation of her faults an icy fist tightened over her heart. Pride turned her expression to stone. *Not a single grain of humanity left....* Did he really believe that? *Oh, Tasha, it was all artifice even then....* Had he really thought so badly of her, even then, when she had been so young and so uncertain of herself?

"I was only seventeen," she said at last, through frozen lips.

"Seventeen going on twenty-seven," came Ben's sarcastic rejoinder. "If I'd known your age I certainly wouldn't have had anything to do with you. Pure poison!"

"Why did you marry me, Ben?" To her own ears

her voice sounded artificial, horrible. "I've always wondered."

Restlessly, Ben shifted on the grass. He propped his elbows on bent knees and stared at his knuckles moodily. "I wish the hell I knew," he said bleakly. "At times I thought I saw traces of something else, the kind of warmth I wanted in a woman. It wasn't until our wedding night that I realized what a terrible mistake I had made. And then...."

His voice trailed into a brooding silence broken only by bird-chatter, and it was a few moments before Tasha regained enough poise to make a response. By then, all defensive mechanisms were in good working order; her inflections were perfectly controlled.

"Why on earth," she demanded with an attempt at lightness, "would you go to all this trouble to renew the acquaintance if I'm so impossible? Really, Ben, you make no sense."

He turned to face her again and answered in no hurry. There was that hostile hatred in his eyes again, and something else—a dark smoky intensity that she recognized as desire. A shiver slid over her skin, despite the tropical warmth.

"Call it revenge," he said slowly. "Call it compulsion. Call it some kind of satanic impulse. I did what I had to do, and I can't explain it better than that. I only know that for years now, you've been under my skin like...like a sliver I can't get out. By now it's festered so long it requires major surgery."

Tasha's pride stiffened her spine. Inside, denials

screamed, and to hide them she voiced a false little laugh. "Perhaps you should go to Eulalie for a cure," she suggested.

Ben's eyes only darkened more ominously. "That's exactly what I hate about you, Tasha. You're so damn superficial it's inhuman. There's just no getting through that layer of civilization."

"Oh?" She arched her brows skyward, masking her hurt with more of the sophistication he hated. "I was civilized last night? That *is* reassuring. Personally, I was afraid I might have been just a little bit human."

"You weren't yourself last night," he said darkly. "In any case that wasn't humanity, it was drink. There's no warmth in you, Tasha; I discovered that on our wedding night. You're too wrapped up in your witty perfect packaging. Oh, I don't deny you have a certain spunk I admire. And I suppose you have the usual biological urges—hunger, thirst, survival, sex. . . ."

Flippancy seemed the only defense against Ben's hateful words. "Do stop! Flattery makes me blush."

She could practically hear Ben's teeth grinding. "Is there no way of getting through that shell of yours?" he grated, smashing the flat of his hand on the ground.

"Oh, it's not so hard once you have the knack." Her voice and her smile were far too bright. The bend of her knees concealed from Ben's view the one hand fisted in her lap, where fingernails were digging furrows in the palm. "Really, it's no harder than sharpening a pencil. A dozen swift chopping strokes—that is what you've been doing, isn't it? And—''

"Tasha!" he roared, and a score of small birds screeched upward to the sky. "Stop it!"

But she could not stop. It was a reflexive reaction, a nervous outpouring of the hurt that could not be told in tears. "Of course, you use a different stroke for someone with meat inside. Fatten me up with a little humanity, you might even be able to demolish me with a single—''

Ben moved with the swiftness and strength of a striking serpent. Before the next word was uttered, Tasha found herself flung flat on the ground and the wind knocked from her lungs. Before she had time to catch her breath or make a single outcry, brutal fingers seized a handful of her long hair and wrenched it painfully to hold her head still for his onslaught. His face descended so swiftly that she received only fleeting impressions—the blaze of golden anger in his eyes, the slash of naked hatred that was his mouth. And in the next instant that mouth was on hers— driving, punishing, possessing, prying her lips apart with a bruising hurtfulness. His tongue ravished her with a cruelty and vehemence that left her pained lungs screaming for air, and when the initial shock passed, she started to struggle with the desperation of a trapped wild creature, uncaring of the hurt this caused to her imprisoned hank of hair.

And then suddenly her lips were free. But Ben's broad shoulders and the long leg flung over hers still pinned her to the ground. Gasping for air, she continued to fight, her long fingernails tearing at his hair, his eyes, his clothing, until at last he released his grip at her scalp.

"You she-devil," he gritted through drawn lips. It gave Tasha only one millisecond of satisfaction to see the abrasion on his mouth where her teeth had fought his kiss, for in the next moment her wrists were seized in a cruel vise and yanked above her head, effectively bringing her resistance to an end. But she lay beneath him gasping, still fighting him with her eyes.

His breath was as ragged as hers, his expression as hostile. For a long moment they glared at each other, antagonists in a battle as old as time, and then slowly Ben's grip on her wrists softened. He transferred both her hands into one of his, holding her easily with the superior strength of his long forceful fingers. Gradually the blaze in his eyes gave way to a smoldering fire, and the mouth that had been so hard turned sensuous and soft. In his long limbs that were flung over hers she could feel a quickening, a stirring that told her hatred had yielded to desire.

His freed hand moved downward, leaving its partner to hold her wrists in thrall. With a finger he explored the curve of her cheek, the indentation of her chin, the hollows of her throat. Slowly he drew the line of her lips that seemed to magnetize his eyes. "So beautiful," he murmured, "so beautiful and so hard. God knows why I want you...."

And his lips descended with none of the hurtfulness of before. Softly they brushed against hers, echoing the aching needs she felt in his body, asking for a response she did not want to give. She remained rigid, denying him the warmth he asked for.

"Don't fight me, Tasha," he whispered against her mouth. "You won't win. I intend to have you, to possess every part of you, you know that, don't you? Don't fight, my love...don't fight and it will be right...."

He released her wrists and sank his fingers in her hair, and that, too, was a gentle touch, seeking and stroking where her scalp still tingled from his earlier brutality.

She felt her shirt pulled free at the waist, and the warmth of a hand intruding in the space between fabric and flesh. He found the soft round rise that was his goal, but the skilled gentling of his fingers awakened no response: the wounds of words were not so easily brushed away. She struggled no more, but she battled him with lips closed and eyes closed and heart closed, too. At last the palm of his hand grew still, curving over her breast, but it was a waiting stillness—as if his fingers listened for the pulse-beat of her desire.

He groaned and tried more urgently to part her lips with his—probing, teasing, touching until she turned her head aside and shoved at his chest.

"Don't fight me!" he commanded thickly, and his fingers tightened once more in her hair. "You promised not to fight. God knows, I don't want it that way, either."

Tasha ran a tongue-tip over her ravaged lips, but the coldness of her expression altered in no other way. "Do you really expect me to respond to you after that barbaric attack? I can't pretend to feel anything for you now."

Ben's voice grew harsh; his hand on her breast firmed its grip. "If you can't respond at least acquiesce. Do you think I give a damn whether you feel anything for me—or even whether you actually feel? You've had your half of the bargain—I've fed you. Now I want mine. Or was that just one more piece of fakery—a promise to be broken at the first opportunity?"

"No," she moaned as the pressure of his fingers became hurtful on her nipple. "I won't fight. I know what I promised."

"Then next time I kiss you I expect some manner of consent," he said roughly, and unexpectedly he rolled away, freeing her body altogether.

She watched, tense and shivering, while he rose to his feet and divested himself of his shirt. Sunlight dappled through the palms, shaking light on the ripple of sinew beneath darkly bronzed flesh. She knew only too well that that virile body could master her at will, and perhaps even draw from her the response she did not want to give. Her immunity of moments ago seemed shaken already, and she knew it would not last forever.

"Must it be here and now?" she asked, trying to keep desperation from creeping into her voice. "In this place, in this way? When I promised, I didn't expect it to be like this."

Ben's hands paused over the fastening of his trousers, as he glanced at her in a way that suggested only hard disdain. "What did you expect, all the trappings of civilization? Sheets and a proper bed? Soft candlelight and words of love? Is that what you expected?"

A hard hurt lodged itself in her throat. "Something like that," she said.

Ben did not deign to answer. With a deep scowl, he turned his attention back to the snap at his board-flat waist. Tasha swallowed hard and played her final card in a last desperate attempt to forestall Ben in his intent.

"I'm still a virgin, Ben," she said.

His fingers paused again in the very act of locating the tab of his zip. She could see the tensing of muscle, the sudden stillness of the body that towered above her. And then there was a hardening of jaw, as if her words had only made him more determined.

"That," he said callously, "is a matter of total indifference to me. It only implies a certain lack in you and one best remedied as soon as possible."

But he did not remove the trousers after all. Instead, he lowered himself to a soft mossy knoll on the warm earth, propped his elbows on his knees and took to inspecting her minutely with narrowly hooded eyes, as if debating his next course of action. "I suspect you're lying," he said. "You were far too forward last night to be as untouched as you pretend."

"Nevertheless it's true."

He laughed scornfully. "Seven years of chastity? And in that fast-living set you associate with? Virgins of your age went out when the pill came in."

Tasha's lips felt stiff. "You put me off men years ago," she said in a low voice.

His next laugh was distinctly nasty. "Which explains Max's appeal, no doubt. Yes, I suppose you could be telling the truth. Well, if no one else has made a woman of you yet, Max certainly won't. So perhaps I'll be doing you a favor. Take off your clothes."

And when she did not at once comply he added contemptuously, "Is it so hard? If you can bare yourself for other eyes you can bare yourself for mine. I saw that magazine cover you did, Tasha. You may have preserved your virginity for all these years, but you haven't preserved your modesty. Now undress and do it properly. Slowly and with style. First the T-shirt."

"I can't!"

"Yes, you can. Would you rather I ripped the clothes from your back? I assure you I'm capable." His voice had become soft with danger signals and she knew he meant every word. "Is that the kind of indignity you want?"

She half turned her head and let her hair swing forward to hide the spots of shame that rose high on her cheekbones. "No," she said.

"Then undress yourself. If it's easier for you, pretend that...that you're doing a magazine layout as Eve, in the Garden of Eden." The bitter mockery in his voice could not be mistaken; nor could the command in his next words. "Now, Tasha, or I won't vouch for my actions. Last night put an enormous strain on my self-control."

Pride and a kind of gritty professionalism now came to Tasha's rescue. With a poise and serenity that told nothing of the cringing sensations inside, she turned her back on Ben and swiftly removed the sandals and then the Hermès scarf and the T-shirt. In the stripping she managed to let her long tresses fall forward, so that her breasts were partially concealed. Her hands moved at once to the tie fastening of her homemade skirt.

"Stop!" said Ben in the kind of voice that called for instant obedience. "Now turn so I can see you . . . that's better. Slow down; you're doing this too fast. Push your hair back."

"Don't, Ben," she pleaded, sick with humiliation. "This is no better than torture."

His mouth twisted into a cruelly sensuous line. "Torture? Self-torture perhaps. Do you know what it's costing me to keep myself waiting? You would be very pleased, my pretty temptress, if you knew what a painful effect you're having on me. I should think you would want to prolong my agony. The hair, Tasha."

She stood still, not obeying. And at last he rose to his feet and walked to where she stood, the leashed power of his body telling her that he had spoken no lies. The hungers in his eyes were naked now. Slowly his hands rose, both of them, and pushed the long fall of hair behind her shoulders; slowly the returning fingers brushed the hollows of her throat. His knuckles grazed her nipples—once, only once, in a movement as light as a moth's wing.

Abruptly he turned on his heel and returned to his mossy knoll. This time he remained standing, and Tasha could not look at him at all, because to do so might be to discover that his eyes were on the revealing tautness where his knuckles had brushed her breasts.

"Go on," he ground out mercilessly at last.

She slipped quickly out of her skirt and bikini briefs, and then it was done. With no more waiting for direction, she lay back at once on her bed of ferns and grasses, heartsick and willing the trembling of her lips to stop. She closed her eyes. "I'm ready," she said.

"Very amusing," came Ben's derisive voice. "Now ask me nicely to make love to you."

"I promised I wouldn't fight. Just do it, Ben."

"Open your eyes and say please," he directed callously.

It was only pride that gave her the strength to answer. "I'll never do that," she said, trying to keep her face empty of any emotion that Ben might want to see. Why was he torturing her so?

"In that case I'll just wait," he said softly, "for I intend you to enter this relationship with your eyes open. I want a willing woman in my arms. There's nothing very erotic about making love to a board."

"Ben, don't do this to me," she begged, every pore cringing. "Just undress and get it over with."

"You haven't said please," he taunted. "I'll be ready when you do. But remember, Tasha, I'm waiting until you ask."

There was a rustle of ferns and grasses as Ben now moved. In her mind's eye she could see the tanned hand on the zip of his close-fitting cotton Levi's; could see the paling of flesh as hard unsunned flanks came free; could see the virile strength of him and the long bronzed legs with their darker dusting of hair; could see the twisted mouth and the burning loveless eyes boring into her as if he hated her for arousing such hungers in him.

In the long minutes that followed she could feel his eyes like fingers on her flesh. She could not bear to see those eyes. In her imagination she could feel every gold fleck, every flicker of desire, every particle of molten hatred she had ever seen in those eyes. And as she lay there, it was as if there were not one pair of eyes but a thousand possessing her flesh—eyes in the heavens and eyes in the softly clattering palm fronds and eyes in the surrounding bushes. Was this Ben's humiliating punishment—to make her lie there, so shamefully naked as he watched? In the humid air she could feel her skin grow moist with apprehension, prickling at every stirring of grass and every crackle of twig as small creatures rustled through the forest floor.

At last, when the silence had gone on too long, and shame had sheened her naked body so that even in the hot tropic air she had begun to shudder uncontrollably, she said, "Ben, I beg you, no more torture, no more. *Please....*"

She opened her eyes, and found she was alone.

CHAPTER EIGHT

PERHAPS AS A TEMPORARY CONCESSION to Tasha's fervent prayer that she would never ever have to face Ben again, he was nowhere to be found by the time she made her way back to the hut in the clearing.

The experience in the coco-de-mer grove had filled her with shame and anger and futility and a whole tangle of emotions that left her sick to her very soul. Oh God, why did Ben hate her so? It was almost as if he was punishing her for something, something she did not comprehend. And if he had married her of his own free will, why had he changed his mind on their wedding night? The answer to everything lay in that night, and yet think as she might, Tasha could not see where she had been at fault.

Did he plan to treat her this heartlessly for all of the next week? As if she were a puppet on strings and he some diabolical puppeteer who could manipulate her at will? It seemed nothing to be grateful for the fact he had not possessed her flesh, when there were those last softly dangerous words to remember: *I'm waiting until you ask.*

She had not even indulged in the luxury of tears. Somehow she had managed to staunch the storm of tears that threatened, by sitting for fully ten minutes with a convulsively heaving chest and fingers pressed to her lower lashes to hold back two fat tears that trembled there. They had finally spilled, to be followed by no more, because by then she had managed to fix her mind on one thing only: her deep hatred of Ben. And pride forbade returning to the hut until her emotions were well under control, so by then there were no more tears to choke back.

After the initial relief at discovering Ben was not around, she began to wonder if his absence was only another twisted and calculated joke of his. She spent her first half hour pacing the hut, first in rage, then in despair, and finally—when Ben had still not appeared—with the beginnings of apprehension. That she was so utterly dependent upon him for this next week added to her uneasiness. Had he gone to the lagoon in search of supper?

"I hope he meets a hammerhead!"

Voicing the vicious wish triggered a whole new round of self-recrimination. Tasha was not particularly superstitious, but all the same, how terrible she'd feel if. . . .

She wrested her mind away from vivid imaginings about the dangers of the deep. No doubt Ben was merely close by, staying away from the cabin because he had some perverse notion of tormenting her with another kind of waiting game. She had a fleeting vision of him emerging from behind a tree, laughing down at her, the cruel mockery in his eyes gradually changing to a smoking, hating, twisting kind of lust as his smile faded. . . .

What was he punishing her for? Perhaps it was true that the years had given her a protective brittleness, a shell of the very nature Ben despised. But Ben himself had helped to put it there. And it was a thin shell—like an eggshell, Tasha reflected bitterly: smooth and hard to the eye, but easily cracked, with nothing very hard-boiled inside. She felt cracked now.

But not broken! she decided firmly after some more minutes had passed. The restless pacing around the hut had restored some of her spunk and spirit, and although her shell was not as intact as it had been, it was still well in place. Somewhat recovered, she devoted a few minutes to searching for her blue jeans and located them where Ben had thrust them—in the duffel bag filled with his own clothes. Not very well hidden after all. She changed into them quickly, feeling somewhat more secure than she had in the flimsy and ill-constructed skirt.

Briefly, in an attempt to think of things other than Ben, she wondered if she ought to remove her contact lenses in order to bathe her eyes, which were beginning to feel decidedly strained. . . .

Was it only imagination, or had Ben said something last night about her eyesight? Something to do with Eulalie, and. . . and. . . yes, the little twist of gold wire in the ear. Another of Eulalie's muddled ideas! Thinking of Eulalie was a relief, and deter-

minedly Tasha turned her mind to the subject. By
daylight, with bright sunshine pouring in the window, all thought of the supernatural seemed extra-
ordinarily foolish, especially when everything could
be so logically explained away. Ben was right about
one thing: Eulalie was an addled old woman with a
good heart. A bit of a crackpot, maybe, but harm-
less. She *had* come to Tasha's rescue in the dark;
she *had* put a poultice on the bruise even if it had
cured nothing; she *had* offered to give away her own
supper; she *had* tried to lead Tasha to Monsieur
L'Horloge, whoever he might be; and she *had* prepared one of those little packets for the superstitious, even if Tasha had not accepted it. And she
had done all these things without demanding payment of any kind.

The recollections about Eulalie were sad and funny and touching and oddly comforting, like a warm
bath to the mind. After today's emotional bloodlet-
ting they instilled a curious sense of peace, and
Tasha knew that, witchcraft or no, she would be in
no way alarmed by a return visit to the old *bonne
femme di bois*. Poor Eulalie, with her herbs and her
potions and her terrible memory; perhaps she
should stock her shelf with rosemary for remembrance!

Thinking of Eulalie sent Tasha to the window that
overlooked the woods, where she spent some
moments trying to pick out the exact spot from
which she had emerged the previous night. Perhaps
it was a subliminal influence of some kind that

caused her to dig her flattened hands casually into the hip pockets of her jeans as she stood there, reflectively gazing through the window. Her fingers encountered something small and unfamiliar in one pocket.

"Now when did Eulalie put that there?" Tasha muttered, staring at the little brown-paper-wrapped packet that emerged from its hiding place in her jeans. Eulalie's *gris-gris*, of course. Well, if it was supposed to be an amulet against enemies, it had certainly not served its purpose today! No wonder Eulalie's customers paid her in wretched castoffs!

And then because that thought had its sad side, too, Tasha had to fight down a little lump in her throat. There was nothing subliminal about the way her eyes traveled to Ben's four sturdy chairs. He certainly didn't need four. And if Ben didn't like what she was about to do...well, she'd face that, along with other things, when she saw him again.

Moreover, perhaps it was best if Ben didn't find her waiting there like a whipped puppy dog when he returned from wherever he was. Let him do some wondering for a change!

Not giving herself time for second thoughts, Tasha picked up one of Ben's weighty chairs, hoisted it over a shoulder and marched out the front door. On closer inspection of the woods it was not too hard to find the narrow path; and soon she was trudging uphill with her unusual burden.

She was winded and panting audibly by the time she saw a thinning of trees. Directly ahead lay a

shelf of land carved out of the hillside—a level area
built up with stones to form a kind of rough patio.
Reaching it, Tasha stood at the edge of the woods,
staring. Her mouth literally gaped, less in surprise
than because she still had a real need to catch her
breath after the strenuous climb with the heavy chair.
All the same, her eyes saucered slightly to see that she
had reached not Eulalie's hut but one of the homes
she had seen yesterday from the shore.

The several people standing on the shelf of land
stared back. There were a number of children; two
younger women roughly dressed with bandannas tied
over their heads; and a sturdily handsome middle-
aged woman with a light brown face and graying
hair. Their clothes suggested poverty and so did the
thatched hut, which was scarcely better than Eulalie's
despite the wooden shuttered porch and concrete
steps.

The first inkling that they found anything peculiar
in Tasha's appearance came from a half-naked
brown child in much-patched pants, who pointed,
covered his mouth with one hand and giggled.

That loosed a few titters from other children, one
of whom ran to hide nervously behind her mother's
skirts, earning a reprimand in the incomprehensible
local patois.

Why were the children so alarmed at her appearance? Ben's doing again, Tasha thought with a
stab of anger. Standing here, puffing and panting
from the effort she had just expended, would only
give credence to whatever he had said about her. And

then she remembered the chair. No doubt it *did* look
a little peculiar! Why would a stranger to the island
be carrying a heavy chair through the woods with no
apparent good reason?

One of the younger women crossed herself surreptitiously. Suddenly Tasha felt an insane impulse
to giggle—what a bad habit that was becoming—and
despite her best efforts the impulse won. Another
child went scooting behind another skirt and peeped
out from behind it with worried eyes.

With effort, Tasha straightened her face—almost.
The choked-down merriment kept trying to bubble to
the' surface, no doubt contributing to the way so
many pairs of eyes were continuing to stare at her. It
seemed very funny that their giggles should have
stopped when hers began. Well, she had to give some
reason for her presence there. And she had no intention of asking the way to a witchwoman's hut—that
might make them think her really mad!

Yet without asking for directions of some kind,
how on earth could she rationalize being there?

"Oui?" It was the middle-aged woman who
stepped forward and spoke. Despite her politeness,
she too was eyeing Tasha askance.

At last Tasha managed to wipe her expression
totally clean, but only by sucking in the sides of her
cheeks and swallowing very hard. The determinedly
blasé face she now succeeded in donning seemed to
set no one at ease. The two younger women ex-
changed knowing glances.

Tasha reminded herself firmly that it was not so

very different from asking for directions in Trafalgar Square. "Can you please tell me," she repeated with a fixed smile and a polite tone of voice, "which path I take to find Monsieur L'Horloge?"

For some inexplicable reason, that evoked more muffled titters, and this time even the adults seemed to have difficulty in restraining themselves. And they thought *her* mad! Tasha looked around, bewildered at the reaction.

She opened her mouth to explain herself, decided there was no good explanation for anything on this cloud-cuckoo-land of an island, and felt a sudden return of rage at Ben for putting her in this impossible position. At least that emotion put paid to all her inner hysteria!

Well, if everyone was intent upon believing her crazy, she'd give them something to think about. With compressed lips and a stubborn tilt of the chin, she stepped farther onto the shelf of land, hoisted the chair off her shoulder, parked it, sat squarely upon it and faced down the staring eyes with an open show of defiance.

"I was afraid," she said angrily, mindful of what Ben had told her of customs on this island, "that you might not have a chair in your home to offer me and make me welcome. I see I was right."

The older woman sobered at once, and it now became clear that this was her home. Taking charge, she turned to the two younger women and spoke a few words, clearly asking them to leave. Then with a cluck of the tongue and a wag of her graying head, she shooed away the children, too. Turning to Tasha, she switched to heavily accented but understandable French.

"I apologize for these things that have happened, *mademoiselle*, and I welcome you to this house. You are at the home of Aristide Bruleau."

"How do you do, Madame Bruleau," Tasha said, rising to her feet with an immense sense of relief that someone was at last speaking to her as if she were a sane human being and not an escapee from a madhouse. She smiled warmly, liking the other woman's dignified carriage and bright inquisitive eyes.

"Not Madame Bruleau, I am afraid," smiled the woman. "Call me Delphine, if you wish. I am the *ménagère* of Aristide Bruleau."

Housekeeper? Perhaps she had reached a household of some consequence, after all? Tasha skimmed a brief glance at the sorry-looking hut; it still reeked of poverty.

"And I apologize, too, for the little ones, that they should laugh at your appearance." Delphine picked up Tasha's chair and carried it closer to the entrance of the house; then, sitting down herself on the concrete steps, she indicated that Tasha join her. "Please," she waved, "it is cooler here in the shade of the takamaka tree. Another time, spare yourself the trouble of bringing a chair, for although we are not rich, Aristide and I, we have four chairs inside—two of them fine and given us by our daughters."

Tasha, who was by now a little confused about the relationship between Aristide and Delphine, blinked in mild surprise as she took her chair. "Daughters?" she asked politely.

"Those worthless two you saw. Pah! That they should raise our grandchildren to be so rude!"

Tasha's slight widening of eyes did not escape her hostess's attention. Delphine's face remained solemn, but her eyes twinkled as she explained.

"This shocks you that we are not married, Aristide and I? Perhaps, in your country, to live *en ménage* is not so common?"

"It's not, er, unusual nowadays," Tasha said, at last understanding the arrangement. "Although by the time a couple have grandchildren, they've generally decided to make it more permanent. But of course our customs are different and—"

Delphine laughed, displaying healthy teeth. "They are not so very different! Aristide and I would marry if we could save the wages of half a year! The *bacca*, the banquet, the wedding clothes... to marry without such things would bring great shame upon Aristide's head and mine. So, it is better to live *en ménage*. And someday...."

There was a trace of wistfulness in Delphine's sigh, but she dropped the subject at once and turned back to speaking of Tasha's extraordinary welcome moments ago.

"You must forgive us," she said pleasantly, "but you do look somewhat... different. It is the eyes and the cheeks. We are not used to such things. But of course, we are unfamiliar with what is the new fashion in your land. Really," she added with excellent politeness, "the black streaks on your cheeks are very becoming when one grows used to them. And the eye smudges, too."

Tasha's fingers flew to her face. Of course! Today's events had worked ravages on the eye makeup she had applied too heavily, in order to annoy Ben. It was a possibility she had never considered, because in the normal course of events she wore no eye makeup at all, except on modeling assignments and during public appearances with Max.

Her little laugh was now one of embarrassment. "Oh, dear. I didn't know...and this certainly isn't the fashion in my country! No wonder everyone stared! I thought it was because you all believed I was...well, *amarrée*."

Delphine chuckled. "So I was told, but I know it is wrong to believe in—" here a moment's hesitation "—*la malfaisance*. Others may believe—I saw my foolish daughter cross herself—but I have listened to the good Father Julien, who tells us to put such things behind us. Wait, do not wipe your face, I will fetch you a little mirror. And a cloth, perhaps?"

When she emerged from her house a little later, she brought not only the wherewithal for Tasha to salvage the damage, but two cracked mugs filled with steaming tea.

"What a mess!" Tasha made a wry face into the mirror, finding some humor in the face that stared back at her. There were great black smudges where

her fingers had been pressed against her lower lids
earlier, and unsightly streaks along her cheeks where
she had rubbed away the two recalcitrant tears.

"And then of course," Delphine noted good-
naturedly as she settled back down on the stoop,
"when you asked for Monsieur L'Horloge... well, it
did seem very funny at the time."

Face now well wiped, Tasha put the mirror and
cloth on the step and darted a puzzled look at Delphine. The humor of that escaped her. "I'm afraid I
don't understand," she said.

Delphine smiled indulgently. "There is a saying in
the Seychelles that has to do with the special clock in
the big city of Victoria on the island of Mahé. *Il n'a
pas vu l'horloge.* It means—" she knotted her brow,
looking for an explanation "—to see the clock is to
see the world. If a person has not seen the clock, he is
a stupid backward fellow, *un rustre.* You understand?"

"Not quite," said Tasha, head spinning. "Did
everyone think me a *rustre*—a bumpkin?"

Delphine's face grew slightly wary as she answered; it was clear she was trying not to insult her
visitor. "Oh, no," she said carefully, "not that. It
was only that they thought it odd you should not
know the difference between a clock and a man. And
if it was a clock you were looking for, why did you
not know it was on the island of Mahé, when you
have just come from there? There are no clocks on
this island."

"But I was told there was a man of that name.... I

must admit I'm somewhat confused." And then, because Delphine had been kind and gracious and seemed understanding, Tasha related some of the previous night's strange events. She debated revealing the whole story and asking for help—surely, after today's events, all promises to Ben were meaningless—but in the end she decided to wait until she was sure Delphine was convinced of her sanity.

"So you see," she finished lamely, "I was really looking for Eulalie to give her the chair. I must have misunderstood her last night when she talked of a clock. I thought she meant a man, a sort of local chieftain."

Delphine looked thoughtful and sipped at her tea. "I can see that you might have misunderstood Eulalie." She sighed a wise sigh, not unlike the sound of the breeze soughing through the fat-leaved takamaka tree overhead. "She is very, very old, you understand, so old that no one on this island remembers a time when she was not old. She talks of the clock very often for she has seen it, and many others have not. It is the defense of an old woman against the scorpion tongues of youth. Perhaps you were laughing at her at the time?"

"No," said Tasha.

"Ah. Well, you see, she talks of the clock when people laugh at her, as they so often do. . . . Oh, it is sad, but people are cruel and they poke fun at an old woman who cannot even remember how to make a proper *gris-gris*."

Tasha stared into her tea, swirling the cup as she

fought the by now familiar tightness in her throat and remembered that she herself had said some flippant words to Ben about Eulalie's ineffective potions.

"And they laugh, too, at her clothes. Perhaps you think this strange, when ours are not so very much better?" Delphine plucked at the patched and mended skirt she wore and sighed again. "But you see, it is different on Sundays. Then, Father Julien comes from the island where he lives, six miles away, and says mass. For that, every woman of the island dons her fine *robe la messe*, her fine *chapeau la messe*... oh, some of the clothes are very, very grand indeed. Most women will do without food in their bellies before they will do without their fine Sunday dress! Eulalie has no such dress and yet she insists on going to the mass."

The mental image was unsettling. All the other Seychellois in their very best clothes, and Eulalie, braving laughter in that old sugarsack of a dress with its variegated patches....

"You think it unusual that a *bonne femme di bois* should be a devout Catholic? Ah, but it is not so unusual; the old beliefs and the new often mix. But perhaps, for Eulalie, it would be best if she stayed hidden in her woods. For it is on Sunday, the day of the mass, that she becomes a laughingstock."

Tasha poked a finger at her tea leaves, feeling almost physically sick from what she had learned. "I don't think *you* laugh at Eulalie," she said quietly.

"No, for I have listened to Father Julien, who says

it is wrong. And Aristide has listened, too. He is kind
to Eulalie, and sometimes takes her pieces of fish
when he cannot sell all that he has caught in his
pirogue. And at times we have a little rice to spare, or
an onion; and when Aristide taps our toddy tree, he
takes her a little *calou*. For what other pleasure is left
to the old woman? Ah, I would make her a dress, if I
could find a few rupees to buy some *aunes* of
cloth...."

Moved by her own recitation, Delphine took a
thread-thin handkerchief from her pocket and
mopped her face, pretending the moisture was caused
by heat. Her expression then firmed. "But on Sundays, we take Eulalie to sit with us, Aristide and I.
Even so, the others laugh at her dress of patches...
my own grandchildren, too, although it gives me
great shame to admit such a thing."

"Children don't always understand," said Tasha.

"Their parents, too," muttered Delphine, now
sounding angry. "There are those who should know
better who still snicker behind their hands! Well,
enough of sad things that cannot be helped. Will you
have some more tea? Then we will talk of you."

Yes, thought Tasha as she handed Delphine her
cup; surely she could talk to this sympathetic woman,
who did not seem to think her crazy. Aristide had a
pirogue; and if this Father Julien lived on the neigh-
boring island....

She was still debating how to explain her predicament when Delphine returned with the two refilled
mugs. She handed one to Tasha, resettled herself on

the concrete step and at once turned to her guest
with a polite but lively curiosity in her eyes.

"After talking to you for a time," she started
with the utmost circumspection, "I can see that at
heart you are a woman of great good sense, not
really crazy at all. So perhaps you will not mind if I
ask you a simple question?"

"Of course not," Tasha said, breathing relief that
her coming revelations would be falling on receptive
ears.

Delphine leaned forward conspiratorially and
lowered her voice to a wondering whisper as if such
matters could not be broached aloud. "Tell me,"
she said with rounded eyes, "as you are so sane,
how did you come to be so badly *amarrée*? Oh, to
turn you mad, it must have been a very, very strong
spell!"

SO MUCH FOR FATHER JULIEN'S TEACHINGS! Tasha's
thoughts were wry as she trudged down the winding
trail several hours later, with revelations still un-
made and chair still in tow.

Delphine's unexpected words had occasioned a
few moments of helpless reaction, and no doubt
Tasha's disbelieving stare had only confirmed the
other woman's thoughts. It was clear that beneath
that layer of common sense, there were some very
deeply rooted superstitions! Tasha had nevertheless
enjoyed the long afternoon's visit, putting her own
troubles aside in the fascination of learning more
about island customs. She had departed only when

Aristide Bruleau—a solidly built, pleasant man of middle years—had returned from his day's fishing.

The tropic sun hung two hours above the horizon when Tasha finally emerged into the valley of the coco-de-mer palms. Surprisingly, Ben had only recently returned from the sea, as if he, too, had been avoiding this meeting. His hair was still wet, the back of his shirt so damp that she knew he must have donned it without taking time to dry himself properly. He was outside squatting beside a newly laid fire, cleaning and gutting fish with an efficiency and determined concentration that prevented him from sparing more than one brief glance for Tasha.

On the slow downhill walk, she had come to the conclusion that it was best to attack the situation frontally. It would be a mistake to hide from Ben or avoid talk of what had happened. Why give him the satisfaction of discovering how thoroughly hurt and humiliated she had been? That, after all, was what he wanted! It was time to salvage what pride she could, and that, Tasha knew, meant putting on her coolest, most composed, most civilized demeanor. With the most casual of manners, she strolled toward the fire.

"Why the chair?" asked Ben. He continued to scale one finny specimen vigorously, not looking at Tasha at all.

She placed the chair on the ground nearby and sat down. "I don't like sitting on the grass," she said. "Well, actually, it was intended as payment for Eulalie, but I couldn't find her."

"Oh?" His monosyllable was dry but suggested no reprimand.

"I found some other people instead."

"I see." Ben's voice sounded grim and his knife paused over his work.

"You'll be very happy to know they all thought me totally mad." There, that sounded appropriately brittle! She was pleased to find that this pretense was not too painful. Perhaps the eggshell was still intact!

"I'm sorry if you were embarrassed." His apology was rough, hardly an apology at all. "I'll tell them the truth at the end of the week."

"Embarrassed?" Tasha pretended incredulity. "Really, Ben, you underestimate me. In my profession I'm quite accustomed to being stared at."

At this somewhat skewed reference to the earlier scene in the coco-de-mer grove, Ben only scowled more intently at his work. He chopped off a fish tail with some viciousness. "I thought you'd broken your promise," he said, "and gone running for help."

"I do have one or two good qualities—honor among thieves, and all that." Tasha watched Ben's bent head for another moment, reminding herself of the mental anguish he had subjected her to, screwing up her courage to continue this confrontation. At length she stretched ostentatiously and simulated a yawn. "Odd, isn't it, how having a nap during the day only makes you sleepier? I was so surprised when I woke up in the grove and found you were gone."

Ben glanced up and a peculiar look flickered over

his face, setting a pulse to beating in Tasha's throat. Her bored smile was a study in dissemblance.

"I thought you were upset," he said.

"Oh, I admit I didn't like it at first, but one gets used to anything, even voyeurs. How long did you watch?"

"Don't you know?" Ben said sharply, and then, as if some tension wire had snapped inside, he suddenly threw down his knife, aiming it so that the blade sliced into the earth six feet away, accurately spearing a leaf. He stood up and tossed the cleaned fish into the iron pot that already simmered over the hot fire, then kneeled down to wash his hands with soap in a water-filled enamelware basin beside him—all small rituals, Tasha sensed, to prevent immediate discussion of what had happened. She felt a bittersweet triumph at having won some small victory by taking the offensive.

Ben stood up again and dried his palms on the sides of his pants, a clean but much worn pair of very faded blue denims that hugged the masculine contours of his thighs as though they had been poured into place. Tasha averted her eyes unhurriedly, wanting nothing to remind her that she had won a skirmish, not a battle.

Ben came to stand directly in front of the chair, looming over Tasha with elbows bent wide and knuckles pressed to his hips in an attitude of exasperation. With the lowering sun, his shadow fell in an oblique slant over the earth, and it was this that Tasha now studied, somewhat ostentatiously, until a sudden cloud blocked the sun, causing her to shiver involuntarily even in the still humid air.

"I didn't stay at all," he said in a low level voice. "I left as soon as you so obligingly laid yourself on the ground. Didn't you hear me go?"

She remembered now the rustling noises she had heard, when she had thought Ben to be undressing. Well, that didn't excuse any of his other behavior!

She put on a purposely distant smile and met his penetrating and unfriendly stare. "I'm afraid not. For the first few minutes I was too occupied in trying to dream up a good Garden of Eden pose. I'm only sorry you didn't see it, parted lips and one knee just a little bent...."

At the sick look that came over Ben's face, she arched her eyebrows delicately. "Surely that's what you wanted? You did tell me to think about being Eve. So that's exactly what I thought about. As you pointed out, I am a professional."

"Another of your good qualities?" Ben said scornfully.

Tasha managed a faintly amused look. "Oh, there are more. I have a wonderful sense of humor. When I found out you were gone I managed to have a good laugh at your sudden show of conscience. Imagine going to such nefarious lengths to get me alone on this island, only to be stopped at the last minute because it turns out I'm a virgin! That is why you walked away, isn't it?"

"I don't deny it. I told you, I plan to wait till you ask."

"Kidnapping yes, rape no—is that it? Then you've gone to a great deal of trouble for nothing, Ben. You might as well take me back to Mahé right away, for I don't intend to ask such a thing—ever."

"Oh?" His mouth quirked cruelly and sardonically. "You'll ask soon enough. I'm not convinced, for one thing, that you're telling the truth about your physical state. But virgin or no, I've decided it's best to wait until you say please."

Tasha's musical little laugh trilled with imaginary amusement. "And you pretend I'm the one who's mad!"

Ben's variegated tortoiseshell eyes turned briefly dangerous, but he curbed his anger at once. "You'll ask. I saw the way your body was beginning to respond this morning. You wanted to undress for me or you'd never have done it so willingly. Oh, a charming show of modesty, but that could be pure fakery. All the same I want to hear you express your willingness in words."

"And that I'll never do!"

"No?" he said softly. "I think you'll ask—by nightfall. From the obliging way you lay down today, I think you must be a very frustrated young lady. And it wouldn't be decent to describe some of the advances you made last night."

At Tasha's enraged expression, Ben smiled with bitter mockery and turned on his heels to attend to the simmering pot. He tested the fish and found it done, cooked almost instantly in the hot juices of the stewing vegetables he had prepared earlier. With considerably more expertise than Tasha had achieved this morning, he hooked the pot from its perch and served its contents into two huge bowls that were in truth merely cleaned polished halves of the coco-de-mer nut. He handed one bowl, with eating implements, to Tasha, and then to her surprise produced some chunks of crusty French bread. At last he levered himself to the ground and sat cross-legged, eating his own meal in brooding silence.

It was ironic, thought Tasha, how he contrived to put her in the wrong, as if the whole humiliating scene had been her fault!

The appetizing and aromatic food soon overcame the initial impulse to throw the bowl back in Ben's face. It was Creole cookery of a kind that Max would never have permitted her to eat, a spicy and thoroughly delicious concoction of chopped onion, garlic, tomato and finely sliced green pepper. Plus a dash of ginger root, Tasha guessed, as she dug hungrily into the dish. She was curious to know the name of the delicately flavored fish, but would not give Ben the satisfaction of asking.

Food seemed to put Ben in a somewhat better temper. He actually looked satisfied as he mopped his bowl clean with a last piece of bread and settled back comfortably on an elbow.

"Bourgeois," he said out of a blue sky.

Tasha blinked, not understanding. "I beg your pardon?"

"The fish—it's bourgeois, otherwise known as red snapper, just to answer your question."

"I don't remember asking," Tasha cut back.

"An island delicacy," Ben remarked, seemingly insensitive to her barb. "Even better if it's baked. Perhaps I'll construct us an earth oven tomorrow."

"Where did you bake your bread today? Or does this island have stores you haven't told me about?"

"Bought it in Mahé," Ben said promptly, drawing Tasha's immediate and angry surprise. "I have a cool storage bin under the hut—boxes and boxes of canned goods, too. Oh, didn't I show you the rest of the supplies? Must have been an oversight." The little half smile that lifted one corner of his mouth was infuriating, and quickly Tasha returned her attention to her meal. "If you hadn't run away last night you'd have seen them all, brown eyes, as they came out of the boat. Canned fruits, canned vegetables, even a couple of canned hams." He shrugged in mock apology. "Fact is, I don't plan to spend too much time provisioning this week, or I won't be able to keep you company."

"I don't remember asking for that, either," she said tartly.

"So I've made other arrangements. Not long ago I talked to one of the local fishermen as he was bringing in his pirogue. A man named Aristide Bruleau—nice cheerful fellow. He's agreed to supply us for the rest of the week. And if Aristide has the kind of luck he's hoping for, you'll have a chance to sample a really unusual fish. Seems he's been trying to harpoon this particular creature for a month now, and he's bound and determined to succeed. A real honest-to-goodness Seychelles delicacy, and something you'll never find in London, Paris or Rome, not even in the finest restaurants.''

Tasha managed to look disinterested as she speared a small piece of fish and carried it delicately to her mouth.

"I'm glad you asked me that question," Ben said dryly, and then proceeded not to answer, except obliquely. "Aristide says this is just a smallish one, only a thirteen-foot wingspread. Well, I doubt that's more than a thousand pounds, horny fins and all. Why, I've seen 'em three times that weight, with monster bat-wings and mouths like jet-air scoops! Would you like me to ask Aristide if you can have the tail?''

Tasha thinned her lips in an expression that was wasted on Ben, who dismissed her silence with a wave.

"Oh, I know you're too proud to ask. So I'll just surprise you with it—it'll make a good souvenir of the Seychelles. And you don't even have to use it as a real whip, unless you want.''

Wings? Jet-air scoops? Horny fins? A tail like a whip? It all conjured up visions of a very strange and alarming sea creature, a Caliban of the deep, but after Ben's sarcasm Tasha felt she could not possibly ask. She bit back her curiosity.

"Ah, well," sighed Ben, "Aristide probably won't catch it anyway; the creature's shy as a violet. On the other hand, there are some people who say it's more like a big butterfly when it flaps those gentle wings.''

"You win," said Tasha, feigning boredom. "What is it, fish or fowl?"

Gradually Ben's mocking smile faded, to be replaced by an expression very much like one visualized in Tasha's imaginings earlier today. "I just wanted to prove to you," he said in a soft and dangerous voice, "that you *can* be made to ask."

He shook himself to his feet and vanished into the hut, leaving Tasha alone. And in the shaky aftermath of that smoldering gaze, it was some time before it occurred to her that he had not answered her question about Aristide's extraordinary-sounding fish.

CHAPTER NINE

ONCE TASHA HAD QUELLED the disorderly sensations resulting from Ben's parting shot, she decided to attend to the day's dishes. She added the few bowls and implements from supper to the partly loaded pail Ben had brought outside for the purpose, and made her way over to the stream, frankly glad of having something constructive to do. The coco-de-mer bowls rinsed clean easily in the fresh water, and the silky sand found at the edges of the stream made for a creditable job of scouring pots. To her surprise, she found herself thoroughly enjoying the homey task. During the past few months as the Fabienne woman, she had had few opportunities to practice the household arts transmitted to her long ago by her French grandmother, a practical woman who had been enormously proud of her household and managerial skills. Thinking now of the melting *crémes caramèles* and delicious flans her grandmother had once taught her to make, Tasha felt her mouth watering. It was months since she had been allowed such treats. What extraordinary things Mystique had done to her appetite! If only Max Fabienne knew!

Remembering Max, Tasha suddenly recalled with

great vividness the way he'd looked when she'd last seen him. Some wicked imp caused her mouth to curl into a smile. Poor Max! How he must have hated to look foolish in front of so many people! No doubt once he had recovered from the shock of finding Tasha had been spirited away from under his very nose, half of his consternation would revolve around the loss of his own personal dignity.

What kind of efforts was Max making to find her now? She remembered that he had been trying to acquire a list of property owners that very first day at the hotel. And Ben owned property. Surely that fact would be on record in the capital of Victoria? Which meant that Max and rescuers might arrive at any time.

The thought gave her hope. If only she could manage to keep Ben at bay! And of course she could, as long as he fulfilled his latest promise of waiting until she asked him to make love to her, for she certainly had no intention of doing that. What overweening arrogance on his part to think she would ever invite his embraces after the kind of treatment she had suffered at his hands!

She was feeling quite heartened and self-confident by the time she turned her footsteps back to the hut, the pail full of spotless dishes in her hand. A storm appeared to be brewing; there was a strange waiting stillness in the air. Great black clouds were gathering overhead, competing with the purplish darkness of Mystique's high mountains. For once, no breezes stirred and clattered in the tops of the coco-de-mer palms. Tasha turned her face determinedly away from that direction. On an impulse she detoured to the far side of the clearing and spent some slow minutes searching more closely for the path that led to Eulalie's hut. Knowing now that it was not the more obvious opening in the trees, which led to the home of Aristide Bruleau, she was able to locate another path half-hidden by heavy overgrowth. A moment or two of checking her visual bearings assured her that this was, indeed, the spot where Eulalie had abandoned her the night before. So perhaps she would yet be able to repay the old woman's kindnesses in some small way.

When she entered the hut, Ben was midway through folding back the covers of one of the beds. That done, he dumped the entire contents of his duffel bag on the other bed, an obvious discouragement to its use.

"Too bad," he noted blandly, rummaging through the clothing thus displayed, "I didn't bring a spare pair of pajamas. So if you don't care for the view tonight you have only yourself to blame."

Tasha compressed her lips but made no comment; instead she went over to the table and sat down.

"On the other hand, it only makes us even." Ben straightened from his task and bestowed a mocking glance on Tasha. "As I recall, last night you weren't too happy about the injustice of my having pajamas when you didn't. Tonight you can rejoice. We'll both sleep in the buff."

"No, thanks," came her tart rejoinder. "I'll use

one of your shirts. As you've laid them out on my bed, I presume I have the right to use them.''

"Help yourself." Ben waved magnanimously. "What do you plan to use on your lower half?"

"Restraint," Tasha returned coldly.

Ben chuckled, but with an arrogance and suggestiveness that told her he fully expected surrender before the night was through. "That'll be a change from last night," he murmured unsettlingly as he started to move about the hut, filling kerosene lanterns for the night that would soon fall. With the last lantern filled, he came to a halt and stood looking down at Tasha in a thoroughly disturbing way. "At least you'll go to bed sober tonight. So when you put the question this time, I'll be able to say yes. You do remember putting the question last night, don't you? You said please more times than I care to remember.''

Despite her surface composure, Tasha cringed inside. Had she really been so abandoned last night as to issue an outright and repeated invitation? "You must have misunderstood me," she said coolly. "I was probably asking for something else, some supper, perhaps. I remember I was starving."

"Some way to sing for your supper," came the deeply ironic response. "Perhaps I shouldn't have fed you so well tonight, if hunger results in such wanton behavior. At least tonight you can't blame anything on a lack of food. You tucked in like a trooper at suppertime. That bread vanished as if by magic! If I'd known, I'd have bought twice as much at that patisserie in Mahé.''

Patisserie? At the very word the juices started flowing again; visions of her grandmother's flaky pastries danced in Tasha's head. It was hard to believe she could still be hungry after the healthy meal she had just devoured, so it must have been nostalgia that produced the apparently idle question.

"You didn't by chance buy any pastries, did you?"

Ben lifted his brows questioningly. "Still hungry? In that case I'll rustle up some dessert before it gets dark outside and before that storm breaks. It won't take a minute."

While he was gone, Tasha reflected once more on the ravages Mystique had worked on her careful diet. As a rule, she was not too discontent to obey Max's dictums about limiting quantities, possibly because she preferred foods with more seasonings than Max was prepared to allow. Well, she was certainly making up for missed opportunities now!

"Sorry, no pastries," Ben said when he returned, thus disappointing Tasha briefly. "I didn't realize you had a sweet tooth or I'd have stocked up. Not that I could have brought the perishable kind, with no refrigeration. This is the closest thing to a cream filling I could come up with. It's a local specialty."

He was carrying a tray with a large serving bowl, two smaller dishes and a bottle of Cointreau. "Handy having that larder under the hut," he said cheerfully, and Tasha came to the conclusion that he had been raiding the supply of canned goods brought from Mahé. The large bowl contained a quantity of a whitish jellylike pudding.

"Aren't you going to ask me what it is?"

"No," she said, remembering that the last time she had asked a similar question Ben had not answered.

His only comment was a quirk of one eyebrow. He sat down, spooned a large helping of the dessert into one of the smaller dishes and laced it with the liqueur. Then, to Tasha's speechless rage, he slid the dish in front of his own place and began to eat with exaggerated relish.

"Help yourself," he suggested after he had taken several mouthfuls. "I wouldn't take too much to start with. It mightn't agree with you. And after last night, I think you'd better stay away from the liqueur altogether."

"There's absolutely nothing wrong with my digestion," Tasha said spiritedly, and reached over to serve herself an even more generous portion than Ben's. A liberal dash of Cointreau went on top.

"Perverse creature, aren't you?" remarked Ben, his eyes enigmatic as he watched her put away a large mouthful. "Obstinate as a mule. You'll never be able to get through that amount. If I'd dished you up a helping that size, you'd have told me you couldn't stand the stuff."

The jelly was bland and sweetish, a coconut-flavored pudding of some kind to which the Cointreau added a pleasant bite. Nevertheless, it was not exactly what Tasha would have selected if she had had free choice in the matter. "That shows how wrong you are," she said, digging in. "I love it."

Ben finished his portion before she did, and he

tilted back in his chair to watch while Tasha out of sheer mulishness worked her way very nearly to the bottom of her generously filled dish. Only when she was scraping up the very last spoonful did Ben say idly, "Crazy, isn't it, that men used to pay so much for a single taste of that stuff?"

Tasha's spoon froze in midair, an involuntary reaction she could not conceal from Ben. The fruit of the coco-de-mer! Could it be? It was so utterly different from any coconut she had ever eaten.

"You tricked me into eating it," she said angrily, putting the spoon down. There was no point pretending now; Ben had seen her hesitation.

"Did I?" His face was a study in innocence. "I don't recall. Surely you guessed you were eating the forbidden fruit?"

"No."

"Ah. Well, I would have told you if you had asked. I do remember saying this was a local specialty, highly prized by the Seychellois even today. Perhaps you've never tasted the jelly from an immature coconut? Or perhaps you didn't realize because of the liqueur—it does conceal the flavor somewhat."

"You're very mistaken, if you think feeding me an aphrodisiac is going to produce the result you're looking for."

Ben stroked his jaw in a way that indicated satisfaction, and he raised his brows in mock surprise. "Surely you don't credit that superstitious nonsense. I've eaten the stuff a hundred times, and...." He paused, and his eyes took on a faraway look, as if old and pleasant memories were reasserting themselves. He allowed a reflective smile to curve his mouth. "Well, maybe there's something to it at that. Now that I recall . . . ."

Knowing full well that he was trying to upset her, Tasha struggled to regain her usual poise, with some success. "Of course I know it's not an aphrodisiac. But I don't like to be tricked!"

"Then you should stop being so ornery." Ben stood up, cleared away the dishes and walked around the table. There was a predatory gleam in his eye as he stood there, towering too close, dominating her field of vision. "It's too easy to trick someone who insists on being as stubborn as you. So why don't you just save a lot of time and ask me to make love to you right away?"

Tasha longed to turn her eyes away but knew that would be defeat of a kind. Slowly she directed her gaze to his belt buckle, which was no more reassuring than those smoking eyes. She was alarmingly aware of every tiny detail about him—the waiting stance, the thumbs hooked into the waistband of his faded jeans, the athletic thighs, the powerful forearms. She tried to focus on the dial of the sturdy expensive diver's watch he wore, but it was a strong plain watch that served only to remind her of his overpowering physique. She felt unnervingly close to asking the question he wanted to hear.

"Can you hand me my makeup case, please?" she requested, thinking to remove her contact lenses. It occurred to her that the night ahead would become a great deal less trying if she could not see with such clarity, for even though it was now growing very gloomy in the hut, she knew that Ben would soon be lighting the lanterns; and certainly the lenses must come out sometime this evening, anyway.

"That's the wrong question," Ben remarked sardonically, but he obliged by bringing the case over to the table. "I suppose you want to make yourself attractive for the coming seduction scene. So this time I won't object. Eyelashes, foundation, the whole damn works if you want. And lots of lipstick, too, for I plan to remove it in the best possible way."

"This time reverse psychology won't work." Tasha forced a light defensive laugh. "Now that I know your technique, I simply won't fall for it again."

The laugh returned Ben to silence, giving Tasha some temporary advantage. A sudden gust of wind chased through the hut's open windows, a reminder that the storm and the night were fast approaching. Tasha did not open her case as yet. She waited while Ben, now in a brooding mood, attended to lighting the lamps. That done, he set about pulling the shutters closed against the swiftly encroaching darkness. He paused at the second window overlooking the coco-de-mer grove. Outside, the wind now whipped at the tops of the palms, tossing the fronds wildly against a gloomy glowering sky. The moaning and clashing of the treetops made an eerie sound.

Ben stood for a moment with his hands braced on the still-open shutters, staring out at the awesome spectacle. "In the Seychelles there's a superstition about stormy nights like this," he ruminated. "They say this is when the coco-de-mer palms mate. They're supposed to make love in the same way humans do. According to local belief, the male palm actually walks over to where the female stands waiting for him."

"What foolish nonsense," Tasha said.

"Most legends are. All the same, there are locals who swear by it, even though they've never seen such a thing with their own eyes. The legend manages to perpetuate itself because it's supposed to be invariably fatal, if one happens to witness the trees locked in amorous embrace. So, the necessary ingredient of all good legends—no living eyewitnesses. And perhaps there's some small kernel of truth to the belief after all. It may very well be on nights like this that the coco-de-mer palms really do mate—according to their particular fashion. The method is wind pollination."

"Highly romantic," Tasha said with deliberate sarcasm. But in truth, Ben's revelation of the local legend had caused a peculiar prickling of the hair at the nape of her neck, reminding her that she must very quickly don her very thorniest defenses for the evening ahead. And the contact lenses must come out at once; she saw Ben's powerful frame far too clearly for her own good. Besides, her eyes felt quite burned out.

And so, with low lamps lit and the wind moaning beyond the shuttered windows, Tasha at last removed the contacts. Ben went to lounge in the chair directly across the table and watched her in cynical silence. Ignoring him, she leaned toward her small mirror and deftly pinched the soft little bits of plastic out of her eyes, preparatory to putting them in soaking solution for the night.

"My God, do you go through that every day? I didn't know you wore contact lenses."

"That's the whole idea of them. People aren't supposed to know."

Ben's face was now a blur of highlights and deep shadows that determined only the rough outlines and none of the expression. But his voice sounded impatient. "Come off it, Tasha. Surely your eyesight isn't that bad."

"Oh, yes it is. Why, even Eulalie noticed." Tasha paused midway through restoring the lenses to their small plastic carrying case, a maneuver at which she was now so practiced she could have done it in the dark. "You did say the little gold wire was for eyesight, didn't you? I seem to remember that."

"That's just a local belief, not confined to Eulalie, I might add. Another piece of superstitious nonsense—an altogether crazy notion."

Tasha pondered, then remembered that Aristide Bruleau had also worn the little twist of wire in his ear. "In that case the gold wire would suit me very well," she noted dryly, "as everyone thinks I'm crazy anyway. All the same, I wonder how Eulalie knew?"

"Perhaps she didn't know at all. A lot of Seychellois wear the gold wire when there's absolutely nothing wrong with their eyesight. Ask them why they do, they'll answer with indisputable lack of logic that of course there's nothing wrong with their eyesight—but there might be if they removed the wire.''

"Or perhaps she detected the contact lenses in my eyes,'' Tasha said reflectively. "She had the most amazing eyesight herself. She could see perfectly in the dark.''

"And imputes it to the wire, no doubt,'' Ben noted wryly. "Night vision doesn't depend on superstition; it depends on vitamin A. There'd be lots of that in the roots and vegetables she eats.''

Tasha sighed and tucked her lens case away for the night. "I suppose you're right,'' she said.

"Why *do* you wear contacts, Tasha? As I recall from the short glimpse I once had, your reading glasses looked quite endearing on you. In fact, it was one of the things that fooled me into thinking you had your human side.''

The bite in Ben's words helped stiffen Tasha's resolve. With some anger at herself, she realized she had been about to relax her guard, diverted by thoughts of the old witchwoman in the woods. Well, no more! How could Ben display such scorn for her on the one hand, and on the other expect her to melt in his arms? Long-practiced defensive mechanisms kept her from betraying that his words had the power to hurt.

"I do have my human side,'' she said defiantly, feeling around in the makeup case for the hairbrush she could no longer quite see. She wanted an occupation for her hands, which seemed to be trying to tremble. "I like to see as well as be seen. Besides, I like to read the menus in restaurants."

Ben made no comment on her pointed reference to the earlier events of the day. He watched in silence for a moment as she began the brushing of her hair, using long smooth strokes for the nightly ritual she never neglected. Licked by lamplight, the hair gleamed like black satin; but Tasha's intention was not for artifice.

"I hear you don't even have to do that, because Max insists on doing all the ordering for you—special diets and so forth. Although God knows why you need a French chef for a breakfast of soft-boiled eggs and grapefruit—or a menu, for that matter."

Tasha's hairbrush came to a sudden halt as something Ben had said got through the top layer of her consciousness. She stared at his indistinct features. "How do you know what I eat for breakfast? And how do you know Max does the ordering?"

"I hear things."

"You paid someone on the hotel staff!"

"Not quite," he said. The dry mockery in his voice was clear to hear. "But the hotel belongs to an old friend of mine—the man who served as my guardian, in fact, during my growing-up years. Oh, he doesn't know exactly what's going on. I told him you and I wanted a week together as we were contemplating patching things up, but Max was making things difficult because of some contract you had signed. He was quite convinced he was aiding the cause of true love. Now do you get the picture?"

Poor vision did not prevent Tasha from seeing the broad white grin that had grown over Ben's face during this recitation. Her eyes widened, then narrowed again. "So that's how you arranged this whole thing!"

"Simplifies matters, doesn't it? Ah, Tasha. I was kept informed every time that elegant boyfriend of yours lifted a finger. Likes to keep people on his toes, doesn't he? Naturally, the hotel manager was instructed to be most cooperative. What the House of Fabienne wants, the House of Fabienne gets!"

Ben inclined his head in a mock bow and faked a French accent. "A charter boat, *monsieur*? But of course! A pilot? *D'accord*—the very best! One who knows these waters intimately and can lead you to the perfect spot! A man called Le Rouge, which is after all only a local expression meaning a Creole of not too dark complexion...."

"So that was you, too," she exploded.

Ben ignored her interruption. "A list of the property owners? Ah, we shall do even better! We shall procure for you a list of everyone of the age to vote! Very official, you understand, and not at all doctored, but a few years out of date—when the elusive Mr. Craig was not living here at all. A—what is your English expression—a rolling stone...."

"Damn you, Ben!".

"Oh, and there's more," Ben went on derisively. "A van to use on the day of the shoot? Ah, *oui, monsieur*, a van that can also be used as a dressing room. And if some mannerless fellow thinks to break the door, the owner will not even charge him. And what else? A copy of the latest book of Mr. Craig? *Mais oui!* An autographed copy, if you wish! No book jacket of course, for it comes from a lady's personal library. Flyleaf inscribed 'To Diana darling, with love from Ben.' The searchers should have an amusing time looking into my amorous exploits, hmm?''

By now Tasha had grown accustomed to Ben's latest surprise; she returned to the brushing of her hair with a renewed vigor that expressed some of her anger. "Of which Diana is only one, needless to say," she said through her teeth.

There was something scornful in the dim dark pools that were Ben's eyes. "I haven't been as celibate as you," he admitted with a shrug of his broad shoulders. "Nature didn't build me to be a monk. There have been a few encounters over the years. But as for Diana, aren't you going to ask me whether she's a real person, or just a red herring?"

"I don't think I'll ask that question," Tasha said with an obstinate tilt of her chin. "I don't want to know about your sexual preferences, herring or otherwise."

This time Ben chuckled fleetingly, a deep, intimate, vibrant sound that held a mocking quality. He leaned forward and propped folded arms on the table, bringing his face more directly into the lamplight. Still, it was only the broad strokes of his expression that Tasha could see—the rugged jaw, the strong well-defined cheekbones, the mouth with its tug of amusement.

"Devilfish," he said.

Tasha's hairbrush paused in midstroke. "I beg your pardon?" she said with a blink.

"Devilfish. That's the answer to the question you asked outside. You did want to know about Aristide's big fish, didn't you? The locals call it devilfish. It gets its name from its looks, not from its nature. In spite of its size, it runs away from danger. Perhaps you're more familiar with its real name—manta ray. Great graceful creatures, and very good eating."

"It was only a rhetorical question," said Tasha, finishing her hundredth stroke and popping her brush back in the case. She considered creaming her face simply to irritate Ben, decided against it and clicked the case closed. "I'm not actually interested. Now to answer *your* question—no, I don't."

Ben's dark brows went up a notch; she could see well enough to distinguish that. "I don't remember asking anything."

"Why, about souvenirs of my stay in the Seychelles," she said mock-innocently. "The answer is no. I want nothing to remember it by."

Tasha's unthinkingly provocative taunt and Ben's response of utter silence awakened a new something in the air between them. It grew as they sat antagonistically staring at each other across the table, enemies in opposing camps exchanging wordless messages. Tension crackled in the air; and both recognized that all the words that had passed between them were only preliminaries for the pitched battle about to be joined. Or was it a battle? The messages seemed not so hostile now. . . .

At last Ben broke the silence, but so quietly that it did not disrupt the electrical current that ran between them. "Isn't it time," he said in the softest of voices, "that you asked the question that's really on your mind? You do have a question, don't you? The one I told you to ask."

Tasha's protective layer of brittle sophistication seemed to have deserted her now. She was mesmerized by the deep shadows of his eyes, as if he were a hypnotist and she under his spell. "Yes, I have a question," she said in a low voice, not breaking the trance, "but I don't think you...know what it is...."

"It has to do with my making love to you," Ben murmured, and the way he said the words was another way of making love. "I knew what you wanted when you came back today. You didn't have to come back today. You know that. I know that."

And in that moment she knew it was true. She could have asked Delphine for help, and if she had not done so it was because she had not really wanted to. Delphine was superstitious but not callous; surely she would have given Tasha shelter.

It was Ben who had drawn her back: Ben, like the pull of the tide; Ben, like a flame to a moth; Ben, like a lodestone to a compass needle. She had come back because she wanted to come back...or perhaps because Ben, like a conjurer of the mind, had willed her to come back....

"Ask me to make love to you," he commanded.

Disturbed, she tried to fight the magnetism of his

attraction, tried to deny the compelling force of her own senses. "No," she murmured in a voice so low it could hardly be heard. "No...."

And yet in this witching hour her protest was too feeble. Slowly, not breaking the mood of the night, Ben rose to his full height and came around the table. The lamplight cast his long and changing shadow around the dusk-dim room, over the walls, over the rough plank floor, over the folded-back sheets of the bed.

Helplessly she submitted to the fingers that closed over her upper arms, drawing her to her feet. Obeying the slow command of his hands, she swayed toward him, still gazing into those gloom-carved eyes. It was a moment to destroy all Tasha's careful defenses—perhaps because of what the lamplight revealed in that sensuous unsmiling mouth; perhaps because of the animal heat of that tall close masculine body; perhaps because of the drugging softness of his words.

"I want you," he murmured huskily, and she could sense the way his eyelids had grown heavy, slumberous with desire. "Your lips, your breasts, your hips, every part of you...to see, to touch, to kiss, to possess...."

And there were other words, wooing words, wanting words, a litany of soft love words as he led her across the room. She surrendered to the arms that laid her gently along the bed, because she could not help but surrender. He stripped her of her clothes slowly, ardently, bathing her in kisses as he removed

each garment, until all of her lay bared to his view—
the soft rose-tipped swell of breast, the slender curve
of waist, the smooth flare of hip, the long, slim
shapely legs.

Modesty forgotten, she shuddered beneath his
touch. A tremulous awareness of her own wants and
his robbed her of wit and reason. Helpless to resist,
she bent to the power and the passion of those
masterful hands that were discovering her gold-
tinged flesh. . . coursing slowly over her, and she with
no will or wish to stop them. In uncharted regions of
her body, shivering sensations rose like wind-stirrings
before a gale. And even as his hands broached forbidden lands, he murmured huskily of what he
wished to do and branded her heated skin with warm
expert kisses.

"How soft you are. Velvet and satin, and breasts
like petals. . . made for a man to kiss. . . ."

His parted lips moved from the silken furrow between her breasts, until they claimed their trembling
tautened goal. Flushed, feverish with desire, she
could only yield to the slow and skillful featherings
of his tongue. And all the while, his hands blazed
trails elsewhere, stroking and seeking and finding
other goals with a leashed ardor that turned her
bones to liquid and her blood to fire. And yet, when
his touch grew too intimate, she made a feeble effort
to turn from his hands.

"Don't twist away, my love. . . you want to be
touched. . . like this. . . ."

Deep within her, a great need grew, a welling swelling wanting need that could hardly be denied, until her soft meaningless moaning told him that she trembled on the brink of some magical marvelous discovery. Drugged with desire, she did not at first understand when Ben drew upward on her body and murmured the insidious words against her mouth.

"The question," he whispered huskily, "I haven't heard the question."

Her dazed eyes came open and she gazed at him through a blur of vision, at first comprehending nothing. Gradually it penetrated her awareness that Ben was still fully clothed, despite his own potent arousal. Against her naked hip, the roughness of denim molding powerful thighs told her his urgency was still being held in check for the moment of her surrender.

"I haven't heard your question," he reminded her in a smoky voice, tracing her mouth with a finger. "I promised I'd wait for it. Say it now. You *do* have a question."

The magic of the night exploded in a puff of smoke, as if it had been no more than the illusion of a master magician. Tasha wrenched herself away from his hands and snatched a sheet to cover the nakedness that suddenly seemed humiliating.

"Yes, I have a question!" Her eyes were large and defiant, her body shaking all over in violent reaction to the interruption of passion. *"Why do you hate me so?"*

Ben eased himself slowly away from her and sat on the edge of the bed, contemplating her with narrowed eyes. The silence seemed immense, despite the weird moaning of clashing fronds outside in the dark night. At last, as if reaching some decision, Ben stood up and walked halfway across the room. He stood there with his back turned and his fists clenching and unclenching at his sides, betraying strong inner tensions.

"Why do you hate me, Ben?" Tasha repeated in a low fierce voice. "What did I do on our wedding night?"

"I thought I'd never discuss that night with you," he said in a remote embittered way. "But perhaps, if I'm to get what I want from you, I will have to tell.…"

CHAPTER TEN

BEN'S MEMORIES of their wedding night were not so very different from her own, but his perspective was different. Sitting there in the dim primitive hut and listening to his drone of recollections, Tasha felt numbed that his reading of her behavior should be so very far removed from the truth. And how could she defend her actions when even now, seven years later, she could not see where she had been at fault?

The cottage they were to use for the first night of the honeymoon, before traveling to a destination Ben had not at that time revealed, had been loaned by a good friend of Tasha's father. It was in Surrey, and after the wedding Ben had driven the distance in a forbidding silence that Tasha had not broken because of the cold sickness curling inside her, a sickness that became acute as she watched Ben's knuckles clenched over the steering wheel. With her new contact lenses firmly in place and her horn-rimmed glasses forever discarded, she could see things now that she had never seen before—the sensitive lines at the edges of his tight mouth, the brooding tensions in his eyes and the dark circles beneath, the controlled flare of his nostrils, the hard set of his jaw. Was he that angry about being trapped into marriage?

He was not driving very well, a matter that seemed to confirm her guess that he had taken a few drinks to bolster himself for the wedding. And yet, being Ben, if he felt so strongly about being trapped, why had he given in to her father's pressures?

The cottage was secluded, no more than a shadowed shape in the darkness that had fallen some two hours before. The scent of roses and verbena was strong in the air. The motherly woman who was there during the day waited only long enough to let them into the low-timbered dwelling.

"I've left some cold supper, though I've no doubt you ate at your reception. I won't be back tomorrow, but if you need me just call. I've left my number beside the telephone," she had added with a swift and unrewarded smile in Ben's direction. She averted her gaze swiftly as if she, too, sensed that some volcanic emotion was bottled in that foreboding face.

"Can we give you a lift somewhere?" Tasha had asked after some brief instructions had been imparted.

"I live only a quarter mile from here. Besides, I'm used to the walk, and it's a starry night. Besides, your husband must be...."

But Ben had already vanished into another part of the cottage, and Tasha could hear the sounds of water running. She colored, then mumbled some excuse, and the woman made a swift exit, pretending not to notice Ben's rudeness.

The awkward moment had left Tasha feeling miserable and thoroughly alone in those unfamiliar surroundings, with a man who seemed to have turned into a total stranger. And she was sure that Ben's black mood could be caused by only one thing.

When Ben reentered the intimately lit living room, he was mopping his face with a towel, and that gave Tasha a chance to put on a brave bright expression. Her sophisticated clothes helped, too, giving her a veneer that told nothing of the sinking sensations inside.

"Can I get you a drink?" she offered. "Mrs. Simms showed me where the supply is kept."

"No, thanks." Something about his voice, though muffled by the towel, discouraged communication of any kind.

Sick at heart, Tasha tried to screw up her courage to confront the problem directly. "Ben...we can call a halt to this right now," she said in a strained voice. "There's still time to get an annulment."

As the towel came away from Ben's face, she saw that his mouth held a bitter twist, as if self-control were difficult indeed. He focused his eyes on Tasha almost as if he had become aware of her for the first time today.

"Is that what you want?" she pressed, agonizing as she waited for his answer.

"I...what?" His strong fingers, not so steady now, ran raggedly over the crisp hair at the back of his neck. "Perhaps you'd better leave me alone," he said thickly and none too politely. "I'm in no mood to discuss anything tonight. We'll have it out tomorrow."

Tasha swallowed. "Tomorrow may be too late for discussions," she said. She locked her hands together in a gesture designed to give her self-confidence. Her knees were practically knocking, but thank goodness, Ben would not be able to detect that. "I don't want to go through with...tonight... knowing you're not willing. We should have discussed it before the wedding, but as there wasn't an opportunity...."

"Do we have to talk about this now?" He sighed heavily. "Of course I was willing. I said the words, didn't I?"

"Oh, Ben, when you almost didn't turn up for the wedding, I was sure that you weren't coming. I—"

"I won't discuss my reasons for being late," he cut in curtly and with unmistakable finality.

Tasha began to feel desperate. "But we have to talk! I know you're feeling trapped, and...that's not what I want."

"Oh, for God's sake, Tasha, I'm not the type to get trapped. You've been around enough to know that."

Tasha took a deep breath and wondered whether this was the time to tell him the truth about herself and her age. But Ben began to pace the floor, forestalling any immediate disclosure. His big body, usually so lithe and pantherish, was tensed in a way that suggested not energy but restless exhaustion. Despite a lingering thickness of voice, he sounded quite sober now, and angry because he was being forced into a discussion he did not want.

"Good God, Tasha, shotgun marriages are straight out of another century. Surely you must know I had other reasons for going along with the whole thing."

And Tasha was sure she knew what those reasons were. But she ached for Ben to tell her in so many words that he had not married her merely because of the pressures her father had been applying. "Other...reasons?" she persisted, begging for the words of love he had never said. "Do you mean you were planning to propose anyway?"

"To be honest...no." He continued to prowl the room, raking his hair. "It would never have occurred to me; I had intended a few more years of freedom before settling down. Oh, there was a spontaneous combustion between us, I don't deny that. I wanted very badly to take you to bed, but that's as far as it went. In normal circumstances, I'd have made love to you, and...walked out."

Tasha's voice grew unnaturally high. "In other words you were trapped!"

Ben halted long enough to look at her with disconcertingly narrowed eyes. "I wasn't concerned about your honor, if that's what you mean," he said slowly. "A woman goes to bed when she's ready and willing, and that's that. I suppose I was trapped, but not in the way you think. Your backhanded proposal took me by surprise; I hadn't even considered marriage at that point. And I took myself by surprise when I agreed. I opened my mouth to tell you to go to hell, and...something else came out. Maybe it was because I'd seen you with your hair and your defenses down, and those silly glasses perched on your nose. You looked...human. Vulnerable.''

Tasha's chin tilted defiantly and her eyes grew very bright. "Believe me, you didn't have to marry me just because you felt sorry for me!"

Ben's restless pacing came to a halt, and he stared at her with shuttered dark-rimmed eyes. "I didn't feel sorry for you," he said levelly. "You're a grown woman, quite capable of taking care of yourself. I married you because I wanted to."

Her fingernails dug furrows into the palms of her hands. He was lying, of course; every insecure bone in her body told her so. "If that were true, you'd have said something about love!"

His long silence was unnerving and so was the brooding way he looked at her. When he spoke, his voice was dangerously quiet. "I told you I didn't want this conversation now. There are some things a man likes to say in his own way, in his own time, without being pushed. I'll say those things when I'm ready."

"And I won't believe them if you do! I happen to know you married me because you were pressured into it, because you want your book published." There, it was out, the terrible fear that had been like gall and wormwood inside her. And more than anything, she wanted Ben to deny it.

"Is that really your opinion of me, Tasha?" he

asked, his eyes decidedly cold. "As it happens you're wrong."

Warring emotions tugged Tasha every which way. Ben's denial left her half-relieved, half-disbelieving; and his unfriendly manner filled her with adolescent despair. Yet none of those things showed in the aggressive tilt of her head, in the too bright eyes.

"In that case, Ben Craig, stop behaving like a cornered tomcat!"

His long body tensed into a deathly stillness, and for a moment some naked and haunting emotion flitted through his eyes. Then suddenly he turned his back and his strong shoulders hunched, shutting her out. He seemed to have created a wall around himself in that instant. "Take my word for it, Tasha," he said finally in a flat uninflected voice, "I married you of my own free will. I intend to go through with it, too. Now do you mind? I'd like to be alone for a while."

And at length, after a few more unrewarded efforts to breach that wall, Tasha made her way to the bedroom, expecting Ben to follow in time. He had declined the offer of cold supper, and Tasha herself had no appetite whatsoever. She was still disturbed by Ben's uncommunicativeness, but what could she do? He persisted in saying he had married her willingly, and it could be true. And surely, all would be right once he came to her in bed....

The nightgown was black, transparent and very, very sensuous. The sophisticated silk skimmed her breasts and her hips, sliding over skin and clinging where it should cling. She looked at her reflection in the full-length mirror on one wall and was reasonably satisfied with what she saw. Would Ben be satisfied too? Her breasts were not voluptuous as she wished them to be, but they were very definitely there, and nicely shaped, too. The softness of the filmy fabric revealed that the long slender limbs had finally lost the gangliness of teenage years and rounded into more womanly contours. And soon, in Ben's arms, she would become a woman for once and for all.

She shivered, not unpleasurably, with memories of the expert kisses that had aroused her so skillfully once before. Then, because she expected she would have no opportunity to do so later, and because her eyes were growing tired, she removed the new contacts and put them in their case for the night.

At last she slid between the sheets in the big old-fashioned four-poster. After a moment's reflection she clicked off the bedside lamp so that Ben would know she was ready. And so began the long wait.

How long had she waited? Two hours, three? It had seemed a lifetime. At last, when apprehension turned to a cold hard ball of anguish in her breast, she turned on the light again, pulled a wispy negligee over her nightdress, and padded across the now fuzzily defined room. When she opened the door that led directly into the living room, she half expected to find that Ben had been drinking. The scene was dim, lit only by the long shaft of light tailing through the bedroom door, and one much lower light that burned near the entrance. She saw well enough to distinguish that Ben was stretched on the couch, still fully dressed, with one arm propped over his face.

"Ben. . ." she started softly, thinking he might be asleep.

He at once levered himself to his feet and walked to the fireplace. He propped his hands on the mantel and stood there brooding into the cold ashes left by some long-ago spring fire. "I thought you were asleep," he said, sounding cold sober.

"As you see, I'm not." She paused, waiting for an answer, and when none came, she added, "Aren't you. . . coming to bed?"

She wished desperately that she could see his face, because the unearthly silence that greeted her words told her nothing of his feelings. Despite everything, she wanted Ben to desire her; to make love to her. And so, with trepidation in her heart, she slid her negligee from her shoulders and walked across the room, deliberately moving into Ben's line of vision, with her shoulders pressed against the mantel and one hand tentatively touching his sleeve. He tensed perceptibly, but made no move to retreat.

"It's our wedding night, Ben," she reminded him softly.

Slowly, his head turned. She knew he was looking directly at her now, although to her unaided sight nothing of the emotion in those gloom-carved eyes was visible. His mouth was straight, totally devoid of expression.

What was it he wanted? What was he waiting for? Did he not think her alluring enough? With her heart in her throat, she lowered the shoestring straps of her nightgown, trying to look seductive.

"For God's sake, Tasha, grow up," he said in a bitter angry voice. "This isn't the time for that. I have something else on my mind."

Her fingers tightened over the straps just in time to prevent the nightgown from falling. "Something else?" she said faintly, not understanding.

Ben's shadow-hooded eyes still revealed nothing, and this time his voice turned deliberately flat. "I was thinking about a cornered cat," he said expressionlessly.

For long seconds Tasha stared at that blurred enigmatic face. Was Ben trying to tell her that he was not willing after all? It seemed a direct reference to her earlier words, a markedly cruel crushing of her youthful hopes and dreams. Or was it just Ben's idea of a joke? If so, it was a bad one. To help her through the awkward moment, she laughed, a nervous artificial laugh that was purely defensive in nature.

The sudden blind rage that seized Ben then took her totally by surprise. His mouth twisted into a snarl and his hands abandoned the support of the mantel to dig ferociously into the soft flesh of her upper arms. Stunned, she could only gasp as he shook her angrily, as if she had been no more than a rag doll. Her nightgown spilled downward, exposing her breasts.

"My God, what is it you want of me, Tasha? My guts. . . . as well as my heart and my soul?"

"I don't want any of you!" she sobbed, her hair streaming over her face as the words were shaken from her body. "If this is your idea of marriage, I've had enough! I'm not ready for marriage, either—at least not to a...a brute like you! I lied to you, Ben Craig! You told me to g-grow up, and you're... righter than you know! I've never been with a man. I'm a virgin, Ben, and I'm not twenty-four, I'm only seventeen! Instead of thinking about a...a cat, you might think about that!"

Her revelation brought none of the mercy she hoped for. His fingers seared even more bruisingly into her arms, and he spat a low and ugly curse through clenched teeth. "You shallow little bitch," he grated harshly, "you may not have lost your virginity, but you've lost everything else. Have you no sensitivity at all? Don't you give a damn about anybody else's feelings?"

"No!" she cried. "I care about mine! You're hurting me, Ben, hurt—"

His mouth came over hers like an explosion, driving the unfinished word back in her throat. There was punishment in that possession, but no love. It was a travesty of a kiss, an intrusive, brutal expression of rage and hatred. It was as if something inside Ben had snapped. She had always known that a primitive part of him existed, lurking not far beneath the surface, but she could never have guessed how cruel he could be, how violent, how hurtful, how indifferent to her struggles.

Ignoring her flailing limbs, he had wrenched her

into his arms and swept her toward the bedroom, his hands scorching her breasts and her thighs, his tongue ravishing her mouth with a ferocity and thoroughness that made it impossible for her to catch a single breath. She felt herself drowning, suffocating in that explosion of hatred. . . .

She lost consciousness in the instant he flung her body on the bed, and when she came out of the faint, naked and shivering, Ben was gone. She was sure she had been raped. She had been too shamed to tell her father, or anybody, much of what had happened; and so it was some time before she discovered the truth.

Her father, not knowing the full story, had defended Ben. "Don't push it, Tasha," Charles Montgomery had said mildly. "Not over some little lovers' spat! I have a feeling something was troubling Ben; he simply wasn't himself. Truth is, I like the man, and although I don't hold with his courtship methods, I confess I was pleased by the outcome. Now promise me you won't try to put an end to the marriage without giving it a fair trial!"

"Fair trial?" Her despairing little laugh held no amusement as she cast her eyes to the ceiling to prevent an outburst of tears. "Don't you see, papa, Ben wouldn't give it a trial even if I were willing, which I'm not. He phoned this morning to say he was leaving the country."

"But he didn't mention divorce?" There was a hopeful note in her father's voice.

"No, and when *I* did, he. . .he just swore softly

and hung up on me. Oh, papa, why didn't you leave well enough alone? Ben would never have married me without your interference."

Charles Montgomery looked at her strangely. "Didn't you know, Tasha? I don't deny I tried to exert some pressure, for I didn't like to see you so unhappy. Ben's only answer was a cablegram telling Jim Arthur to go to hell—well, not those words exactly, but that was the general drift of the message."

Which was why, Tasha supposed now, she had not sought a divorce immediately; some subconscious part of her had hoped Ben would reappear. It was not until some months later, when she at last found courage to put an outright question to the family doctor, that she learned she had not been violated at all. By then, Ben's whereabouts were a total mystery. Knowing she could secure an annulment whenever she wished, Tasha made no move to seek a divorce. The marriage had its useful side. In the intervening months, men had become something of a problem; contact lenses had turned the ugly duckling into a beautiful swan.

"YOU MIGHT HAVE WAITED around long enough to make sure I came out of the faint!" Tasha accused now.

"I didn't even know you had fainted," Ben responded with not a quiver of remorse. He was standing by the window near the foot of the bed. He had opened the shutter a few inches and stood with his hand propped on its edge, brooding out into the storm-lashed coco-de-mer grove much as he had brooded into the fireplace on that night so long ago.

"You must have suspected something of the kind when I accused you of raping me," Tasha said tightly. "But when I mentioned that and spoke of divorce, you simply hung up. You might have defended yourself."

"Why?" Ben shrugged and turned to look at her. "I wasn't interested in your good opinion. As far as I was concerned, our marriage was nonexistent. But just to make sure, when I sailed around the world I took a small side trip and secured a Mexican divorce, because I could hardly prove grounds for annulment without your cooperation. And I was damned if I'd ask for that."

"So that's where you got the divorce!"

"Quick and not too tidy, I'll admit. But at that point, I only wanted to be rid of you as speedily as possible."

Tasha looked at the tall outlines of his body and wished she had not removed her lenses earlier. She could see little more of his expression now than she had been able to see on that long-ago night; it left her feeling at a disadvantage. She averted her face slightly, sure that he was subjecting her to a sensuous smoking scrutiny of the type that held detestation as well as desire. She tried to void her face of expression.

"You still haven't told me why you hate me," she said.

"Because I had reason to be upset that night. You seemed insensitive, to say the least."

"You might have told me what you were upset about."

"Would it have changed things?" His voice was callous, indifferent. He raised his shoulders tensely and then the hunch changed into a shrug. "Oh, I'd have told you in time, if I'd found one grain of the warmth and understanding I wanted in you. Perhaps not that night, even if you'd been receptive. It was hardly a topic for a wedding night. And it was too close, too hard to talk about."

"Tell me now. It might help me to understand why you attacked me. . . why you walked out on our wedding night."

"Understand?" He gave a harsh unfeeling laugh. "Frankly, I don't suppose you'll truly understand now, any more than you understood that night. Understanding is not one of your strong points." Then, raking a hand through his hair, he added roughly, "But yes, I can talk about it now. Why not? It's time you learned that the whole world doesn't revolve around your face and person. It all came about right after I'd come to inspect this property. It was about a week before our wedding. . . ."

Ben had returned to Mahé with the former owner of the coco-de-mer grove, intending to make connections on a regular outward flight to Mombasa and thence to London. Delayed by some aggravating red tape to do with sale and transfer of the property, he had missed his flight.

"It happened that I couldn't get another flight immediately—those flights aren't an everyday thing, and for some reason the bookings were heavy that week. I wanted to leave my ketch in Mahé for use on our honeymoon, so that method of travel was out, too. I discovered that there was a down-at-heels tramp schooner bound for Mombasa and leaving that same day. It was to deliver some stores to an island in the Amirantes group—those are low coral atolls that form part of the Seychelles—but after that it would be heading directly for the east coast of Africa and should get me there in time to catch a flight for London. It wasn't a regular passenger ship—none of the comforts of home—but I booked on.

"A small family group had also taken passage on the old schooner: a grandmother, mother and two children, one of them a baby still in arms, all of East Indian extraction. They were on their way to join the father of the family, a shopkeeper who had decided because of assorted financial difficulties to emigrate to Mombasa, where he had relatives. The father had gone on ahead to establish himself; the rest of the family were following in leisurely but unluxurious fashion, with all their worldly possessions.

"It was a stinking old tramp that smelled of iodine and copra. The captain, two Malagasy natives for crew, the five passengers and an old one-eyed ginger tom—one of those fiercely independent ship's cats that's more at home on sea than on land."

The cat, of course. Ben had been thinking about

that cat, the memory no doubt triggered by Tasha's own words on their wedding night. There was no need to ask Ben if some disaster had befallen; the instinctive knowledge vibrated through Tasha's bonuses.

"It was wretched weather, mean seas, and in that stretch of water, the currents come at you from two continents, even at the best of times. At some point during the first night the engine conked out altogether, leaving us with sail power only. I wasn't concerned at the time; I'd seen worse seas. And I was busy below with the East Indian family, who were huddled in the fo'c'sle cabin, miserably seasick. The baby was bawling, and the others were too prostrated and terror-stricken to do much but huddle into their bunks and whimper. They were all nearly out of their wits, for they'd never been at sea before. Well, at that point, what was happening up top was the least of my worries. So I didn't discover until later that the captain had taken to the bottle that night due to personal problems. The Malagasy natives were very handy with the sheets, but neither of them had a master's ticket to sail in those dangerous shoaling reefs; only a small handful of men do. I might have helped if I had known, but. . . ."

Ben sat down heavily on the end of the bed. He seemed almost to have forgotten Tasha's presence; it was as if he was recounting the ordeal to himself. His voice was flat, unemotional.

"The seas grew calmer during the night. The Indians slept and I did, too, just curled in a corner on some old gunnysacks, because the old grandmother begged me not to leave them alone. We struck the coral reef just at dawn. Ripped us open like a giant can opener. The coral kept us from sinking at once—we were impaled on it—but that was a temporary situation; one wave and we'd be done for. I herded the family up top. That took a few precious minutes, and by the time I got them all onto that slippery deck, the crew had already swung the lifeboat out on its davits...and somehow the damn thing had landed upside down, hurting one of the crew in process. He wasn't unconscious, but he was bleeding badly.

"There wasn't much choice, because the next wave sucked up the wreck and there we were, all in the water. The Indian family couldn't swim, but the captain had sobered some, and between us we got them all to the lifeboat—the baby, too. The wounded Malagasy managed to make it on his own, but the other crewman just...vanished into the seas."

"And the cat?" Tasha said in the lowest of voices, when Ben fell silent with his own painful recollections.

"The cat made it, too...somehow. He had a strong instinct for survival, and cats can swim when forced. So there we were—seven of us and a half-drowned cat. It was a very small lifeboat, and upside down, but at least it was floating, and free of the coral—a big, jagged, dangerous reef we couldn't possibly take the lifeboat over. There was a low coral island within view—we could see the tops of the cocopalms as the dawn broke through. We didn't know if it was inhabited or not. And if there were inhabitants, they couldn't know we were there on the other side of their barrier reef unless they had a lookout in a treetop.

"Our only hope was to find a channel through to the lagoon, and that meant circling the reef. We had no oars—they'd been lost in the confusion—and we knew we had to kick our way through the water. Besides, there wasn't room for everyone to crowd on top of that tippy boat bottom. The Indian family were on the keel, all hunched over it like dripping sacks of potatoes, along with the wounded Malagasy. That wasn't because he was incapable of helping; it was as a precaution—a futile one, as it turned out. The captain and I stayed in the water.

"Two men kicking and a tippy burdened useless boat with a bunch of frightened people who couldn't swim crouching on top.... By last light, we still hadn't found a channel, even though the island looked so close. By then there were cries of thirst—not from the mother or the grandmother, but the children. The mother nursed the baby, and that helped. Oh. . . I don't think you want to hear the rest. Perhaps you can imagine it."

"Please tell me," said Tasha quietly.

"The sharks came just before sundown. Tigers—not big ones, but vicious. That's when the captain went. Why him and not me? I don't know. I was wearing dark trousers, and perhaps that helped. He just. . . went. . . with a shocked look on his face, and then there was fresh blood in the water, so. . . .

"I climbed on the keel with the others; there's a difference between courage and sheer foolhardiness. None of us could sleep that night for fear of slipping from the boat. By dawn the tiger sharks had gone. And so I went in again. Well, it had to be done, didn't it? The backwash of the tide had pulled us farther from the reef, and the others were beginning to suffer from exposure. I realized by then that I should have struck out for shore the previous day—I could have made it over the reef on my own—but by this time, I didn't know if I had the strength to make it to the island and back again, should it turn out to be uninhabited. So I stuck with the boat; I had strength enough to hang on and kick.

"It rained some that morning and that helped; at least nobody went mad with thirst. At noon the wounded Malagasy went in the water, too; he was no longer trailing fresh blood, and he could see I was getting nowhere much on my own. That day it didn't happen until midafternoon."

"The Malagasy?" whispered Tasha when the silence had stretched to breaking point.

"First it was the East Indian boy, the nine-year-old." Ben's voice was bleak and blank now, devoid of emotion entirely. "I guess he fell asleep and dragged his foot in the water, and. . . who knows why sharks attack one thing and not another. First thing we knew, he was in the water, screaming. It was a small hammerhead that time. It circled for another attack. We got the boy out of the water, but the blood brought more hammerheads, and makos, too.

They got the Malagasy—he was too weak from his wounds to move very fast—but I managed to get out of the water.

"The boy died that night, and the grandmother, too, from exposure. I think it was that night, or, or...I don't know.... I lost track of time. It only comes back in flashes. And then it was morning again...I think it was morning. I remember the sun hot on my head and my body waterlogged and salt caked on my mouth. The baby cried a little—he was the only one with strength to do so, for his mother had nursed him off and on, and he had been able to sleep in her arms. I didn't attempt to push the dead bodies into the water—not because of sharks by then, but because I just...didn't care. I sat there for a long time, doing nothing. And then...I looked up and I saw that ginger tom. He was looking at me with that one eye—just looking at me, in that accusing way cats have, as though he expected me to do something."

"So you got back in the water," whispered Tasha, knowing.

"Somebody had to do it," Ben said dully. "By then I didn't care about sharks. I only cared about sleep. I think I did sleep, too, hanging there in the water, kicking out of sheer reflex. We never did find the channel. They told me later that I passed right by it, and that's when somebody spotted us from a coco-palm. The island was being worked for copra, and there were men in the trees—we'd finally reached the inhabited side by circling the reef. I just remember waking on the way to shore in a pirogue. The woman and the baby were in the boat, too. And the one-eyed tom.

"There was a radio on the island, and they called for help, a flying boat. The mother died before it arrived. I really don't remember much of what happened after that, except little snatches. Delivering the baby to its father in Mombasa—that was the worst. Catching a flight to London.... I shouldn't have tried, I suppose, but I was working on sheer nerves by then. I knew I had to be somewhere, and I could hardly remember why. I was numb, too; the horror hadn't struck me yet. Somewhere I acquired a bottle of pep pills, and that kept me going. I took handfuls of the things."

"Then you hadn't been drinking."

"No."

"Oh, Ben, if you'd told me that, any of that, I'm not inhuman, I'd have—"

Ben's fist smashed into the soft surface of the bed, obliterating her words. His voice turned thunderous, too. "What difference would it have made? What the hell difference? You didn't walk out on me. I walked out on you, remember?"

Tasha placed trembling fingers to her mouth, as compassion for those long-ago sufferings warred with a great coldness caused by the unforgiving anger in his words. Ben did nothing to make the moment easier for her. He stood up, leaving the bed, and returned to a moody contemplation of the storm-battered coco-de-mer grove beyond the window.

"Ben," she whispered at last, with hurt in her heart and in her throat, "please... please make love to me now."

CHAPTER ELEVEN

HE CROSSED THE ROOM—lithe, strong, silent—and stood towering beside the bed, looking down at where she sat, a sheet still clutched to her breast. In his very silence was contempt. Outside, the wind howled and the great fronds clashed, but here there was no sound save the wild beating of Tasha's heart.

A hard hand reached down, bronze against the white sheet, and plucked it away from her fingers. She did nothing to hide herself now. But when his silent scrutiny went on too long, she turned her head slightly away toward the wall, letting her dark hair swing forward a little to conceal her anguish. He reached for her then, pulling her to her feet until she stood naked beside him in the lamplit hut, her tall slender body matched and dwarfed by his greater height. His hands ran slowly over her breasts and her hips, a wordless proclamation of possession that she did not try to deny.

And then, leaving her standing, he shed his own clothes and thrust them aside, revealing the virile body in all its intimate detail. What Tasha with her dim-sighted velvet eyes could not see, she could imagine—the memorized textures of roughness and smoothness and hardness that had such power to disturb.

Standing close once more, so close that she could feel the warmth of him even where their bodies did not touch, he insinuated his fingers into her hair. Taking his time, he started at her ears and combed his way down the length of the dark tresses, unhurriedly, letting his fingers linger along the way. And then, he wound a silky skein around his wrist, issuing a silent command with his hand that forced her nakedness to melt against his and her face to tilt upward toward his smoking loveless eyes.

"Open your lips," he commanded roughly as his mouth descended to claim its promised due. This time there were no soft phrases of love, no gentling with words of praise. His tongue took her with a deep mastery, extracting her submission with a kiss that did not end even when he pulled her down to the waiting bed.

It took no more than his hands surging over her breasts to turn her taut as a bowstring, no more than a nudge of his knee to ready her for their union. She clung, moaning, uncaring that he made love with his hands and not with his heart.

"So you weren't lying," he murmured in that poised moment before he made her his. His face hovered close, inches close, so that she could discern the thick separate lashes, the texture of his skin. Against her bared breasts lay the heat and the weight of him, the rough male hardness of his chest. In her hair his fingers were twined, holding her in readiness for his onslaught. "I wasn't sure before. Should I say I'm glad there's been no man before me? Then I'll say it. I'm glad...."

But was it only another way to hurt? His sensuous mouth crushed down over hers to still the soft incoherent cry that parted her lips. There was punishment and passion in the way he took her then—ardently, urgently, imperative in his needs. The virile strength that pinned her to the bed cared only for its own appeasement. And yet, when his hands coursed over her breasts, when his deepening tongue plundered her mouth, when his male body drove to possess her flesh, she forgot all else but the rising rapturous enslavement of her senses.

He cared for his pleasures, not hers. The illusion of love was there in the commanding lips, the demanding hands; and yet he had brought no part of his heart to bed. She knew it was so, and yet she forgot as some primitive part of her answered the savage surge in him. And if it was an illusion it was a sweet one, rising like a true strong song within her, until she found the magical moment that she sought, shuddering with ecstasy in his arms....

With passion slaked, Ben's body at last grew still. Tasha lay clasped in his embrace, moving her hands slowly over his muscled shoulders, not wanting the moment nor the illusion to end. Unthinkingly, she whispered what was in her heart.

"I love you, Ben."

And in that moment she knew it was true, that it had been true for many years; that in her heart she had never stopped loving him at all.

Ben raised his head from the hollow of her throat, until he could see into her eyes. "Tell me how much you love me," he murmured with those lips that had tortured her so exquisitely. "Tell me. I want to hear."

Perhaps the twist of his mouth should have warned her, or the smoking intensity of his gaze. But Tasha was as possessed in soul as she had been in body; she wanted only to please. "I think I've always loved you," she whispered.

"More," commanded Ben. "Tell me more."

"I love you with every breath in my body," she trembled, fearful of her own vulnerability even as she said it.

"Again," he directed.

But she had admitted too much already, and so she remained silent this time, sickening inside as the cruel twist deepened on his mouth, and the body that had spent its passion on hers at last rolled away. He came to a semi-reclining position beside her, lamplight gilding his long naked body to a pagan bronze, gleaming on the hard cording of muscles and the lean masculine flanks whose power she now knew so well.

With his free hand he forced her face to turn to his. For a time he lay in silence, studying her, raking her with contemptuous eyes.

"Love, Tasha? For all your fine words I don't believe you're capable of such feelings." His voice was harsh, his words hateful, his intent hurtful. It was as if he, too, had been possessed, but by some demon that wanted to wreak vengeance for the past. "Desire, arousal, physical passion, mating instinct, sexual fulfillment. . .call it what you want, but don't pretend your emotions were involved in what just happened between us. Don't confuse love with your primary biological urges.''

Some vestige of pride kept the tears from trembling to Tasha's eyes, but that was her lone defense. Ben had penetrated the shell too well; there was no going back to the brittle artificial exterior that had protected her for so long.

''I was a virgin, Ben,'' she whispered, begging for some compassion from that remorseless face.

''So I remarked,'' he noted callously. ''Aren't you going to thank me for making a woman of you? Say something light and clever, chalking it up to experience? Surely it amuses you to lose your chastity to the man who used to be your husband! Come, Tasha, laugh at least; show me how shallow your feelings are. You're not really capable of love, are you? If you were, there'd be tears.''

''Ben, please. . .!''

Perhaps some note of misery in her plea reached him then. Suddenly the glint of scorn vanished. His voice softened, and his expression, too. ''Could it be that I've been mistaken about you?'' he murmured. His hand began to toy with a long strand of hair that lay against the pillow; he touched an earlobe fleetingly. ''Possibly your feelings are quite genuine. If so, I've done you an injustice. Can it be your emotions are true. . .?''

He leaned forward and his lips brushed against hers softly, slowly, temptingly, until with a small sob deep in her throat she responded, clinging with relief that his small cruelties had come to an end. Surely, now, he had had his vengeance?

"Don't you realize," Ben murmured after a time, "that I can't trust myself to admit how I feel until I'm sure of you? You're so invulnerable, my love, so capable of destroying a man with that bright laughter of yours. Surely now you can understand how I must have felt that night."

"Yes, oh yes," she whispered, happiness singing in her heart. She stroked the nape of his neck, telling her love with her eyes.

"Then you still love me, in spite of everything I've said? It takes genuine feeling to survive such bitter words."

"Yes, I do."

"Then tell me so," he muttered, closing her eyes with a trail of tender fiery kisses.

"I love you, Ben; I always will. . . ."

His kisses came at once to a halt and he detached himself from her arms. "Good," he smiled mockingly. "I told you I wanted to hear it once again."

Tasha stared at him, dumb with horror at her own lack of perception. Her heart contracted with the cold knowledge of how much she had put herself in his power; but now, there was no taking back what she had admitted—once too often.

"Forgive me if I don't return your feelings. Do you expect me to vow undying love, just because you've put your heart—what there is of it—into my keeping? Do you think I care for you at all? Or that I ever will?''

There was no refuge for her now but the pretense that his words did not wound. Somehow she managed to empty her face of emotion as she listened to those words, each one a knife twisting in her heart.

"I wanted you physically and I took you—physically. I'd have done the same for almost any woman who asked. And you did ask, just as you'll ask again, next time I decide I want you. Just as you'll tell me you love me when that's what I want to hear. A very amusing situation altogether...."

"Do you hate me so much?" she whispered, her face a frozen mask.

"Hate?" He laughed softly, smokily, and bent his head to her breast. She tried to twist away, tried to hide the quick response of her flesh, but it was too late; already his hand was seeking and stroking and arousing her anew, and she was gasping with needs she could not hope to conceal.

"Does this feel like hate?" he muttered huskily, as his tongue teased and a treacherous nipple sprang to the touch. "It's only desire, my sweet. Illicit desire. The forbidden fruit of the Garden of Eden...."

EULALIE MATERIALIZED late the following morning. Over breakfast Ben had been silent and brooding, and shortly thereafter had vanished in search of the fisherman Aristide, leaving Tasha resting alone in the hut to nurse a throbbing headache.

The headache was the aftermath of a poor night's

sleep. Lying beside Ben in the darkness of night, sick at heart and wakeful long after his rhythmic breathing told her that he slept, she had relived every agonizing memory a thousand times. Knowing now of the terrible nightmare he had lived through so long ago, she found it easy enough to excuse his past behavior. But why did he find it so impossible to excuse hers? Why did he still hate her? She knew that no pleas and protestations would alter his contempt; he wanted to hate her.

And she wanted to hate him, if only because hatred would be a defense against many things. Yet in the night, despite his intentional cruelties, she had longed to cling to him, to cry out the sorrow in her soul and the hurt in her heart... but how could she express such emotions to Ben, who had been the cause of them all? And so this morning she, too, had taken refuge in silence, not wanting Ben to know the depth of her feelings.

She was lying on the bed, fully clad, when the sensation of being watched became very strong. She opened her eyes, and there was the wrinkled raisin of a face, peering at her through one glassless window where the shutters had been opened to admit the warm humid air of a morning where storms were only a memory.

"Oh, oh, oh," moaned Eulalie sadly, shaking the wispy halo of white hair that was framed by the window, against a backdrop of trees. "To see you makes an old woman weep."

Tasha overcame the moment of initial surprise and

struggled to a sitting position. "Eulalie! Please, won't you come in?"

Soon they were sitting at the rough table, sharing the coffee Ben had left warming over a spirit burner. Eulalie ran a loving hand over the chair Tasha had pulled out for her.

"The wood of the takamaka tree," she said in a tremulous wistful voice, "makes a very fine chair."

"I tried to find you yesterday," Tasha told her, "to give you one of these in payment for your *gris-gris*."

"*Gris-gris?*" Eulalie looked vague for a moment. "Did you ask me for a *gris-gris*? I forgot to bring it. You see, it is so long since anyone has asked—"

"You already gave me one," Tasha reminded her quickly.

The old eyes turned crafty. "But you must be mistaken," she wavered, "or perhaps you are trying to make fun of this old *bonne femme di bois*? If you had a *gris-gris* you would not have the eyes of sorrow. Or...." Her face crumpled a little and her eyes started to wander as she tried to recollect. "Or... is it that I gave you a *gris-gris* and it did not work? For I can see that it did not work."

Eulalie's expression of self-doubt tugged at the heartstrings, and Tasha answered carefully, trying to be truthful and kind all at once. "You wanted a pinch of sand from someone's footprints," she said, "and as I couldn't provide it, you made the *gris-gris* without. So really, it's my own fault."

Eulalie looked enormously relieved. She patted the

lap of her patched dress as if to remind herself that she was still there and said, "Oh, of course. Now I remember. Well, give it back to me and I will fix it for you. And this time, I myself will find the pinch of sand, for I saw the tall man going toward the beach. Oh, oh, oh, it will be a good *gris-gris* then."

"I'm sorry, Eulalie, I...lost it," Tasha euphemized, "and really, I don't need a *gris-gris* at all."

"No *gris-gris*?" Eulalie looked disappointed all over again. "Well, then, I cannot...." She eyed the chair longingly and fought a visible battle with herself.

"It's yours anyway," Tasha said.

"No, no, no." Eulalie shook her aged head emphatically. "First, we solve your problem."

"I don't have the kind of problem anyone can help me with," Tasha said, despairing. "It's very good of you, Eulalie, but—"

"Oh, oh, oh. Do you think there is no wisdom in this old gray head just because my memory is gone?" She contemplated Tasha, blinking and sighing plaintively. "Oh, you need help. I have seen your eyes of sorrow and I know. Tomorrow I will make you a proper *gris-gris*, say some spells perhaps, and if you will only let me pierce your ear...oh, that will bring happiness to your eyes."

"My eyes are fine," Tasha protested, beginning to feel trapped. "It's just that I have a headache. I don't want my ear pierced and I don't want another *gris-gris*. I have no desire to destroy an enemy."

Eulalie leaned forward and peered probingly into

Tasha's face. "Why do you pretend to an old woman?" she asked, her voice trembling. "When you asked for the first *gris-gris* it was not to bring down an enemy, but to capture the heart of a man. You are trying to confuse me."

Oh, Lord, thought Tasha, feeling hysteria and despair rising inside. How could she be kind to Eulalie without accepting her offer of help?

"Oh, oh, oh, you think me an interfering old woman. But it is only because I wish to see you happy. Do you think I know nothing of love? I will tell you a story I once heard, and then you will understand...."

Eulalie closed her eyes and began to rock back and forth, crooning and curving her frail arms in front of her patchwork dress almost as if she were cradling a child. When she spoke her voice was a singsong, her words chosen more surely, as sometimes happens when the very old speak of the past. It was as if she had traveled to some other time and space in her mind.

"She was so small, that little baby, so small and so helpless. Why did her real mother leave her there in that basket woven of palm leaves at that little hut in the woods? It was a poor little hut without a chair, but perhaps someone knew that the woman who lived alone had love in her heart to give. Oh, she was a witchwoman and not too young even then. Many thought her mad, but if she was mad it was only with loneliness, and because she longed for a child of her own. And oh, how she loved that little baby, as if it were her own daughter...."

With a certainty as clear as if Eulalie had spoken in the first person, Tasha realized that the old woman was speaking of herself. How many years ago had these things happened? Eulalie was a very, very old woman and yet, oddly, it was not hard to visualize her in her middle years, lavishing a foundling with love.

"She left her own plate empty to fill the belly of the child. And when the child grew, she cut up her own *robe la messe* to make a little dress, so that the girl could go to school without wearing rags. Oh, she wanted her daughter to read and write so that she would not be ignorant, too. The old witchwoman even stole at times, though she knew it was very very wicked...oh, oh, oh...but perhaps the saints will forgive that sin, for did she not do this from love? It is hard to see a child go hungry. And she taught the child things, too many things, about the roots and herbs she kept in the hut. Oh, if she had not taught those things...."

Eulalie wrapped her arms around her body, as if comforting herself, and spent some minutes moaning softly before she resumed her narrative. Tasha's throat lumped with sympathy; for the time being she was not thinking of her own problems.

"As the child grew," Eulalie went on at last, "she became very lovely, until many of the young men of the island looked upon her with lust. There were none who wished to marry, for who would want the daughter of a *bonne femme di bois* who had not a single chair in her home and who could not afford a wedding? But there were some who wanted her to leave her mother and live *en ménage*. Oh, her mother warned her. Being a poor girl, if she wished to find a husband, she must remain a virgin. For what other reason would a man take her to the church? Oh yes, her mother warned her! But she was sixteen, and she had gone to school, and...oh, oh, oh...I think she was a little ashamed of her ignorant mother the witchwoman....

"One day the girl saw a fine tall man emerging naked from the sea, wrestling a large turtle. He was a young man but a man full-grown, not like the lads who had courted her until then. The water shone on the strong young rippling brown of his arms and lay in beads on the hard flat belly, and these things filled her with desire. She wanted him; but in that moment she remembered the words of the witchwoman who was her mother and with a heavy heart she turned her footsteps away."

Eulalie's eyes now came open, wearing a faraway and rueful look. "But the man saw her and wanted her, too. Oh, she was beautiful, with her hair so long and black and sheened like a pearl...like yours...." Here, Eulalie reached forward and touched Tasha's hair once, lightly. "Oh, yes, you remind me of her, with her limbs so straight and slender and her breasts so proud! Is it a wonder that he wanted her? Oh, oh, oh...and because he was filled with desire, he followed her and spoke to her of a love he did not feel in his heart. He took her then, and again, and again at other times.... Oh, oh, why did she not tell her mother, who could have given her wise potions of love to win his heart? She might have been saved if she had told.

"For at once, when they had lain together that first time and she had lost that part of herself that all men want in a wife, she knew that the man's words were no more than the whisperings of the wind, and that his hand on her heart was no more than the pulse of his own pleasure, and that the lovemaking of his body was no more than the crashing of a wave on a lonely reef. Does a wave care where it crashes? Does the wind care where it blows?"

The parched eyes had closed again, and Eulalie spoke as if in a trance, with a poetry in the quivering cadence of her words that added to their haunting sadness.

"Sometimes, after he had taken her, she would cry quietly in his arms. And yet, when he kissed her tears away and told her to meet him again, she forgot that he had not offered marriage...oh, oh, oh. And she told none of these things to her mother until it was too late. One day the man decided to go to Mahé, and he asked the girl to go with him. What was she to do? She would have followed him to the ends of the earth, to the four corners of the winds. She bore the seed of one month in her womb, and she did not want her mother to know. She went with the man and she did not even say goodbye to her mother. Oh, oh, it broke the old witchwoman's heart."

Eulalie's recitation came to a halt as some memory

appeared to move her deeply. "Did she never come back?" Tasha asked quietly at last.

Eulalie came out of her trancelike state, blinking with confusion. "What? Oh...yes. The witch-woman stole some money and went to Mahé, too, and found her daughter. The man had deserted her to take a job on a ship. And it was then that the *bonne femme di bois* learned of all that had gone before. She brought her daughter home, sorrowing in her heart. Oh, the *gris-gris* and the incantations then! But it was too late. For who can win the heart of a man when the man cannot be found?"

Eulalie's purse of a mouth trembled with emotion. "Too late the girl learned that there is sometimes much wisdom in the words of an ignorant witch-woman. And too late the witchwoman learned that there is sometimes little wisdom in teaching a girl the arts she is not ready to know. For, in the sickness of her heart, the girl waited until she was alone in the hut one day, and then she took something that her mother had taught her would start the cramp and finish the life that grew in her womb. The poison in the bark of the avocado? Ergot? Yes, I think it must have been ergot, for there was a little ergot in the hut until I threw it out afterward, along with every other poison I could find. Oh, oh, oh, it is so hard to re-member, it is too sad to remember...."

Had Eulalie's daughter died? It seemed a painful but inescapable conclusion. Ergot could kill. In the Middle Ages many thousands had died, and many more thousands had been driven mad, during epidemics of ergot poisoning caused by disease in grain. That much Tasha remembered from old French history lessons; even in this century there had been an outbreak of ergotism in the south of France.

And no doubt Eulalie blamed herself for her daughter's death. She was wringing her hands now and moaning softly; and in the tracery of wrinkles on her face, there was a very real pain.

"Oh, oh, oh, I think she wanted to die, for yes, she had truly loved her faithless lover...and you think I cannot understand about love?" Eulalie's lashless old eyes were rheumy with tears, and a claw of a hand clutched at Tasha's sleeve. "Do you think I ask for payment in chairs? I would give all the chairs in the world if I could undo the great evil that was done that day. Do you wonder that I wish to see a lover happy? Oh, oh, oh, I am an old, old woman and it is all I have left to give. To make a lover happy, that is all I ask...and when I see the look in your eyes I see...those long-ago things...."

She shook her head as if to straighten her thoughts and seemed to brighten at once. "A good *gris-gris* will help you," she said hopefully. "Surely you will not refuse it now, as a favor to an old woman? Please, say yes."

Tasha nodded her acceptance, unwilling to trust herself to speech. At the moment she could have refused Eulalie nothing, not even the piercing of an ear.

Eulalie's face crinkled into a pleased smile. "This time you must not lose it," she warned. "And when it works... well, perhaps one little chair.... Oh, oh, oh, why are you upset by the ramblings of an old woman? It was only a tale told to me long, long ago, when I was very young.... I think...yes, perhaps my mother told me...or did I imagine it all? Yes, perhaps I imagined it, it is not really true...."

When Eulalie took her leave a few minutes later, Tasha threw herself on the cot and indulged in a good cry.

CHAPTER TWELVE

BY NIGHT SHE SUFFERED the practiced cruelties of his lips, and by day the caustic bite of his contempt. Tasha plumbed the depths of misery and soared to the heights of passion. She could not say him nay. She had tasted the forbidden fruit of the Garden of Eden, and the taste had become an addiction, a drug to her senses—as if the fruit of the coco-de-mer was indeed the aphrodisiac men had once believed it to be.

Between those times he claimed her, it was only the remnants of a pride stretched too thin that kept her head high and her eyes dry in his presence. It was as though he wanted to hurt her, to humble her, to destroy her. When they lay twined together in the night she could deny him nothing. Those were the heights—when his fevered kisses scorched her flesh and his warm breath mingled with hers and his strong arms forced her to submit once more. And it was force of a kind: not the force of superior physical strength, but the force of a love she could not hide from herself or from him. The need to know Ben's embrace was like jungle drums pounding in her blood. At one touch of those masterful hands, her pulses leaped with desire, her flesh trembled with ardor, her body melted and cried out for completion.

And yet, in those dark nights were also the depths.

"Do you think," he murmured once, as she drifted into sleep in his arms, "that because I enjoy making love to you I'll never let you go? Oh, my sweet, you're wrong. I turned my back on you seven years ago and I'll do it again—as soon as I've had my fill of you. But I'm not sated yet. Turn this way, Tasha, I want to kiss you again...."

His kisses were wine, his hands like brands, his lips like instruments of exquisite torture. And she soared once more, reaching the heights—only to be dashed to the ground.

"There have been other women, but then, you know that, don't you? Some that pleased me more than you. Strange that for all your sophisticated airs, you're so naive in bed. Come, I'll show you what pleases me...."

He seemed to have control not only over her body but over her mind, over her soul, over her very being. How could she want to please him? And yet she did.

The little defiances of the first two days seemed like impotent gestures now; the artifices of her other life were put aside. Other life? Max seemed a million light-years away; it was he who now seemed unreal, and the otherworldly bewitchment of the life she led the only reality. She longed for the week to end, and yet she dreaded it with every fiber of her being. How could she leave Ben—lover and torturer, captor and conjurer, whose very touch set her trembling flesh on fire? She loved him, and all the unhappiness in the world could not change that.

She longed to put herself beyond the reach of Ben's dark influence, and yet, and yet. . . .

Eulalie had delivered another *gris-gris* as unsuccessful as the first. For three days Tasha, unsuperstitious though she was, kept it in her pocket. Why not, as nothing else seemed to penetrate Ben's ironclad affections? And then one morning when the week neared its end, she crumpled the brown paper into a small ball, flung it into the dying coals of the breakfast fire and watched it burn with a hurting heart.

"What was that?" asked Ben, emerging from the hut in time to see the gesture and the hungry flaring up of flame that licked and devoured the useless charm.

"A pair of eyelashes," Tasha lied.

"Could it be," Ben said mockingly, "that you're trying to please me?"

"I don't think that's possible."

"Yes, it is." He stood leaning against the wall of the hut, tall, desirable, exerting his virile attraction with no physical contact at all. Obeying an unuttered command, Tasha turned her head until her eyes locked with his. He tilted his head in the smallest of beckoning gestures.

"Come here," he said in a husky imperative voice that seemed to travel to the roots of Tasha's being and left her helpless to disobey.

And when he had parted her lips in a deep kiss and

run his hands over her body in a journey that proclaimed her his once more, he murmured, "You pleased me last night."

"More than—" But she bit back the question; she did not want comparisons with other women. She buried her face against the roughness of hair in the V of his shirt. "How well did I please you?" she whispered, aching for a compliment.

"Well enough that I'm considering keeping you after all." His casual words awakened a quick joy, as did the idle way his hands asserted ownership of her body. Then, with the studied cruelty that had become a part of the bitter game he played, he added, "You've become an amusing plaything, Tasha, now that you've fallen in love with me."

"I haven't," she tried to lie, despairing.

"Can you deny it now? You told me so again last night... and again, and again...."

"Only because you... told me to say those words."

"Have you no mind of your own?" he taunted, lifting her chin to look into her face. His eyes were darkly derisive, scornful. "Only a few days ago you were all tart tongue and bright defense." His mocking smile faded and he commanded, "Tell me now. I want to hear it once again."

"Ben, don't," she said, suffering and trying to hide this with the droop of her lashes.

"Tell me and then I'll decide whether to keep you."

"I love you," she said in a low voice, knowing in

advance that there would be no like response from him.

"How much?"

"More than is good for the safety of my soul," she said, her voice barely audible.

"Do you want to stay with me?"

"Yes," she said, cringing inwardly even as she made the admission.

"Good—because then you'll be in accord with my plans." His voice turned cold, deliberately hurtful. "Yes, my love, I think I will keep you a little longer. Not very long, but long enough."

Tasha pulled right away and turned, pulses pounding, so that he could not see her face. It was terrible, the power he had over her. Terrible, the way he could raise her hopes and then dash them all at one time. "Long. . . enough?" she said, trying to sound casual.

"A month, two?" Ben's hands came from behind and captured her waist, pulling her back against him. His brown fingers spread possessively over the hollow of her stomach. "Long enough to confirm that my seed is growing in you. And it will be soon, if it isn't already. It amuses me to think of you bearing my child, tied to my child—"

"Ben, please. . . ."

He bent his head to tantalize an earlobe. "Oh, you can pretend for your smart London friends that the child is Max's, that you and he anticipated your vows." He murmured the words softly, as if they were love words instead of daggers in her heart. "That should make an intriguing piece of gossip. Or you can tell them the truth—that might be even more amusing. I can imagine you laughing about your love child with that bright sophisticated little laugh of yours. Why don't I hear it now? Laugh, Tasha.''

She longed to laugh if only to conceal the power he had to hurt her. But the capability for such fakery had been destroyed days ago, when Ben had made her his.

"Aren't you enchanted by the idea of a love child...my child?'' Skillfully, his hard hand manipulated the zip of her jeans, allowing his spread fingers to intrude against bared flesh. "A little memento for when I walk out of your life—as I will. Laugh, Tasha.''

"Ben, don't! I don't feel like laughing." And yet, she seemed incapable of preventing his invasive fingers from having their way.

His other hand moved to explore the agonized face he could not see. "Tears, then? No? You never cry, do you? The feeling simply doesn't go that deep.''

She should have fought him then, but with his hands roving so intimately and his lips laying moist erotic patterns in the hollows of her throat, it was hard to think; especially when he was already leading her toward the hut, and the whole world was whirling in a vortex of feeling, too much feeling. . . .

Perhaps it was true that she was *amarrée*. For what but a spell could account for the fact that she could not stop him when he undressed her, and kissed her breasts, and took her once again?

"Do you think we made our little love child today?'' he murmured after it was done. ''But then, it won't truly be a love child, will it? Just a bastard. For I don't love you at all, my sweet, and I never will.''

She tried to twist away, but Ben's hands trapped her in such a way that he could watch her face. ''Ben, don't talk of a child as though. . .as though it were a bad joke.''

''A bad joke,'' he agreed with a bitter twist to his mouth. His hands dug hurtfully into the fistful of hair he had seized in order to prevent her head from turning. The brooding hatred he had once tried to hide now darkened his eyes with no attempt at concealment. ''My joke. . .living in you.''

IT WAS AT NOON of that same day, when Ben had gone into the palm grove to collect coconuts and kindling for later use, that she finally sought help. Driven at last to desperation by the cruel exchanges of the morning and finding some strength in Ben's absence, she fled the valley of the coco-de-mer.

Eulalie could not help, but perhaps Delphine could. Tasha had visited Delphine on two other occasions during the past few days, both times with intentions of asking for help. Some deeper power had always prevented her from saying the words, possibly because in her heart she had not really wanted to leave Ben. The visits, however, had served to confirm a growing friendship; and Tasha had taken comfort in Delphine's kindness, optimism and warmheartedness.

Today, because Tasha was too desperate to explain

her reasons or trust to sympathy alone, she carried with her several one-hundred rupee banknotes she had stolen hastily from one of Ben's pockets.

Delphine's eyes rounded at the sight of so much money. "But that is more than Aristide makes in a year. You will pay him so many rupees to take you to see Father Julien this afternoon, when Father Julien will be here on this island tomorrow? No person that is in her right mind would...."

Delphine bit her lip and eyed Tasha's wild and haunted expression, letting silence serve for what she was too polite to say.

"Please ask Aristide," begged Tasha. "He'll be home soon, won't he, for lunch?"

"It is not right to take money from a person who does not understand what she does," said Delphine, resisting the hand that tried to thrust the banknotes upon her.

"Delphine! With this much money you and Aristide can marry. And yes, I do understand what I'm doing. I'm not crazy, really I'm not. Oh...."

Tasha's sense of hopelessness became acute as she realized that her blandishments were not working. Seeing the stubborn and disbelieving look on Delphine's face, she switched tactics. Could she play on Delphine's superstitious nature? "Well, perhaps I am...a little. But...but...I have some magic power too."

It was no more than a bluff, but it kindled a slightly different expression, one of mild awe, in Delphine's eyes. Tasha quickly tried to follow through on her brief moment of advantage. "With the power that is in me," she declared, "you can't refuse me...*anything*!"

Delphine backed away a foot or so and looked at Tasha's slender waistline, measuring it. She pursed her lips, and shook her head knowingly. "But you do not look as though you are with child. It is true that, if you are with child, it would be very bad to refuse, no matter what you asked, in case you caused me to break out."

Was there some Seychelles superstition involving pregnancy? In her desperation, Tasha had no qualms about misrepresenting her physical state. She pounced on the opportunity, even though she was not sure what kind of an outbreak she was supposed to cause. "But I am expecting a child," she lied, "even though you can't see it yet. And if you refuse me, I'll...I *will* cause you to break out, you and Aristide Bruleau, too!"

"Oh," moaned Delphine, wringing her hands. Her honest face looked unhappy but as stubborn as ever. "All the same, we cannot accept your money, not even to prevent the pimples."

"What is this talk of pimples?" came a deeply modulated man's voice in understandable but accented French, deferring to Tasha's presence. Tasha turned to see the well-knit figure of Aristide Bruleau emerging from the trees, the morning's catch in his hand. He smiled and nodded pleasantly at Tasha, then handed the string of fish to Delphine.

"Now, what is this foolishness?" Like many

Creoles, Aristide spoke a Seychelles patois most of the time but was capable of switching to traditional French when the occasion demanded.

"She is pregnant," said Delphine, her normal cheerfulness fully restored. "And she will give us pimples if we refuse to help her."

"I offered money," Tasha inserted quickly.

Aristide turned his attention first to Delphine. "Foolish woman!" he scolded her sternly. "I wonder that this fine young *dame* does not laugh at your never-ending nonsense! I refused you many things years ago when you were with child, and I never had a single pimple."

"That is because I always forgave you before they had time to appear," Delphine said complacently.

"Pah! It is a silly superstition!"

"You call it superstition today, but look in the mirror tomorrow!"

"And if I see a single pimple," warned Aristide, "I will throw you out the door and find a *ménagère* who has put such nonsense behind her! Now, why have you refused to help?"

"If she had just asked for help I would have said yes," returned Delphine, sulking a little at Aristide's reprimand, "but she offered so much money for your service that I thought it was only the *malfaisance* speaking. Remember, she is mad."

Aristide rolled his eyes to heaven and turned to Tasha. "Forgive my silly woman. It is she who is a little mad, when money is so scarce! Now, what is this service for which you wish to pay?"

THE PIROGUE WAS ANCHORED in shallow water, about twenty feet from shore. It seemed markedly prone to tipping, and that Tasha clambered in at all was perhaps a measure of her need to escape. As a non-swimmer, she certainly should not have done so without a lifejacket. But at this moment in time, the torments to which Ben had been subjecting her seemed potentially more destructive than any dangers of the deep.

Aristide pulled in the great stone, noosed with rope, that served as an anchor; the pirogue rocked alarmingly. Tasha crouched in the bottom of the boat and hardly noticed when some water slopped over the side; her jeans legs and sandals were already thoroughly soaked from wading through the shallows.

"How long will it take to reach Father Julien's island?" she asked anxiously.

"Not too long," said Aristide cheerfully. "True, there is little wind today to push my sails, but there is always the paddle. And as you see, I am a man of strong arms. I have paddled that distance and more many a time."

Tasha curled low into the pirogue, too miserable with her own thoughts to pay much attention to the course Aristide was setting. As he had predicted, the sail was of little use. He remained in the lagoon, aiming northward in order to round the island of Mystique; the second island could be reached through a channel on the far side. There were several channels through the reef surrounding Mystique; that had been explained by Delphine who in the last analysis had overcome her initial reluctance to help, perhaps because of Aristide's sarcastic but affectionate suggestion that if a woman were indeed *amarrée*, she could do worse than commit herself to the good auspices of Father Julien.

Why was Ben trying to destroy her—if not in body then surely in soul? Instinctively Tasha knew that his hatred stemmed from that false little laugh she had uttered so long ago on the night of their wedding. And yet, if he had given her any clue as to the thing that had troubled him that night, she would never have laughed. Even now, knowing the full story, it seemed incongruous that he should have been thinking of a cat that survived when so many people had died.

True, it was the cat that had sent Ben back into the water, and no doubt he had been reliving that horrendous experience, but how could she have known?

Occupied with her own thoughts, she did not at once react when Aristide's strong stroking of the paddle came to a sudden halt.

After a few moments, the canoe began to lose its forward impetus, and it was then, only then, that Tasha stirred herself from her troubled reverie and raised her eyes. They were still within the lagoon, in limpid mirror-still water. Puzzled, she looked at Aristide. He was poised and watchful, his attention riveted by something beyond Tasha's head. The paddle was already back in the boat, dripping over a naked callused foot.

Even as she watched, Aristide's hand, almost visibly itching as he flexed his square brown fingers, inched toward a black metal harpoon. On his face there was an expression that reminded Tasha of the way Ben looked at her at times—an obsessive, possessive look. Only in Aristide's case it was directed at the mirror surface of the lagoon behind Tasha's back.

She turned, following the direction of his covetous gaze. Her heart stopped for fully a second.

"Devilfish," whispered Aristide, but she had not needed to be told. The canoe was sliding noiselessly toward the largest sea creature she had ever seen. She held her breath—not in alarm now, but certainly in awe. Ben had said the manta ray was not dangerous. It was impossible to do anything but admire the creature's eerie silent beauty, the slow graceful motion of the black-and-white shape gliding through the limpid turquoise water directly ahead of the pirogue's prow.

"No, Aristide," she begged, disquieted lest he should be seduced by his own cupidity to capture this creature he had been stalking unsuccessfully for so long.

"Hush," murmured Aristide, "I have never been so close."

"Aristide, you can't, not until after—"

In the next moment the harpoon sliced unerringly through the water. Tasha's first instinct was horrified pity as the beautiful ray lurched, flapped frantically and then plunged toward a clearly visible sand bottom starred with bright sea anemones. The harpoon rope uncoiled and slithered into the sea at a frightening pace, then continued to unfurl as the creature reached bottom, leveled and swerved toward the reef with all the mighty strength of which its wings were capable.

The slack was taken up in seconds, and the harpoon rope pulled taut where it was attached to the pirogue. Tasha gasped and gripped the gunwales of the boat as the ray pulled the canoe completely around and started to tug it toward a channel into the open sea.

Aristide had come to a crouch in the stern of the pirogue, and he was roaring with triumph and laughter. "Down in the canoe!" he shouted at Tasha.

"But he's pulling us out to sea!" she screamed.

"And who cares if he pulls us out to sea? We can always tow him back. Ha! He only thinks he can escape! He is dead, that devilfish, as sure as my name is Aristide Bruleau!"

"But your promise to me—"

"I will have you to Father Julien before the day is through! Ho! But he is a wild one. Ha! But look how fast he pulls us. He wears himself out, and in minutes now, he will die!"

The manta ray was no longer within the range of visibility. Its progress was strong and steady, not quite the frightening joyride Aristide's ebullient and gleeful remarks suggested. Nonetheless, it headed swiftly and surely toward its escape route, and soon the pirogue was coursing at a steady six knots over the somewhat choppier waters of the open sea.

Tasha's first premonition of terror, real terror, began the moment the pirogue left the protection of the lagoon. The second premonition came some minutes later when the towing rope went suddenly slack. At that sign, Aristide gripped a second harpoon and came to a standing crouch, ready to place a second barb.

Tasha turned her horrified gaze to the point where his eyes were fixed, right beside the pirogue. And there in the sea was the giant shape, looming upward, still thrashing, far too close to the boat. Terrified, she leaped to her feet and heard Aristide's angry oath. . . .

And in the next instant her scream was drowned by the sea. Instinct closed her mouth and her eyes and set her limbs to flailing. It all happened too swiftly to sort out the sequence until later: the scream she could not voice; the great pain as Aristide seized her long floating hair; the pull upward; the finding that her head was free of water; the choking; the helping hands; the warning shouts.

"Stay away from the lash of the tail! *Diable!* Can you not swim? Hurry, onto the boat. . . here, I will push. . . hold on. . . don't scream! That was his last lash. . . . Can you not see, the devil is dead?"

She was a sorry-looking figure indeed by the time Aristide had pushed, pulled and ladled her onto his overturned pirogue. "Sit still," he commanded from the water. "*Mon Dieu,* where is my paddle? The tail must have tossed it away...who would have thought the old sinner would have so much life in him then? Sit still! Would you faint now when you are perfectly safe?"

Aristide removed his shirt, slapped it over the far end of the pirogue and then spent several minutes swimming around the canoe, looking for his lost paddle. At last, giving up, he dived beneath the surface for seconds only and came up with a loop of rope over one shoulder. He climbed onto the overturned pirogue in some haste, squatted at the far end Hindu-fashion, and looked at her with a sad accusation in his eyes.

"Why did you stand up?" he said softly. "The pirogue is no more than a log, dug out to make a boat. It upsets very easily."

"I thought...the manta ray...." Her words came out in great spasms, between gulps of restorative air. "I thought...it...was going to...upset...the boat...."

Aristide smiled wanly and fatalistically. "Ah, well, perhaps it would have. It happens sometimes with a small pirogue like mine. So perhaps it was meant to be."

"I'm...sorry."

"What is done is done," he said ruefully but philosophically, and set himself to pulling in the rope to ensure that his catch was still intact. "We are lucky after all that there is so little wind. And I do not think it will start to blow; it is not in the air. Have courage! Rescue will come before dark."

"D-dark?" repeated Tasha faintly, her teeth chattering from nerves.

"There is no worry, you will be safe," Aristide reassured her. "True, others on the island cannot see us now, but the tide is with us. Soon enough we will drift back to where the houses are. But I am afraid, very afraid," he added wistfully, as his eyes skated toward the water where he had brought the devilfish nearly to the surface, "that by then, I will have no catch at all."

And that was when Tasha looked and saw the sharks.

How DO YOU MEASURE true terror—in seconds, in centuries, in light-years? For to Tasha it seemed endless, and yet it ended, to be replaced by a numbness that stretched through the long afternoon hours of huddling on top of the capsized pirogue.

Perhaps the numbness began shortly after Aristide prodded her with his callused toe and warned her not to close her eyes. "Because then perhaps you sleep, heh? And that is not good. To watch the sharks feed, that is nothing. But to be their meal...."

And at last his repeated importunings reached her enough that she opened her unwilling shock-dilated eyes. She had not wanted to watch the sharks in their feeding frenzy; and yet once she did so she could not wrench her gaze from the boiling of water around the body of the manta ray. At that point, with pure terror still possessing her mind, it had seemed like a bad dream come true, each nightmare facet of the scene distinct and separate and macabre beyond imagining: the slippery boat bottom lapped by small waves; the paddle floating out of reach; Aristide shaking his fist and cursing, not the fates, but each and every hammerhead and mako that tore at his long-coveted prize.

"Cursed thieves!" he cried from his miserable perch. "Can you leave a man nothing of his catch? By nightfall there will be nothing left of my beauty. . . . Oh, that a man should be so unlucky. . . ."

Tasha watched the sharks, hypnotized, horrified. The little wash of wavelets was rhythmic, rocking, cradlelike. Haunting snatches of Ben's description of his experience came back, like prophesies of her own living nightmare. *It was the boy, I guess he fell asleep. . . I lost track of time. . . by then I didn't care about sharks, I cared about sleep. . . .*

Sleep? How could a person sleep? It was when Tasha realized that she had jerked herself back from a hypnotic trance that some numbed part of her mind took over. Numbed? Perhaps simply objective; the mind was capable of absorbing only so much horror. Now her brain seemed totally clear, capable of reason. She recognized that the pirogue bottom was not so slippery after all as it dried in the sun; that if anything it was less unstable now than it had been right side up; that rescuers were sure to come, probably before nightfall, especially as the drift of the sea seemed to be taking them back toward the part of the island where they might be sighted by other inhabitants; that the sharks, though close and frenzied, were not attacking the pirogue; that they were interested in one thing only, the devilfish; and that the devilfish was dead. The sharks tearing at the carcass could even be watched with a detached and clinical admiration for the efficiency of their streamlined primeval design, one of the early marvels of genetic evolution.

At what point in that long afternoon did she begin to equate the devilfish with Ben? It was a strange transference—or possibly it was not so strange. Perhaps it occurred because she had once in anger wished a similar fate for Ben. Perhaps it was because she now knew that Ben had once nearly suffered such a fate in waters not so many hundred miles from here. Perhaps it was because of the manta ray's size and power and unconscious grace, qualities Ben, too, possessed.

And perhaps it was because, over these past days, she had begun in her subconscious to think of Ben as the devil incarnate, whispering temptations and torments in her ear. . . .

The devil is dead, Aristide had said; and Tasha watched it being devoured with a benumbed objectivity that left no room whatsoever for emotion. Only when the last of the devilfish carcass had been torn from the harpoon and the last of the sharks scattered did Tasha realize how exhausted she was.

Tired, tired, tired, weary to the very bone.

The sun had long since burned her skin and dried her hair and turned her clothes to salt-caked stiffness, and these things contributed to her fatigue. But the tiredness she felt reached deeper than her marrow; it reached into her very soul.

In one direction stretched an unending vista of blue calm water. In the other direction lay the lumping shape of the island of Mystique. The sun had slipped behind the island's uppermost peaks, advertising the swift advance of nightfall. By now the pirogue had drifted close enough that the tops of the tall coco-demer palms were perfectly visible in the cup of the valley that Ben owned. The sun told her that she and Aristide were due east of the valley.

The island no longer pulled the senses as once it had. Without emotion Tasha turned her eyes away; the peace of the blue expanse held more appeal. She did not try to fight the bone weariness that assailed her; she welcomed it.

How ironic, she thought mildly as that great peace washed into her soul, that they should be east of the valley of the Garden of Eden. For east of Eden lay the land of Nod....

CHAPTER THIRTEEN

SHE OPENED HER EYES and Ben's demoniacally lit features came into focus, leaning over her. For a disoriented moment she believed she had reached her own personal heaven, or hell. Whichever it was, it was a curiously peaceful place. She felt totally serene, as if viewing everything from a small distance, a detached space in her head.

And then she realized she was once again in the hut. There was Eulalie in the background, buzzing worriedly in her uncomprehensible patois; here was the solid bed; there was the solid plank floor; across the room were the solid chairs and the solid table; and in Ben's hand was a lighted lantern, and that was what was casting those strange upward-slanting shadows on his face.

With a detachment devoid of emotion it came to her now: Ben had arrived at the capsized pirogue just at the last moment of purple light. She remembered Aristide advising her that help was on its way, and that this had stirred her briefly out of her unutterable exhaustion and the dangerous lethargy induced by the narcotic rhythms of the waves. She had been conscious but groggy at that moment Ben pulled his ketch alongside the pirogue. What had happened after that?

"You fainted," Ben said now quietly; and she realized that there was something in his face she had never seen before. There was an ash-grayness about his mouth, despite the gold cast of the light emanating from the kerosene lamp, and his eyes held no mockery, no cruelty, no hatred now; only concern.

She knew that Ben was wrong. She had not fainted, she had merely gone to sleep. But it seemed too much trouble to tell the truth; let him think what he wished.

Tasha licked her lips. They tasted like tears; had she been crying? With a mild sense of relief she realized it was only sea salt. That was as it should be, for she could not conceive of allowing emotion to intrude into the pleasantly numbed and protected realm of her mind. It was odd that for the first time in days she felt no desire to cry. Shock-induced or no, the mood of objectivity of the afternoon had stood her in good stead, and it still persisted. It was as though the nightmare events of the day had been a catharsis of some kind, cleansing her of the turbulent emotions of the past week. Even the hypnotic bond that had bound her to Ben seemed snapped.

Perhaps there had simply been too much emotion for the mind to assimilate; she still felt numb.

Her eyes turned toward Eulalie slowly and questioningly. What was she doing here? It was odd how Eulalie looked different, too, seen with new unemotional eyes. A very old woman in a patched dress; not so much to cry over. With a sense of dispassionate wonderment Tasha realized that despite her lack of superstition she had half believed in Eulalie's magic; or perhaps she had just wanted to believe.

"How are you feeling?"

"Very well," she said placidly.

"Delphine fetched Eulalie after we came in." Ben's voice was still low and concerned. It struck Tasha as vaguely incongruous that he should be concerned when he hated her so, but the thought seemed too unimportant to pursue. The inner workings of Ben's mind were of no particular interest now, except as a mild curiosity. He was not the Devil incarnate after all; he was only a man. He could hurt her in no way because she felt too little to be hurt. It was odd: the realization that she could not be hurt should have made her happy, except that happiness was an emotion, too, and therefore beyond the realm of Tasha's current capabilities.

"Delphine says Eulalie has a very good potion for settling the nerves. Something to make you sleep. Take it now; you'll feel better in the morning."

"I feel very well now," Tasha said calmly, but she made no demur when Ben supported her with his arm and raised her to a sitting position. With some part of her mind she noted that she was wearing Ben's pajama top; she made no effort to conjecture what was on her lower half. She simply didn't care.

For once body contact with Ben affected her in no way. It only confirmed what she had so objectively known: he could not touch her now, not really. She should have felt gratitude for this imperviousness, but gratitude was too strong a word for the neutral reaction she was experiencing.

As Eulalie approached with her potion, Tasha's accepting smile had a faintly ethereal quality. Why did they think she needed something to settle her nerves? She had no nerves at all, or if she did they were already nine-tenths deadened.

It was a herbal tea of some kind, or perhaps an infusion of barks. It tasted musty and not unpleasant, and Tasha drank it obligingly. Eulalie's mutterings as she urged the warm clear liquid down Tasha's throat seemed inconsequential, and they penetrated that sense of floaty detachment very little.

"Oh, oh," Eulalie worried, "what happened to my *gris-gris*? It was a good *gris-gris*, it should have worked.... Oh, I troubled so hard to make that *gris-gris*! Surely I made no mistake this time?"

"I burned it," said Tasha mildly, feeling nothing but an obscure relief in telling the truth. Eulalie's crumpling expression caused no emotion whatsoever, not even remorse. How nice it was to feel no emotion. There had been too much emotion for too long—too much agony, too much ecstasy, too much desire, too much despair.

"Oh, oh, oh," mourned Eulalie, with the wrinkles around her eyes bunched as if to prevent tears. "And you wonder that you nearly died? I shall have to make you another. Tomorrow...yes, tomorrow I will bring it. Or is tomorrow the day I go to mass? I am confused now, I forget...."

"Tomorrow is Sunday," Ben reminded her quickly.

"Then the day after that," Eulalie wavered. "The third *gris-gris* will work, I promise it. But this time you must not treat it so lightly! You must believe, you must have faith...."

Eulalie stood up to go, still moaning worriedly at Tasha. Ben pressed a kerosene lantern into her shriveled hands despite Eulalie's protests that she could see her way in the dark.

"I have good eyes," she said, tugging her gold-wired lobe and casting a last longing look at Tasha's ear. And then she was gone, still muttering to herself as she vanished into the night.

"Why is she making a *gris-gris* for you?" Ben asked in a quiet voice, coming back to sit on the bed beside Tasha after letting Eulalie out the door.

"Oh...I remind her of someone...I think..." Tasha said in a vague unconcerned voice. "It wasn't my idea. She wants me to be happy."

"Are you unhappy?"

"No," she replied with total truthfulness. What was unhappiness? Only a trap for people who had feelings. And to think she had once been hurt because Ben accused her of having no feelings. Having no feelings was a state of mind and heart devoutly to be wished.

Ben frowned, but with concern not anger. "You must have had some reason for running," he said, probing her expression with oddly intent eyes.

How silly he was to be concerned, when she was no longer to be pitied. She rewarded him with a distant little smile. "I don't like you," she said.

And why did that simple statement cause such a churning of conflicting emotions to cross his face? Poor Ben. He hadn't learned not to feel. For once, he was more vulnerable than she, and had she not been anesthetized against feeling she might have even felt a remote sense of pity for him.

"Tasha, I'm sorry for...." There was a long choking pause, as if his words came with difficulty. His perturbation left Tasha unaffected; she watched with a polite but clinical interest, until he recovered his equilibrium and his voice.

"I'm sorry for...deliberately setting out to hurt you. Yes, I admit it...and...good God, if I could take back some of the things I've said, I would. When I finally went looking for you...when I sighted that capsized pirogue from up on the hill... when I thought about what could have happened out there...what nearly happened...."

"Why did you worry?" she murmured indifferently. "You don't like me, either."

For some illogical reason, her words caused Ben to bury his head in his hands. Tasha could see a furrow digging a deep groove between his brows, and the swallowing muscles working in his throat. To her it seemed irrational and a little pointless for him to react so strongly to a statement that was very patently the truth. She watched with untouched eyes and saw every detail of his bent head with great clarity, just as she had seen the sharks in their feeding frenzy.

At last Ben raised his head; his eyes looked haunted. "Tasha, you have to understand. It was the way you laughed that night. It hurt...oh, God, it hurt. For seven years I've been in some kind of purgatory, all muddled up with that laugh. Until... this week...I used to wake up in a cold sweat every night. And always in my nightmares was that cat's reproachful eye, and you, hovering somewhere near, laughing that brittle little laugh...."

"Only because you mentioned a cornered cat," she said with total calmness. "It seemed...pointed."

Ben balled a fist and pressed it into the palm of his other hand, in a too intense gesture. When he spoke again his voice was forcedly controlled, unaccusatory. "Why did you laugh?"

"I couldn't think of anything else to do." Remarkable how even that old memory had lost all its pain, very much as if a shot of novocaine had been administered.

"You might have.... Oh, what difference does it make now? But I was upset about the cat that night. I had just remembered what happened to the cat. The memory had been buried; I think I was in shock after the rescue. Or perhaps I was just too exhausted to remember. But the memory came back that night, triggered by your words. And somehow...it seemed to crystallize all the horror."

"Oh?" said Tasha out of politeness, not curiosity. She cared about a cat no more than she cared about Eulalie, or Ben, or anything else. How pointless it was to suffer for a cat. And yet, Ben's face and voice suggested suffering even now, seven years later.

"They drowned the cat," he said in a low strangled

voice. "The copra workers on the island. The cat killed one of their chickens. They cornered it and caught it. And then they put it in a sack and drowned it."

"Oh," said Tasha.

"I couldn't forget that—the way it had looked at me with that one eye. It saved my life. And then, I couldn't save it...for God's sake, I didn't even try. I just...watched...too numb to do anything. I watched it die, no more able to save it than I had saved anyone else. Can't you see how your bright little laugh was just the last straw? I almost wanted to kill you that night...and then today, I almost did, by driving you away." He passed his hand over his eyes and then pressed thumb and forefinger over the bridge of his nose. "Oh, God," he said thickly.

"It doesn't matter." Listlessly, Tasha closed her eyes. She knew she should remove her contact lenses, but her fingers felt pleasantly paralyzed. An immense torpor was stealing through her limbs. Some analytical portion of her mind concluded that Eulalie's sleeping potion, at least, was effective.

"Nothing matters, really...."

She cared neither one way nor another when she felt Ben's warm palm close over her benumbed fingers. Her last thought before she slipped into sleep was:

At last the devil is dead, truly dead....

TWELVE HOURS OF SLEEP cured the paralysis of limbs, but not the paralysis of emotions. She remained apathetic. It seemed mildly ironic that Ben's desire to hurt her appeared to have evaporated along with her ability to be hurt; but the train of thought was too irksome to pursue. She was as inured to his sympathy as she would have been to his scorn.

"Come for a walk with me, Tasha...into the coco-de-mer grove. Or do you feel up to it?"

Why not? The body was functioning perfectly well today, and so were the reflexes. She had dressed herself with no trouble at all, using a fresh shirt and the homemade skirt, because the jeans were too encrusted with salt. She had even managed to wash the jeans in the brook while Ben prepared breakfast. She had also rinsed the salt from her body and her hair, although for once felt too lethargic to use shampoo.

And she had eaten breakfast. All the right chewing muscles had worked; even her appetite had been normal. Why not a walk in the coco-de-mer grove? It held no fears for her now.

"All right," she said listlessly.

This time the cathedral grove struck no particular chord in her heart. It was beautiful, yes; but seen with this objective detachment of which she now seemed capable, it awakened no sense of awe. It was merely a stand of unusually tall palms with unusually large nuts. The soft breeze that clattered the fronds was like breezes everywhere, and the sunlight sifting through was the same sun that shone in London. And the birds were hardly worth a second glance.

Ben walked slowly to allow for her laggardly pace and came to a halt before they had penetrated the

grove too far. It was not the same place they had
stopped once before.

"Sit down, Tasha," he instructed, "we have some
talking to do. You feel up to a talk, don't you?"

"Of course. I'm quite recovered," she replied. She
lowered herself obediently onto a mossy fallen log
and spent a moment arranging her skirts, a slow and
gentle occupation that pleased her as much as she was
capable of being pleased.

Ben himself remained standing, looking down at
her, his hands jammed into his pockets. "All the
same, yesterday must have been a terrible shock to
your system. I don't want to tire you out, but...
there are things to be said, and I don't want to put
off saying them. There are some matters that must be
put to rights. I don't want you to be unnecessarily
upset about...things I said yesterday morning."

"I'm not upset," she said tranquilly.

"But you were at the time?" His eyes were on her,
probing.

"Was I?" Her voice was politely disinterested;
past states of emotion were of no moment now.

"I think you must have been. What I said about
forcing you to stay with me...I won't do that,
but...oh, God, I think there's been a demon in me
ever since that first time we talked on the telephone,
long distance." Ben ran tanned fingers around the
back of his neck in an anguished gesture, and spent
some moments looking up into the coco-de-mer trees
as if for strength or inspiration. "Perhaps it's best if
I start from the way I felt that day," he said.

"It's unimportant, really." She wanted to consider his past emotions no more than she wanted to consider her own. To avoid looking at that tall tense body that spoke of too much emotion, she plucked a piece of fern and started to denude it of its little leaves, very slowly and very methodically. "You say I can go, Ben. That's all I want to know. You don't need to explain."

"But I do. Hear me out, Tasha, that's all I ask, and then. . . make your decision."

"Decision?" Another little leaf fluttered to the ground.

"Whether you'll go. . . or stay."

"I already know," she said calmly. "I'll go."

"Just listen," he said with an intensity that seemed faintly ludicrous. "Hear what I have to say, that's all I ask. And then if you still want to go you can."

She was already wearied of his suppressed passion, but too apathetic to resist listening. "Talk then," she sighed, pinching another small leaf from the stalk of the fern.

He took his time, pacing the forest floor, ruminating for a while before he started his persuasions. When he came to a standstill his back was turned to Tasha, his sinewy length taut with tension. "Do you remember enough of last night to recall what I told you. . . about the cat?"

"Yes."

"Good," he nodded. "I was afraid you might be in a state of delayed shock; it sometimes happens. A kind of numbness of mind."

"I was perfectly rational," she said, nipping away another tiny leaf. She was doing it in a very orderly fashion, alternate leaves on alternate sides, creating a symmetrical and pleasing pattern on the stalk.

"Then perhaps you understand why something that happened seven years ago still affects me so strongly. I...haven't spent seven years dreaming of revenge, but...when you laughed on the telephone when I returned your call, that very same artificial little laugh I kept hearing in my nightmares, I—" the shoulders hunched higher "—it was as if something inside me snapped. I knew then that I had to exorcise you from my mind if I was ever to exorcise my nightmares. I wasn't sure at that moment how I would do it, but I knew it required a turning of tables. I felt a compulsion to see you upset, and then to laugh at you as you once laughed at me. Does that sound heartless?"

"No," she replied, lifting her eyebrows a fraction of an inch. "It sounds very logical."

"Then you do understand the...the motives behind my behavior? And you can forgive that much?"

She reflected a moment, soberly and with a perfect clarity of mind. "Yes," she said at last, "I can forgive that much."

Ben nodded, temporarily satisfied with that first concession. "Instinctively I sensed that this would require luring you to my home territory. I knew that surrounded by all the trappings of civilization you'd be immune. Does that make sense, too?"

"Yes," she agreed placidly, knowing that she was immune now, even without those trappings.

Ben turned at last so that he could see Tasha, and then because her face was bent a little in concentration over the leaf, he dropped to the ground near her feet and sat cross-legged, watching her intently.

"I used the first thing that occurred to me on short notice." His words were slow, as though he wanted to gauge her reaction. "You seemed to want that proof of divorce pretty badly. The bait is real enough—I have the papers in a safe-deposit box in Mahé—but I'm not sure it's valid in England. I think it is, but I don't know. Mexican divorces aren't recognized everywhere."

"Oh," she responded with a reaction too pale to be surprise.

"Don't you care? One way or the other?"

"Not particularly," she said indifferently. "Max will arrange something else, if necessary."

"Tasha!" Ben exploded. "Hear me out before you say things like that, will you?"

"If you insist," she agreed, but with a total absence of enthusiasm.

"When I saw you arriving at the airport at Mahé you seemed so cool, so invulnerable, so unapproachable, so... protected by your phalanx of civilization. And it was then that the rest of my plan took shape. I knew I couldn't reach you, really reach you, unless I got you away from Max Fabienne and his human wall.

"Making love to you wasn't part of my plan at first; that was pure conjecture on your part. That particular... obsession didn't arise until your first night here, when you were drunk and made some advances that were—'' his voice tightened with the recollection "—very hard to refuse. I wanted you badly, and I decided to have you. So I tricked you into agreeing. It didn't occur to me then that you'd be a virgin still; that kind of inexperience didn't fit with what I knew about the jet-set life you led. Perhaps if I'd known that at first, I'd never have gone so far. . . .''

She listened with no particular interest while he recalled some of the happenings of this past week from the point of view of his own emotions, his own misgivings, his own motives. How clearly she saw him now. The dark forelock falling over the wide brow. The hollow questioning eyes. The mouth, unmocking now. The khaki shirt, sweat-dampened, rumpled, as though it had been worn in sleep. The unpolished textures of face and hands and hair. Why had these things ever moved her? He was a man, no more, and a fallible one at that.

"Please come to the point, Ben," she interrupted wearily. "I'm quite aware of the fact that I invited your embraces.''

"Tell me, Tasha. Did you fall in love with me. . . a little?''

"Yes," she admitted unenthusiastically, because prevarication would have involved too much invention. "I was very infatuated, although now I can't think why. Yesterday quite cured me. Now I want only to leave.''

"Tasha. . . can't you understand? This is hard to

say after all I've put you through... but... I'm asking you to stay."

"Why?" she asked with a wan show of interest, lifting her eyes fleetingly from the nearly denuded fern stalk. But the intensity of Ben's gaze and the working of his jaw were too fervid for her liking, and so she turned her attention back to her task.

"Because I need you... and... can you deny it's been good in bed?"

"You said it's been better with other women," she reminded him out of a mild intellectual curiosity to know the truth.

Ben had the grace to drop his head, and it was a time before he spoke. "That was a lie," he said in a thickened voice, "perhaps the worst lie of all. I've never wanted any woman as I want you. You're an obsession, a madness, a poisoning in my mind. It's why I told you yesterday I wouldn't let you go." He laughed harshly, remorsefully. "It wasn't because I had any real intention of making you pregnant.... Oh hell, perhaps that's not true. Somewhere deep in my subconscious I think it must have occurred to me that a child might bind you to me. And I do want to see you bearing my child someday. My child. I made it sound like a punishment, but... dammit, Tasha, can't you see? My real motives go far deeper than the motives I talked of yesterday."

"It doesn't matter," Tasha said, not caring to hear any more. Abstractedly, her fingers pinched away another leaf.

"But it does," Ben said too fiercely, looking up

again. "I did a lot of self-examination last night. It's a sad fact of life that it so often takes a near catastrophe to make a man see how he really feels. I want you for my wife. I'm asking you to stay of your own free will. . . to marry me again."

Daintily she plucked off another leaf to balance the emerging pattern of the fern. *He loves me not*. It looked like a skeleton now, the slender spine with only a few symmetrical leaves remaining. It satisfied her aesthetic sense, that stripped-to-the-bone look. "All the better to hurt me?" she murmured contentedly. "It won't work anymore, Ben."

"Tasha! That's all done with now—those demons that were riding my back. They're exorcised. I don't want to hurt you anymore."

Her fingers idled at yet another leaf and pinched it off. *He loves me*. She glanced up, her eyes untouched. "Does this mean you're in love with me?" she asked unconcernedly.

A slow flush rose over Ben's face, and he answered reluctantly. "I'm sorry you asked, Tasha, for I'm trying to have done with lies. I think love would come. At the moment I only know that the prospect of a life without you is a very empty one."

"Then you don't love me," she concluded unemotionally. Another leaf fell. *He loves me not*.

"I didn't say that, either. Dammit, I just don't know! I'm still wrestling with the question. Perhaps I've spent too many years hating you, hating the kind of woman you are. From hate to love is too much of a jump. I can't change overnight."

"Then it seems your low opinion of me hasn't changed, either," she remarked dispassionately. In truth Ben's opinion of her no longer concerned her at all except as a matter of trivial interest, evidence that while his mind was behaving irrationally, hers was not.

Ben studied a blade of grass too intently. "I didn't say that," he replied with a forcefulness that did not seem called for. "Perhaps I'm mistaken about you. There must be warmth somewhere beneath that beautiful, clever, icy surface of yours. Perhaps I can learn to...take more pleasure in the qualities I admire. And yes, there are some. There's physical passion, and that's a start. A good start. We're good together, Tasha. Can you deny you enjoy my lovemaking?"

"No, I don't deny that," she said serenely, because to lie would have been foreign to her current mood of objectivity. "I find it quite a pleasant pastime."

"Pastime...!" Ben tore his eyes away from the blade of grass and regarded her with a thunderstruck look that gradually faded, to be replaced by a guarded expression. "I don't think this is the time for sophisticated observations," he said at last in a dry controlled voice. "I'm asking for a decision that affects both our lives. For the love of heaven, be serious, Tasha."

"I am being serious," she pointed out seriously, with her fingers poised at the second-last leaf. "And I'm considering your offer seriously, too, from a logical point of view."

"I don't want to push you into instant decisions," Ben said carefully, watching her fingers and not her face. "And I want you to understand what's involved in my offer. I can't lavish you with the things Max can give—the furs, the jewels, the private jets. But I'm not a poor man, either. There'll be weekends in Paris and Rome, if that's what you want. Designer originals, if that's what you want. Nannies and private schools for our children, if that's what you want. I'd like to settle here—I have a mind to put down some roots. I'd build a proper bungalow, of course; I would have done so years ago if our marriage hadn't gone awry. But...."

Ben frowned down at his fingers and flexed them. "I can force myself to adapt to a big city somewhere—if that's what you want."

"I see," said Tasha thoughtfully, considering his offer with total objectivity and a computerlike clarity of mind. The second last leaf succumbed to her fingernails and fluttered to the ground.

"And I can give you something I don't believe you'll get from Max, something I think you've come to need despite your little... joke of a moment ago. Sex is a very basic drive, and there's a spark between us that turns to fire very easily. Do you really want to live a life without that fire?"

She thought about fire; and she thought about Ben's face lamplit by flame as it had been last night; and she thought about a cool gray-suede existence.

"And if I decide to go?"

Ben's knuckles whitened perceptibly and the tinge

of grayness returned around his mouth. "If that's what you decide...I'll...take you back to Mahé tomorrow."

"The law will be looking for you there," she mused. "Abduction is a very serious charge."

"I've always known that," he returned in a low level voice. "It was a risk I took. I could ask you to say you came with me willingly, but I won't. If you decide to go back to Max...well, I suppose you've earned the right to some kind of vengeance."

She considered that, too, with all the logic at her disposal. "Vengeance takes too much effort," she decided with a small sigh. "I'll tell Max I agreed to a trial reunion."

"Don't decide now," Ben interposed quickly, perhaps sensing some decision in her words. "Think about it; take your time. We'll discuss it again tonight."

"I don't need time. There's only one rational decision." Her fingertips closed daintily over the very last leaf and pinched it from its stem. *He loves me not.*

"No, thank you," she told Ben with immense civility. "I'd rather be married to Max."

CHAPTER FOURTEEN

"I STILL FIND IT hard to believe," Max said, "that you went with the man of your own free will."

"Do you?" Tasha murmured unconcernedly. Truthfully she was indifferent as to whether Max believed her or not, and she had no intention of elaborating on her lies. It had been an effort to lie at all, and if she had done so it was only because in this instance telling the truth required far more effort.

Aided by favorable winds, the ketch had arrived back at Mahé several hours before, in early afternoon. Ben had delivered Tasha directly to the hotel and left at once before anyone noted her presence. Within minutes there had been a swirl of concerned faces and excited questions from several members of the entourage; and soon Max himself had arrived on the scene with Morley. Soothing unflappable Max. It was with relief that Tasha had allowed herself to be led away from the others.

Solicitous as always, Max had asked few questions at that time; instead he had escorted Tasha directly to her own room. He had insisted on an immediate and thorough medical examination, which Tasha had been too enervated to refuse. The previous day's mood of apathy persisted; she wanted only to be left alone in peace. Perhaps sensing this, Max had decreed an afternoon's sleep.

For dinner, he had ordered a small carefully chosen meal to be served in the sitting room of the cottage they shared. They were seated now at an immaculately laid table, on which sat platters with gleaming silver lids opened to reveal morsels of this and that—exquisitely cooked, but morsels nevertheless and not all of them to Tasha's taste.

"Calves' liver," Max urged as she refused one course especially prepared for her, "is very good for stress."

Tranquilly Tasha waved the dish away. "No, thank you, Max. I don't like it broiled, and I don't like it without salt. I like it smothered in bacon and onions. I'll eat something else."

To Tasha's mild surprise Max did not insist. He put the liver on his own plate and helped Tasha to some creamy Coquille St. Jacques that had been intended for his own consumption. "I recommend that you return to dieting tomorrow," he reprimanded mildly. "You've gained two pounds, Natasha my dear. I would have guessed it even without seeing the doctor's report. All in all, the report was good, despite that unsightly sunburn on your nose. It seems you've not been mistreated, although I'm concerned to see two fingernails broken. And the remains of a bruise on your leg! Did your loutish ex-husband cause that?"

"I fell against a rock. I've told you, Max, I went with him willingly."

"Hmm," said Max, with a tiny lift of one smooth brow. "You did not appear so willing at the time, from what I could see of your face. And it is not like you, Natasha, to be so...unprofessional as to vanish during a working session. So...shall we say, inconsiderate? I confess, my dear, that you left me in a somewhat, ah, difficult position."

"I'm sorry, Max. I know it's been very expensive to keep the crew idle. You've been paying me well, and I have money put away now. Would you like me to reimburse you?"

"Reimburse your own fiancé?" he chided gently. "Surely, my dear, you know me better than that. Or perhaps you have forgotten that we plan to be married?"

All at once Tasha's appetite evaporated. It would be too strong to say that Max's words upset her; she was still beyond the reach of such emotions. But his slightly sarcastic reminder had brought to mind that there were things she had to reveal about the happenings of the past week. She put down her fork, patted her mouth with a snowy napkin and faced up to it.

"There are some things I have to tell you," she said calmly. "Perhaps, Max, you won't want to marry me when you hear them."

Other than a look of faint reproach that conveyed some disappointment in her, Max did not seem overly alarmed to learn that Ben and Tasha had been living as husband and wife. Nor did he seem surprised to learn that the divorce, though extant, might present some difficulties. By the time Tasha's story was told, they had retired from the dining table to more comfortable chairs in the large sitting room, and Max had allowed Tasha a thimbleful of pale chartreuse—a liqueur he considered to be almost medicinal in nature.

His eyelids drooped reflectively when he had heard all of Tasha's unemotional revelations, which included an account of her own willingness. "I confess a mild surprise, my dear, that the invitation to, er, indulge came from you. It makes me wonder if you really wish to become Mrs. Maximilien Fabienne. Please understand that this puts a new complexion on our relationship."

That reprimand, too, left Tasha indifferent. "I expected you might want to break it off under the circumstances. I understand, of course. Morley's holding your ring; I gave it into her keeping on the day of the shoot. You can get it from her."

"You seem unperturbed," murmured Max, "that you may have jeopardized your future as my wife."

"It can't be helped now," Tasha responded halfheartedly. Really, what did it matter? Max's rejection moved her no more than Ben's entreaties had done.

Max smiled in that gentle soothing way he had. "Ah, Natasha. I confess I was curious to see your reaction. But I have no intention of altering my plans in any material way. The decision to make you my wife was taken in the belief that your marriage had been consummated many years ago. And you tell me that this past week was in the nature of an experiment you do not wish to repeat; that you have, in fact, refused all suggestions that your former marriage be renewed. Perhaps it is best that your, er, experiment came prior to our exchange of vows and not after.... Jealousy, my dear, is foreign to my nature. I still plan to proceed."

"I see," said Tasha with no more enthusiasm than before.

Max went on smoothly. "If details of this past week become known to the press, it is easy enough to put it down to an attempted reconciliation requested by your ex-husband. You would announce, of course, that you decided in my favor. Yes, I believe that will do very well. In fact I may see to leaking the story myself. It will do as well as anything to account for the developments that have taken place in your absence."

"Developments?"

Max's nostrils flared slightly, a sign of unusual emotion for him. "I need to give some rationale to account for the fact that you are no longer the Fabienne woman," he said in a voice stiffer than was his wont. And then, because the announcement put no question marks on Tasha's face, he added, "Yes, Natasha, for you that particular role has already come to an end. Are you not surprised?"

"I suppose I am surprised. I thought we'd have to start shooting again soon. What are you going to do about your photographs? You must have deadlines to meet."

"The shots for the Drenched Look are already done," Max announced through tight lips. "We finished them yesterday."

"Yesterday?"

"With Lisette," Max said.

That did surprise Tasha. "Lisette?" she asked with a faintly wondering expression.

Max nodded with a vehemence Tasha had never seen in him before. "Astonishing, is it not? I admit I was enraged at first at the idea of using that... that. . . ." For once words seemed to escape Max; he took a healthy swallow of his liqueur before he continued, clearly in a cold fury, "Lassiter's mistress is not my idea of what the Fabienne woman should be. And now, for the first time in memory I find myself saddled with a Fabienne woman not of my own choosing."

"Lisette," murmured Tasha again. "But why—"

"I prefer not to discuss the details," Max said coldly. "Let it suffice to say that Jon Lassiter was in possession of some, er, material that I did not wish to see published. The material was not exactly damning, but had it come to light it would have tended to make me look ludicrous."

Tasha puzzled briefly and then remembered the candid photographs Jon had been snapping with such delight on the day of the shoot. Max minus the toupee. So Jon had had some kind of revenge for Max's critical words; and Lisette had also had her way. Under normal circumstances the whole situation might have amused Tasha, but her sense of humor, like everything else, seemed deadened. "I suppose you mean blackmail?" she inquired politely.

Max drummed his manicured fingernails on the well-padded arm of his chair, the sound muted by the soft upholstery. "Perhaps the term is too strong," he admitted, "in view of the fact that Jon insisted only on making some trial shots. No doubt Lisette put him up to it. As the crew were idle I allowed him to proceed. And despite my initial objections—my continuing objections to her moral turpitude, I may add—I had to admit, once I saw the contact sheets, that Lassiter was right. The trollop photographs excellently. I am not pleased, but I am an objective man, a rational man. I have come to the unwilling conclusion that Lisette is perfect for the Drenched Look, better even than you would have been. Moreover, she has no troublesome reservations about modesty. Frankly I was astonished to find that you did."

"I apologize for that," said Tasha.

"It is as well to discover it now. My new perfume, Fabienne Nude, requires being photographed in dark silhouette—very tastefully, of course, but nude nevertheless. Oh, I am resigned to Lisette's tenure as the Fabienne woman; perhaps she represents the new morality. But for the first time in thirty years I find myself with a Fabienne woman I can not bring myself to court, even for public consumption. Perhaps you understand now why I wish to continue with our arrangement, despite the happenings of this week? In fact, I intend to marry you as soon as possible—as soon as my legal advisers determine whether your divorce is recognized.''

Tasha blinked slowly and wondered how she could have been so stupid. "I forgot to ask Ben for the divorce papers," she said, worrying a little. How could she have neglected such a thing? That sense of floaty detachment, she supposed...and yet, in every other way it seemed to have clarified her thinking processes.

Max dismissed her moment of concern with a small wave. "They arrived by messenger this afternoon. The man also sent a short note declaring his intention of staying at Mahé for some time in case the matter presents difficulties. He promises his cooperation should it be necessary to secure a more binding divorce. Not that we need the man's cooperation now. In seeking his whereabouts during this past week, my investigators came across several evidences of infidelity: an Austrian divorcée, a Parisian cabaret singer who holidayed here for a season...."

"Oh," said Tasha, feeling nothing. She knew that Max was watching her closely for signs of any reaction; there were none.

"I confess some pleasure in seeing that you are not upset by these infidelities," Max noted smoothly.

"I'd hardly call them infidelities considering the circumstances. Besides, I expected as much." Although Max's revelations made no impression on the numbness inside, Tasha felt suddenly exhausted. She listened with no real interest while Max recounted a few other items of news, mostly to do with

the House of Fabienne and their return to London,
planned for the following day.

"As soon as the doctor assured me you were in excellent shape to travel, I instructed Morley to make
the arrangements. No doubt it's been done. In thirty
years Morley has never let me down; an admirable
woman altogether. Although I wonder that she has
not seen to returning your engagement ring; it's not
like—"

"Max," interrupted Tasha with no preconception
of what she was going to say, "please kiss me." ·

She could hardly believe her own ears; and from
the look on Max's face it appeared that he could not
believe his, either. Gradually his startled expression
faded. "I think you have been more affected by this
past week than you care to admit," he murmured at
last. "You surprise me, Natasha."

"I can't think why I said that. Unless...." She
paused, trying to sort out the reasons for her im-
pulsive request with the same kind of detached logic
she had been applying to everything else. Certainly, it
had nothing to do with wanting to experiment with
Max. She looked at him consideringly for a time and
saw him with the same clarity and objectivity with
which she had seen Ben and Eulalie. A likable aging
perfectionist who was not the dashing Lothario he
wished to project. Egocentric and demanding, but
still considerate in many ways. All in all, she liked
him. But despite what she had told Ben, did she really
want a life of being married to Max?

"Unless I was giving you a last chance to take back

your offer," she finished slowly. "You see, Max, there's one question you haven't asked me since I returned. You haven't asked if I still want to marry you."

Max steepled his fingers, leaned back in the soft chair and closed his eyes tiredly. He looked as if he felt very old at this moment, and a little sad, and a little remorseful. "Perhaps I have been afraid to ask it," he murmured. "I am too tired to do any more looking, any more public romancing. And yet, I confess the need of a companion for the years to come."

"If you want a companion," Tasha said, surprising herself again, "Morley would be a better one."

"Morley?" Max, too, looked surprised, as though he had never considered such a thing. And yet, thought Tasha, why not? The relationship between Max and Morley was platonic, but it was a strong bond. Logic told Tasha that her intuitive suggestion was a good one. After thirty years of working for the same man, of catering to his every whim, of putting up with his idiosyncracies and smoothing every difficulty in his path, Morley knew Max almost better than he knew himself. And she was devoted to him in a way that Tasha would never be.

"Morley," said Max dryly, "is not exactly the image of the woman I ought to marry."

Tasha sighed. "No, I suppose not. But I wasn't thinking about your image; I was thinking about your comfort."

Max sat swirling his liqueur in its tiny glass, silent for a time as he contemplated the liquid beading on the crystal. To Tasha, he looked more unsure of himself than at any time in her memory. "I confess I have no desire to be rejected," he murmured at last in a soft wry voice. "Nevertheless I repeat my proposal, if I must. Is it so much to ask? To tell the truth, I am a lonely old man. And perhaps the years will be fewer than you expect. You see, my dear, I lied to you about my age."

Max's admission was a little pathetic, but pathos was at that moment beyond Tasha's ken. If her emotional reflexes had been in good working order, she might have thought it was pity that dictated her answer. But they were not, and therefore it must have been her logical mind that produced her response.

"All right, Max, I'm willing. Now do you mind if I go to bed? I'm very, very tired."

"YOUR GUESS IS PERFECTLY CORRECT," the Harley Street specialist confirmed a few weeks later. "Moreover, you seem in excellent health. I presume there's been no trouble with nausea? You seem to have gained a few pounds, according to your chart."

"I've been eating a lot. And no, I haven't been sick very often. I've been eating a crust of dry bread before I get up in the morning."

"And you've been sleeping well?"

"All the time, it seems. Ten or twelve hours a night—and afternoons, too. Another three or four hours every day."

The doctor's bushy brows lifted no more than a quarter inch. "Well, it does seem a little excessive," he smiled, "but no doubt your body needs it. Nature has a way of telling us these things. Perhaps you were under some strain prior to your pregnancy? And yet I take it the pregnancy was a planned one, for I see you stopped working around the time of conception. Well, well. It's always nice to be the bearer of good tidings!"

Max was as delighted about Tasha's condition as if he himself had been the father. He insisted that she move into his Mayfair mansion at once, and Tasha agreed without enthusiasm, mostly because she could think of no good reason not to. In her state of emotional and physical torpor, it was pleasant to be cosseted. Max certainly did that. He showered Tasha with advice and gifts—perfumes, flowers, jewels, baskets of fruit, an antique French cradle purported to have belonged to a Bourbon prince, an exquisite layette that consisted of a great deal of handmade Brussels lace. He immediately launched into plans for nursery quarters, prospective nannies, future school enrollments. No detail escaped him. To Tasha's unborn child, he transferred all the attentions he did not wish to lavish on the current Fabienne woman.

Plans for the wedding proceeded, too, although the ceremony could not be performed as soon as Max wished. The Mexican divorce had presented something of a problem: although it was recognized in certain countries it was not recognized in England. Tasha could have remarried immediately by flying to Mexico with Max; but that was something he would not hear of—not only because of Tasha's condition, but because it would leave her child in a legally ambiguous position. If Tasha remarried outside of England she would not be charged with bigamy, but a second marriage would not be officially recognized in England, where according to law she was still married to Ben.

In order to prevent future complications, Max's battery of barristers set about procuring a second divorce that would be beyond question, using evidence gathered during the stay in the Seychelles. The delay seemed to trouble Max more than it troubled Tasha, possibly because he was anxious for the divorce to be secured before Tasha's child was born. His thoughts revolved almost incessantly around the impending birth, and he already talked of the child as heir to his cosmetics empire—a circumstance that Tasha would once have found rather touching and sad, because it revealed certain yearnings in Max that the years had never fulfilled.

"Goat's milk—that's the thing," Max decided. "I've arranged for a fresh supply to be delivered every day. You will drink it, hmm? I confess you do look well with those few extra pounds—not photogenic, but blooming, Natasha, blooming! I've chosen some books for you to read. It's very important, my dear, to formulate the mind of an unborn child. Quiet, lovely literature, nothing brutal or upsetting. I recommend you avoid watching television altogether, especially the news. We want nothing untoward intruding upon your frame of mind, hmm?"

Nothing did. Tasha's continuing detachment, something that manifested itself in a good deal of daydreaming as well as sleeping as she reached the end of the second month, did not seem to alarm Max; he considered it a suitable frame of mind for a pregnant woman. Tasha herself was mildly concerned. She was not as totally immune to feeling as she had been some weeks before, but there was still a numbness inside her that left her wondering, in a purely intellectual way, whether she would have the ability to mother a child.

Max also concerned himself with plans for the wedding itself, which was to be reasonably simple but by no means secret. Once Tasha might have been amused, because it was clear that Max quite fancied himself walking a pregnant bride to the altar.

"Would you like to see the sketches for the bridal gown?" he asked one evening near the start of the third month. He handed a sheaf of sketches to Tasha, who was reclining at Max's insistence on an elegant Recamier couch in the sitting room of the quarters she had been assigned. "I commissioned ideas from several designers, but this is the one I've chosen. As you see it's been sketched from several angles. Somewhat medieval in appearance, don't you think? Very clever, those folds over the front, hmm? White won't be suitable, of course, so I've chosen a pale shell pink, in velvet—pure silk velvet, especially woven in France. Velvet is an unusual touch, I think, for a wedding dress! With the seed pearl embroidery it should be altogether stunning. The embroidery for the bodice and the sleeves is to be started right away, but the final fittings will have to wait until closer to the date. Well, are you pleased?''

Tasha managed an appropriate show of interest and handed the sketches back. As if sensing an underlying lack of enthusiasm, Max studied her thoughtfully for a time through narrowed eyes. Finally he said, ''I confess a certain curiosity, Natasha. When I entered your rooms this evening I noticed an envelope on the escritoire. Would you like to tell me about it?''

''I suppose you're talking about the letter with the Seychelles stamp,'' sighed Tasha. ''It's not from Ben.''

''I hardly thought so,'' Max said.. ''The hand-writing is trembly and rounded, far too childish for a man. I must assume it is from some other person you met during your stay on Mystique. I think you mentioned an old woman?''

''It's not from her, either.'' Tasha attempted a smile that barely curved her lips. ''It's from another woman I met. It's an invitation to a wedding that's taking place very soon, in a little more than two weeks to be exact. I've written a letter of regrets. Perhaps you could mail it for me? It won't arrive before the wedding, I'm afraid; the mail reaches the island only when a boat happens to call there.''

It was Delphine's wedding to Aristide, of course, which had been made possible by the money Tasha had insisted they keep. So some good had come of her stay in the Seychelles; Tasha had been mildly pleased to learn that. The carefully penned letter had not mentioned Ben, but through Max, Tasha knew that Ben was still on Mahé, having remained true to his promise to make himself readily available in order to expedite matters. Through Max she had also learned that Ben had put the coco-de-mer grove up for sale at a sacrifice price, apparently wishing to rid himself of it as soon as possible. Not that Tasha wanted to think about Ben.... She turned her thoughts back to the matter of Delphine's approaching nuptials.

"I'll have to send a gift," she said.

"I'll attend to that," Max offered promptly. "It's best if you remain away from the stores, hmm? One doesn't want to run the risk of being jostled. I have no wish to jeopardize the heir to the House of Fabienne! Have you any suggestion as to what gift might be appropriate?"

"A pair of chairs." This time, Tasha's smile held a small degree of spontaneity. "But I'd like to pick them myself, Max. And I'd like to pay for them myself. Call it a last gesture of independence."

"As you wish." Max's brows didn't lift a notch. "But as to going in the stores, no. You can make a preliminary selection from photographs, and then I'll have the actual chairs delivered here on approval. I'll have Morley see to the details. What type of chair?"

"Not upholstered, but handsomely carved. Actually, I want six chairs altogether. Four of them are for someone else—the old woman I told you about—and they should be really special." Tasha's brow knotted briefly as she considered a new problem. "Oh, dear, I suppose the shipping will take months. And she's so very old, Max. I want her to have the enjoyment of them for as long as possible. Could we make special arrangements? I'll pay for that, too."

"Consider it done," Max said softly. "I'll phone Morley right now and ask her to attend to everything; possibly she can start making arrangements tonight."

"That would be wonderful, Max. And can you tell her price is no object? I imagine it's the very last time I'll have a chance to spend my own money."

"Morley knows price is never an object," came the smooth reply. "Now rest, Natasha. Rest and read, while I make the phone call. Have you started that book of poetry I brought you yesterday? I think you'll find Kahlil Gibran an excellent choice for a restful half hour or so. The language is quite beautiful; thought provoking, too. There's a fine passage on children, the fourth section, I think. Now, where is that copy? Ah, here...."

It was a full half hour before Max returned from his conversation with Morley. He started to say something as he came through the door, checked himself at once when he saw Tasha, and crossed the room to where she lay on the couch, the copy of *The Prophet* drooping open on her lap. Max pulled a chair close to the couch, much as a doctor might have, and plucked the beautifully illustrated book from her nerveless fingers. His eyes ran down over the page she had been reading.

"I see you got no further than the second section," he murmured. His voice was soft, reassuring, nonaccusatory. "A very beautiful passage, the words of the prophet on love." He folded the book over a finger to mark the place and began to quote from memory:

"But if in your fear you would seek only love's peace and love's pleasure,

"Then it is better for you that you cover your nakedness and pass out of love's threshing-floor,

"Into the seasonless world where you shall laugh, but not all of your laughter, and weep, but not all of your tears."

As he finished quoting the passage, Max reached into his breast pocket and extracted the immaculately folded monogrammed handkerchief that had peeped from its edge. Without comment, he handed it to Tasha. It was only then that she became aware of the unhurried slide of tears over her cheeks. They had been gentle tears, slow tears. She did not particularly care if Max saw them, but she wiped them away obediently. New tears oozed back to replace the old. But because they were not all of her tears, they soon came to a halt.

Max watched her gravely for a time, his eyes thoughtful, and then he replaced the book quietly on her lap. He left the room without another word.

PHOTOGRAPHS OF A SCORE OF CHAIRS were available by the following day. Max appeared in Tasha's quarters in late afternoon, at an hour he was normally at the House of Fabienne, and presented them with a small flourish. He sat back in silence while Tasha riffled through the prints in leisurely fashion. She was in a pleasantly numbed state, still half-drugged from her long afternoon nap.

"What's this?" she asked, extracting the envelope that did not belong in the pile. It bore her own handwriting and Delphine's address. "I thought it had gone in the mail. Oh, dear."

"Open it," Max prompted softly, drawing Tasha's attention to the fact that some person had already freed the envelope's flap. Inside, the letter had been shredded into small bits.

"I took the liberty of tearing it up. I decided it was best for you to attend this wedding and deliver the chairs in person. Then there will be no trouble over shipping delays, hmm?"

For a moment, just for a moment, Tasha's brain swirled with sensations of light-headedness. And then the numbness returned. "Max, I won't go back to the Seychelles," she said with a positive gesture.

"But my dear, I must insist. All travel arrangements have been made. Morley and I intend to go, too. She has chartered a large yacht out of Madagascar, and I intend to spend two weeks cruising in the Indian Ocean. Call it a much needed rest. Do you know how long it has been since Morley or I have had a holiday? It will be easy enough to

arrange our schedule so that we anchor off Mystique
for a few hours while you attend the wedding.''

"Then we wouldn't be going to Mahé," Tasha said
thoughtfully.

"No."

"But what if Ben...?"

"He will not be returning to Mystique," Max
assured her blandly. "My sources tell me his valley
has been sold. Yes, he found a buyer. Did I forget to
tell you that?"

"Sold?" Tasha repeated numbly. "Then someone
else is...living there?"

"Who knows? Perhaps not yet. The transaction, I
am told, is a fairly recent one. But even if there is a
new owner in residence, it should not prevent your
attendance at a wedding."

"Ben might be attending, too," she said.

Max steepled his fingers, and a small smile played
over his lips. "Did you think such a thing would not
occur to me, Natasha? I am aware that you are not
anxious to see him. Therefore, when Morley made
plans, she also had my legal firm in Mahé contact
Mr. Craig and set up a meeting for the very day of
the wedding on some pretext or other to do with the
impending divorce. He agreed. I suspect, my dear,
that he has no desire whatsoever to return to this...
enchanted island."

Tasha mulled over the things Max had told her.
She still had come to no decision when Max added,
softly, "Surely you must know I could not possibly
wish you to see the man. I want nothing to interfere

with the smooth progress of your pregnancy. But I do wish for you to attend the wedding."

"Why, Max?" asked Tasha, looking at him, a small puzzled frown troubling her brow. "Why do you care?"

"Call it a whim." Max was smiling gently, but despite that his eyes looked sad and old in a way he seldom allowed others to see. "Perhaps I wish you to see the scene of your seduction, in order that I may assure myself you really wish for once and for all to... enter the seasonless world."

CHAPTER FIFTEEN

"So... THE ISLAND OF MYSTIQUE," Max murmured smoothly. During the approach, he had not even stirred from the canopied deck chair where he lay stretched, with Morley seated at his right hand taking dictation so that he could catch up on his voluminous personal correspondence. Nor had Max commented on the island until the yacht, a large and luxurious one, had reached that part of the lagoon where it would weigh anchor, not very far from where Ben's ketch had once been moored.

"I think it's best," Max directed now, "that we see to the delivery of your gifts immediately, hmm? With the wedding this afternoon, to leave it until later today would only create confusion. One of my men will accompany you ashore in order to do the carrying. Naturally you will have to direct him."

"Won't you come ashore, too?"

There was a sizable boat being lowered over the side of the yacht for the trip to shore. In the distance, across a sparkling expanse of turquoise water, Tasha could see a pirogue resetting sails in order to approach the newcomers to the island—driven by curi-

osity, no doubt. Surely not Aristide's boat when today was his wedding day?

Max eyed the island askance and shuddered slightly. "I think not," he said. "The surroundings are a
little too primitive for my liking. I prefer to stay
here."

"And you, Morley?" asked Tasha, turning to the
older woman.

"I'd prefer to stay with Max," decided Morley,
with a small watchful smile trained on Tasha.

"Yes," concurred Max, closing his eyes. His face
was totally serene. "Yes, that is as it should be.
Morley will keep me company."

The man who accompanied Tasha carried one pair
of chairs, while the four chairs for Eulalie were being
ferried ashore on a second trip from the yacht. Not
being familiar with alternate routes through the
island's dense growth, it was necessary for Tasha to
traverse the coco-de-mer grove and the clearing once
owned by Ben in order to reach the path to Delphine's hut. Walking through the valley triggered no
particular emotion, nor did the sight of the tidy
dwelling she and Ben had once shared. Had such passion and such pain really existed beneath that very
ordinary thatched roof? The memories seemed
remote, unreal, no more than a dream once dreamed
and half-forgotten.

Delphine welcomed Tasha with an effusiveness
that in former days would have warmed her heart.
"But you did not need to bring such a gift!" she protested, after exclaiming with delight over the two

heavy and handsome chairs. "That Aristide and I will be able to marry at all after so many years, that is gift enough! Ah, and only because you insisted that he keep the money, for something he did not even do. If I had not learned by then that you were not *amarrée* at all, I would have made him return it."

On Delphine's instructions, Max's man carried the chairs into the hut. Tasha then dismissed him after arranging to meet him back at the coco-de-mer clearing, where he was to wait with the four chairs to be delivered to Eulalie. "I'll only be a few minutes," she told him, thinking that Delphine would be too busy for an extended visit.

"Surely you can stay longer than that?" Delphine asked as the man departed through the trees. She spent some time oohing and aahing over the Paris original Tasha had worn for the wedding—a cool floaty silk in shades of taupe and brown, draped over a flattering fullness of breast that was the only sign of Tasha's pregnancy. Delphine herself still wore her everyday dress—but then, as the wedding was not until the afternoon, that was only to be expected.

"Come inside and sit on one of your fine presents, and we will drink some tea together while I tell you of the wedding plans."

"Really, Delphine, you must be far too busy today. I won't—"

"Busy? Pah!" Refusing to take no for an answer, Delphine urged Tasha into her abode. While the older woman bustled to and fro making tea, Tasha looked around the tidy spare interior and reflected that Delphine seemed to be in a very unprepared state, considering that the wedding was to take place within a few hours. But perhaps the marriage feast was being set up elsewhere—possibly at the home of one of Delphine's daughters?

"So, you received the letter," Delphine noted with satisfaction as she settled herself on one of her new acquisitions. "It is good that you gave me your address before you left! I am hoping that you will be able to attend."

"Of course I will." Tasha's face reflected a touch of puzzlement. "That's why I'm here. I won't get in your way, Delphine. I intend to go and visit Eulalie until the hour of the wedding. It is all right if I attend with her, isn't it?"

Delphine looked briefly puzzled, too. "But that will be a very long visit indeed," she chuckled, "when the wedding is not to take place for months!"

"Months?" Tasha blinked at Delphine in disbelief and then began to rummage in her Louis Vuitton handbag for the letter of invitation. She found it and confirmed that it contained today's date. "But there must be a mistake. Look, right here. My letter says today."

Delphine was nonplussed for a moment and then burst into a peal of laughter. "There is no use to show the letter to me! Oh, it is Eulalie's doing. She has got things wrong again. I do not read or write, you see, and so I told Eulalie the words I wished to say. I was very careful, and I told her several times. Oh, dear. The wedding is not for six months."

"Six months?" Tasha repeated in dismay.

"Ah, to plan a wedding, that is the work of half a year. That I sent word so far in advance is only because the big boat calls here so seldom. But I am glad to know you will be attending." Then, more anxiously, "You will still come?"

"Six months! No, I won't be able to attend after all," Tasha said regretfully. "I'll be far too close to my time by then."

"Then you are still expecting a child?" Delphine paused delicately, sounding somewhat surprised.

Now Tasha recalled that the Creole woman had believed her to be pregnant during their last meeting. How ironic that it had indeed been so!

"Yes, I am," said Tasha.

"And yet you are still so slim, so pretty! I was sure it would have been lost on that dreadful day...and then when the tall man came back and told us that you were no longer together, and that the valley of the coco-de-mer was to be sold, we thought perhaps it was because you did not wish to return to the scene of such tragedy."

"I heard the valley was sold," Tasha said, wanting to turn the conversation away from its more personal aspects. "Do you have any idea who bought it?"

Delphine frowned and clucked her tongue. "There have been people to see it only once, so I suppose they are the buyers. The tall man of yours, when he returned that time so many weeks ago, it was to show the valley to some fat men in suits. Aristide, he says they were from a land called...." Delphine paused, reflecting, then came up with the name. "Germany. Yes, Germany. Aristide heard them talking about cutting down some of the trees to make room for swimming pools and rows of thatched cottages. So I suppose they will build a big hotel someday."

"Oh." The tiny wrench of feeling was not really regret, Tasha told herself—only a brief disappointment that Ben would sell the valley to entrepreneurs.

"But enough of such unhappy matters. I am sorry that you will not be able to come for the time of the wedding. When is your child expected?"

"About two weeks after your wedding." Tasha changed the subject. "Now tell me, how is Eulalie? I take it she's as confused as ever."

Delphine sighed heavily. "Oh, she is being very difficult. It is hard to talk sense to her. Perhaps you will have more success than I."

"I doubt that," smiled Tasha. "What's she being difficult about?"

"With some of the money you gave to Aristide I purchased some *aunes* of cloth weeks ago, when the big boat came to call. I made Eulalie a dress for everyday, and also a fine *robe la messe*—oh, very nice, in a pretty blue color, with fine embroidery. I took them to her hut, but she keeps them in a box under her bed and refuses to wear them at all."

"Why on earth would she do that?"

"Oh, that Eulalie!" Delphine cast her eyes to heaven. "Her lip trembles and she tells me that I am like the others, that I must have been laughing at her dress of patches all along. So of course I have to tell her that it is not so, that her own dress is very fine indeed. So, says Eulalie, if her own dress is so very fine, why have I made her others? I could not insist too much for fear of insulting her. Perhaps you could talk to her? She seems to have a special feeling for you. She talks often of the lady with the long black hair."

"I can try," Tasha agreed dubiously. "There must be some way of convincing Eulalie without upsetting her. I don't like to see her unhappy."

"Unhappy?" Delphine sighed again, too heavily. "Eulalie is not unhappy most of the time. She loves her plants and her roots, and she loves the birds and the small creatures that live around her hut. With these things to keep her company, she is not lonely, as a sane person might be. So, you see, there is some good in being mad."

Tasha was surprised at Delphine's use of the adjective. "Mad? Oh, I know she's old and forgetful, but...."

Delphine wagged her head in a very positive way. "Oh, yes, she is quite, quite mad. Did you not realize? Eulalie has always been like that. My own grandmother used to talk of Eulalie's confusions when I was just a little girl. And that is forty years ago. Why, I can tell you a story about the time my great grandfather went to Eulalie with a sprained wrist and got treated for falling hair instead. Is it any wonder that she mistakes a simple wedding date?"

Delphine's musing and unmalicious recollections

went on for some minutes and were interrupted only by the arrival of Aristide Bruleau.

After a brief exchange of civilities, he said to Tasha, "A man on the big boat told me you were here, when I took my pirogue to see what new thing was arriving at our island. Ah, I was in fear that it might be the men of Germany coming back to lay claim to the valley! But it seems I had nothing to fear. The man of fine manners and soft tongue gave me a message for you."

"Max Fabienne?"

"He did not tell me his name." Aristide had the pleased look of a man who was the bearer of good tidings, delaying the telling of the news in order to savor it more fully. "He asked me to bring you a message, but he told me not to deliver it until I had done a task for which he paid me well—which was only to deliver some chairs to the hut of the *bonne femme di bois*, whose name he did not know. And that task is now done. Eulalie has the chairs, which he said to say were from you. She seemed very pleased, although I had a little trouble to get the old chairs away from her to make room! So now, I have come to you with the message from the man on the boat."

Tasha struggled with a twinge of annoyance at Max; she had wanted to deliver the chairs herself. But it was not Aristide's fault, and at the moment the honest fisherman was looking so pleased with himself, fairly bursting with good news, that it seemed wrong to comment on Max's unilateral rearrangement of plans. "What was his message, Aristide?"

"He said I was to tell you that the coco-de-mer grove now belongs to you," Aristide announced triumphantly. "The man said he himself bought it through an agent in Mahé and had it transferred to your name."

Tasha stared. Why would Max do a thing like that? "I don't believe it," she said.

"The man said one other thing I did not understand." Aristide's face grew more sober now and betrayed puzzlement. "He made me repeat it, so that I would get it right. He said one week should be enough for you to decide whether you wished to laugh all of your laughter and weep all of your tears."

"One week...?" As the deeper meaning of Aristide's words penetrated, Tasha stood up with a hasty apology and hurried outside to the terrace, from where the moored yacht would be visible. One glance confirmed her guess: it was moving slowly toward the channel and would soon leave the lagoon.

Aristide and Delphine had followed her out the door. "The man asked me to see that you were well looked after for the week," Aristide remarked pleasantly. As Tasha's eyes were still turned seaward, he did not note her expression, which was considerably more emotional than any she had displayed for some time. How dare Max desert her like this!

"He gave me some other things, too, which he asked me to place in your hut. Supplies, a very fine small cookstove with special fuel...and there was a

suitcase, also, with an envelope attached. Perhaps
was addressed to you? I could not tell because I ca
not read, and so I left it in the hut. If you wish, I w:
go there with you now.''

Ten minutes later, having refused Aristide's off
and saying a hasty goodbye to Delphine, Tasha w.
back at the coco-de-mer grove, alone. The envelo]
did indeed contain a message from Max. It read:

Please forgive the deception. I confess the
motivation is selfishness, pure selfishness on my
part. Frankly, I am alarmed at signs that your
previous visit to this place may have affected
you in a manner unbecoming to the woman who
is to be my wife. I sensed that you should return
here for a time in order to reflect on whether or
not you can come to terms with the future we
have planned. I knew you would not come here
alone, nor without some intervention on my
part.

I believe you will find that Morley has provi-
sioned you adequately for a week of roughing
it. Do not feel I have altogether deserted you; I
will return in seven days. In the meantime
Morley and I will enjoy a much needed holiday
cruising around these islands—yes, that much
was true. Consider well, Natasha, and remember
that you will be letting me down only if you permit me to make an unfortunate and irreparable
mistake. Max Fabienne cannot afford to make
mistakes.

The letter was typewritten and unsigned. It had
been dictated to Morley, who had added in her own
no-nonsense handwriting as a postscript:

Don't let Max fool you, he's not as self-centered
as he pretends. Do what's best for you. No more
now, Max is calling me. Good luck! Morley.

Tasha could not entirely agree with Morley's
estimate. Max must be doing this for his own sake,
or he was certainly not doing it for hers! No doubt
he had gone to a great deal of trouble and expense to
purchase the coco-de-mer grove and plan the cruise,
but somehow she failed to feel grateful.

It took Tasha very little time to realize that Max
must have been planning this deception for all of the
last two weeks. The suitcase contained casual
clothes, many of them brand-new, which Tasha had
certainly not packed herself. The propane stove,
along with a number of other pieces of equipment,
all bore tags from a famous London supplier. Moreover, the elegantly packaged prepared foods—jars of
preserves, caviar, canned goat's milk—were all from
Fortnum & Mason's. Max's idea of roughing it in
style, thought Tasha without even being able to raise
a smile. Certainly it was quite a departure from the
down-to-earth foods she had eaten during her past
day on Mystique.

Mystique. Why had the name ever held such a
magical fascination for her? During her previous stay
on the island, Tasha had had a strong sense of the

fates taking over, but this time she was under no suc
illusion. It was Max, autocratic egocentric Max, wh
was rearranging her life against her will—with a litt
unwitting help from an addled old woman who ha
not even been able to get a wedding date straight.

While thoughts of Eulalie no longer wrenched h
heart as once they had, Tasha still experienced son
feelings verging on poignancy as her reflectio
turned in that direction. As she toyed with a co
luncheon of canned prawns, melba toast and goat
milk, Tasha mused on the problem Delphine ha
presented. Surely there must be some way to get t
old woman to discard her ancient sugarsack witho
hurting her feelings.

There was nothing wrong with Tasha's analytic
processes, which perhaps accounted for the spe
with which she concocted a plan. Within minutes s
was on the path to Eulalie's, wearing a straw-belt
smock that was somewhat more expendable than t
expensive designer silk she had intended to wear
Delphine's wedding. All the same, it caused son
twinges of remorse when she stopped by a thornbu
along the way and deliberately snared the smock
the prickly branches. Tasha was not destructive
nature, but her simple plan required a ruined dre
By the time she reached Eulalie's hut, she certai
had that. The smock was in total tatters, and seve
large patches of cotton had been left behind on t
thornbush.

Eulalie was squatting outside her hut, communi
with a nondescript bird, which was perched on c

frail finger, eating from Eulalie's hand. It winged away in alarm at Tasha's approach.

"Oh, oh, oh," wavered the old, old voice, "and just when he agreed that I could pluck a feather from his tail. Well, no matter, he will come back...I think...."

Her face, like a dried berry, turned to Tasha, its halo of sparse hair snowy against the wrinkled brown. She rose to her feet and shuffled slowly closer. She blinked at Tasha's face and moaned softly to herself; then looked downward at Tasha's hemline.

"I had an accident," Tasha said, expecting some comment on her ruined clothes.

"I remember," quaked Eulalie just as if she had seen Tasha only yesterday. "Did you think I had forgotten? I told you there would be no bruise by today. Oh, oh, oh. And you thought old Eulalie's cure would not work! Yet see, there is not a single mark on your leg. Oh, come into my hut. Yes, do come in. Did you come to return my piece of string?"

"I...lost it," Tasha said, entering the hut a pace ahead at Eulalie's urging. The four new chairs occupied pride of place, and Eulalie stopped stock-still in her own doorway, blinking at them uncertainly.

"Oh, such lovely chairs," the old woman exclaimed in a voice that trembled with genuine pleasure. "How did you carry them up the path? And you, who should be carrying nothing so heavy. It is enough that you carry a fine little girl child inside. Where did you put my other chairs? Oh, no matter...you can keep them if they make you happy. Oh, oh, oh. And to do so much, just because you lost my little piece of string.''

"I'm glad you like them," Tasha said, ignoring all Eulalie's misconceptions. It no longer seemed strange that she could be so confused about some things and so perceptive about others. No doubt Eulalie had noted the small evidences of impending motherhood—the fullness of breast, the gained pounds, the glowing complexion—that Delphine had missed. And there was no point telling Eulalie it was impossible to guess the sex of the child at this point in time!

"Or are the chairs because of my third *gris-gris*?" came the trembling and somewhat troubled question. Clearly, Eulalie's mind was moving back and forth in time, with a fine disregard for the actual sequence of events. "I did make a third *gris-gris*...I think... Did I give it to you?"

"Er...."

"Oh, oh, now I remember. I could not find you. Now where did I put that *gris-gris*?" She padded over to her shelves and began a fruitless search. "Oh, yes, it was a very fine *gris-gris*, that one. I remembered what I had forgotten the first two times. It was a lock of my own hair. Oh, not this thin white hair you see today. I have been saving that lock for many years, so many years that only the big *cèdre* can remember.... I cut it from my head when I was a young girl, just to make the *gris-gris* for you...."

Eulalie's probings through old tin cans and chipped jars turned up nothing that could possibly pass for one of her paper-wrapped charms. "O-o-oh," she moaned to herself at last, sounding totally heartbroken. "Why have I lost it, just when she came to get it? Oh, if I do not find it she will think me mad...she will think I forgot to save her the lock of hair...."

"I'll get the *gris-gris* another time," Tasha said quickly in an attempt to distract Eulalie. "I came for something else today."

Eulalie stopped her searchings immediately and came back across the floor. "Something else?" she quaked uncertainly.

"A favor," Tasha said. "There's something I'd like to borrow. I hope you don't think it's an imposition."

"O-o-oh." Eulalie looked at her new chairs with unmistakable regret, sighed from her very soul and squeezed her eyes closed as if she could not bear to see. "Take them, then," she trembled out. "Although I cannot think why you brought them here, except to break an old woman's heart."

"No, no, Eulalie, I don't want your chairs. ...you see, I've had a very bad accident with my dress. I ripped it on a thornbush and I have absolutely nothing else to wear." Tasha crossed her fingers, mentally if not literally. She knew that after the lie, she would be unable to wear any of the clothes Max had provided, for the next few days at least. Knowing this in advance, she had closed her suitcase to conceal its contents before coming to Eulalie's hut. "I wonder if I might, er, borrow a dress?" she finished pleasantly.

The ancient eyes came open and investigated
Tasha's tatters, as if seeing them for the first time.
"Oh, oh, oh. Why did I not think at once? I will give
you one of the dresses that someone made for me.
Now where did I put them? Under the bed? Yes,
under the bed." She kneeled and pulled out a sal-
vaged wooden packing crate with a few possessions
inside. The dresses were carefully folded in paper, as
though they had been put away lovingly. "Oh, yes,
such pretty dresses. Which one would you like?"

Tasha swallowed, smiled and said pleasantly,
"Those are very nice, Eulalie, but they look too small
for me. Besides, I've always admired the dress you
have on."

"Oh!" Eulalie chirped in a surprised pleased
voice. "Why did you not say so at once? And you do
not need to return it. Oh, oh, oh. Do you really like
my dress?"

TASHA TRAVELED THE DOWNWARD PATH slowly and
reflectively, scuffing at roots with the practical low-
heeled shoes she had worn for the visit to Eulalie's
hut. The pathos of the scene had not touched her
very deeply; nor had the ridiculousness of finding
herself wearing Eulalie's much patched dress. In any
case she was aware rationally that with the addition
of the straw belt from her wrecked outfit, and with
her height and her flair for wearing clothes, the loose
dress no longer looked so much like a long sugarsack.

She knew that three months ago she would have
been unutterably moved—either on the verge

tears, or on the verge of laughter, or perhaps balanced somewhere between. How little Ben had understood her. How little of her true self he had seen. But then, in the grip of his warped hatreds, he had not wanted to see. And now that true self had gone; she preferred the gray-suede existence.

She walked across the clearing, idly remembering that first time she had done so by moonlight, but recapturing none of the mystical sense of inevitability that had gripped her then. Slowly she mounted the steps, crossed the veranda and opened the door.

As she entered, the tall figure bent over a duffel bag straightened; then froze into a deathly stillness. Tasha recovered her self-possession first.

"Ben! I didn't expect to see you."

"Tasha," he muttered, his lips scarcely moving as they formed the word. His face had turned utterly gray beneath the tan; his eyes were haggard with dark circles beneath. In his hand he held some charts he had been about to thrust into the duffel bag; evidently he had come to clear out his possessions.

"Ben...." Concern washed through her, surprising her because it was by far the strongest emotion she had felt for some time. "Have you been ill? You don't look well at all."

Ben made obvious efforts to regain his poise. "No, I.... What are you doing here? On Mystique?"

Tasha hesitated, wondering how she could explain. "Max and I are on a cruise through these islands. He chartered a boat so I could come to Delphine's wedding, but it turns out there's no wedding at all—at least not today. There was some confusion, and somehow I got the wrong date.''

"Boat? I didn't see a boat. Where is Max?"

Tasha sighed; there simply seemed no way to avoid telling Ben about Max's treachery, despite the fact that she was not anxious to do so. She gave the sketchiest of explanations and finished, "So you see, Ben, I came ashore all ready to attend a wedding, thinking it would be only for an afternoon. And now I find Max won't be back for a week.''

"You can't...stay." Ben sounded strained. "My agents have sold this property to some English fellow. I was told only yesterday that I'd have to clear out my belongings within the next couple of days. I thought these things lying around must belong to the new owner.... Oh, God, they're not yours, are they? I'm afraid they'll have to go.''

Tasha smiled. "Don't you see, Ben? Max is the man who bought your property. He bought it for me; it's in my name now.''

Ben turned whiter, if that was possible. "A wedding present, I suppose? Then you and he....''

"No, we won't be coming here together. Can you picture Max in this setting? He only did it because he wanted me to be very, very sure. And that's why he's arranged that you'd arrive, too. Oh, Ben. He's throwing us together for one last time—just to make sure that I don't harbor any regrets.''

Ben was silent and somber for a time, reflecting on the import of her words. "I don't know quite how to take that statement,'' he said slowly. "Does it mean you *have* been harboring regrets?"

"No, I haven't, but Max seems to have some silly notion. I assure you none of this was my idea."

"Then you haven't changed your mind?"

"No. Do I look as though I've been pining?"

His eyes probed her face, then traveled slowly to her feet, and back up again. A brief pain ghosted through his eyes, to be replaced by a kind of bitter anger. His mouth twisted with a cruel irony and no humor. "No. You look remarkably well, except for the outfit. My God, Tasha. Is that your idea of a smart London joke—to attend an island wedding in a copy of Eulalie's wretched dress? You did say you came ashore ready to attend a wedding. Oh, very cleverly done; flattering enough to you, yet so, so cruel to her."

Once, Ben's scathing assumption would have been unbearably hurtful. Now it only sent Tasha's chin stubbornly high. "For your information, Ben Craig, this isn't a copy; it's the original item. Eulalie gave it to me."

"You can't expect me to believe that!"

"I don't give a damn whether you believe it or not." In a defiant gesture, she jammed her hands into the pockets of the voluminous patchwork dress. The fingers of one hand at once encountered an obstacle and closed over it. Tasha drew the object from the pocket, knowing even before she saw it exactly what the little packet was. The third *gris-gris*. It was somewhat larger than the two Eulalie had provided before. Tasha began to unfold the wrinkled paper, hardly hearing the suppressed fury in Ben's words.

"It's one thing to direct your laughter at a man like me—I'm big enough to take care of myself. But my God, Tasha, what kind of twisted humor can you find in making an old woman the butt of your jokes? At a gathering like a wedding? You haven't changed, Tasha, you'll never change...."

His words hardly penetrated. Tasha was staring at the opened packet in her hands and the lock of hair. Eulalie's hair. It was long, straight, glossy; it might have come from Tasha's own head. *Oh, she was beautiful, with her hair so long and black and sheened like a pearl, like yours....*

Droplets of memory trembled on the surface of Tasha's mind like rainwater on a windowpane. And then the drops began to form new patterns as they slid slowly out of place, forming new rivulets—joining things said today with things said months ago; and together they seemed to lead to a conclusion very different from the one Tasha had reached once before.

Oh, the witchwoman wanted her daughter to read and write so that she would not be ignorant, too. And Eulalie had written the letter for Delphine. And according to Delphine's grandmother Eulalie had been mad since... when?

Ergot? Yes, I think it must have been ergot, for there was a little ergot in the hut until I threw it out, afterward, along with every other poison I could find.

Who had died and who had lived? Ergot was a hallucinogen; it did not always kill. It could as easily have been the mother who had died so many years ago—from shock or from grief, or from natural causes. Was it Eulalie herself who had once wept in her lover's arms? Eulalie who had wanted to die when her faithless lover deserted her? Eulalie who had driven herself not to death but to madness with self-administered ergot? *Do you think I know nothing of love? Oh, I would give all the chairs in the world if I could undo the great evil that was done that day. Do you wonder that I wish to see a lover happy? I am an old, old woman and it is all I have left to give....*

And all these thoughts coursed through Tasha's mind in so few seconds that she looked up in time to see the snarl on Ben's face as he ground out the words, "And to think I've been in absolute hell over you for these past weeks. Yes, it's true. Once it was only purgatory, and now it's hell, pure hell. I've been obsessed with you, devoured by thoughts of you night and day...."

Suddenly, Tasha's feelings welled up like an underground spring too long contained. The corked-in emotions choked to the surface—knotting her throat, tearing at her lungs, stinging at her eyes. With her fingers still curled around Eulalie's charm, Tasha trained one tortured look at Ben, turned, and fled.

She hardly knew where her frantic footsteps were taking her until she stumbled over a concealed stone in the coco-de-mer grove and sank, sobbing, to the ground. Tears blinded her eyes. She buried her face in her hands and gave in to wrenching, soul-deep sobs.

Ben had been only paces behind. "Tasha—why don't you look where you're going? Oh, God!" The explosion of his words accompanied the hands that now seized her shoulders from behind in an intense grip. "I'm sorry.... I swore I'd never talk to you like that again.... I love you, Tasha. I love you."

Kneeling close, he turned her in the circle of his arms and she allowed it, abandoning herself helplessly to the choked-up miseries within. With fingers spread against the firm warm bulwark of his chest, she wept while he rained tender, fierce fiery kisses against her tear-streaked cheeks.

"God knows no one of us is perfect.... I love you, Tasha, all of you, the good and the bad, and most of all you.... If I could take back those things I said, I would. I didn't mean to make you cry."

It was a time before Ben's urgent murmurings of love slowed the anguished sobs enough that Tasha could speak. "I'm not...crying...because of you," she choked out at last. "I'm crying because of... Eulalie. I wasn't making...fun of her...ever. Oh, Ben, I'm sorry...I can't stop...."

He drew his face a little away from hers and looked at her wonderingly, his fingers tracing the tears that still coursed down her cheeks. "You were crying over Eulalie?" he muttered disbelievingly.

"I...can't explain.... It's as if...I've been saving...all of my tears...for her."

And through a new wave of weeping Tasha began to laugh, a rueful, self-deprecating laugh that soon changed to one bordering on hysteria. Ben shifted his hands to her shoulders, gripping them as if to steady her.

"Oh, Ben...this is so silly. I couldn't cry about m-myself, but...oh...you can't understand, can you...I d-don't suppose you've ever...c-cried in your life."

Suddenly Ben's whole body went still, only the fingers digging deeply into her upper arms betraying his tension. "What did you say?" he asked. His voice was deathly quiet.

"I said...you don't know what it's like.... Men like you...n-never cry."

All at once Tasha's tears and hysteria stopped and she began to shake all over with reaction. "Oh, Ben, hold me...please. Hold me tight." And when he had folded her close against his chest once more, she said in a trembling voice, "I'm s-sorry. I think I've been in some sort of shock ever since...ever since that last day on Mystique."

Whatever emotion Ben was experiencing, it seemed to be one he could express only by burying his face in her hair and tightening the hold that enclosed her in his warm virile arms. And at last, there in the circle of his embrace, Tasha's violent shuddering ceased. Gradually a great peace descended, for she knew she was where she was meant to be.

"I wasn't laughing at Eulalie, Ben," she whispered after a time. "This really is her dress. Delphine made her some dresses she wouldn't wear, and I wanted to get this away from her, so I ripped my own.... I couldn't think of another way."

"I'm sorry I ever doubted you," Ben said in a husky unsteady voice.

"I love you, Ben," Tasha said, gladness rising because she knew that this time Ben would answer in kind. Hadn't he said he loved her? And that was what she had always wanted to hear. "Of course I'll stay with you...if that's what you want. Here or anywhere. I'll follow you to the four corners of the earth if that's what you want. Ben, kiss me...if that's what you want.... Ben?"

The question in her voice was because he had suddenly shifted position, and now held her a little apart, looking into her eyes still shining from her tears. "Yes, it's what I want." The timbre of his tone was low, intimate as a caress. "But first there's something I'd like to know. It's important. Tell me exactly how bad your eyesight is."

"I've told you. It's terrible. Without my contacts I can't see properly six inches in front of my nose."

Tasha's face took on a puzzled look as Ben spent some minutes studying her in a warm, intent silence.

"And I suppose you didn't have your contact lenses in on our wedding night," he asked at last thoughtfully.

"No, I took them out," Tasha replied. Gradually a germ of suspicion began to grow in her mind. "But why does it matter?"

"Because I thought you could see my face...and I thought you laughed at what you saw." Ben's voice was level, contained, revealing little emotion. "A man may cry only once or twice in his adult years—and for me, that was it. I was under strain, just coming out of shock. The full horror hit me that night. I didn't want you to see in the first place, and then, when you did—"

"Oh, Ben." She buried her face in her hands. "That must have been awful for you. How you must have hated me. I understand everything now. You don't need to explain. Please forgive me, please. I'm so ashamed."

"Ashamed...?" Ben issued a contrite humorless laugh. "I'm the one who should be ashamed, for a thousand things. It seems you've done very little to be ashamed of. Poor eyesight isn't exactly a sin."

Tasha raised her head and managed a shaky smile. "I wonder if Eulalie knew all that," she said. "She always seemed so concerned about my eyesight."

Ben laughed again, this time vibrantly, affectionately. "Surely you're not beginning to believe in her magic."

"Of course not." But she paused, and added with some wonderment, "And yet, if I hadn't started to cry about Eulalie, we'd still be back at the hut, trading nasty words."

"Why did you start to cry about Eulalie?" Ben asked somberly.

Tasha reflected for a moment. She thought of Eulalie, of what the *bonne femme di bois* had known or had not known, of what she had been or had not been, of what she had done or had not done. Everything could be explained so rationally and yet... was any part of life completely rational? Many of the thoughts were poignant and bittersweet, and Tasha knew this was not the time to tell Eulalie's sad story to Ben, any more than it was the moment to tell him about her own pregnancy.

"I started crying because of her third *gris-gris*," Tasha said simply. "It was such a sad little collection of charms that couldn't possibly work."

Ben remained silent, watching her as if seeing her for the first time; and perhaps indeed he was. Tasha sensed he needed that silent moment to shed the misconceptions of the years, and so she respected it, talking no more for the moment. She looked up at the coco-de-mer palms, seeing the indistinct and stirring patterns of light and shade, trying to keep a new round of ready tears from springing to her eyes. Ben loved her now; surely the time for tears had passed. The sunlight breaking through the fronds high above seemed to say it had.

And yet, when a burst of silvery birdsong sounded, flooding the sun-dappled grove, she found her face tear-wet once more.

Seeing the tears, Ben closed the small distance between them and gathered her comfortingly into his arms. "Don't cry about Eulalie's *gris-gris*," he soothed, stroking her hair. "Somehow, I think she'd be very happy to know we worked things out—for whatever reason."

Tasha smiled and spent the very last of her tears against the thin cotton of Ben's shirt. She rubbed her face against the little roughness of hair prickling through. "I know. I wasn't crying about Eulalie that time...or about us. It's that bird, the one with the beautiful song. I have a feeling it's the one I saw today at Eulalie's hut, feeding out of her hand. And oh, Ben, this is silly, but I have the odd notion that she sent it to make sure things were working out."

"The bird that's singing is a black parrot. It would never feed from a person's hand."

Tasha laughed shakily. "Then of course it can't be the same bird, for Eulalie's little friend certainly wasn't black. He was gray and very ordinary, just like a bird that flew away one day not so very far from here, when you threw a stick at a laurel bush. I almost cried that day, too. Which shows you what a silly romantic I am."

Ben pulled a few inches away and caught Tasha's face in his fingers. He spent a moment gazing at her in a wondering way, stroking her cheeks with infinite gentleness. "Are you? You just described a black parrot exactly—and yes, it was a black parrot we saw that day, too. I told you it wasn't much of a looker to inhabit the Garden of Eden. I didn't think you'd even seen that little bird."

Gravely, he traced the line of her trembling lips and studied the signs of emotion that had always been hidden to him before. "I wish you *had* cried that day. I might have made the attempt to understand you months ago." He paused briefly. "Do you know, the black parrot is very, very shy. You're lucky to have seen one. There's an old Seychelles superstition that says you'll now have a long, long life.''

Tasha managed a tremulous smile. "Then tha should include you, too," she said. "But I though you weren't superstitious.''

"I'm not, but that's one superstition I'd like t believe in. I think I'm going to need a lot of years t make up for the heartache I've caused.''

Luminous with love, Tasha buried her face in th crook of his arm. "Oh, Ben, you already have," sh whispered. "Do you know, I half begin to believe i Eulalie's magic after all.''

"Silly woman," he muttered, pecking a line of lit tle kisses along her brow. "It's all nonsense.''

"All the same, if she hadn't led me to you that firs night, when I thought she was taking me to Monsieu L'Horloge. . . .''

Ben's chuckle held a vibrant affectionate deptl "So that's why you kept calling me Big Ben," he said

Tasha froze. "I. . . what?''

"Big Ben," he repeated. "Is that so odd? Especia ly if you had clocks on the mind. Eulalie certainl does! That night we rescued you and she gave you th sleeping potion, I spent some time trying to ascertai its contents. She couldn't remember. I suppose sl thought I was trying to bait her; she kept telling m she had seen the clock on Mahé. At length I decide to take Delphine's word that the stuff was harn less.''

"All the same," said Tasha wonderingly. "Ol Ben, do you think. . . ?''

"No, I don't." As he pulled her down to the earth beside his large frame, Ben's voice held a warmth Tasha had never heard before. "At the moment I don't want to think about anything but you. Oh, darling, I love you more than I can tell. And there's no special magic to that."

Tasha wound her arms around his neck and let every part of her soul show in her liquid eyes. "Yes, there is," she whispered from the fullness of her heart. "A very special magic indeed."

And then the black parrot fell silent, and even the softly clashing fronds high above seemed to hush their sound. And it was as if a thousand eyes were watching, eyes in the heavens and eyes in the surrounding bushes and eyes in the towering palms, while all creation waited, breathless, for the joining of their lips.

SUPERROMANCE

Longer, exciting, sensual and dramatic!

Fascinating love stories that will hold
you in their magical spell till the last page
is turned!

Now's your chance to discover the earlier
books in this exciting series. Choose from
the great selection on the following page!